CW01617500

DEAD MEN'S BONES

Siân Jeffreys

Paperback Edition First Published in the United Kingdom
in 2020 by aSys Publishing

Hardback Edition First Published in the United Kingdom
in 2020 by aSys Publishing

eBook Edition First Published in the United Kingdom
in 2020 by aSys Publishing

ISBN: 978-1-913438-29-6

FOREWORD

There are, and will only ever be, fifty copies of this little *tragici fabula*. Where and when the one you hold now in your hands found you, I do not know. But the list below will tell you where it found its way into the big wide world. How it got to you is another story.

1 – the author keeps, of course
2 – sent to Rhiannon, Goddess of Horses
3 – sent to Conor, Master of Hounds
4 – left on the 4.20 from Euston to Edinburgh
5 – donated to a bookseller on Pansodan, Yangon
6 – sent to 222B Baker Street
7 – left in the Caffe Greco, Rome
8 – left on the trig point of Coniston's Old Man
9 – left on Emirates flight from Bangkok to Heathrow
10 – donated to St Cuthbert's Church jumble sale
11 – left at Archipelagos restaurant, Rhodes Old Town
12 – donated to HanThar Gardens, Bago, Myanmar
13 – left in a London taxi cab
14 – left at Juan Borgia's tomb, Santa Maria de Popolo
15 – donated to charity shop, Sidney Vancouver Island
16 – left in the British Library Reading Room
17 – left besides Jeremy Bentham at UCL
18 – left on a seat after *The Book of Mormon*
19 – put down the back of the sofa, Wallabarrow Farm
20 – listed on eBay

21 – buried on Ambion Hill, Leicestershire
22 – left at Judith's feet, Piazza della Signoria, Florence
23 – sent to Cooling Castle Farmhouse
24 – left at the feet of Saint Zeno (quietly)
25 – left on pew, Holy Trinity Church,Stratford-upon-Avon
26 – left behind on the floor of The Globe
27 – donated to Chetwynde School library
28 – left outside the Castelvecchio
29 – left at the church of St Giles in the Fields, London
30 – sent to 3 The Fairways, Soi Chonlaprathan, Phuket
31 – left on steps of St Mary Matricolore
32 – left on the Ponte Fabricio, Rome
33 – sent to Ms Ingrid, Siem Reap
34 – left on plinth of monument to Savonarola, Florence
35 – left on the circular train, Yangon
36 – sent to Bea Cassimer, Taipei
37 – left in Café Salween, Yangon
38 – sent to Palau dels Borja, Valencia
39 – put on shelf in Waterstones, Oxford Street
40 – left on shelf at Sea View, Well House Farm, Bardsea
41 – sent to Richard Booth's Bookshop, Hay-on-Wye
42 – sent to Professor David d'Avray, UCL
43 – listed on Amazon Second-hand
44 – left in Merton College library, Oxford
45 – sent to Ms Aryal, Manila
46 – left at the London Book Fair
47 – left at the church of St Mary Ovarie, Southwark
48 – left at St Marcello al Corso, Rome with Bishop Michiel
49 – sent to Matt in Bangkok
50 – sent to Moe Thin Shwe Thant (Ree) in Yangon

Dead Men's Bones

For Moe Thin Shwe Thant whose idea it was

and

For Matt whose company in Lockdown made writing it possible

Hope is the pillar that holds up the world. Hope is the dream of the waking man.

Gaius Plinius Secundus (Pliny the Elder)

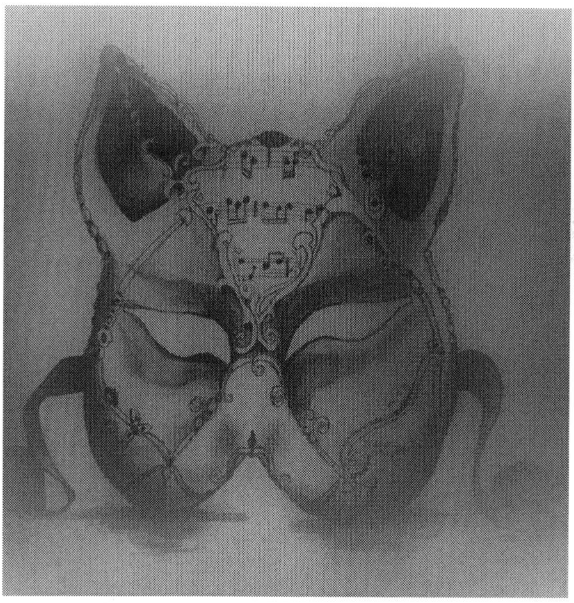

DEAD MEN'S BONES

1495; as summer fades, an Italian town.

PROLOGUE

A day of disappointment in which a priest dies unpleasantly, the crowd go home unhappy but an old woman seems content.

It starts – or rather it ends – with the execution of a man. He died reasonably well, and quietly too, to the disappointment of those who had travelled to the Piazza Duomo to witness. Now, a good day – one worth three or even four days re-telling – was the man who cried and groaned and whose guts spilled blood like great pumps, sometimes splashing to crimson the faces of the front row *curiosos*. And those who had travelled from Marzana, from Castel d'Azano, from Mantua even, had high expectations of this particular judicious civic killing being perhaps even a four-day tell. For the man to die was godly, a man of God indeed and as such wore the glamour and glare of a Church which held its great celestial heel above the faces of those it liked to crush into *oboeditione*. Because *ex nihilo nihil fit* and from nothing came such a life as theirs; trembling, bowing, cursing, rutting. Rutting, retching and then rotting in unmarked graves, ripe and stinking with hell eternal. And men of God like this one – this one who now swung back and forth, back and forth like God's own pendulum – was no doubt one who had raised the stick in time and time, and in time and time had brought it crashing down.

So indeed, it was always a satisfying thing to see one of the Almighty's minions crying out for help which did not come. Especially in times like these. No man watching thought it might lessen his own chances of eternal damnation but it was somewhat cheering to think that the sinners did not walk Eurydice's path alone but sometimes got to clutch at the trembling paw of one who had assumed himself journeying upwards.

So, those who had dared to come from neighbouring towns and dusty, war-ravaged villages jeered a little and threw some customary fruit and other rotting things, even as the Thing that had once been Man swung red, and as shining things like snakes unravelled from within him to clump obscenely upon the wet wooden boards beneath. Because to murder a man was to kill God. And to poison was to take the way of Eve, the serpent in the garden upon whom we could rest all of our blames and sorrows and misdeeds. Poison was surely a *woman's* way. A woman's way to bring about death by means of cowardly potion, a death which might manifest itself as natural sickness and allow the dealer to go unpunished and live amongst the decent. But worse of all was the sin of treason. Of conspiracy, of the desire and action to bring down the government put there by the Almighty. What did Paul say '*Obey the authorities for they have been put there by God*'? And it was for this last sin – the sin of treachery – that the swinging man had been most reviled. Rumours concerning the man's true identity had also fueled the fire of excitement.

The actual citizens of this town however were quiet. Just as Cicero had sat still and slightly nauseated as the gladiators bled, so the people of this town watched the corpse tell the slow, sad tale of seconds passing with a furrowed line between their eyes. Children with jaundice, women with the passing sickness, old men with flaming liver; many of the eyes watching the shiny pendulum had gone to this man. A frothy draft. A poultice of crushed herbs. A pungent mixture of nameless pulpy things mashed into paste. A splint for a boy's misshapen leg, set to rights and poppy to follow for the nights. Some cured, others not but all remembering . . . a gentle man.

So all were disappointed that day. The brave travelers who had made the journey in the footsteps of the French King's retreating army and in expectation of a show, of crying, beseeching, perhaps even a cursing of the Almighty! (Now that was always the greatest treat. The man of God cursing the maker who had set him up so highly and immune, to beseech with eyes skywards and to be turned away!) But they were disappointed this day. The man hung from the gibbet and disemboweled by the town butcher did not cry nor curse his maker. He was quiet and still and made perhaps just a little groan as they brought him down still choking and hacked him across the belly, ungently then hoisting him back up again. But such an amount of blood! The ignorant gawped in delight but the *cognoscenti* looked at each other with eyebrows raised.

And the people of this town who had known this man personally were disappointed too. Disappointed and yes, fearful and full of guilt, because many roads had led to this one man paying the price for them all. They had come to watch Aaron's Goat bear the town's sin upon his gentle shoulders and not one was brave enough to step forward and share the weight. They had waited for a Just Reprieve and they had been disappointed. They had waited for Princely Intervention and they had been disappointed. And they had waited for God to reach out his hand to save his own. And as usual, God was the biggest disappointment of them all.

However, one of the townspeople was not disappointed. Old but not ancient, plump but not rotund to ridicule, she was stood by the side, one or two mossy teeth showing as she sucked salvia leaves bought from this holy man's own garden. The condemned man had seen her as he was marched between the rows of onlookers, his eyes had flickered in recognition and she had tilted her head, just a little. Had he made a small sign? With that damnable finger of his? She was not wholly sure. It was too late for him to reach out and pull her down with him now anyway. He had tried and he had failed. The great lords would have their day. The English lawyer, the mighty Duke-Bastard and the long-nosed Bishop had squabbled and preened and screed through great and ancient volumes to find the words that would rescue or condemn this man and the Great Lord who had demanded condemnation had found it. Who could argue when the ancient tongue which condemned him was also the tongue which labelled the great potions and poisons and herbal concoctions he himself had used? *Cui bono? Habius corpus? Damnatio populus? Opius majoriam. Fluidium lethalum.* There was a fitting symmetry. The woman by the side of the platform knew no Latin but she knew an amusing irony when it came her way. *Clever lives as clever dies*, her long departed husband had said with that stupid, self-satisfied grin on his bovine face. Well, mayhap – on occasion – the stupid live whilst the clever die. Mayhap, just on occasion.

The sun was fast setting. In the Piazza Duomo before Santa Maria Matricolare, the crowd's mood was turning to the expectation of food and drink and whatever entertainment could be found. This was one of Italy's safest city-states after all and their lords and bishops and princes and emperors had but recently made a great peace. The League of Venice had seen off the French Monster and he was even now dragging his blood-stained soldiers west of here through Genoa. And peace brought more food and better food and strange wonderful food from the south even. People began to shift away from the wooden stage. The plump woman's tattered leathers stepped slowly into the wide and spreading pool of blood that had dripped and gathered just beneath the platform. She would have liked to have dipped her nose rag into the bloody earth but a decree had already been spread from the Lord-Podesta, the Great Families and the Bishop himself that there was to be no soaking up of the blood, no turning this common little poisoning traitor into some kind of a martyr. This town had martyred dead enough to worship, who knew that better than they these last six months? The crypts were still overflowing with blooms, some fresh, some rotting, all stinking to the high vaulted ceilings of the churches. No, the town did not need another martyred, worshipped Dead.

And so she stood still, looking upwards as if in contemplation of her soul. She could feel the still-warm stickiness begin to seep through the holes in the leathers and into the woolen stockings within. Another few warm, sweet moments. It began to moisten between her toes, *seep, seep*. For the first time in many years she felt a warmth begin to glow deep inside her cunni. Oh but that was nice. *Seep, seep*. She swapped feet just to make sure she had it all and allowed the other stocking to become saturated. Then walking carefully upon her heels so as not to lose what was beginning to thicken and grow sticky within, she hobbled from the square and took him home.

(One week earlier)

Thursday

CHAPTER ONE

In which the Bishop is told his Lord's demand and then has to converse with a woman in his cellar.

The Bishop of the least important of all Italian states examines this most tragic and tortuous case.

It is at first glance a case of a holy man gone beyond his sense and place. But it is at the same time also, the case of a foolish woman complicit in all sorts. And over both their wooly bloody heads hangs the spectre of many dead bodies (*how many was it? Five? No, six, we must not forget her at the very end, the foolish boy's mother...*). Bodies gone beyond rigidity and softening now into musty, airless petrification. *Pulvis et umbra sumus.* We are but dust and shadow. True, true enough but no one wants to hurry to the state, let alone be dragged there through malice.

So half of the town are wanting one punished, the other half demanding the other. The Bishop himself–standing awkwardly, not knowing quite what to do with his hands–is unsure of whether anyone left alive is guilty of anything at all but the truth of the matter is that six citizens–five of them not yet twenty and five–are dead. The city state's worthy Lord-Podesta is soon to be absent, negotiating the fragile northern states' peace with the Holy Roman Emperor. He wants the matter settled before he returns. Not even brave enough to publically wash his hands – as Pilate did of the Nazarene – the noble Lord makes plain his moral ablutions in a dusty ante chamber deep within the heart of the Castelvecchio Fourth Tower as his men scurry round packing chests.

---------- ∞∞∞ ----------

'Someone must be punished! It seems clear – *no, boy! Not the cerise but the cerulean! Do you wish me to appear before the Holy Roman Emperor in war colours? Do you wish me to flick my finger at him before I am even asked to sit? Shall I join the very French and bastardise our entire city with shame? The cerulean! The blue, God's Wounds, the blue!* – no, no, no, my Lord Bishop. You see how things stand here, you are a man born of this city-state, I think – no? of Milan? I did not know that. And how long have we known each other . . . ? If I'd known, I might have taken you with me . . . But it makes no odds – you are enough a citizen of this fine city-state to realise how the calm seas bubble and churn beneath. How the tinder can be light and small enough and yet the blaze so fierce. Aye, fierce enough to not just bring down the rafters but to bring down your Podesta even! So, guilt must be assigned and the guilty assigned to the appropriate fate. I care not how it is done. Court of law, judicial review, *Magnorum Quaesitum,* it matters not, I'll be fifty leagues hence, a thousand leagues hence if the Emperor sees my worth and takes me back to Austria . . . a public trial? No, no, no, I think not. I don't want the Council of Ten involved. The voices here are too fond of themselves, best not to give them air and audience. No, no, an episcopal review, an episcopal judgement, a Church burning. A long time since we've had a burning but it might serve a multitude of purposes. Witches abound, my Lord Bishop, and not just in Albion where I think one of their number sat her daughter upon the bloody throne not ten years ago now, a witch's daughter destined for hell if ever there was, that Queen of Discord. *Christ's Wounds, wrap the blade in cloth before you sheath, imbecile! That is my third best sword and as such will travel with me but wrapped. And a sword cannot travel well rattled in its sheath can it? Damned fool boy! Not the damask cloth, the cotton. Cotton! Pauper child, gutter snipe, not knowing cotton .... Around the blade!* ***The blade****! If you cut your God Forsaken fingers upon my sword and stain the cloth brought all the way from India, I swear the rest of your blood will join it and not long after ... my third best blade tasted French flesh just six weeks ago at the Battle of Fornovo! Would you not accord her due respect? Damn Paulo for getting the shits when I need him do my packing.* My Lord Bishop? Still here?

A burning, my lord?

Of course, how not a burning? Poison is a witch's weapon. '*And thou shalt not suffer a witch to live*'? The witch clearly has an evil tongue. Didn't Saul die at the hands of the Lord for listening to a witch? And does the Holy Book of Leviticus not tell us to burn witches?

I think it recommend stoning. But if I might ask ...

But in Revelation I think I remember that those who practice magic arts face the fiery lake of Sulphur. What is that if not burning? We merely do the Lord's work for him.

He remembers again at this point to tread carefully. This Lord-Podesta is pacing the small room like a caged and thick-headed bull, his unfortunate manservants white-faced amidst the chaos of packing, but he is no fool. He is a learned student of many things and has ruled this city well, given its difficulties and dangerous proximity to the greater states fought over so viciously by the voracious Charles Valois, the machinating Borgia Pope, the exiled and beleaguered Medicis just a few hundred leagues south ... And now Aragon, Rome, the Emperor and the northern city states – come to oust the French and save them all? It is true, this lord has much on his mind, a balancing act of great precision if they are not all to fall. The French are not yet gone from Italy, not quite ... The Bishop coughs his disagreement.

Burning for witches, yes, yes my lord. But am I right in thinking . . . it is a long time since we burned a priest . . . even for witchcraft.

The Podesta's dark eyebrows have drawn themselves low and fierce.

'You'll not be burning *him!* You'll be burning *her*! You do know who he is, do you not? This humble priest's proper name? Well, if you do not know, I'll not say it now but be warned! And if you think I go now to sit down with the King of Aragon himself, traitorous Italian blood still fresh on his sword and carry with me the stink of a burnt priest . . . yea gods, man! They call him Ferdinand the Catholic, you know that, yes? Burn the woman, she is clearly guilty of . . . '

Yes, Lord-Podesta?

At last the great man stops pacing. He is tired beneath the sweat and action. Grey skin shifts and shimmers beneath the ruddy tan of the man who detests the dictatorship of confinement. Yes, tired, so tired. So tired of the petty squabblings of this city's citizens that taking the knee before a hated conqueror now seems preferable to staying and mopping up mess from his own streets. (And he had so nearly kneeled. Milan had kneeled, the Sforzas had sought French gold and he himself had so nearly . . . but enough of that, no one knew, he had held fast and had backed the right horse. No one knew he had considered the other nag.) The Lord-Podesta sighs.

I know not. I know not of what she is guilty but six are dead. Six breathed 'ere we last took Christ's Mass but this Mass of Christ coming soon, those six will already have well begun their rotting wait for Judgement. Christ's Wounds, my Lord Bishop! Six noble-born dead! And this woman at the heart of the intrigue, no doubt her baseborn fingers upon the poison, no doubt some common, womanly *plebeian!* ambition at the root of her deeds. I cannot . . . I will not plunge into the mire of detail. That is for you. Your reputation . . .

My lord?

(Does the great man have the grace to look a little discomfited? No, a trick of the autumn's sun thin and weak across his mouth. But even so . . .)

Well, your reputation is of a man of God who finds the way. Who separates the Sheep from the Goats. Who apportions blame and due censure where it is due. And who understands – listen now most carefully, my Lord Bishop – who understands the delicate politics of the position. Yes. Delicate politics. You have read your *Secretum Secretorum*?

This is unexpected. But perhaps not so . . . This great tower, this solid ugly lump of a fortress, houses a great library or so he is told. Almost as good as his own in the cathedral of Santa Maria de Matricolore. Almost.

Of course, I am well versed in all the surviving letters of Aristotle. But political advice given to the pagan Alexander on the governance of a city . . . A great work to set before a student to translate . . . But I fail to see . . .

No, sir, no, you do not! I am Podesta of this this *infernum foraminis* of a town and I must do what it takes to bring order to these streets, aye and to the walkways and to the alleyways and to the very gutters so clogged they are with the shit of my citizens that neither mouse nor louse might run free. I shall answer to God, aye willingly, but until that blessed day I answer to my new lord, whether that be Venezia, Ferdinand of Aragon or the Holy Roman Emperor Maximilian himself, I shall not be the one who comes to him on knee bent with hands and fingernails dirty with the excrement of an ungoverned city.

The great man sighs. Runs clean white fingers through thick dark hair.

I cannot burn the priest. We cannot burn the priest. No matter what poisons also ran through his hands or were concocted in his apothecary mind, no matter which great family screams for his blood, he is protected by the great Mother Church and the holy Father of Rome and the *Sanctae Romanae Ecclesiae cardinalis*, and the bloody heirs of the Seventy Who Knew Our

Lord and the teeming multitudes of miserable boy-buggering pederast hypocrites we shelter and from whom we accept the blood and the flesh each day. And most of all he is protected by his blood, stinking and rancid though it might be. Do I shock you, Sir?

Not at all, my Lord-Podesta. The Holy Mother Church is perfect but it is an earthly perfection that allows sin to flourish within. We must not ignore it, we strive to overpower it, we ... we see through our glass yet darkly.

Hah! (The princely finger was pointing. An arrow aimed at his heart.) I knew you were the man! '*The Church is perfect but it is an earthly perfection that allows sin!*' What a tautology, worthy of Cicero himself! And with such a convoluted and tortuous mind, I shall leave this perfidious investigation in your hands, confident that you will apportion blame where it can do least harm. Any defense from the opposing side, I see now you will twist and pervert and cast down into confusion! Yes. I think three days and I will smell the roast of the old sow's burning teats even from Milan. Now are we of one mind? Will you keep the Council of Ten out of it? Might I attend to the thrashing of at least three of these useless boys who cannot tell a cannion hose from a ruff and who seem hell bent to crease every fine linen I own?

I understand Lord-Podesta. I shall undertake your requirements. I cannot see an impediment to your desired conclusion.

Our desired conclusion, Lord Bishop, our desired conclusion. And that of God in his Heaven and the Son by his side. *Gratias Deo.*

Of course. *Gratias Deo.*

And so the interview ends. Not surprising but perhaps ... *disappointing.* As Servant of the Holy Mother Church, the Bishop knows full well the symbiotic and yet often tortuous relationship that seals the City of Man to the City of God. That these city states are tossed like toys betwixt this French king and that Spanish prince and yet also beneath the yoke of the Papal Father in Rome and the mighty Emperor in Austria, is a sore of constant itching. And this particular Holy Father . . . Alexander VI to the faithful but always always Rodrigo Borgia to those who had watched his meteoric rise. Mindful of the great works that ambitious men could encourage, the Bishop is cautiously admiring of the present incumbent of Saint Peter's Seat. The rumours of women and bastards were of little moment. God tests us all, we all fail, we beg pardon, we are forgiven, we are tested anew. It is the Grand Plan, God's very own *magnum opus*. If we do not allow sin, then the holy Nazarene would have had no reason to bless the shit and vomit of the earth with his pure and shining feet. Yes, Alexander VI is a formidable proponent of God's work on earth and the princes of these city states and counties and countries and kingdoms do well to acknowledge his papal powers. And so they have no choice here in such a humble, second-rate city but to throw the nobody, the peasant, the woman to the wolves. But even so . . . As he treads softly away, the Bishop thinks that this particular lord might have put up more of a fight.

---------- ∞∞∞ ----------

She was going to die. Cicero himself could not have defended her successfully, Even the man who with such brilliance conjured an impossible freedom for Sextus Roscius the Patricide would have thrown his hands in the air at the impossibility of this defense. She was all that her sex was. Weak, ignorant, tearful, sullen. She even attempted a mild cunning, a child's cunning, so easy to eviscerate. He had had her brought to the episcopal palace next to Santa Maria, a mean unfurnished room towards the back of the great building but even so, she seemed to diminish its meanness with her own. *Lord, what was her name? He really must find the damned woman's name* . . . He had been tempted to pass over the onerous task of interview to his secretary Lucius, thinking it would take but an hour and then be over, but he remembered the keen eyes of his temporal lord and worse, the stinking fear of displeasing the Mother Church by a careless, ill-considered, lazy investigation . . .

So here she was. And here he was. The Bishop in a humble wooden chair, a chair devoid even of damask and velvets, not even a cushion. Perhaps he should have thought to awe her into tearful confession with the glories of his audience chamber; the tapestries, the armoured suits, the busts of emperors, the statues of popes and saints and Zeno himself casting indifferent judgement from plinth upon plinth.

But he realized as he took his humble place – hard, oak, kept rough through underuse beneath his soft palms – he realized now that this could not have been a better place. The walls were unplastered, the grey stone shining slightly with September's damp, the flagstones unadorned by the simplest homespun rug. Firstly, he could see from her eyes as she was dragged roughly within, that it might appear to the uneducated like some place of torture. True, there were no instruments to threaten and cajole an early admission but perhaps the imagination was the greatest of all instruments. And he could see that her imagination – stupid though she clearly was – was in a fervent of creation. And secondly, in that grey, sad, wintery chamber, his own gaudy magnificence shone like God's light from Heaven. Red became carmine, blue became topaz, green the turquoise of peacock feather. He could not have designed a greater background for the opulent omnipotence of his office than these grim, hard stones.

She was on her knees. Four feet away but close enough for him to smell sweat, unwashed clothes, the stain of shit and urine, some womanly horror that seemed almost to take on a wispy shape as it snaked towards him upon the fetid, closed airs. He closed his knees. *Keep the door open.*

Lucius stood by his side. The two episcopal guards by the door. The stinking woman starting to sob on the floor. The Bishop sighed. He had little to do with women. They were the intangible ghosts at his side when he had finished his repose, they drifted like spirits through the palace corridors with purposes and tasks he did not comprehend or even consider. They prepared him food and dealt with the waste his food eventually became. Ghosts. Swift, heads bowed, smelling of nothing, saying nothing, leaving no trace. Of course, the women of the city streets were different. Occasionally he watched one from his covered sedan as he took the air. He liked the women who swung their hips in time with their unbound hair. He had no desire to fuck or even touch them. But there was something about their primeval joy in simply *being* that amused him. They were dead in childbirth or of the pox or from the final husbandly beating soon enough but for ten, twenty years, they swung their hips in time with their long, unbound hair and seemed to love this miserable life beyond all common sense.

This woman, this woman no longer loved life. And her hips were wide and packed with solid plebeian fat, her hair tucked beneath a simple white cap but greyish and wispy. He could not imagine her swinging those hips in time with life's pendulum. She was boring him already.

He could see that she had been beaten. Her lips were swollen and there was a vivid bruise distorting one eye. It was not surprising. Whatever her guilt, she had been instrumental in the deaths of six people, one a child – and all six way above her in station – and her ignorance and lack of status gave her a greater vulnerability than it perhaps deserved. By rights of course, the learned, the quick of thought, the privileged involved in this horrid, never-ending case should pay the price but God had ordered every estate so that his creations all had a divine price to pay. Noble man and shepherd, lady and whore, their estates were full of purpose and not one immune to divine judgement. Women such as this needed to understand that the conclusion of whatever trial she might be afforded was of absolutely no consequence. She was guilty because she was poor and common. She was beaten because she was poor and common. She could however determine her heavenly fate by showing obedience to it all. He looked at her sadly. She would never understand even his words, let alone their theology. But it was his divinely ordained task to at least try.

'Do you understand why you are here?'

She looked up. Nodded. Shook her head. Cried a little.

'Speak up. I cannot hear you. Do you know who I am?'

This time she nodded. 'My Lord Bishop. I have seen you. On the steps of the . . . the cathedral. Mother Maria's house. The holy day of the maculate concession. I was with my lady. My pretty pretty lady. Blue ribbons that day. But then the bow came loose . . .'

'Good, good. Then you know why you are here. That you are charged with the most grievous conspiracy either by intent, or by gross neglect amounting to intent, of causing the death by poison of your lady. A young girl, no less.'

He could see that she understood little of this but was gratified that she did at least flinch at the final phrase.

'Well? How do you plead? 'Twere as well you speak only the honest truth because to lie before a bishop is to lie with your hand upon the holy book or upon the relic of a saint's bone or Saint Zeno's silver mask.'

At this, the miserable creature began to cry in earnest. He could make out a few simple words; 'love', 'my sweet one', 'nursed at my dug', 'poor little ladybird', something more about a blue ribbon and 'a secret letter'. It was cloying stuff. The Bishop was a decent man; he shut his eyes at passing children being thrashed by angry fathers, he could not even abide cruelty to horses, the deliberately wounding of hounds for sport. But he had never come this close to pain that smelt and looked so . . . well, so *ugly*. The woman's eyes were red and puffy as if suffering infection, her stubby nose dripped with white snot and green mucus. She was even starting to dribble a little from her swollen mouth. Ugly. Highborn grief was contained. Elegant. Exquisite and composed. He had seen and admired no shortage of that these past few months. But common lowborn grief was…well, it seemed cruder than the howling of injured animals.

Lucius – a good boy but a little eager, some distant Medici blood nudging him into arrogance despite recent, rather sobering events – Lucius prodded her gently with a distasteful toe.

'Answer your bishop, woman. He is giving you fair hearing which is more than you deserve or should expect.'

But she sobbed on a little more. He could just decipher her blaming the apothecary, blaming the monk, blaming even the very dead themselves.

'But what of you? Are you spotlessly clean of blame?'

She stared with dumb bovine eyes. And then shook her head and he had her. No. She was to blame. This was her fault. And this. And that and this and that and all the things going back a decade and more. Ribbons and letters and toy dogs let loose under carriages and unhealthy passions for her master's nephew. He stopped listening. She had confessed. To quite what, he would fashion with more precise wording later but she had confessed and her soul was safe and the Podesta's approval was safe and the city streets might even be safe when the citizens had watched her hang. Yes, he would hang her as a conspirator to murder. Because he had no intention – and had never had – of trying her as a witch. Did his worthy and most estimable Lord not realise how time-consuming and downright infuriating a witch trial was? There was no righteous golden glory, just paying surly boys to shovel up the stinking, sticky mess left over at the end. And it would tie up this city in a state of unhealthy furore for weeks, perhaps months. It would involve Rome, the Magisterium, the Inquisition and a cardinal or four. By the saints, that madman Torquemada might even sail over from Spain…Was this poor peninsula not suffering enough after fifty years of war? Was the French enemy not still on Italian soil? If he could quietly deliver the accusation, the case, the pleading and the confession to the Council in one sitting, then they could sign off the vote and the penalty without even having to see her. Not quite according to the *Promissione Maleficarum*–the labyrinthine Venezian law code they were forced to follow–but it was close enough. Did they really want to sit through weeks of raking tired eyes through ten centuries of legal codes which contradicted each other and made no sense? No, the damned peasant could swing at the end of a rope and let that be an end to it all.

CHAPTER TWO

in which an English traveller docks at an Italian port and meets an old friend

Four days earlier – before the woman in the Bishop's dungeon had received her third beating but was yet newly glowing from her second – a ship from London docked at the Free Port of Livorno. An Englishman of approximately forty years disembarked, slightly green about the gills for it had been a rough autumn journey all the way from Spitalfields and the Southwark Pool. He spent one night in port and then at dawn found himself a place on a six seat carriage *en route* for Firenze. Livorno had thankfully escaped the ravages of the invading French army which had now passed this way twice but it was still bearing the closed-shuttered grimace of a town facing siege. The fifty or so miles to Firenze were uneventful although the Englishman was overheard refusing the *osso buca* offered him at the roadside tavern in favour of *ribolitta* with water. This rejection of traditional, if rich and fatty Tuscan cuisine was noted. Also noted was his quiet refusal to be goaded and the belligerent fellow passengers who had tried, soon gave up. The countryside still bore the ruts of war carts, a thousand horses and forty times as many boots but Mother Nature was bravely beginning to fill in the muddy traces with new-sown grasses and saplings.

Firenze that year (now that the French threat was gone) was a place of huge hope and godliness. Or alternatively the city was now a nest of vipers spreading sin. Opinions varied.

As the carriage approached the ancient city walls, the road began to deteriorate. Carriage wheels rocked, passengers clutched at the sides, the ceiling, even at each other. Mud, stones, unmended paving split under by cracks; the coach driver shouted down that *give another winter and another bloody war, they wouldn't make the journey at all. That they were lucky he was brave enough to venture forth, that God was watching over them, that they were approaching the most holy of all holy city states. That God Himself had saved the city from the French Beast! That friends of Alexander the Borgia Pope might as well jump out now and head back to Rome*!

One of the pieces of leather luggage snapped its ropes and bounced down the road behind them. Curses, horses complaining, a brief respite from the rocking as the driver shouted his boy to run back. *No time to mend the rope with knots, they're too close to the city now, the dusk is upon them, the gates will shut. Signor Brooke needs to carry his case upon the knee*. The passengers looked expectantly at the pale Londoner, for Signor Brooke could be a name owned by none other than he. *Signor Brooke!* The broken toothed boy held open the door with his knee and lifted up the case with both hands. Still the quiet man with the grizzled chin and deep eyes made no sign, seemingly lost in his thoughts.

Ehila! Ciao! Signor!

At last light and sense returned to the Englishman's eyes.

'Oh. Oh of course, my papers, books, thank you, grazie, grazie.'

That the boy had been at fault for not tying the box more securely and needed a slap around the ear seemed not to occur to him. The other passengers shook their heads and exchanged derisory looks, sharing an unspoken but universal contempt at the Englishman's arrogance that he was 1) too deep in thought to care about possessions and 2) too rich to care if they perished in the mud. *Bloody English!* One king and then another and then another and then back to the first and then another and then his brother. And then butchering one in a cold chapel before God and the one before this one in the mud of the fields. And all the time expecting the people of Flanders and Burgundy and Brittany to feed and shelter and keep safe this pretender and this exile and this usurper so that the petty squabbles of a cold, wet island had to become the problems of all Europe. *Bloody English.* All they had to do was sit back and count all that money they made from woolen cloth, money stolen from the Low Countries and the Italian valleys, but no, no, they had to squabble and fight and kill their kings. *If there was one thing they all hated more than the French* . . . but no, that was old cursing. The French were the real beasts now. After what had happened at Mordano . . .

The Englishman was unaware of their hostility. Or rather he was well used to it, having travelled all over France, the Low Countries and these Italian states. And in any case, a contemptuous reference to the York-Lancaster wars from a citizen of the most fractious and violent peninsula in Europe would only have had him smile a little at the irony.

Groaning, the coach was rumbling forwards again. The Englishman – we should call him Mr Brooke for the moment at least – could only see backwards. His quiet demeanour, his inferior race and the ebullient belligerence of his fellow travelers had seen to it that he faced backwards. He could see the hazy September sun just hovering over the skyline of trees and a few rows of simple houses. They had passed great stripes of vines and olive trees earlier – some showing signs of an army on the move but not as many as he had feared – but these had retreated as they neared the city walls. And so because he was facing backwards, he heard rather than saw the tumult of jeers and cries as they drew nearer to what was clearly the city. The noises got louder as the coach persisted. He tried to get a better view but the other five passengers were doing the same, jostling against one another. It sounded as though a not-insignificant crowd was shouting insults at a smaller group who were in vain attempting a valiant exchange.

Ladri! Maiali pigri! molestatori di bambini! vai all'inferno! puttana sporca!

Contadini ingrate! animali sporchi!

Quite disgusting taunts. Although imaginative.

The coach was forced to come to a bumpy halt. After a second or two of incoherent grunting, the Englishman's co-passengers began to heave and squeeze themselves out onto the mud and pave. Allowing himself ten seconds or so to savour the emptiness and rapidly clearing air, the Englishman mentally shrugged and deftly hopped out too.

What a sight. None of them had seen anything quite like *this*. The six – and their driver and his gaping boy – squelched around the side of the carriage and took it in.

They were on a wide road of barely adequate paving which led reasonably straight towards the high, grey walls of the city, maybe half a mile eastwards atop a small incline. As it headed towards the walls, the road soon became swallowed up by rows of two story houses but where they had stopped there were still flat expanses of common land and a few browning fields turning gold in the sunset. Along the road, clearly coming from the city, rolled a crowd. Maybe a hundred or so drably coloured Northern Plain Italians, browns, greys, dull hues, simple hoods and cloaks, rough woolen hose. But in the centre of this drab collection swum a smaller centre that glowed and shone. Twenty or so people – mostly adults but some smaller figures that had to be young children – moved quickly along the road trying to extricate themselves from the larger swarm and this smaller cluster was dressed in all the colours of God's rainbow. Bright jewels caught the dying sun, soft furs glowed, pinks, saffrons, scarlets, titians, the azure blue of the very sky itself. A little crowd of gods, their cloaks, doublets, gowns and hose singing out in the brightest shades of every colour. Even the children glistened and sparkled, their hair shone smooth and clean, their cheeks made pale and sleek by good food and shaded rooms. Servants, almost as gaudily dressed, were trying to force a way through the outer ring. The Englishman could see now that the larger circle of townspeople and peasants were calling out, even throwing the occasional clod of earth. Weighed down with bags and pushing carts on wobbling wheels, the serving men tried to steer a way through and at the same time protect the others from mud, stones, insults, the world.

'*Sancta mater Dei'*, breathed the driver. 'It is the Medici. Firenze has rid herself of the last of the Medici. Who would dare this thing?'

Whilst the Italian passengers swore and gasped and grunted in every shade of amazement and incredulity, the Englishman allowed himself a small pursing of his mouth. But if you knew Mr Brooke, you would know that this was the equivalent of a wide-mouthed gape.

'The bloody Medici,' said the driver again.

'The bloody Medici,' aped the boy and got a slap around the ear.

---------- ∞∞∞ ----------

It took another hour or more for Mr Brooke and his fellows to rumble slowly through the Porta Romana, across the Ponte Vecchio to the first of their lodgings. Mr Brooke exited upon the fourth, a decent enough tavern deep in the heart of the nameless alleyways surrounding the Piazza della Signoria and because it was now very dark and the city streets awash with all kinds of refugees, soldiers itching for a fight and women mourning the loss of camp-follower earnings, he took immediately to his bed.

Firenze was unusually noisy. He had stayed in the city perhaps half a dozen times and yet it seemed most unfamiliar. She seemed to taste different somehow. There was something upon the night air…an arrogance, a fresh smell he couldn't quite define, a buzz of voices at once uniform and at the same time indistinct. At last the cathedral called the midnight offices and he drifted off. But in the streets he could hear singing.

---------- ∞∞∞ ----------

Firenze without its Medici was a nervous filly of a town. She twitched and stop-started in her excitement as if she didn't quite know which way to trot. Just after dawn, the streets and dirty alleyways were as full as he remembered but somehow the people were both louder and more exuberant and yet also more subdued, laughing and then cautiously flicking their eyes this way, that way, laughing again, crossing themselves. Yes, that was one thing new; so much crossing of themselves! And was he mistaken or were the shades of cloth now more somber, as if all the colours of Ancient Rome so long preserved had been packed away into one great chest and been taken on the road with the last of the Medici.

Mr Brooke bought himself some bread and goats cheese from a stall in the alley outside his lodgings. The cheese seller seemed an affable sort of fellow despite the ragged weeping flesh wound across his cheek and so our Englishman sent a tentative hook down.

'I saw a crowd leaving the city last evening. The Medici, people said. Good cheese. A very fine cheese.'

The Firenzi rolled his eyes and expleted both words and spit in a torrent of exasperated contempt.

'That is what comes of sucking French cock! Yes, my friend, the last of them. Hiding behind the skirts of their serving girls but now out and on their way. A damnable shame. Medici thrown out into the streets like dogs! For how many years have we respected our Familia Primum? For how many years have we paid our dues? Who could have thought they would let us down so badly, heh? Deals with the French, may God curse them! The Medici shitting down upon us from such a great height! I remember Old Piero and before him Cosimo the

Great, incredible man, how beautiful is this city because of this man, the most beautiful city in the world because of Cosimo the Great.'

'Yes indeed, you have patronized the best here, the painters, the sculptors . . . '

'And Lorenzo too, died just three winters ago now. Died too young, too young, God bless him, my age, forty summers and a few. But such a lord! I remember when the bloody Pazzi tried to overthrow him. I was twenty years old or thereabouts and the Pazzi a bloody scary lot, no respect for Man nor God but we stood firm here, told them where to fucking go. I was at the Duomo itself when they slaughtered Lorenzo's brother at the fucking altar, nineteen fucking stab wounds and Lorenzo covered too, nearly bled to death next to poor Guiliano. Such a golden boy that one and dead at twenty-five. But we rose up, us Firenzi, my good old dad was one who locked the sacristy door on them.'

'Yes, we heard. Even in London . . . '

'And Lorenzo not scared to take on the ones right at the top, the Archbishop of Pisa, that fucker Salviati–*yes, my love, fresh from the Tuscan hills last week, no the blue veined is more expensive*–hanged from the Palazzo della Signoria just behind us. Didn't give a shit, Lorenzo, about ecclesiastical bloody privilege, no, you plot against the Medici, you hang in your archbishop's robes, you fucker.'

'Yes. I remember the Pope of Rome being quite upset.'

'Hah! I like your words, Englishman. Quite upset. Fucker excommunicated the whole bloody city! Every single one of us banned from Holy Mass, no baptism, no communion, no extreme unction. What a devil. But our priests did us anyway, our priests are Firenzi first, dogs of Rome second. *A couple of pennies, my love. Smile at me again and you can have another inch. Yes, that's lovely, there you go.*'

'And the group leaving yesterday . . . ?'

The cheesemonger ignored the question, gesturing happily with his knife. 'Did you hear, all the way over in London Town what Lorenzo did with Jacopo de Pazzi? The fucker escaped but Lorenzo sent out the Medici dogs – his cousins that is – and they caught him and brought him back. Three weeks tortured in the cellars of the Duomo, then hanged next to Salviati's rotting corpse. Buried at Santa Croce but then a group of lads dug him up and chucked him in a ditch. Bigger group of lads comes along and finds him, drags him – bits falling off, mind – all the way through the town – over there, I was watching over there through the archway by the piazza and then, then, they propped him up against the door of the Palazzo Pazzi itself and used his head as a door knocker! Nearly pissed my hose.'

'Yes, very amusing.'

'But then, then – and this makes me proud – it was thrown in the Arno, good and gone but a group of kids, just kids, fished it out again and gave it a good whipping! Even kids, you see, even kids know that you're loyal to your lord, you don't side with the bloody Pisans. Pisa is *our* tributary commune, we don't answer to them.'

'But with the Medici now gone . . . '

'Yes, yes, Englishman, new times, new times. Well, Piero the Younger isn't a patch on his father. Trying to do deals with the French! After what they did at Mordano? Children spitted on pikes, old men blinded, nuns raped; Lorenzo is spinning in his tomb, Englishman, spinning. But it's not easy to be the son of a great man. Or a weak man in a strong family.'

'No indeed.' And was there a flicker in the pale, still eyes of Mr Brooke?

'Lorenzo would never have made that deal with the Bastard Charles, with the murdering French, no, he'd have cut his own throat first. But Piero . . . . well, it's done now and they're gone. New world, new world.'

'Indeed. And now might the Pazzi family return?'

The cheesemonger hawked, deep and rich, then spat a dirty green lump, worryingly close to his wares. 'I see you keep your ear to the ground, Englishman, yes I've heard they're sneaking back in. People who should know better think this city is now on the table for any *canis filius*. I've heard that bloody Giovanni Borgia was seen in a covered litter not a week back too. He won't find much of a welcome here. Lock up your daughters!'

At this, Mr Brooke blinked. His lips most certainly turned downwards in a micro-second of derision but then it was gone. The more sensitive might have noticed a sudden chill in the warm morning air. 'Giovanni Borgia, the young Duke of Gandia. In Firenze. I had not heard that.'

'Could be wrong, could be wrong. Now, I can't be talking to you all day, my good lord, cheese to sell to ladies like this gorgeous creature here. Where are you off to?'

Mr Brooke licked at his upper lip. 'I believe that an old acquaintance of mine, an old colleague of long standing, a friend even . . . he is from Ferrara, was lately of Milan, longtime resident here in Firenze. Humble priest but . . . but I hear that he is now a man, the man perhaps of influence here in this city.'

'Tell me his name and I'll see if I can help. If he's French, Pazzi or Borgia, you can go fuck yourself.'

'Of course.' A miniscule pause. How tricky were names and the weight they balanced upon their fingertips. Who knew the power of a name better than our Mr Brooke?

'My friend is Girolamo. Girolamo Savonarola.'

There was a little crowd around for alongside the cheese-seller there was also a fruit stall and someone mending broken leathers. And so it was not just the cheesemaker who swore and gawped.

'Piss on the Pazzi, Englishman! You know the *Dominus Holocausta*? You know him to call him Girolamo?'

There was a tangible taste of keen interest in the ether. Mr Brooke tasted it and found it relatively unthreatening.

'I am honoured to called him Giramo. And to also call him Friend.'

'Well, well, well,' A cheesy ham of a fist thrust forward and took the slim white fingers, enveloping them in sticky rind and melting fat. 'Calling the Dominus, Friend! There's an exalted road you're taking!'

'Or the lowest road of all,' muttered someone else, 'Be careful we don't all end up taking the Infernal Path, it'll be us burning then, not Father Savonarola.'

'Yah, shut your mouth, Jaco, you want the Medici back? You one of the *Bigi*, you *Compagnacci* coward? End Times are coming, we're not far off now. War, rape of children, spoiling the land, plague killing cattle – it's what the Dominus has been saying for years. Might look like the bloody French but it's the Anti-Christ himself. And we know where he's perched his fat arse . . .'

There was clearly a general consensus in this admittedly small group that the Devil had perched his ample behind on the seat of Saint Peter himself. The cheesemonger was in full flow and Mr Brooke, relieved to find himself no longer the centre of attention, began to slip away.

'Bloody Rodrigo Borgia! Pope Alexander the fucking Sixth, my royal rectum. How many whores bouncing on his papal cock? How many bastards getting the sinecures? *Hey Englishman! You might find your Dominus in the Plaza de la Republica, mate! Go on through Signoria, take the far left exit, keep going. He's preaching there most mornings! Or he might be with Judith in the Palazzo Medici gardens! Talks to her for hours on end! People stand and watch him, now there's no Medici left, the gardens are for the People! You can piss in the fountain all you want! Try Judith first.* Will you get you filthy hands off that ragusano, that came all the way from Sicily two days ago, first in since the French went north and I know for a fact that you, Pox-face, cannot afford it . . .'

---------- ∞∞∞ ----------

The hub of stinking, belching, living, breathing humanity receded as Mr Brooke made his way through the covered alleyway beneath five floors of cramped apartments and came out blinking into the wide expanse of the Piazza della Signoria. In his wide travels – some from choice, some *per vim* – he had visited Firenze at least half a dozen times but the wide expanse of the world's greatest piazza in the world's greatest city never failed to please. It was just so huge. And so clean and clear of unnecessary nonsense. Smooth ochre-red paving, clean lines, high white facades like the full morning skies of winter ... Mr Brooke was no architect unless one could construct a city of words and concepts – and surely Mr Brooke's piazza to his shame would then be a labyrinth of snaking pathways and hidden turns! – but he had enough learning to appreciate the sheer, almost monstrous bulk of the Palazzo, its crenellations, its huge square clocktower reaching up to God. Named The Cow, she was indeed an ugly beast. To the Palazzo's right, the three curved arches of the Loggia; smooth and soft and dark like the hidden reaches of a woman's body. To Mr Brooke, these two – the palace and the open loggia with its triple arches – represented nothing if not the contrast and sympathy that existed between man and woman, male and female. Seemingly so at odds, the Palazzo so harsh and brutal and almost crude in its simplistic bulk. The Loggia graceful, drifting upwards, lost in dark shadows.

Somewhat unwillingly Mr Brooke then thought of the women in his life. Dear dependable Eliza, back at home in Clerkenwell, soft mountainous breasts, laughing eyes, big meaty hands covered in flour. Twenty years together but they had never shared a bed and had she complained? Not once. He rarely bothered to ask himself why. And his mother, that poor neurotic shrew, complaining, complaining, always looking over towards the Other Family, the Brookes, who sat on the sunny side of the ancestral tree, free from the knock that comes in the darkest hour of the night and which might yet come for them. His mother had lived her life in anticipation of the past waking itself, shaking off its 80-year slumber and remembering where she lived. When he was old enough to be told the story of who they were and who they had been and the story of *him*, Old John, he had tried to paint her – with words – the passing of the years and the flimsy gauze that was men's memories. But she had never really let the fear pass. Fear but also a vicious envy that the Cousins could walk in the daylight whilst *her* children lived still in shadow. And as usual he refused to think of the third woman in his life. The light was too bright this morning, the noises too vivacious, the appetites too voracious. Eleanor belonged to the hours between Matins and Lauds.

If he wished to find the Piazza de la Republica he needed only to cross the square, take the corsa towards his left and continue on. But he had a feeling that Giramo was here, here somewhere in this wide expanse of red floor and white marble walls. A long time since the narrow alleyways of Oxford's Inns of Court and three years now since their last meeting in Rome but still . . . sometimes he could smell Giramo's vitality, his living, breathing rage. It was early but there were small groups of people in the piazza, even a few on horseback. Stalls had been set up around the edges, deep into the dark depths of the Loggia arches even, vying for space with the newly carved statues, white gleaming marble shining out from the shadows, slender arms and fingers visible even from where he was standing across on the other side. The Palazzo had a small entrance, scarcely even noticeable from where he was now strolling. But in front of it, Mr Brooke – if he squinted – could just about see a sizeable crowd . . .

Carefully avoiding horse shit and the various detritus of human passage, he crossed the square. As he passed children, merchants, women with wares, whores of the night on their sleepy way home, he could hear her name. '*Judith*!' '*Judith has come to the Palazzo de la Signoria!*' Apparently Judith was on the move.

The crowd became a little more dense as he got closer but it was apparent to Mr Brooke that there were as many people hurrying away from the Palazzo front doorway as heading towards it. Being thin, not over-tall and innocuous with very little personal scent, slipping through crowds whilst causing no offense was one of our friend's many skills and so just a few minutes after entering the square, he found himself underneath the squat, solid walls of the palace itself.

There she was. Judith. How uttering incredible to see her here. To see her at all outside of a penny sketch. Mr Brooke gave himself over to appreciation.

Well over seven feet high and gleaming bright in the new Italian sun, she was golden. Golden and terrible. Holofernes had his head and neck twisted awkwardly round, the better for her to choose the place to sever. *How quite strange to see every side of a statue,* Mr Brooke wondered. *I do not think I have ever see every degree of the three hundred and sixty. How very remarkable. To see something from every place one stands and not just from the front…here I can see Holofernes' face, eyes closed, proud moustache drooping in almost loving submission. From this angle, her arm and the blade are dominant. But if I just move to my right….* – Such a crowd! All talking, some approving but he could hear some calls of dismay too – *from here I can see her other hand, clutching with such calm possession his hair. And his kingly braid that falls all the way down his back. He must have been so mighty, for a king who fails in battle must cut his braid back to the nape and here is his, so long and proud…*

The gold-on-bronze statue on its heavy square plinth had clearly only just been deposited in its position, just to the left of the wooden doorway. There were scored marks of a heavily laden cart deep in the paving, mud everywhere, the scuffing of heavy horse hooves, deep marks on the ochre stone. Mr Brooke could see where some of the statue's gold had been scratched away to reveal the greenish bronze beneath. The figure herself looked a little unsteady.

'Behold the neck of pride served by the hand of humility! Does it not say in the Book of Psalms, my brothers, that the wicked wear pride like a necklace and violence wraps them round? Look at him! *Look at him!* His pride falling away with his blood into the sands of Israel!'

Ah. There he was. Right beneath Judith's elbow, leaning on the very stone cushion of Holofernes' last rest. Gesticulating of course. Gesticulating wildly and spitting not a little, his bulbous eyes straining in their sockets. Good old Giramo.

'Read what it says here on this plinth, my brothers, my Firenzi Brethren! '*Kingdoms fall through luxury, cities rise through virtues. Behold the neck of pride severed by the hand of humility.*' Are ***we*** virtuous? Are ***we*** humble? Do we wipe our arses with the hands of humility? Do we pluck our noses with virtuous fingers?'

The crowd responded as crowds do with ribald jeering and many a 'No! Shame!' and 'Yes we do!' 'Help us, Dominus! Help us towards virtue!' But there was also a low murmur, almost like the growl of a cat who has put up with your stroking just this far but who now evinces her discomfort.

'Be careful, Savonarola, you go too far!'

'Be careful, Father, that you yourself do not fall into the sin of pride.'

This led to an angry exchange and a bit of scuffle between those who disagreed, finally interrupted by the great man's roar.

'Save your ire for those who deserve it, brothers! Where did this great woman, this Lady of Courage and Virtue and Revenge and Justice, where of yesterday did she reside?'

'In the bloody Medici's garden!' 'She was in the middle of a fountain!' came an immediate reply to the laughter of those around. Savonarola nodded, shaven head now coming clear of the godly habit.

'Yes. Since our proud Firenzi forefather Donatello carved her virtuous lines, this great lady has been held captive in Babylonian slavery! As a water fountain in the Palazzo Medici, a *water fountain*! In their palace to taunt the citizens of this republic that one family and one family alone ruled us. Against the laws of God and Man, one sinful family ruling all. But where are they now?!'

There was a communal roar of approval at this. 'Gone! In Hell! On the road with the tarts and whores! Sucking cock in the gutter!'

But quieter voices muttered; 'Yes and as like to return before we know it. Be careful where your tongue gets you, Master of Flames.'

Savonarola now – with the strength and grace of a much younger man and seemingly uninhibited by his robes – swung himself up to the plinth of the statue and, perched like a predatory bird, seemed to be sharing the stone cushion with Holofernes himself.

'What does it say on this very plinth? What did the hypocrites dare to carve upon the base of this fine Lady's greatest hour?'

There were a few *sotto voce* comments about the little boys urinating and other rather pastoral scenes included on the plinth reliefs but generally it was a partisan crowd.

'Liberty and fortitude! The Medici dared to lecture the Firenzi on liberty and fortitude!'

'Yeees!' the great hooked nose swooped downwards and a thin white finger pointed at the successful heckler. Who happened to be standing next to Mr Brooke. The sweeping gaze held him like a hawk locking on to rodent pee in a meadow and then released him with a flicker. But Mr Brooke knew instinctively that he had been seen.

An hour or so passed, perhaps less, and the statue was heaved more firmly into position and given a ceremonial wiping down by every man, woman and gawping child. Girolamo Savonarola kept to his position, half sitting, half kneeling on the edge of the plinth, reaching out to touch people in blessing, to remonstrate those women wearing face paint, to clasp the forearms of men promising all of Earth's obscenities falling upon the Medici. At last as the nearby monastery of San Michele rang out the chimes of Sext, the great man slid from the plinth and strode over to Mr Brooke.

'Giovanni! Giovanni! My dearest John! You came.' A simple statement. He had known he would come. There had never been a doubt.

'My old friend. Giramo. You look . . . thinner.' But in truth the man was a veritable reed, a wire, a wisp of grass, 'thinner' did not do his corporeal disintegration justice. The man's skin was almost transparent. Savonarola shrugged, huge teeth like a wolf's in receding gums.

'Things of this world, John, things of this world. So much corruption of the purity, so much distraction and obfuscation. When I pared myself down to the very bone, I *saw myself*. Heh? Heh? I actually saw my soul. Have you ever seen your human soul, John? It's a dark, slimy thing, it hates the light, it slides away from our introspection and examination. But in the heart of darkness – if you look very carefully and in a state of bliss – then within this dark, slimy thing, John, you can determine the faint, glorious glimmer of God.' He stopped, eyes half closed. '*Non est ad astra mollis e terris via*. There is no easy way from the earth to the stars. But the way is there, John, it is there.'

'I remember how you loved your Seneca. I was worried with your new fervency that you would abandon the voices of Old Rome. And what then would we talk about, old friend?'

'Hah!' the gaunt arms clamped themselves firmly to both Brooke shoulders, 'Never! The ancient aesthetes and Stoics had more of God about them than the pestilential whoremongers who dare to lecture us on virtue today. And anyway, *Fas est ab hoste doceri*. One should learn even from one's enemies.'

'So even Ovid is allowed in the new Savonarola Republic?'

'Pah! Ovid? I thought that was Terence?'

'No. Most assuredly Ovid.'

'Well then . . . that makes my point exactly! Ovid is my enemy and I would burn every carnal, licentious page but if I can learn about the carnal and lascivious Beast from him, then I shall. Does Rodrigo Borgia love Ovid? Hah! Do bears shit in the Vallambrosa? Come now, Sir John, you look like an Englishman in Firenze. Hungry as Hell but not quite knowing how to order. Come with me and we shall eat and talk and talk and eat and I shall tell you why I have called you all this way.'

---------- ∞∞∞ ----------

Mr Brooke ate and drank but unsurprisingly the great man touched only watered wine and some bread. It was a dark, unpretentious tavern and the proprietors and other diners obviously knew Savonarola well enough to nod, cross themselves and leave them alone. But Savonarola clearly had need of casual protectors for as they ate, a tall, quiet man Savonarola called Casale came and sat close by, eating nothing but looking up when the door opened. They talked a little of the French army, still on its way northwards, out of Italy, the devastation and the terrible atrocity of poor unfortunate Mordano. The peace brokered by the League of Venice and what it might mean for power-sharing in the future. Savonarola was not as vitriolic as the cheesemonger had been. He leaned forward and spoke quietly;

'You know, John, and I can say this to you, I am not sure many beyond my closest brethren are quite ready to hear yet, but the French King is not our enemy.'

'No? But the invasion? Mordano?'

'Yes, yes, terrible and these terrible things happen when man is given license to behave like a beast as he is in war. Ask my friend Casale here, he was at the fight at Fornovo just in the summer, a nasty business and with no winner though both sides are claiming it. Look at King David himself. '*And he brought forth the people that were therein, and put them under saws, and under harrows of iron, and under the axes of iron, and made them pass through the brick kiln.*' Children, John, just children! War is the most terrible thing, then and now. But the direction of hatred towards Charles Valois merely diverts our attention away from the true enemy. Which is the Great Ape of Rome.'

'Hmmm,' Mr Brooke had his mouth full but nodded, 'Ah . . . Rodrigo Borgia?'

'Of course, of course. But not just him, pox-ridden son of a harpy though he is. Every Pope. Every Cardinal. Every Bishop. They throw shit in the face of Our Lord, John. They defile his footsteps with their foul, filthy, silk-shod shoes. When did Peter rise up so high above his brothers? Where does it say that the few must rule the many and with such disdain and grandeur? When did Christ live in a palace? When did he father bastards on whores?'

'Giramo! Hush! Your words may well be true but have some circumspection. I may only have been in Firenze a morning but I do not think the populace have turned our way just because they have thrown out the Medici.' He wiped his mouth on his sleeve. 'I saw them on the road, you know.'

His friend wiped sweat from his pale brow. 'Yes. It was the last of them. We found them hiding in a secret apartment, fed by loyal retainers. We gave them the count of one thousand to be in the street and over the bridge. Amazing how much tawdry wealth one can pack in one thousand heart beats.'

'Indeed. It was as if a rainbow had fallen to earth. So much silk. I did not know it came in so many shades of pink.'

Savonarola laughed. 'You know, Sir John, I have a plan. The moving of Judith was the first of many stages. But I wish to rid this whole city of its vanity. Every silken hose, every pearled doublet and fancy ruff, the nonsense that men and women hide behind. The lace and earbobs, the perfumes and shoes fit only for sodomite dancers. I would have every citizen of this republic gladly, joyfully empty every chest and drawer of these things and bring them here to the Piazza della Signoria and throw them into one huge bonfire. This city is to be the beacon of hope for all cities. She shall be the New City of God, just as Augustine of Hippo prophesied could come if men embraced virtue. Here! In this place. *I have seen it*, I am blessed with visions and dreams every night, I hear voices of angels lifting me up. This place, this great city, can be cleansed of her vulgar pride. I shall do it, you know, Sir John Oldcastle, I shall do it.'

He had observed the slight wince.

'Still not travelling as yourself, John Oldcastle? If I had a name so steeped in the glory of God's true word and practice, I would have it emblazoned on every travel trunk and every cloak.'

'And you would not survive the week, my revolutionary friend. No, I am still John Brooke of Spitalfields for the moment. When I travel at least. My friends and neighbours, my woman; these all know I am of the Oldcastles but it is still too ... *hot* in England for the legacy of Old John to be too widely cheered. And you know full well, Giramo Savonarola, that I have never been and will never be a knight.'

Savonarola shook his head. More a skull than a human head. 'Your grandfather ... such courage. And foresight for such times. You must not despair. Yours is still a name to be reckoned in parts of this continent.'

'Which is why I travel under Brooke!'

'Not Lord Brooke of Cobham then?' Now the skeleton was smiling warmly.

Mr Brooke raised his eyebrows. 'Now that would most surely have me in the Tower. My cousin Lord Brooke of Cobham would rather piss on me dying in the street than acknowledge bastard Oldcastles still polluting his family strain. No. Brooke is a name I can claim rightly from my sire and Oldcastle one I claim proudly from his. Proudly but not openly. Such are still not the times, Giramo. The Catholic Church has a tighter hold now than even in my grandsire's day.'

'And yet we trust in our Lord that one day ... *sole scriptura* ... '

'*Sole scriptura*.'

They sat quietly for a time. Both remembering a small, cluttered room in the Oxford Inns of Court and two young men who for a short time shared that room and talked under the stars – on the ledge than ran across the roof from the eaves – talked about a world that would surely come in their lifetimes. Ran their hesitant, trembling fingers across the spines of forbidden books and rolled pamphlets, smuggled into England in crates of cloth and barrels of salted roe. Pelagius, Jan Hus, Peter Bruys, Wyclif. How many toasts – silent, secret, their half-unbelieving sincerity shining like stars in the night – to the wonder that was Gutenberg? To the sheaves and sheaves of *incunabula* pamphlets whose print now allowed freedom to the thousands of godly thoughts held back for so many years by the slow stumbling gait of the monk-copyist's skill and the sharp unforgiving eye of the Bishop-censor? The wind held the salt of true change upon the tongues that dared to taste. For young men like John Oldcastle and Giramo Savonarola it was as if a tightly iron-bound chest had been prised open, thin slivers of bright, quick-silver truths slipping out like streams of mercury to swim out into the world. Young men like them, young men all over Christendom, could now share in the wine-rich depths of God's own mind without having those pure Absolutes diluted – no *polluted* – by the constrained and censored priestly filter. But what irony; that the ideas once so vulnerable to that primal essence of Fire should now be impervious to the threat of oblivion but that those brave souls at the forefront of these new creations should themselves face the flames. Segharelli and Fra Dolcino the Fraticelli Spirituals. Jerome of Prague and Hus himself. Thomas Bagley and William Sawtrey the Lollards. Sir John Oldcastle, Lord of Cooling Castle . . .

The fear of the flame hung over them all but young men like Giramo Savonarola claimed passionately to be warmed by it, that it gave him strength, that without it he would be but a cold, passionless thing. *To face the flames for the glory of God's Truth*, he would enthuse as they drank cheap wine and cursed the ignorance of their tutors, *to have such a cleansing of the soul that all possible filth and dirt be burnt clear away!* And his eyes would gleam with a mad desire that both entranced and repelled. But John

Oldcastle had grown up in the flickering shadows of the flame and had not felt it warm nor cleanse him. Sometimes his grandfather came to him in his dreams and showed his outstretched hands with the flesh melting and dripping like candle fat.

'How is my beautiful Eleanor?' Savonarola broke the silence at last. But she had been there all along, quiet as a leveret, soft as fur, and John – for we can now call him John – was not surprised.

He chewed a little on his lip. 'As well as I can hope or expect. When she took holy orders – well, you know how it is, how we feel about such vanities – it was difficult for us all. But she seems more content. I am less frightened for her eternal soul and the deep waters of her mind than I was. Her abbess knows. And is kind.'

'If I could have killed a man …'

'I know. I too. Without hesitation. But it is three years now. '

'Yes. And yet not so very long. I still remember … I did not truly understand Abelard, I thought him alien and weak and tormented by such foolish nonsense in his love for Heloise. But Eleanor … when I met your dear sister, I understood how even a devout man of God might be tempted to love a woman. Or at least the woman all could see she would one day become.'

'I know you care deeply for her.'

They sat quietly again. Soon, thought John, he will tell me why I am here and then it will be all work and travel and reading and burning the candle to the end of its wick in the earliest hours. So before he tells me, I need to ask … as we are on the subject of her anyway …

'Giramo.'

'My friend?'

'I heard this morning. From a man selling cheese. That he had been seen entering the city. Did you know?'

The huge eyes strained against the pale skin. 'Here? In Firenze? Giovanni Borgia? I had not heard this, no. I would tell you, my friend, I would not lie to you on this. Casale, have you heard this?' The thin man with the opaque eyes frowned slightly and shook his head. Savonarola spat on the floor and a thin, grey whippet-dog reached out its thin neck to lick. 'I will ask questions, I have many many spies in every household. Giovanni Borgia, Juan, Spanish Duke of Gandia, here. That is no coincidence if it is true. Just as the Medici leave. I sense his father's hand in this. The Anti-Christ of Rome. Sniffing out another city-state to swallow down into his capacious belly.'

He fed a strip of bread to the dog now at his feet. Allowing himself a smaller portion.

John Oldcastle reached across the table and firmly took the skeletal hand. '*His flesh and blood, through his subtle works, is there in the form of bread.*'

Savonarola sighed. '*In what manner it is present need not be debated, whether as subject or as accident.*'

'*But as Christ was when he was alive . . .*'

'*So He is truly there.*'

'Amen.'

'Amen, my friend, amen.'

Savonarola wiped away a yellowed tear. No, he did not look well at all. He nudged his earthenware against John's in tired toast.

'To Sir John the Loller.'

'To Sir John.'

'We shall deal with the Papal Father's bastard another time, my friend. But no, that is not why I have called you. That is what you were hoping, yes? That he was here and we could finally avenge your sister? No, my friend, I have heard nothing of this wretch for many months now.'

He finished his drink and threw the last of the bread to the whippet, sitting back quietly with scrawny haunches backed into a rippled spine. It struck John that they could have been brothers, this thin hungry dog with the huge eyes, and his friend.

'I have a task for you. A task in the north. I received a letter from a friend who is master of a noble household. There has been a spate of killings and as usual the Podesta wants a quick solution, an arbitrary justice, an innocent head upon which to let fall the axe. A peasant woman, a servant of some kind, a non-entity has been chosen to act as the sacrificial lamb. If nothing happens, she will die in a few weeks, days even, and that will be that. But my friend – who is a great lord – is not happy.'

'No?'

'No. You see there is another in the picture. A Dominican monk. And a far more likely culprit than our sad, stupid woman. But this priest of course . . . '

'Protected by ecclesiastical privilege. And his sex. And his birth.'

'Hah! There you have it but you do not even know you have it! His birth, yes, yes. This priest is a lowly sort, a Dominican friar, not an abbot even. And as is so typical in these cases, a bastard. No offence, John, your blood as a bastard is more precious than many whose blood is sanctified by the sacrament, you know this! But this priest is not just any bastard. His name is Lorenzo. Lorenzo de Borgia. And he is the Pope of Rome's cousin, bastard born to his uncle, the late Pope Callixtus.'

'Ah. Now I see.'

'There are many ways to strike at the Anti-Christ and this may well be a small blow but if it is a blow we can take, then as Christians we must take it! No one can argue the law like you, John Oldcastle! No one knows Leviticus and the ancient skills of Cicero and Hortensius and every scrap of Justinian minutiae like you, my friend. Even that damned . . . what is it now . . . *Promissione Maleficarum* those damned Lombardi hide the law inside. And no one is – I am sorry but still I say it! – as devilishly cunning at twisting the ropes of these laws and case studies and precedents into such a Gordian Knot that the enemy across the Forum throw their hands in the air and concede rather than listen to you twist their own words like snakes around their necks anymore! You and your words are the serpents of the Gorgon, John! And I need you, my own Medusa, to go north and see to it that this murdering Borgia priest pays the price. So that all might know that the name is not a shield but a target.'

CHAPTER THREE

In which a young woman tries to escape this world

Wrapping strips of linen tightly around her breasts hurt but worked. She pulled the roll of bandage tighter still, winced slightly as skin and fat was pushed hard against muscle and bone.

'Tighter, sweetheart? Can we pull even tighter?'

The little sister, not yet eleven, had clever fingers but they lacked power. 'I'm trying, Rosa, that is as tight as it will go. Turn around. Let me look at you.'

The older girl – or woman, for despite the current attempt at concealment, she clearly was a woman – lifted her arms up and then down, turned in a half-pirouette. The little girl with the big eyes and clever mouth pursed.

'Definitely better. They are much smaller.'

'Hmmm. I wish I had the Lady-Podesta's half-height glass. I don't think the Podesta's steward will let me into their chambers though. It's all a-chaos there with the packing now that the Podesta's wife is following him to Milan. You will have to be my eyes, sweet little Livia.'

'Put the habit back on.'

Grey and shapeless, the rough hempen-cloth fabric fell over her soft, smooth skin. Skin that had not seen the sun, had not seen hardship, had not seen malnutrition, just attar of roses and milky creams. Roughspun to the floor, only her toes peeping through. A simple belt of hemp-rope around her waist. But ten years of womanly custom dies hard and she pulled the rope tight. *Suck it in, my lady, suck it in.* The younger one laughed.

'You are silly, Rosa! That makes them look big again! You look like Mistress Florentina!'

Mistress Florentina? That would never do. The woman attracted every eye in the piazza by simply walking from one side to the other. She was pushing forty at least, well beyond her childbearing age and had indeed born seven but you would think her a pear ready for plucking the way she swung. Low-hanging fruit indeed. The young woman with the disobedient breasts – Rosa – undid the rope belt and tied it once more, this time to hang loose and unbeguiling at her hips.

'Better.' The little sister cocked her head like the little sparrow she was. *Chitty, chatty, flying from perch to perch, sit upon my finger little sister-sparrow so I can save you from the cat.* 'Now you look more like Marcia who works in the kitchens.'

'Oh.' This was the goal after all but still slightly disconcerting that it could have been so easily reached. 'Well that's all well and good. I cannot have the Abbess think me unsuitable. I need her and the Podesta to guarantee my application. After all that has happened, I am frightened they might think me … well, a disruptive influence in the Order. I cannot have that, sister mine. You know that.'

'I know,' the little sparrow knows more than ever she lets on, 'but is it true that I will never see you again? That I must consider you dead? Like Eurydice and Orpheus. Can I not come and fetch you when I wish it? I promise not to turn around!'

'Sweet Lamb.' Long clever fingers ruffling hair the colour of honey. 'I shall always be with you. We are sisters. But when I enter the order I take my vows and am the Bride of Christ. I shall be Rosa no more. I shall be … another name. And you might see me in procession on Holy Days, in the Piazza delle Erbe – and I hope that you do – I shall tilt my chin, just so, in order for you to see me! – and although I shall make no sign, be sure that I shall see you send you the invisible spirit of my kiss. Like this.'

And she kissed her sister's brow. And although there was no one else in the little room they shared, with its overflowing chests and boxes, the signs of impermanent living, still it was like a little scene from a travelling Mystery; the Angel and the Christ-Child perhaps, St George and his Maiden. The young woman with the magnificent breasts and narrow waist assumed the face of a woman within a shapeless shroud; chin down to facilitate a double one, eyes squinting to add age, mouth down to imitate discontent. From siren to shrew, every woman can do it if the need is great enough, she thinks. Another age–just a century or two on–and this woman could have turned her skills to a life upon the English stage or in France as a travelling player. But it was not that time and she was not in France.

'Rosa, you look old and ugly! How do you do that? Show me! Show me!'

They both laughed; easy, flowing, as slick as molasses. That's what their father had called them, up to and until a French blade entered his gullet and ended his breath. *Slick as molasses, my girls, slick as molasses.* And they all knew that he was boasting not just of his girls but of the molasses in the great jars of his cellar.

'See. Bring down your chin. Like this, yes. And frown your brow like Jove himself. And purse out your lips like Nurse Angeline bless her eternal soul.'

'Bless her eternal soul. *Gloriam Deo.*'

'*Gloriam Deo.*'

'Am I ugly yet?'

'Oh I am so sorry, child.' She cupped her sister's chin, a golden phoenix egg in a marble palm, the pale flesh-not-flesh of Pygmalion, the bright feathers of the anqa-bird. *Così per li gran savi si confessa, che la fenice more e poi rinasce,* It was all her duty, to protect this little feathered thing. Hide her low, hide her far, let her resurrect when the streets were clear of this city's men. 'We have failed.'

'What?'

'You could never be ugly, Livia. You are the beauty of the family. You must bear the weight of your beauty, carry it like a cross, lift its heaviness with brave shoulders.'

'Like Saint Philomena? Who was so lovely she was adored by the Emperor Diocletian himself. But the Lord through his angels helped her escape and they mended the scars from her tortures.'

'Most surely, like Saint Philomena. But unlike the blessed saint, you will not die at the hands of a lustful man, the angels will keep you safe. And then …'

'And then what, Rosa?'

'And then you will be the huntress, Atalanta of Italy, and you will catch yourself a prince!'

She swung her around so the little legs flew out. *Fly, sparrow, fly away*.

'Which prince? Which prince shall I marry, Rosa?'

'Well,' she took her sister's hand and they passed through into the corridor beyond. Stone, cool, secure, safe. It was not home but the Podesta had offered them sanctuary in the Castelvecchio after the summer's troubles and she had welcomed his generosity given the problems her family had gifted him.

'In England there is a Prince called Arthur. He is a little younger than you but he will be King of all England one day. And the English believe that he is the Coming-Again of their greatest king of all the ages gone, King Arthur of the Sword and Lake. You know the stories.'

Livia began to skip and swing her sister's hand. 'The same Arthur as in Le Morte d'Arthur? Which we acted before Father last Lammas-tide? And I was Sir Gawain and you were Guinevere and … and …'

Yes. ***He*** had taken the place of Launcelot, of course he had. No one else could have dominated the little stage with its home-made curtains in the drafty hall and before the indulging eyes of their father. He had glided across the stage, had given the childish little lines invented by Livia a smooth, sexual grandeur, had made the trite seem profound, the amusing seem hilarious. But Rosa could not think of him. He was dead and she was marrying Christ Jesus and that was all there was to it.

'And now you will marry Prince Arthur of England and be Guinevere for real! But remember not to fall in love with Launcelot!' *Not as I did. Never as I did.*

---------- ∞∞∞ ----------

The Bishop is taking his leave of the Podesta's palazzo too (they call it a palazzo but they all know it is just an ugly wing of something greater). The brutish beast which was for a century the della Scala family fort is still three-quarters empty. No one knows if or when they will ever return but no Podesta dares to be the first to announce his belief that they won't. The Castevecchio was built by the notorious tyrant Cangrande della Scalla a century and a half before. There had been a fort on the site since Roman times–it was a perfect location for supervising the gate of the old Roman town which was tucked snug within the loop of the river. Cangrande however was ever suspicious of the loyalty of his populace, cruel to them as he was. The small, dilapidated 12th century fort had been uncomfortable, unimposing, it had welcomed kings, emperors and doges but it was an embarrassment when compared to the great residences of Venezia and Firenze. And so Cangrande had built this huge red-bricked monstrosity to both dominate and inspire.

Simple to the point of brutish ugliness, the castle had seven towers–which in itself was an insult to both aesthetics and to God himself for four and eight and twelve even were all holy numbers but *seven*? What would the great God make of seven? Perhaps the architect had been honouring the seven days of Creation in his own less-than-humble creative imitation and perhaps he was considering the seven holy sacraments of the Blessed Mother Church. But surely, even the most ignorant of passers-by would count the seven and think not of Seven Virtues but of Seven Deadly Sins? Not of Creation but of the Book of Revelation where the lamb has seven eyes and seven horns and the dreadful dragon seven diadems upon seven scaly heads? But whether from ignorance or arrogance, seven towers there were, separated by simple redbrick walls with strangely high and disproportionate merlons. Merlons shaped like the letter M or like birds' wings about to fly. It was intended that these merlons demonstrated the daring and innovative mind of Cangrande but in truth, the citizens found them ugly. They rose up from the top of the four long walls which encompassed the giant square of the castle keep within and the seven towers like misshapen teeth. True, people came from fifty leagues to see the Castel Scaglieri but very few returned home and demanded the same.

The southern wall faced the Old Town and the great ruined arena where once gladiators and lions and Christians had met their bloody end. The northern wall backed on to the river and so Cangrande della Scala also built a huge bridge. The bridge was also lined with the same M-topped merlons, again too tall for the height of the wall, like red fingers rising up in some ancient insult. Cangrande had insisted that this bridge, his bridge, be a thing of moment. The greatest bridge in Christendom. And so he had commanded that the span of the arches across the water were the widest ever constructed. The architect – one Guglielmo Bevilacqua – had protested in vain that such a thing was courting disaster but Cangrande had brushed his fears aside. His was not the greatest city-state, his was not the greatest republic, his was certainly not the greatest castle but his would damn well be the greatest bridge. And so it had been built, the span of the three arches an incredible – for the time – one hundred and sixty feet. At the grand opening it was said that Bevilacqua arrived on his horse, not so that he might tower above his della Scala master but so he might make the quickest of all escapes should the bridge collapse on its first day. But it did not collapse, amazingly it stood and stands still, the merlons visible from the first floor chambers of the Podesta and his household who – after the flight of the della Scala family across their very own bridge – then occupied the tower of the south-east corner.

Now, one hundred and fifty years later, the bridge still stands, the merlons are still ugly and the castle is mostly empty. Its halls and cellars are filled with town supplies of horseshoes and gunpowder and barrels. The militia occasionally marches around the keep, grizzled oldbeards train youngsters to wield swords in the dust of the yard. The moat is now more of a ditch; it fills if the river wishes it, otherwise it is mud and grass. The Podesta has lived in the Fourth Tower – why it is called this no one is quite sure for surely it depends where one starts counting? –and has made a comfortable home of the two-story block. He has a small household, twenty or so including his wife, and refuses to consider expanding into the long red walls and the other red towers. He is a practical man with a demanding role. Why run his household from within fifty rooms and spend his whole life shouting and receiving cold food when he can live in ten and eat hot?

This particular autumn morning the Podesta and his household are finally on the move – complete with third best sword wrapped carefully in cotton and a very pale Paulo Steward – and it is time for the Bishop to put the Little Matter of the peasant woman to rest. A confession simply but cunningly contrived. A signature (or cross if that is all she can manage). A quiet hanging on a day when something else more thrilling is happening elsewhere. He stops at the Tower's great double door as Lucius fusses with a cloak, trying to swing it over the prelate's shoulders but in truth the Bishop is too tall and Lucius too short. As he waits, he steps aside to let a plain young woman in the grey of a novice nun's habit slip respectfully out into the street. A pretty child holds the nun's hand, she is chattering about knights and dragons and holy grails. The Bishop allows the little girl to give him a pretty curtsey. The nun attempts one but is gauche, uncomfortable, an ugly crow trusted with the care of a little dove. And why is a novice out of the cloister unchaperoned, or out at all? He will have words with the Abbess for sure. But as the ugly crow raises her eyes to continue her way, he notes them flash and turn. Lightning strikes the plain lines of her commonplace features and just for a second...And he knows her. So *this* is where she has been hiding! As a novice in the Podesta's own household, soon to be assigned to the chapel of the Poor Clares no doubt and anonymous by virtue of her sexlessness. But there was no disguising those eyes...How intriguing. This Podesta is indeed a man of some depths. Not that the Bishop suspects anything untoward or immoral. The Podesta is known to be a good, honest husband, loyal to his wife with transgressions only in the other city-states upon his travels. And the scandal of any liaison with this one would complicate an already fractious and tinder-dry city. But intriguing that he had offered her sanctuary...

The Bishop forgets the young woman and has so scarcely registered the smaller one that forgetting her is not even necessary.

The law on complicity...how then does it go? One could take the scriptures of course. It was not necessary for Caiaphas to actually have crucified the Lord Jesus Christ to bear the eternal weight of unimaginable guilt. *Better for this one man to die than for the entire nation to be destroyed*, indeed. One only needs to observe the pitiful vermin that are Caiaphas' descendants today to see that guilt can be transferred to those with intent but no blood stain on their fingertips. And the same is true of Pilate. By literally washing his hands, he passed on the deed but surely bears the burden all the same. Hmmm...best not to speak too lengthily on Roman guilt. Such things could be so easily misconstrued and politicized, especially in this feverish climate. And of course the Bishop has heard rumours of the monk's identity–Lord help them! How had they not known that a Borgia was living amongst them all this time? *Per deos immortalis?*–so any perceived attack on Rome needs to be curtailed before it breathes life. No, he will start with Caiaphas, even the most ignorant know the name, and then any defense of the woman–and who would mount it? Who in this city has the skills to take on their bishop?–who would run the risk of defending Caiaphas himself? That will be the road he will take. Intent to harm, intent by malice or even by neglect of care–and this is the important thing–necessitates a sharing of the effect. Cause and effect, just as Aristotle and his Thomistic Five tell us. *Here is the cause, here is the effect, see the shining thread between them and name it causality*. And causality, in this woman's trial, at least will determine collusion and therefore guilt.

Does he need to look at the ecclesiastical canons to bolster this tawdry business? The law codes of the great Gregory himself, the speeches of Marcus Tullius Cicero? Perhaps a perusal through Justinian's Pandects might be in order, perhaps even a review of Accursius' great work of summary and subsumption, the *Glossia*. The Great Families were well educated after all and it would not do for the Awkward Family–the *inconcinnus familia* as he termed them in his mind–to throw a little poorly-understood but impressive-sounding learning into the circus ring. A little reminder-reading would do him no harm. But let us all remember too, exactly what she is. A peasant woman of the lowest stock, damned in deed, speech and soul, damned by the curse of Eve and damned by the stupidity of all her sex.

Do not be mistaken by the abrupt dismissal of this woman's case. Our Bishop is not a cruel man. He does not delight in rape or the servitude of the lesser sex, he does not amuse himself with lascivious touches, spiteful slaps, muscular beatings. And as we have already determined, he either likes women (a certain type of woman) or he simply does not see them. The little girl called Livia is worth remembering; she is the type of girl who inspires not just love but adoration, not with wily arts but simply by exhaling the air that she breathes and thus purifies. But our Bishop–although he passed her by, just a finger's breath from touching, and was honoured by a dancer's curtsey–our Bishop has forgotten her already.

He forgets women because it seems to him that God himself forgets them. They are, as Moses tells us, an afterthought. And there is so much else to think of in this *insanus mundi*, why would a learned man weighed down with the burden of temporal and ecclesiastical power bother with an afterthought, a spare rib bone, the *parce costa*? No, it is a misfortune of life that this miserable serving woman will die but all men are mortal and women more so. He has no doubt saved her from penury and a not-so-old death from neglect and starvation. Certainly the Great House that once fed and clothed her will not reach out their grieving hands. They might not want her accused – plebeian mud sticks after all – but they will not stick out their thin, white patrician necks in her defense. Not after what she has done.

Lucius and two deacons scurry around him as he finally leaves the Tower that is the Podesta's house. The covered litter is cool against the Italian sun; opaque silks lift slightly in the breeze affording him the occasional glimpse of the plebeian life without. And they are without, these plebs of the North's smallest city-state. Without certainty, without security, without dignity most of them, and some even without the discipline of faith. He sees it as his divinely ordained role to bring them these things. *But the greatest of all these is faith.* The Bishop shakes his greying head. No, that was not right. The Damascene had said that the greatest of all virtues was *agape*, charitable love for soiled, sinful humanity. Love was greater than faith, love was greater than hope. It was a hard lesson, perhaps the hardest of lessons. *Does he love his people?*

The silk curtain catches a breeze and blows upwards. Just a breeze, the air is full of them after all, but the Bishop is a man who sees God's hand in all things, He is not just the Creator, the Prime Mover, the First Cause but also the Sustainer, the Great Encourager of all new chains of causality, not just the first. We call it Providence, he thinks, but it is better we see it as the hand of God dipping into every small thing of this world. And so because the curtain lifts at just the time he is considering

Paul's exhortation to put love above faith and hope, he makes a clear, mental note of which grubby, sorry persons his fine litter is passing by.

A threesome of solid workmen, covered in white dust, sat outside a drinking house built into the crumbling walls of the Roman arena on three-legged stools. Their mouths are wide open with bread, crude joy and not many teeth but does he love them? Yes, assuredly he does. These men are what Moses calls the salts of the earth, they are but of small moment themselves but what in their multitudes they contribute to is all to God's great glory, whether it be the great cathedrals, the newly paved piazzas, the gleaming statues of venerable saints. How could he not love them with their filthy nails and sweaty brows?

And darting in and out of the piles of stinking refuse, the small boys running countless errands. Bent bronze coins for bolts of ribbon, for jars of honey, for sheets of newly printed parchment. Here, there, under every foot, under the very hooves of the horses, they are the blood of the city, pumping through her veins, keeping the beating heart alive. He loves the small boys assuredly. Not, he quickly adds to himself, in the foul carnal way of some of his colleagues at the seminary or even – God help them! – at the Offices of the *Magnorum Quaesitum* itself. No, not in that strange perversion of love that seeks to dominate and allows in Satan, the Greatest Perverter of all. No, he loved the boys for their rude delight at the joyful crudities of life, their ebullient refusal to be beaten down even when cruelly beaten down. For the men of God – in all their variants – that they would become.

And so he sinks back upon the soft fine cushions and is reassured. He does love his fellow man. And he even loves the servant woman with her wide, stupid face. And because he loves them all, he will soon see her dead.

---------- ∞∞∞ ----------

As the episcopal litter, with its fours bearers and two attendants all running alongside, passed down the Street of Zeno towards the great Basilica of Santa Maria, the silk curtains sank back down before the great man caught sight of Rosa and Livia as they also hurried along. There was no real need to hurry; the Abbess of the cloistered nunnery of Poor Clare did not know that they were coming at this particular hour (although she was not surprised, poor lady, when they did arrive). No, rather they hurried because even though it was six weeks or so since the terrible troubles of the summertime, Rosa and her little sister were still unaccustomed to walking the streets of the city unchaperoned, without so much as a serving boy to hold their parcels and safeguard their virtues. And since the invasion of the French army and the battle of Fornovo just a few months since, the narrower of the streets were likely to be blocked by angry, unpaid soldiers, drunk and spoiling for another fight. The Podesta was as good as could be expected at using his powers to keep the peace and not afraid to put a judicial noose around the neck of any thug who broke it. But as both Rosa and little Livia knew to their very personal cost, young men were a willful lot.

'Rosa! Slow down!' Livia was panting and pulling at her sister's hand. They were circling the great curve of the amphitheatre with its two storied arches and great white rose-white blocks. Some of the stone had fallen from the upper levels during an earthquake many years before, other huge blocks bore signs of quarrying by locals keen to apportion free stone for their building. Rosa had lived in the city her entire life and gave the theatre no thought at all, so used was she to circling it on her way through San Zeno Gate and into the Old Quarter. Livia however had rarely left their palazzo house in the west of the city, the other side of San Zeno basilica. Mass and festival days, she had emerged with the familia but only to San Zeno, no need for a small child to be taken into the old walled city with its warren of streets and alleys and cloistered churches.

'Rosa, slow down, I want to see the theatre.'

'It's not disappearing, Livia, it has sat on that exact spot for over a thousand years now without so much as spending a week in the mountains so my guess is it will still be there another day.'

'Father said that they are going to mend all the cracks and put all the fallen stones back into the walls. And then when it is all beautiful again, like it was in the Roman times, we shall have music and tragedies and players.'

'That will be very nice.' Rosa had been forced to slow down, she gave her sister an exasperated nudge which was reciprocated. How she loved her funny little bird! But how she went on so. And how she swallowed down histories and poems and stories, the girl was a ravenous wolf not a trilling songbird at all.

'I hope very much that they perform the Greek plays.'

'Livia, you do not know any Greek plays.'

'I do, I do! The Cousins act them out in the garden sometimes, they have to learn them in Greek and they get their knuckles hit with a switch if they get it wrong, so they used to play the parts in the herb garden. There was a funny one about frogs and the Cousins all did silly voices and then another one about birds and a pot of gold and then they read out a horrible sad play about all the women left behind after the fall of Troy . . .'

Rosa looked down in no small horror. 'The Cousins performed The Trojan Women in front of you? Did Father know? They would have had more than their knuckles rapped if he had found out.'

Livia skipped past a dead cat with a little 'oooh' and pulled up her skirts. 'I didn't hear much, it was all wailing and crying and then Valentio pretending to be the baby and Lucio had to try to throw him from the garden wall . . .'

'Enough Livia, you should not have been watching.' They had left the shadow of the great arena now and were making their way north-east towards the bend of the river. It was busier here and their progress slow.

'When they put on plays again, will you be allowed out of the House of Poor Clare to watch?'

'Not if it is The Trojan Women, my love.'

'But if it is a mystery play like the one in the great hall at Easter? *Quem Quaeritis?* it was called, do you remember? The women were looking for Christ's body and they had to ask the gardener–who was Jesus in disguise–and the guards and the stableboys and everyone and no one had seen him. And then Mary Magdalena was left all by herself and she was crying and the man she thought was the gardener came up behind her . . . do you remember what he said to her?'

'No, little bird, I do not.'

'You must! He said it three times and everyone clapped.'

'I must have slipped out to the closet.'

'While the three holy women were looking for Jesus?'

'Yes.'

'Why are there three sad women in the Greek play and three sad women in *Quem Quaeritis?*'

'Because three is a very holy number.'

'I know why! Do you know why, Rosa? It is because God Himself is three-in-one, Father, Son and Holy Spirit. But when we put them altogether we still say God the Father which I think is very confusing . . . '

'You can ask the sisters all about it, we are nearly there.'

'Can I? Can I ask them about Clare and Saint Francis? And there is a saint called Gobnault which I cannot believe. I can remember all seven of the blessed women we pray for at Mass; they are Felicitas, Perpetua, Agatha, Lucia, Agnes, Cecilia and Anastasia!'

'By Zeno, my little sparrow, the sisters will want to take you today not me. You had better hush a little before they dismiss me as a foolish clod outshone by a sunbeam. And that means being quiet.'

---------- ∞∞∞ ----------

The cloistered house of St Anne the Mother of the Immaculata was half-hidden down a side street, close to the Pietro Ponte. Currently home to a small community of Poor Clares, it was not like the great Dominican abbey-church of Santa Anastasia just a few streets away with its huge towers and solid rose-cream walls, built as much to glory Man as against the dark arts. The cloister was much more akin to a private house, except it had no windows opening out into the narrow alleyway. No windows, just a dark, wooden door with a simple arch of stone above, crowned by a figure in bas-relief of the Mother of the Mother herself.

Rosa had entered this way once before, six weeks ago now, tearful, hair awry, pulling at her lovely skin with jagged nails. The Sisters of St Clare had taken one look at her and blanched. No, they would not take her! Yes, they knew her plight, the whole sorry city knew her plight. But they were a simple Order, an Order uninterested in the troubles of this earthly city and certainly unprepared to deal with them well or wisely. Watered wine had been offered, a chance to pray quietly, two novices had even pulled apart the wild braids, combed her chestnut hair and braided it anew. But the Abbess – a timid creature made stern and fierce by fear – was adamant. She could not join the Order simply to avoid a domestic tragedy! There was no threat to her life, the culprit (or was it culprits?) were now dead or behind bars and the whole sorry mess should be swept away with the autumn leaves. *Come back if the city is still harsh come the end of September,* the Abbess had finally conceded. *If you still feel that they cannot forgive your part in this bloody affair and if the Podesta and Bishop give blessing, then and only then might you join.*

Well, the city had not forgiven. Despite the hundreds of young men who had died at the Battle of Fornovo, still the deaths of just six citizens by poison and sword could not be forgotten. Rosa was tired of being called a whore. Tired of Temptress and Cock-teaser. Tired of young men who had heard some small part of the drama – for that was what it now was – and assumed that would be willing to play her part for them too. She was tired and she wanted rest. She was out in the wide open plains beneath the all-seeing sun and she wanted to curl up, quiet and grey, in a small dull hole so that the hawks could fly by unfed. Mother long-dead in childbirth, father dead at Fornovo, cousins dead in the maelstrom that had swept through them all over that wild summer month – there was only Livia and she would be taken in by the Podesta himself, his wife having only given him sons and desirous of a little doll as pretty as this one.

Her knock was calm, convincing, calculating. She was not the wild, crying, weeping thing they had dragged in before. No longer was she in fine dyed woolens, tight-waisted and jeweled, now she was in shapeless grey sacking, hair scraped back into an unflattering and ageing bun. (But if she had only probed Livia a little harder, she would have known that for some classic faces, to be denuded of paints and plaits and ribbons was to illuminate, not to make ugly.) A hesitant door revealed a hesitant hand. They were admitted into the dark, narrow hallway; the lingering perfume of disappointed reluctance seemed to seep from the simple brickwork. They waited for perhaps a quarter of the hour on a wooden bench in an empty cell, white-plastered and featuring simply the last words of Clare of Assisi herself; *Blessed be You, O God, for having created me* beneath a poorly painted frieze of St Francis blessing Clare in as Abbess of San Damiano.

They could hear the chant of Compline. It sounded like the soft complaints of unmilked cows.

'So. You're back then.' Not the Abbess but a younger one. A sharper eye and no doubt sharper tongue.

'Yes, Sister. As I was advised.'

'Domine dirige nos.'

'Domine dirige nos.'

'And the citizens have not yet forgiven you?'

She hesitated. 'They are not as unkind. The summer is over now and perhaps . . . '

'Perhaps their minds turn to other things?'

'Perhaps.'

'But still you are here. And in stolen robes, I think. A habit to which you are not yet entitled, even though the belt be but a novice's.'

A little flush but she never flushed deep enough. Once she had been glad but now she wished she could pinch seemingly deep contrition into her obstinate and willful cheeks. There was no answer. The habit was not strictly hers.

'The Podesta . . . he seemed supportive . . . he directed me to . . .'

'A chest of walnut with a carving of the twins suckling the wolf? Yes. That was where I left it. After I made my own choice to leave the world. And my brother.'

'I see.'

'I am Sister Clement. If you join us as novice, I will be your mentor. In the world, I was known as Sophia. It seemed strange to me at the time that I was to abandon Wisdom to become Mildness. I stubbornly resisted the exchange for too long in fruitless argument and debate. When I finally submitted to the will of God, I felt a great peace flow over me like a mighty river. My wish is that my novices feel the same.'

'I will that too. More than anything.'

'Really, my child? Even here within these cells which we do not leave, we hear whispers. Stories are thrown over the walls for us to peck at like starvling chickens. They are like worms, these gossipy pieces. But juicy with it.' And she smiled, not unkindly, at Livia who was gaping at her as if at some holy vision. 'We hear of young men and women falling into unwise loves, of disobedient liaisons, of *yay*s and *nay*s and *I-know-not-whether*s. It seems even more of a cess-pit out there than when I stepped out and cleaned the dirt from my feet, fifteen years now. We hear, you know.'

Rosa did blush then, deep and plum and true. 'It is hard. So hard to know what to do when the Scriptures tell us to be chaste and the Romances tell us to be . . . to be . . .'

'To be chased? And then to be won? I know. It is not easy to be a woman in such a world. But marriage is the sacrament sent to most women by God to save them from temptation and sin. And children are the blessed fruit of the sacrament which cleanses the sin which brought them into being. Can you not see yourself as a wife? And a mother? To one as pretty as this little dove?'

Although she instinctively reached out for her sister's hand, the woman in the novice's drabs shook her head. 'I know the men planned for me, their types, and I do not wish to share any of their beds, their lives or their hearts. We have all been here before with these forced unions! You say you hear the rumours over the wall, you must know that any union with me is cursed. With any of the great households. Enough is enough.'

'Curse is a strong term. But yes . . . I think you may be right. Your father fell at Fornovo, I think – my sorrows go to you but he is with God, Amen.'

'Amen.'

'And you are the ward now of your father's cousin?'

'I would not say ward, I am nineteen years old. But I am brought under the protection of his family and Livia here is his ward. But he has agreed to be bound by my lord the Podesta in all things. My father's cousin is recovering from a wound and so we are in hiding within the Podesta's house. His wife does not wish to be burdened with another child and so Livia here will stay with the Podesta's family. Your family, Sister Clement.'

'In the circumstances, a wise choice. '

There was a stillness. A comfortable silence in the coolness of the cell. The plaster smelt like damp cheese. There was a heaviness in the air as if the doors and windows had not been opened in a millennia and would not now til Judgement. And yet Rosa felt a lightness of heart, something she had not felt since before the summer.

Finally.

'I shall support your case before the Bishop. I am confident that the Podesta will do the same. And with the three of us backing your application, I cannot see that any member of the Great Houses could complain. But what of you, little wren? How do you feel that your sister will become a Bride of Christ?'

Livia was clearly giving this much thought. Her chin twisted slightly to the side, her forehead wrinkled a little. 'I think . . . I think that I shall miss her. But I know that she will have a place with Mother Maria in the Last Days and will be saved. And with Clare too. And when I am done being Queen of England and Arthur's wife, then I shall join her perhaps. If the Podesta and the Bishop agree.'

'Oh, child! I think they would agree. Our order would have another Sophia if you were to join us! But I think you would take the name of the blessed saint, Hypatia. Now, I must speak to the abbess and we will send communication to the Bishop's deacon, Father Athanasius, to set the process in motion. It should not take more than ten days or so. You may wear the habit if you choose until then but not outside on the street. We already had news that you were coming this morning! A novice, alone on the city streets, outside the convent walls! We could not think who you were.'

'I am sorry. I did not know. I did not think. But it was pleasant for once to walk amongst the citizens and for them to . . .'

'To not see your face? And know who you were?'

'Yes.' *If they could have had but a single neck, I'd have sliced it clean through.*

'Then stay within the Palazzo Podesta. Do not venture forth until your last journey. Now stand and kiss me. Praise the Lord.'

'Praise the Lord.'

'*Christo et Eccelsiae.*'

'*Christo et Ecclesiae.*'

'Well then. Wait here and I shall find a boy to walk back with you. The streets of the city are not safe in the middle of the day let alone dusk and it is nearing Vespers already. God go with you, sister.'

'And with you.'

CHAPTER FOUR

In which an awful boy arrives, very late, to plague the peace of the Bishop

Hours pass. Our Bishop is a busy man in a busy world. Firstly, a monastery to the south is late with tithe payments and it is not the first time. He doesn't think they are cheating him, it is just that their prior is a lazy fellow and cannot count. But if payment is late to the Bishop then the Bishop makes his own payments late to Venezia and that will not do. Secondly, deep within the old Roman city, a bookseller is thought to have a manuscript which mentions Pelagius the arch-heretic. Lines cleverly concealed in orthodox philosophy but when looked at more closely, apparently resembling something thought to be from *On the Defence of Free Will.* Some misguided or even deliberately seditious nonsense denying Original Sin and praising human will. Arrogant foolishness! If Men were taught they were not sinners, that they did not need to confess their sins and baptize their children, then why was the Mother Church there? Why were priests accorded the divine ability to perform the miracle of transubstantiation? Free will made no sense. It denied the omnipotence of God. This book–if it exists–needs to be found and burnt. He has sent deacons out; they should return soon. Thirdly, the Bishop of Venezia, our Bishop's Patriarchal master, is angry at somesuch discrepancy with the accountings sent before the summer. He cares not that the whole of the west and centre of Italy was turned upside down by the French army. He demands that the figures in the columns agree today as they did yesterday and no amount of excuses – war, pillage, rape, pulling down of walls and bridges – will assuage his petty counting.

The French invasion scarcely touched Venezia, her power remains as inviolate as a virgin's pride. But she does not have the sympathetic pity of the Virgin, instead the miserly spite of the dragon, always wanting more. And so a day passes. The wretched woman in the cellars remains there. (*He **must** ask Lucius for her name!*) She is rarely beaten now, there is no amusement to be had in it. And her virtue remains intact dispute her offering it up many times in exchange for better vittels. He has not yet had time to fix the names and number of the tribunal – he is loath to elevate the matter to the standing Council of Ten who are puffed up with self-importance as it is – but he has found a suitable date for her death. It has been decreed that when the northern city-states get word of Charles Valois and his army stepping foot once more upon French soil, there is to be a great celebration in the streets. Countless trestles of food, wine flowing from fountains, revelers and jugglers and deceivers of the eye, the citizens can have it all and on the other side of the town, he will quietly have a woman hanged.

Our Bishop – and remember he is not a bad man, he simply wishes for the peace of heaven to be reflected at least on occasion in the peace of his streets – he is now, an hour later, sat with the charred remains of Pelagius. Pelagius himself is of course still burning in hell everlasting and has been for a millennium. But the wretched bookseller tried to throw the offending book into his fire. He claims that he bought the tome in good faith from a German merchant from Saxony and that the cover claimed a harmless title of Boethius' *Consolations.* This may well be true. There are disturbing ripples flooding the godly seas between Italy and Germania, most of which lands are governed by the Holy Roman Emperor. But it is a vast estate and Maximilian cannot be everywhere and the Germans have long been a troublesome people, not suited to any sort of vassalage, just ask Augustus where his eagles are. The ripples whisper of priests denying the holy bread and wine as flesh and blood, denying that penitential punishments have either purpose or effect, denying the existence even of Purgatory! Chantries are mocked, holy monks derided, papal supremacy debated by scholars in far-off universities, the holy tongues of Hebrew, Greek and Latin translated by arrogant *impudenti* into their own crude *sordidum linqua.* And now heresies made corporeal by the damned Gutenberg press, a true Trojan Horse if ever there was one.

The Church has long had her tapeworms of course; *disputandi pruritus ecclesiarum scabies.* Scabies indeed. A loathsome itch. And the Mother Church has occasionally had to scratch, scratch out and then purify as any man would with a body not quite so clean. Pelagians, Arians, Waldensians, Cathars, Illuminati, Lollards; so many tapeworms sucking at the very bowels of the poor Mother who only wanted to love and protect them into obedience. His own congregations–*benedicat eis*–had resisted the heresies of the north (Germans, French and English! Always the Germans, the French and the bloody English!) but as a good shepherd he has to be ever-vigilant. He has decided. This bookseller is no heretic. A thorough search of the tawdry little shop revealed nothing untoward apart from the single book. And the man's terror when the book was ripped open and the offending lines read out loud–well, it was apparently as genuine as the utter shock at what they had uncovered. He will do a full pubic penitence at the altar of San Zeno and then an obeisance on the steps of Santa Maria. That will suffice.

Our Bishop sighs. It is late. The fire is burning low and Lucius has already retired. By rights, one of his many–far too many, what *do* they all *do*?–deacons should be sat outside all night in case the great prelate is visited by some heavenly thought in the early hours. But that practice seems to have died a quiet, unmourned death, he knew not when. Now when *he* had been a humble deacon in Milan, he had sat outside Bishop Nardini's chambers for ten hours at a stretch, never daring to leave his seat, never daring to close his eyes for more than two heartbeats, lest he snooze and be discovered derelict. Now **there** had been a hard man. Stefano Nardini. Toughest *filius canis* ever to wear the cardinal's hat. An ex-soldier, he used to bark at them as if they were boy recruits on the parading ground. He had the reputation of a man who had killed with his bare hands, strangled French, Swiss, Lombard, Castilian men on the field of battle. Probably hyperbole, thinks our Bishop now, with some regret but even so. How much had he learnt from that old monster? How many times had he watched in awe as he dominated papal chambers, gave orders to terrified archbishops, countermanded princes, flirted with duchesses and all on three hours sleep, never more, never – God help them all – less. Our Bishop shakes his head. We truly squat like rude and impotent gargoyles upon the shoulders of greater men. No wonder our deacons go to bed and leave us be.

He looks back down to his desk. There is yet much to do before he acknowledges defeat but then there is always so much to do and his eyelids are becoming heavy.

'My Lord Bishop?

'Yes, boy?'

'A visitor at the door, my lord. He apologises for the lateness of the hour but beseeches me to give you this, his signet seal, and says he has every ... *expectation,* my lord, of being admitted. I think that is the whole of it. I think I got it right.'

The Bishop is not a superstitious man, he believes in the devil of course and in Providence but he does not believe that the body itself determines Signs and gives notice of them. And yet it is undeniable that as his fingers take the scrap of paper with its splodge of still-warm and soft wax, he sees it for just one second as not wax but blood. Congealed blood given pattern by a familiar seal.

'He is without? This lord?'

'Yes, Lord Bishop. With a small retinue, just four manservants and the horses already liveried.'

'I see.' This cannot be good. There is absolutely nothing in this turn of events that can be good. And yet with the tumult of the last six months, so many nobleborn on the road, deputations here, ambassadors there, you could not take the air without tripping over an emissary or three. And with the expulsion of the Medici from Firenze, of the della Scala from this very city, who knew who one was supping one's chianti with?

'Bring the lord within, the great hall I think but prepare the corner table with the half screen around. The silk screen from Araby.' *I'll not have this lordly man–with a seal I know only too well–think me a peasant.* 'And some bread and oils. Fruit.'

'My Lord Bishop.'

It is late as we have already said. Somewhere across the towers, Roman gates and church spires, an exhausted child on the highest roof of San Lorenzo is late in calling out for Vigil and will see a beating before Lauds. The Bishop is sitting very still. He is still telling himself that this unexpected visitor means little–a slight demand upon his steward-cellarer, no more–but in his true heart he knows this is a lie.

'My Lord Bishop.' The dark shadow of the night rises up, parts and becomes a man, this man. The Bishop himself rises. Gives half a bow. Perhaps a little more than half. For whom does a bishop bow? For the Bishop of Venezia certainly, there is a clear hierarchy enshrined in city state statute, just as his own Podesta would bow before his Venezian counterpart, the Doge. Before Archbishop, Cardinals, Pope, of course, just as Christ Himself left the apostolic succession to the Twelve and the Seventy. Before the dukes of this many-lorded land? Perhaps. Probably. But a courtesy curtsey, a bend to say '*I do because I choose, to display my humility but I do not do because you ask me.*' To Lords below the rank of Duke, then no. As Bishop he would not bow. A flick downwards of the episcopal head might of course be diplomatic on some occasions... So, what to do with *this* man? A duke, the

Duke of Gandia indeed despite his extreme youth. And Grand Constable of Napoli. And Captain General of the Holy Mother Church. My, how those tithes must roll in . . . A bastard of course but newly legitimized by his father, the Holy Father no less. So here we have Giovanni Borgia, known to all as Juan.

Here before him is a strong, beautiful man. It is not often that our Bishop concedes that beauty can be male. He has travelled to Firenze of course, he has seen the newly-fashionable statues by the likes of Duccio with their sensual sinewy lines, he has even seen Duccio's Hercules although he wishes that he had not. Why did the Lord God send his only-begotten son to reign over us and replace the pagan heresies and vanities of the ancient world if we were then to resurrect them as sexual beasts in terracotta, marble and bronze? And before him, this dark autumn night, is a dangerously sexual beast, Duccio's Hercules come to life.

'Lord Bishop,' A low bow; he knows how to play the princely game this Bastard-Duke. 'I apologise for my interrupting your repose. Rest, I know, is a rare indulgence for you Shepherds. *And yet a field well rested gives the more bountiful crop*.'

It is apt that the first Ancient to be used in this night of gambits is Ovid. And yet the Bishop is not wholly surprised, knowing what he does of this young Adonis.

'My Lord of Gandia. This is a pleasant surprise, indeed. Please take a humble seat. We are but the least of the northern city-states and yet what is ours is surely yours.'

In sitting, the sharp cheekbones and fleshly mouth sink closer. A swiftly snatched scent of something alluring – is it lily? – and then gone. *Were I a young maiden*, thinks our Bishop, very thankful that he is not and as far as he knows, has no daughters, *then I would lie myself at the feet of a serpent such as this.* Lucifer, Star of the Morning, must have looked just like this man. And suddenly our Bishop realizes, or perhaps remembers, that Lucifer in another tongue is Venus and that Venus is both love and the venial. Yes, it is the root of those sins the Church terms venial or pardonable. He is not wholly sure however that whatever sins this young man has, or will, commit are entirely to be forgiven.

'How were the roads?' He asks, thinking of the camp followers and whether they themselves are safe. 'And you found entry into the city? Although the hour for barricading the gates is surely long past?'

Juan Borgia, Duke of Gandia, a Spaniard in Italian hose, shrugs an entitled dismissal of all those things in life that disturb and disrupt the lives of petty mortals. 'A ducat here and there, most gates open, do you not find, Lord Bishop?'

'I am sure you are right.'

'The best gates are the ones at first held tight and closed. Or that is my experience.'

He has no doubt that although this boy cannot be more than twenty, he has had the experience. He would not be his father's son if not. Which reminds him . . . best to nail one's colours early . . .

'And how is the Holy Father, your . . . uncle?'

Juan Borgia laughs. 'I think we may now all call him my father and now that he is also our Holy Father, there is no disrespect or error for he is Father to us all.'

'Indeed. How then is . . . our Father?'

Reaching casually for a peach, the young man takes slow, calculated bites. Yes. The Bishop is happy not to have daughters.

'The Holy Father is well, returned from establishing the League of Venice which gave us all peace and sent the enemy packing as you know.' This was not an objectively accurate version of Pope Alexander's flight from Rome, a flight from the very French he had so foolishly called over to Italy in the first place. And the League of Rome was surely at the feet of the Emperor Maximilian and Ferdinand of Spain. And the Battle of Fornovo had been no one's victory save the crows . . . but what did it matter, these were just words.

'And now he turns his all-seeing eye towards Firenze where a viper long-since hatched is starting to spread its venom through the populace.'

'A viper?'

Borgia yawns, peach juice dribbling. 'It need not concern you here in the north-east. I have come from Firenze this very night. My wise father wanted me to observe this viper and ascertain its intention and promise as it were.'

'And, my Lord Duke?'

'An insane rabble-rouser. Italy has seen her share. A priest called Savonarola. Preaching in the Piazza della Signoria that we are all doomed, that we are in the Last Days, that we must burn our vanities and become as Adam and Eve in the Garden. I think he would have us all naked under the stars!'

And I think that you would like that.

'I watched the fool froth and fulminate to his simple-minded crowd. He tells the people of Firenze that their city will be the new City of God, that at Judgement it will be in Firenze and not Jerusalem or Rome that Christ will walk again. He even had the statue of Judith and Holofernes moved so that he could preach whilst aloft its plinth. Can you believe such errant arrogance?'

'It seems in defiance of Christian supplication and modest obedience.'

'I was tempted to deal with him then and there – I could have got through the crowd and the thugs he calls his Soldiers of Christ, his Piagnoni Wailers, but who are in truth peasants with pitchforks – but I am an obedient son.' A wolfish grin. 'So I report back to my father first.'

'And yet . . .'

A pause.

'And yet . . . ?'

'And yet this city is in quite the opposite direction.'

Peach stone tossed to the floor, an unshaven sticky chin wiped with obscenely red and long tongue. How fitting that such a beautiful façade should hide such clear evidence of such an ugly soul . . . *in horto iacabat in colubrum*, the Lord was indeed wise in his creation, in the Garden He had hidden a serpent; the truths were hidden but they were there to be seen by those with faith.

'So. Good Bishop. Your perspicacity has unmanned and defeated me! You truly wear your training with the Magnorum Quaesitum like a cloak of power. Yes, I admit it.'

I had not questioned you, impudent pup. Don't presume to treat me as a child.

'I was sent north on the wishes of the Holy Seat of St Peter with two errands. One to witness the errant foolishness of the Firenzi and to judge whether these preachings constitute a heresy.'

You are but a score and a half! How might **you** *determine a heresy?*

'The second errand is my business here.'

'I am listening. Wine before you shine light?'

The serving boy – the Bishop thinks his name is Luigi and he is a nephew of Lucius – springs forward and they wait whilst the deep red of loosened tongues is poured.

'So,' says our Bishop who has a deep and broken feeling that he is going to need some fortitude after this night's work is out, 'You were sent by Rome. The Podesta is away; sealing our city's place under the terms of the new League. He will be gone a month or so. Perhaps less.'

'Pah. I do not bother with podestas. They are but a few steps up from the churl who saddles my horse. No, this is an ecclesiastical matter.'

An ecclesiastical matter and the Holy Father of Rome sends his eighteen-year-old bastard son as its inquisitor.

'You see, my Lord Bishop. We heard a little of your disputes between the Great families – we would call them the *Arrabiati*, the Noble Ones – although we of course in Rome were consumed with the defeat of the French and their expulsion, still we heard some talk of your little troubles. To be truth, it all sounded like a great romance, a tragedy; Euripides came to mind. I do so love *The Trojan Women*, do you not?'

Not so much as you do, I think.

'But news came south just two weeks ago now. There is to be a trial, is there not? A trial to spread the guilt a little further than those who are already guilty and dead.'

'Yes, but . . .'

'And we heard the strangest rumour. Hear me out whilst I say it. You will agree with me that it sounds like the talk of fools and cannot possibly be true because no Lord Bishop under the jurisdiction of the Holy See and *Christo et Ecclesiae* . . .'

'*Christo et Ecclesiae.*'

'Would dare to even countenance such a thing. So hear me out though I know we will both be sharing mirth when it is said. We heard in the Holy See that a priest – a goodly man of God, a holy Dominican no less – was under scrutiny in this thing. That one of your *Arrabiati* – jealous, fractious ingrates – was attempting to pass some kind of blame onto his innocent shoulders, shoulders currently clad in the habit of a priestly-monk. Now; can you believe such foolish talk?'

'And yet you ride one hundred leagues in the middle of the night . . .'

'And yet I ride one hundred leagues in the middle of the night.'

'Curious. But reassuring that the Holy Father sees all and hears all and considers all his duty.'

'No one sees what Pope Alexander sees. And Rodrigo Borgia sees even more.'

'So the Pope has four eyes?'

He thinks at first that he has gone too far. There was a twitch, a flash of something deep and dark. But no . . .

'Four eyes! Yes, my father truly has four eyes. A pair at the back of his head to see his enemies. I shall be sure to tell him that you said this.'

Yes. I am sadly certain that you will. A blessing I did not mention his two faces.

'So. Back to our priest. Now, Lord Bishop ...' Juan Borgia leans closer. Yes, it was lilies. 'We can speak as men here tonight. Your boy there by the wall, he hears nothing and I think he knows that if he does hear, you as Bishop can cut off an ear or a nose. Is that not right?'

'Luigi is about to leave the wine and retire anyway. He will be yawning tomorrow if he does not sleep. Go, boy.'

'Good.' Even closer. And now the scent is something without a name. 'We both know that my Papal Father is the greatest of all popes save Peter, that he has the only mind capable of the requisite machinations that keep balance between families, cities, emperors, kings, heretics and saints. His mind – Bishop! If only I could show you! – his mind is like the universe itself. It is as if it contains all things, a *mappa mundi* indeed of Humanity; miserable that it is. He holds us all in his mind, he directs our small and petty purposes, he spends every waking hour bringing order and harmony to this earthy City of Man so that we might all enter the Heavenly one.'

'Indeed. High office is a heavy burden.'

'Yes, indeed! And although the greatest of men, he is but a man. A man with the carnal desires of Adam. The need for spiritual companionship, for the meeting of like minds and the occasional ... meeting of companionable bodies.'

Occasional was an interesting way of describing a twenty-year relationship with Vannozza dei Cattanei, four bastard children labelled as his nephews and niece, another five or six children not yet acknowledged and a current amour with the Duke of Orsini's wife, Guilia. But the affairs of state lie heavy as the boy says ...

'We are none of us perfect.'

'Although the Holy Father is closest to that state.'

'Of course.'

'Well then, you understand! And the . . . wards of our great father all have his great zeal to spread the gospel of Lord Jesus Christ in whichever way we can.'

I wonder which way is yours.

'And as my father seeks mortal companionship, so did his great father; Gioffre of Aragon. And his even greater brother, Alonso, my father's uncle who of course became the Holy Father Callixtus of blessed memory, four papal fathers ago now; even the blessed Callixtus – lying as we speak in his most sacred tomb beneath St Peter's Basilica – even he needed occasional female comfort. It may come as a surprise to you, Lord Bishop – and I hope after the shock has worn off, a pleasant one – that this humble Dominican, this homespun priest of your little city-state, is the meanest of my brethren. A cousin, you understand, natural son of Callixtus himself. Much older than I, assuredly, but sprung from the same auspicious family line. My cousin.'

'I am amazed. And honoured that he chose to make this . . . little city-state his home.'

Juan Borgia slams his palms down. 'Then we are agreed! No cousin of mine, no son of a Holy Father could possibly be guilty of such a heinous crime – whatever the crime is, I forget. A Good Man. A Heinous Crime. It is an ontological impossibility as Anselm himself would say; Like the Fool who has God in his mind but cannot conceive of God in reality! What a fool!

A small education is a dangerous thing in hands with such long fingers.

'My Lord Gandia. I fear that you have travelled so far north with fears unfounded. It is true – may God forgive them – that in their grief, one of the injured families in this affair did call for the monk to be castigated in some way for his part in our little trouble but I have investigated the deeds of all concerned and it seems clear to me that to blame is another.'

'The woman.'

So. You have your spies. And this far north, pretty lordling, I am impressed.

'Yes, a common woman of another great household. It seems clear that she bears some guilt for what occurred over the summer months and she will be tried and, if found guilty, given the appropriate punishment.'

'She will die at the end of a rope, my Lord Bishop.'

'In this matter, you and our Podesta are in absolute agreement.' Best not to put the idea of burning into this unpleasant young mind.

'Hah!' Another thumping of the table. 'Then this is a happy evening indeed. We are all in accord and God smiles down on this world.'

'You are of course welcome to rest here at the palatum this night. It is a long ride back to Rome and you will wish to make an early start after Aperire Porta. The gates open early here in the North.'

The Duke of Gandia seems intent on marking a little pattern in peach juice upon the table. Soft fingers and smooth, polished nails go this way and that; swirls and loops and swirls again.

'My Lord of Gandia?'

'Do you know…' The long forefinger completes a sticky series of figures of eight. 'Do you know, I have a fancy to stay; I could help in some small way with your trial preparations. I am not the great mind that is Rodrigo Borgia now called Alexander the Sixth but I have some mean talents that could be put to use. I could advise you. Be Atticus to your Cicero.'

'I see.' And he does see and he does know that it was all decided long before the ducats exchanged hands at the gates and that it is completely useless to envisage an alternative path. And when all is said and done, he wants the same end result as the Pope and this awful boy. Where is the harm?

'My offer of lodgings is then extended indefinitely, my Lord Duke.'

'Oh no,' the Duke of Gandia is on his feet, 'If you say that the Podesta is away agreeing terms with the Emperor and Spain, then I shall have his house. The Castelvecchio, once home to the illustrious della Scala family. What could be better? Your seal please, to afford me entry although I should imagine mine own would now be good enough, even in this most ignorant of cities.'

The red wax upon the cream vellum allowing Juan Borgia, Duke of Gandia and Papal Gonfalonier, free access to all parts of the town cools quickly as they press their two rings into its softness. It does not look like blood this time. Instead it now looks like the freshly shat excrement of a very sick man.

Friday

CHAPTER 5

In which we sit in a cell beneath the basilica with the old Pope's Bastard and wait for his visitor.

So here we have it. John Oldcastle of Illustrious – or Heretical – name is on his way to ensure the guilt and earthly end of a Monk. He will be here within the day. He has been sent by Savonarola, Master of the Firenzi Flames, *Dominus Holocausta*, busy burning vanities on bonfires. But already here is Juan Borgia, Duke of Gandia and he is quite determined – as only a Borgia can be – to ensure the exoneration of this monk, his never-met but apparently well-loved cousin. Borgia and Oldcastle, Pope versus Heretic. Surely the meeting of these two cannot be accident but God's unfathomable mind needing some delicious entertainment? But we have met John – and he seems a quiet, unassuming soul with troubles aplenty on his mind – and we have now met Juan, a second John! – not so unassuming perhaps, and although the cause of many troubles, probably not allowing any to stick. And we have met the Bishop of this, the meanest of all northern states, a man caught between Podesta and Pope on the one hand and his whispering conscience on the other. And we have met a young woman and a girl, a child who chatters like a sparrow but who soars with the phoenix, both fleeing some tawdry local scandal and who will both now surely fade from sight and be of no more moment in our story.

But we have not yet met our monk. Lorenzo *Ordo Praedicatorum*, distantly yet not acknowledged a Borgia, a man who took the path of the blessed St Dominic so many years ago he himself can hardly remember a time before the tonsure. Who is this man to cause an English lawyer and a licentious Bastard-Duke to travel so far? Why should his guilty death or innocent reprieve matter to anyone at all? And does he even know, what we now know, that despite his impoverished life and anonymous name, he is at the very epi-centre of a spider's web worthy of Ariadne herself?

The monk will be questioned, hard and harsh. Oldcastle is a canny lawyer of twenty years' deliberation and knows his stuff. He is also going to be paid well – if quietly – by the Great Family wishing to see the monk suffer. If Juan, Duke of Gandia, and the Bishop and even the Podesta now far away in Milan, had known of the unassuming traveler on his way north, then the trial of the foolish old woman would have been hastened forward, held and concluded within the day. Her flaccid body would even now be hanging from some convenient hook in one of the lesser piazzi. But they do not know. Only Savonarola knows John is coming and he is telling no one. And so the monk will be questioned hard and harsh, even our not-so-holy Trinity of Bastard / Bishop / Podesta will be unable to spit in the face of *Jure et Justitia* when John Oldcastle gets his hands on them.

But before John Oldcastle arrives, perhaps we should pre-empt the good Lollard and – with the help of a newly stirring saint – ask some questions of our own.

---------- ∞∞∞ ----------

Let us see in our mind's eye, a small room in the Basilica San Zeno, a small, squat and yet not unlovely church next to the red-stone abbey but herself sitting serenely in cream and pale pink.

Central to the upper façade is a rose window, in the shape of a Wheel of Fortune, the work of one Brioloto of whom we shall hear no more, although it is an exceedingly impressive window. Our monk – dare we call him Lorenzo de Borgia? – would no doubt have entered under this twelve-petalled glass marvel, perhaps wondering at the cruel and perhaps ironic spin of the Wheel that has led him to this pass. Somesuch armed men, grim-faced retainers from the Great Family so keen to see him pay, would then have ushered him quickly through the great bronze doors with their forty-eight accusing faces. The Dominican has long lived in this city and will no doubt be familiar with this mismatched and cross-stitched collection of wooden panels, cobbled together from so many other doors and walls and chests and rood screens. He no doubt knows the names of nearly – no one knows all – but nearly all forty-eight. But it is likely that of all forty-eight – four for the gospels multiplied by twelve for the blessed disciples – it would be the smoothened face of Zeno himself that he reached out to touch as he hurried by.

The Basilica of San Zeno is of three huge floors, the presbytery, the nave proper and the crypt beneath. No doubt our monk knows all three well, living for many years as he has in the sister–abbey of Dominic just a few minutes' walk into the Old City. He will see the church proper as he enters hurriedly through the doors of course and he will see a great deal of the crypt beneath for many days to come. But it is likely that it is the presbytery that he truly wishes to visit at this point in his life. Not for its earthly remains of saints – Lupicinus, Lucillus and Crescentianus to name but three – and not even to witness, for perhaps one last time, the Mantegna altarpiece with its Virgin, Child and myriad of chubby children. No, it is most likely that our priest would have paid good money to spend just five minutes in the presbytery to give the little red statue of Zeno himself a 'please-give-me-fortune' rub.

But short of time and patience, the noble henchmen would not have acceded to this priestly request and would have pulled /

pushed/dragged our man down the marble steps, under the monstrous creatures of Adamino screaming froth upon the arches, to the dark cool depths of the crypt beneath. And within one of the eight aisles – long before he came to the tomb of Zeno himself, more's the pity – he would have been stopped before a small door of English oak and the other side of that strong, hearty wood, he would have found himself his new home. Pallet, desk, pen, plaster, tiles, rushes, a mattress, – his captors want him to feel like the guilty prisoner he is but they are political and self-preserving enough to acknowledge, even if privately, that there is a very good chance that he will walk free, and they cannot therefore be accused of anything but Christian forbearance.

Does he feel their forbearance, we wonder? Does he consider himself fortunate with the mattress and the rushes, the desk and the pen? Or is he cursing into the straw that an injustice – any injustice – screams into the eye of God Himself? He is thinking about that very thing, even as we join him …

I feel guilt. Ergo I am guilty? Guilt is a by-product of my informed conscience, a gift given only to Adam from God but Catholic guilt, I know too well, is often confused with over-zealous scrupulosity. An overly scrupulous conscience is an exaggeration of healthy guilt. I feel guilt, I do, it consumes me so much that sometimes I wake in the middle of the night and cannot breathe. Why I can hardly breathe now … Satan himself is sitting upon my chest and pushing downwards. But by itself, surely guilt can be nothing but destructive? It is rather ***contrition*** *that I must endeavour to feel, only contrition is constructive. Contritus. To be ground to pieces. To be crushed.*

I sometimes think I have been crushed my whole life.

The monk's breath comes short and fast. He takes a moment to exhale through his mouth, to inhale through his nostrils. Slow, slow, calm, calm. *You shall not win. Beatae Mariae semper virgini, you shall not win, Satan I reject you and all your wiles.* The monk slowly lifts his old body upright. There is no light save a fat tallow candle, sometimes spitting, sometimes spluttering, always stinking of animal sweat. He is used to the smell. Although the candles he is skilled in creating for the abbey's altars are sweetened with herbs and honeysuckle, he does not waste such luxury on himself. Closing his eyes, he stretches his arms upright to touch the rough plaster of the rounded ceiling above. If he could just reach out a little more he might touch the sky above, feel the soft blue of a late Italian summer on his fingertips, sense the honey-glow of the sun's resting rays as she sank slowly to the west. He so misses the breeze. To feel fresh air upon his grizzled old cheeks. The rain.

He sits back down again, heavy, labored, limbs unwilling.

I miss my little garden.

Closing his eyes, he paints himself a picture. Raised borders filled with pungent rosemary, St John's Wort for well-being, echinacea for skin rashes and eczemas, the tiny white flowers of the common yarrow for headache. Snakeroot for diarrhoea, gentian to aid digestion, juniper for hot infusions so efficacious when a brother had fever. Pale pinks, flashes of cadmium yellow, glorious berry reds... in his dank place of shadows, he could almost smell the colours... High twisted canes above his head laden with beans and sweet pea. A few ancient vines kept for nostalgic pride for he had been told that they were cuttings of cuttings of cuttings going back as far as the time of Augustus. And beneath his now spindly butt, the old Roman seat with its weathered, anonymous beasts, species now lost to wind and sleet. Blue. A hundred blues. White, saffron-yellow, every hue of green.

Confiteor Deo et beatae Mariae semper virgini...

What use him confessing to himself? He had already confessed so many times to his Abbot, God already knew the depths, heights and leagues of his contrite heart. His crushed heart. His heart ground to pieces. But of course he had never quite confessed everything.

At the end of the summer, when the last of the bodies had been discovered, when he had been dragged in front of the lords and the Podesta to explain his sad, sorry role, he had been called a 'holy man'. Even after confessing to all that he had contributed to the *humano clades*, the human disasters of the summer, still the Podesta had called him a holy man. Men had clasped hands and promised friendship and an end to feuding, women had wept for the dead children and had twisted the stems of flowers into wreaths. And then he had retreated. He had sat in the dim light of his beloved cell, deep within the warm beating heart of the Abbey of Santa Anastasia. Sat and waited for his own heart to beat again.

I waited, he thinks to himself. *I waited and waited. But it was as if when the children died, when their strong, passionate, irrepressible hearts stopped beating, then mine ceased too. It was as if the leaden weight of my guilt pressed down so hard, so heavy, that my poor little cor devastatum had not the strength to do its job. I lie awake at night, waiting for it to forgive itself. But then the questions come;*

Why did I put my earthly pride before my God-given common sense? Why did I allow myself to get talked into such a risky enterprise? Such a lack of humility! What did I envisage? The praise of the Bishop raining down upon my blushing cheeks! Honours and prizes from the Great Families? My name spoken of in hushed awe in the corridors of Vatican City? Is that what I truly wanted all along? That my cousin, the Papal Father, should at least hear of my name and learn of my worth and call me into his service? Or did I simply want to do one truly good thing so that the awful guilt which has sat upon my shoulders for forty years might at last begin to weigh less heavy?

He tries to think for a while and because he does not want to brood any more about the events of the summer, tries to remember when he first knew who he was. If there ever had been a defining point, a name spoken, a short terse meeting, an insult scrawled on paper squeezed under his door. But if there ever had been such a moment, it was now lost in time. He had never known who he was and he had always known. It was crucial and it meant nothing. He had wondered once, long ago, if his rapid elevation to *herbarius secundus* had had something to do with his father's name and he had felt a momentary panic, a terrible fear that he was not worthy. But Ufffizi had gently cuffed him on the shoulder. *Name this plant!* And he had. *What is it for?* And he knew. And this one and that one and this book and that book. No, he had been a worthy candidate, the best candidate, surely? Old Brother Guillaume, Herbarius for so long, would never have allowed him to learn if he had not been the very best. But over the years there had been glances, fingers making signs against evil, ambitious brothers flattering his work, a conversation he knows he was not supposed to hear involving a monthly stipend from Rome in his name.

Fortunately, and thanks be to God, he had not been cursed with vanity nor ambition. And Uffizi his friend had been such a sublime talent as a young illustrator, so praised and admired and rightly so, that his own small contribution to the Abbey's glory was easy to downplay and forget.

But over the years, had he become complacent? And had that sense of sweet, sad acceptance of his life and place at the heart of Santa Anastasia's brotherhood been the chink through which the sin of pride had slipped? The Devil needed only an inch, everyone knew that. And he *had* felt proud that the nobleborn young had come to him for their Latin, their Greek, their herbology. He had used his paltry knowledge of human nature to advise them on their little problems. And when the time came, he had felt proud that his small, daring actions might help to end the town's feuding.

And where has this pride got us all now? Six dead, one of them a child... o domne exaudi me, please hear me Lord, show me how to make good what I have done.

The dank, dark cell remains silent. The Lord does not hear, or if He does, He is not in the mood to answer.

The monk tries again.

Zeno, Saint of this city, you who were the greatest fisher of men since the Twelve, hear my prayer. You, Father Zeno, who fought Satan himself and snared him in your nets to keep this city safe from the wiles of the evil one, hear my prayer.

The body of Saint Zeno – holy relic beneath a silver mask – lies just yards away from this very cell. Soft. Soft as a sigh, a wisp of sorrow comes floating down the crypt nave, past the aisles and arches, under the stout door of English oak . . . Soft and sad. All people in mourning for the dead. The dead of Mordano, tortured and slaughtered just a few months past, the dead on the field of Fornovo, the dead in childbed, on sweat-drenched pallets, upon pox-ridden mattresses. All call for Zeno, Zeno and their mothers, but very few are heard. The monk tries to see his little tragedy as part of a bigger plan, the piles and piles of dead lie in a ghastly tower reaching up to God Himself as His Son weeps down upon the fleshly mountain. So many dead. So much pain. It is simply the way of this Earthly City. One must endure.

Saint Zeno however – soft-hearted though his shade might be – sees his little game and is having none of it. *Mordano was not your fault, Priest. Fornovo was not your doing, Priest. The death of all men in penance for Adam's disobedience, this was not your deed, Priest. But the deaths in this little city this summer past . . . how clean are your hands, Priest? And what of that other death, so long ago?*

Without volition, the old man on the pallet turns his hands. Dark are the shadows cast by the fatty wax of the stinking candle, they flicker like young birds testing their wings. His palms are dark. Is it blood? He peers closer. When they came for him, he had not time to fetch his eyeglasses . . . It is hard to see. He sniffs. Is that iron? The unmistakable sharpness of blood's scent? Perhaps. Yes, perhaps that is a stain, there, a long mark three inches by two from the knuckle of his index to the rise of his palm. It may well be blood. Instinctively he rubs his hands together as if in water. Again, again, flesh against flesh, bone to bone, a palmer's kiss. Holding the offending hand up, he looks again. It is still there. Long and jagged, like the shadow of a blade.

*Who would have thought that a little girl could do **that**?*

He sits back, suddenly tired and defeated.

When they had come for him – their protestations of undying love unsurprisingly finding that love was indeed harder to sustain than hate – he had welcomed it. The knock upon his cell door, the feeble protests of his Abbot, the scowling countenance of the bereaved lord himself, yes, he had welcomed and expected them. If they had predicted calls for help, tears, angry blows, then he confounded and disappointed them all. Rising, he had remembered his bound books of the four Gospels, of Boethius' *Consolations* and of the sermons of Zeno. He had remembered his posy of lavender for the headache which would come, he had remembered his hair shirt, his second undershorts and his dignity. But his eyeglasses. But how he wishes now he had remembered his eyeglasses.

As they took the hurried walk through the dark streets from Santa Anastasia abbey to San Zeno's Basilica and then down to the crypt – with the abbot trailing them all the time bewailing this sacrilegious flouting of ecclesiastical privilege – the bereaved lord was a pacing, clenching, sweating mountain of rage. The monk was expecting the rope to snap, the volcano to explode, at a much earlier pass but the lord held on until the oak door swung open and the old man made as to enter within.

'How could you dare!?' The ancient ceilings shook. 'You are a Man of God! How could you think to warp the mind of my daughter? To poison such a sweet innocent flower? *She was my life!* My only child. What do I do now, eh? Tell me you rotting sack of Satan shit, what do I do now?'

The Dominican realizes that – ecclesiastical privilege or not – he had been close to death at that point. A swift beating in the bowels of the basilica, a new corpse amongst the rows of corpses, another death after a summer of slaughter; a few may well have called out for the lord's excommunication, the hangman's noose or Podesta's swift sword perhaps but none of that would have deterred this grieving tower of fury from his righteous kill. He waited for the blow, perhaps it would be the dagger he saw snug to the lord's waist and belt, perhaps an ignoble throttling. He had dropped his eyes in apology and supplication.

The heavy, calloused hand around his throat. So, it was to be by throttling. That was apt. He did not deserve the blade. Squeeze became hard pressure became excruciating choke, he felt the bones in his neck begin to creak and crunch, his eyes bulged.

'My lord,' a timid voice behind, '*My lord!*' a little louder. The Abbot. 'My lord, think of your immortal soul if you murder a priest! It is the very deepest circle of hell's realms for priest-killers. The frozen lake of Cocytus itself. You would be the very last of all to reach the Kingdom of God. Think of your wife. Think of your daughter's soul.'

One last vicious, angry squeeze. Falling to his knees, he was then booted through the door, ignominiously collapsing backside in the air, chin rough and bleeding against the gritty stone.

The door had slammed shut. Harsh sounds without. The sounds of a grown man weeping.

How many days ago, that dreadful noise? Six, perhaps seven. He had kept the Hours and Offices as best he could, hearing sometimes a few murmurs above but soon losing track of all time and days from nights, Vespers from Matins. The Abbot had tried to see him a few times but had been curtly turned away. Bread and water shoved through the door once a day. A new candle even. The cell a world entire, a flickering flame its sun.

And so here he was. Imagining his little herb garden and being scolded by Saint Zeno.

More hours passed. Or perhaps days or perhaps just the flutter of a butterfly wing. The monk neither knew nor cared. Every so often, there was a grunt, a fart, a sniff from the man outside. He began to look forward to these little human noises, to welcome them when they came, he tried to anticipate which would come next. Once there were three farts in a row which amused him in a detached, dream-like way.

Above him, the city's community attended their services, sang their hymns and prayers, listened to the Bishop deliver his orations, his exhortations, his readings; sometimes a low hum could just be ascertained and the priest strained to hear the communal responses, trying to make out the familiar words. *Ave Maria, gratia plena, Dominus tecum, Benedicta tu in mulieribus et benedcitus frustus ventris tui.* But the ancients had built this church fair and strong and good and the stone and marble allowed him little escape into the still-living, still-breathing, still-beating world above.

---------- ∞∞∞ ---------

'Come on, Brother, wake now. You need some food. Come on now,'

A gentle hand gently shaking. He has fallen into some strange kind of un-sleep, a state previously unimagined; even as a novice fifty years ago now he has been able to immediately fall into deep sleep between the Hours, bounding out of dreams like a diver coming up for air, instantly awake and ready to accept God again and again and again. But this somnolent half-state, neither in one world nor the other…

'That's it, take a little wine. I am here to share blessed sacrament of Penance and hear your confession, if you so wish. No man, no matter his estate can be denied the sacraments…'

The kindly voice tails off. Explaining sacraments to a monk of over fifty years standing… foolish. He realizes with a growing flood of shock that this must be his bishop, the Bishop of the City, his superior's superior, a great man he had only seen from the distance of quire and nave. He struggles to kneel and half falls to the stone. A cool hand on the back of his head.

'*Fili mi*, be calm, my son. Your ordeal will soon be over.'

The shock of it hit him, a swoosh of cold air. Expecting and then hearing are not the same thing.

'My Lord Bishop. How … will they do it? Am I to hang? Please not the pyre. There was no witchcraft in what was done … *in nomine Patri*, no witchcraft …'

'Eh? The pyre? No, no, no, *mea culpa, fili mi, mea culpa.* I meant that your ordeal down here with the rats and the dead is soon to end. Dear God, man! What do you take us for? To bow down to the angry whims of a grieving lord? To supplicate the ecclesiastical to the temporal? To ignore ecclesiastical privilege?'

The man on the floor sniffs a little. 'But in Firenze they hanged the Archbishop Salviati. Do you remember? The Medici so angry, they cared nothing for privilege and church courts, they just hanged him from a post.'

He feels rather than sees the Bishop cross himself. The soft holy air of God himself conjured up by any of us, all of us, anyone with an arm and a hand to genuflect.

'And thanks be to God that our noble families are not Medici. Our own most terrible and corrupt della Scala are still under the Emperor's heel in Vienna and none of the families left behind in their wake are of similar power or arrogance. No, no, no, the Podesta and I have … allowed this little disrespect, this small outrage – a priest imprisoned by a temporal lord! – we have allowed it so that tempers can cool. *Ignosce me, fili mi*, forgive me if you can.'

He is helped up back to the pallet, finding himself concerned that the vicious mites in the straw and already feasting on his flesh, will now smell and find their way to episcopal blood.

The Bishop sighs. 'So much grief. We can hardly blame the parents, even the men who died … well, they were children really. And what the little girl did … such a shocking act.'

Tears come hot and unexpected. 'I have tried not to think of her. To do that. She must have felt that she had nothing left to live for.'

'Terrible, terrible. But you will not bear the weight of this, be assured. I am one with the Podesta. And . . . and we also have the support of the Holy Father in Rome.'

There is a loud, mocking silence. 'The holy . . . Pope Alexander?'

'Yes, Father, Pope Alexander. And he has sent his own son, the Duke of Gandia, to supervise the investigation ensuring your complete exoneration.'

'Gandia? I do not think I know of this one . . . I am confused . . . '

The Bishop holds out his hands, palms upwards as if to illustrate the indecipherable ways of popes. 'Juan Borgia the nephew is now Juan Borgia the son and Juan Borgia the son is also now the Duke of Gandia. Ours is not to reason into the great minds of great men, so far above us both. We can only be grateful and offer prayers to the Almighty that the Holy Father has chosen to remember you.'

'I see. He remembers me.'

There was a hesitant glow of soft and shy pleasure at this. The Bishop wondered for a second if the man was a little simple. Surely he didn't think that the Pope was acting from some kind of family loyalty? Surely this Dominican realized that his tawdry little dilemma was just a tiny gambit in a game so much bigger? But perhaps he was being harsh. As Bishop he was exposed to the crude politics of the ecclesiastical world so much that he had stopped despairing but this little Dominican . . . no, he probably still believes that the Pope is a holy man, that princes keep promises and that rubbing the red belly of Zeno will bring you luck.

'Of course, of course, he remembers you. So, you will be questioned – briefly, very briefly – by whichever advocate the Great Family has found hiding under a stone, whichever half-a-ducat lawyer is willing to incur the wrath of Pope, Bishop and Podesta combined! Such a man, I do not think, can be found! The shade of Cicero himself might baulk to take on the task! But my poor attempt at humour aside, the desire for vengeance will not be directed at you, no, no. Now, here in this basket I have cheese, grapes, some meats of some kind. First I will hear your confession, then we shall share the Body and Blood of Christ in the Eucharist with full and faithful knowledge that He is with us, even in this dark prison cell, even as He Himself sat, alone and betrayed, in a prison cell perhaps not unlike this one.'

'*Gratias Deo.*'

'*Gratias Deo.*'

'Then kneel, my son, and I shall begin. What is it?'

'You said that the desire for vengeance will not be directed at me?'

'As I said, no. You are protected by ecclesiastical privilege. And by your innocence, of course.'

'Yes. Yes. *Confiteor Deo et beatae Mariae semper virgini, et beato Michaeli archangelo et beato Iohanni baptistae . . .*'

'My son?'

'But . . . is it to be directed at another then?'

A deep sigh. 'Someone must pay the price. There is much anger in the city. And some fear too. You yourself know better than any man alive that she was deep in the morass of this thing. That she encouraged at least some of the unchristian behaviours that led to the murders and other deaths. And when all is said and done, there is little other future awaiting her anyway, she is reviled. Friendless. Despised. A quick death at the end of a rope will be a mercy.'

'Yes. Yes, I see that.' And so he kneels.

CHAPTER SIX

In which we wake and spend one morning with the Duke

Ordinarily we go inside the heads of men we are following, those with such important parts played and yet to play. The Bishop is rational, obedient, sympathetic and yet often torn between duty, conscience and reason. His mind is cool, a lily lying placid upon the surface of a milky pond staring upwards at the temperate sun, admiring and yet unblanched. By nature, and yet not by label, a Thomistic Dominican, he strives for synthesis and cohesion in all things. Like his great spiritual master, Aquinas – long dead and yet still living – he wishes to acknowledge the role of both his God-given *ratio* but also the *gratia spirituali* given to humanity by God to temper reason's arrogance. But how hard it is as a man of intellect not to err too close to the impudent heresies of those men – Jan Hus, John Wyclif, Averroes – who placed the reason of Man ahead of the Grace of the Almighty which alone could guide it away from error. Our Bishop works calmly and at all times to keep his febrile, fertile mind from straying. He has faith. It can be done. The calm lily pond of his consciousness seems without ripple. But beneath the surface ... well, we shall see.

The Podesta however is impatient, emotional, hot-headed and ambitious; his head is like a ferment of wild seas lit by a stormy sky. With no time for the labyrinthine twists and turns of philosophy, he bends his head, says his pater nostra, confesses his venal sins and tries to keep his streets and alleys safe. With every stabbing, every brawl, every show of disrespect to Church or State, he feels a sudden swell of rage, a sea wave of crimson, flame, vermillion, looming over his head to crush him. He roars at it to stay its path, to retreat, to sooth itself and the wave recedes. He glares, he glowers, he grimaces and the rage becomes stern resolve, he becomes princely, he has *gravitas*, he is their *princeps solennes*. His mind is always on the precipice of the next roar. It is an unquiet place to visit.

John Oldcastle is quiet, still, hesitant and loyal. Inside his head it is as if we have stepped into a warm room, lit by a cheery fire but with a dark, sad shape sat nameless in the corner. The tongues of the flames sometimes lick out as if to caress your limbs but although they warm and warn, they do not scorch. One hundred years this fire has now been burning and for Old Sir John it was an unimaginable, animal terror of a flame – flesh, skin, fats, hair, eyes, all a-burning, all a-crying out for God's mercy. For the Young John Oldcastle – our John – the fire is burning low. There is the threat of scorching one's fingers if one gets too close but for the most part, the fire in his mind brings great comfort. It reminds him of who he is. Of who, if he has but the courage, he might yet be. The sad, dark space in the corner of his mind is hard to distinguish. The shadows seem to shift, change, re-gather, change again and so they defy the eye. If you sit awhile in John's mind, you try to stare into this dark place of raging sadness but like magnet repelling magnet, your eyes are sprung away.

But inside the head of Juan Borgia it can seem like a dark formless place, the swirling nothingness of Chaos before the Logos and the Light. And there are also foul smells, dark sticky patches upon the walls of the dungeon, nails torn from desperate fingers still embedded into the walls... If Virgil had accompanied us deep beneath the ice lake, Cocytus, past Cain and the betrayers of kin, past Antenor the Trojan and all those who betray their country, past even the Kingdom of Judecca where traitors against God reach up in contorted frozen cries, if, with Dante, we had held Virgil's hand even *ad vexilia regis inferni* and stood before Lucifer himself, stood and screamed wordlessly and silently with Brutus, with Longinus and in the centre with the Iscariot himself, still we would have to dig beneath the long, bloody claws of the Beast to find the black, moist soil of Juan Borgia's mind. And so, one lifetime alone is probably not enough to wash oneself clean after venturing in, even for just one day. Which means that we need not . . . But this is what Juan Borgia did on the day he woke up in the Podesta's best bed in the Podesta's best chamber.

He broke his fast late, still drunk from the early hours when he and his four men sampled the drink, dance and debaucheries on offer in two of the whorehouses closest to the episcopal palatum. (And although our good Bishop might claim ignorance of both their existence and their proximity to his austere and chaste lodgings, the truth is that on a good night he could almost spit from his holy window to theirs.)

He then pulled down onto the bed the young woman who brought him the bread and dry meats, managing to insert two rough fingers inside of her before she pulled herself away and exited the chamber. Ordinarily he would have quite happily have chased the little bitch and had her on the stairs but he had indulged himself more than usual the night before and was unsteady on his feet. And anyway he needed a piss.

After eating and then shitting to huge satisfaction in the commode chamber off the Lord's Room, Borgia opened the various wardrobes and chests, taking out the few – very few – pieces he deemed in any way good enough. He had never met this town's Podesta but he could only assume that he had packed and taken with him his most bearable clothes. Certainly what was left behind would scarcely do honour to some pox-ridden burgher or even one of the mangy peasants they had passed in the fields. No matter. He would send Vincenzo to find a decent costumier and set up a papal account.

Then, he peered out of the mullion window for a while, scornfully noting the less than impressive lead work and glass panes, bubbled with imperfections, giving the outside world the look of a world stewing above a boiling cauldron. It was a fair little town – he wouldn't give it the pretension of city – and from where he was on the fourth floor he could see across to the remainder of the Castelvecchio, her ugly towers and crenellated battlements, as yet unclaimed since the departure of the della Scala family nearly one hundred years before. Our brazen young man could have flashed his ducal signet and gained entrance to the whole palazzo of course but he was concerned that the rooms would be damp and the beds unmade and the remaining women old and ugly. No, this Podesta-tower was warm, reasonably luxurious and seemed to have an adequate complement of staff despite its lord's departure. Certainly enough to keep him in suitable comforts for a week or two which was all this tawdry little business needed. He leaned out of the window and took in a deep breath. To his far right beyond sight over the rooves of the town, was the basilica of Saint Zeno with its rose window and where his new-found beloved cousin lay imprisoned. How dull but he would have to visit the man this day. No avoiding it. Straight ahead, he could see the round of the Roman arena – not a patch on Rome's obviously and in an even worse state – and to his left the Duomo's piazza of Santa Maria. In between was the usual messy maze of narrow streets attempting to follow some careful plan, some respectful nod to Rome's great architects and planners but the podestas and lords of the past had clearly not enforced their law quite well enough because he could see all sorts of dwellings springing up here and there, destroying the grid.

After shouting in the corridor for his four companions – Matteo he knew had fallen into the Lady's Rooms by accident rather than design but had seemed well pleased at his find, although sadly the lady herself had left with her lord – the five young men, not one over twenty and five, snarled at the terrified staff they encountered and made it known exactly what would befall them if the horses were not well fed, watered and brushed down. Carlo found the kitchens and gave orders for a constant supply of foodstuffs, Raf took some shaking lad by the ears and was shown the cellar. 'Not bad, some decent Spanish reds,' was his verdict and the boy was ordered to fetch up three barrels for when the young lords returned.

Whilst the wine was finding its way to the main hall, Juan Borgia himself ordered the full remaining staff to assemble in the hallway. From pot-boy to hearth-chit to cellarer and head cook they bowed their heads as he took their sorry states in and told them – in case they did not know – exactly who he was. The Second Steward, Horto, was a bundle of nerves and kept rubbing sweaty palms against rough breeches. Slightly more impressive was the aura of matronly disapproval emanating from the stiff figure of the First Steward's wife. She was too old and stout for his tastes but he appreciated the waves of dislike she was struggling to contain. Standing just a foot from her downturned head, he spoke softly to her white cap. He liked clean linen and freshly baked pies washed down with wine from home – Spain that is, not Italy. He waited for her to nod, casting a slow, leisurely glance around the little group as if daring the lads to hold his eye but in reality he was choosing the sweetest, youngest, least pox-ridden girl to warm his bed for the next few nights. Not a great choice. The girl who had brought his breakfast seemed the most bearable. Reasonable teats from the look of them stretched against a tight bodice. Wide, slightly stupid forehead, pug nose, reclining chin but pretty girlish curls escaping from her cap. He gave her a look which made it extremely clear what he was expecting and was gratified to see her bite her lower lip. Another arrogant young lord would have fooled himself into believing that the gesture spoke of nervous anticipation and bashful joy but Borgia knew his women better than that. And anyway, the more unwilling the bitch, the more delightful the sport. A shame he had not time to test her unwillingness out there and then but he was in this miserable northern shit-hole on errand for his father. There were very few things that Juan Borgia would put ahead of his own pleasures and they all involved – in some way or another – obedience to his father.

After waiting for Carlo – the least even-tempered of the four, none of whom to be honest had a patient bone in their body – after waiting for Carlo to break the nose and then with his boot the cheekbone of a random page who had not accorded him quite enough respect (though how Carlo quite knew given that all dozen or so of the household still had heads and eyes bowed), Juan Borgia sent the half-pretty girl one last long and unblinking stare and then they were out in the street.

And so we can follow the five young men towards the western quarter of town where the pink stone of Zeno's basilica glows in the mid-morning sun. Italian youths are hot-tempered, they are quick with their fists and, as this city knows only too well, even quicker with their swords and daggers. But these five Spaniards seem to usher a miasma; a hot, foul odour of threat before them as they swagger through the crowds, crowds which now part like Pharaoh's seas. It could be of course that word had spread. The name of *Borgia* carried with it a low growling timbre, the stench of underground rooms, shackles and fine metal instruments, groans, cries, pleas and supplications. Mayhap indeed, the populace saw the five and knew them for who they were and which apostolic shadow flew over them. But it may also be true that evil can adopt a face. And although we might not know exactly why we avert our eyes, why we step back into the shit of the gutter, why we hold our breath and turn our heads away, still we seem to know exactly when that face appears.

CHAPTER SEVEN

In which the young Duke talks to the old monk and neither mind is set to rest

'Morning my Lord Bishop, well met,' The young Duke of Gandia took one disparaging look around the cell, the crypt, the sarcophagi and – down the nave – the tomb of the blessed Saint Zeno himself and spat. The Bishop winced. Sat next to him upon a ragged-looking stone shelf with a lousy mattress was a sorry-looking creature that the Duke took to be his entirely-beloved cousin, Lorenzo Borgia, *bastard.* He honoured his newfound relative with a cursory glance that took in a grubby white tunic beneath the worn black cloak and scapular that marked his membership of the Order of St Dominic. Tonsured scalp with thin grey wisps of hair to the back, untidy eyebrows, admittedly intelligent eyes but a weak mouth. Juan Borgia considered himself an excellent judge of character and he was not too impressed by this newest member of his kin.

'Yes, my Lord of Gandia. This is Father Lorenzo, *Ordinis Praedicatorum*. I have informed him of our Papal Father's generous interest in his case.'

'I don't want to have this discussion here. It stinks. There's monk shit in the bucket. I am the Duke of Gandia, son of the Papal Father, Gonfalonier, Constable of Naples and Captain

General of the Church and I do not conduct conversations over buckets of monk shit. *Ordinis Praedicatorum* shit or not.'

'Of course. I am sure the guards will allow . . . that is, this is my jurisdiction here, this basilica, so the cloister perhaps . . .'

'Yes, my Lord Bishop. This is your ecclesiastical jurisdiction. You are Lord-Spiritual of this miserable little town. But as I say, I am Captain General of the Church and a Papal Gonfalonier. This man, this wholly beloved cousin of the Papal Father, is protected by ecclesiastical privilege. And yet you have allowed not just the defamation of his character but the loss of his liberty. So now he shits in a bucket.'

The Bishop bristled. 'My Lord Duke, we have had much disturbance this summer and many tragic deaths. The populace has been much unnerved and unsettled. Before he left to renew the city's fealty to the Emperor, the Lord-Podesta decreed that there was to be full and proper investigation into each man's part and portion and as Lord Spiritual I concurred. You know full well that the northern states have long recognized the temporal authority of the Holy Roman Emperor as equal to that of the Papal See. And so in microcosm and mirror, I must acknowledge the authority in these matters of my own Lord Temporal *in localis*, the Podesta. And although we have suffered two centuries of unholy turmoil between Emperor and Pope, I have every confidence in the grace of the Holy Spirit guiding us that both the City of God and the City of Man can concur in the procedures respected here. Father Lorenzo has been accorded due comfort and procedure. We are nearly at the end of our investigations and I have no doubt that the Friar will be exonerated of all blame, malice and misjudgment.'

'There are others who think not, my Lord Bishop.'

Borgia swung around at this new voice, angry that he had not heard the silent footfall behind him. Glaring at Raf Salamanca who should have stopped this man twenty yards away from the ducal person, he drew himself up to his six feet and one. Far too late, Raf slipped himself between the two men – his Duke and the newcomer – as the Bishop got to his feet.

'Ah, my lord. There is no need for umbrage. The Duke of Gandia and I are simply interviewing Father Lorenzo as is our right and proper due process.'

'Without informing me that you were doing so.'

'As a Lord Spiritual investigating the case of malpractice involving a member of a religious order, I have no need to inform anyone but my Lord Bishop of Venezia, the Papal Father in Rome and the Emperor Maximilian. It is a courtesy only that we have even allowed you to secure his person.'

The dark, dank air began to swim with the heady musk of testosterone. Juan Borgia took in the newcomer, shoving Raf roughly to the side. 'And you are, my lord?'

'A grieving father. A lord of this city. Of ancient lineage. This priest is in my view guilty of many crimes, many crimes and most heinous misdemeanors. All of which resulted in the death of my daughter. A child.'

Ah, the grieving father. The stubborn local nobody shaking up a dead and buried case instead of accepting its demise and keeping his mouth shut. Which of course was the reason that he, Juan Borgia, was in this pestilential midden rather than enjoying Firenze. Ignoring the Bishop's hasty introductions – there were no family names worth remembering outside of Borgia, Pazzi, Sforza and Orsini after all – the young duke smiled a straight white challenge.

'Your daughter seemed handy with the blade. Takes strength to do what she did to flesh, muscle, sinew and heart. More strength than most women can muster. I should have liked to have met with this creature.'

The father sucked in a ragged breath. Clenched his thin pale fists. 'Well now you cannot. And I hold this man at least partly responsible.'

'I find that unlikely Lord ... *Quaesemper*. Lord Whatever. This priest is my well-beloved cousin, long-time my kin and ergo kin to our Papal Father. So it seems to me that – how was it? Your phrase, Lord Quaesemper? – *crimes and hideous misdemeanors* are not within his capabilities. That the scion of a goodly house such as my father's should be ungodly is surely a tautology. An anti-tautology indeed.'

'He is a man.'

'No. He is a Borgia.' Turning to the Bishop. 'The cloister you say? Some fresh air for this rank and mouldy cousin of mine?'

The grieving father still stood in their way. Skeletal head, dark blonde and thinning hair, cheekbones stretching taut as if pain itself could take form as a fleshless canvass. Half a dozen in his retinue, all decked out in some mulberry and gold affectation. Sheathed blades at their belts and three with longer blades hanging to their knees, fingers outstretched, affecting something casual. *How in Hell's name had they got this close without warning? Another entrance clearly but he should have heard them ...*

Furious with his failure, Raf Salamanca was almost bursting out of his shirt and doublet, ready to explode for want of a fight. And Carlo Roja, whose temper matched his hair and skin, hovered hungrily at the bottom of the crypt steps, small narrowed eyes sharp as a fox, just waiting for the ducal nod. Stupid bastard, he too should have got between these northern peasants and his Borgia lord, what in the name of St Catherine's cunni was he paying them for?

Gandia did not use papal guards from Rome, he picked up lads from gutters and whorehouses. They stole for him, they extorted money, they frightened tavern-owners and cardinals alike. They owed nothing to God, nothing to his father, nothing to Rome but everything to him. Sometimes a protégé didn't work out, got greedy, started to believe his own renown. You couldn't return them to the gutter or midden, they didn't belong there anymore, like the cur you trained up from the feral pack to hunt, to guard, to bring back the pheasant. If the pup then couldn't make the cut, lost the bird, rolled on its back to another man's dog, then you couldn't just send the dog back to the feral family from which you'd taken it. No, a quick, kind slice across the throat and the body in the Tiber. So had sunk Michele, Tabio, that stumbling idiot Paulo, a dozen boys he had tried out, tested and returned to the oblivion from which he had so temporarily rescued them. Raf had been with him almost a year now, he wasn't bright but he was solid, loyal. The other two – Carlo, and the giant Matteo – he had known since childhood, running wild and loose in the alleys of Rome, Spanish blood setting them apart from the other kinless, loveless, ungovernable urchins. Vincenzo he had found in a whorehouse four years ago now, carving up the face of the pimp trying to take his boots. He could see Vincenzo now in the corner of his eye, slipping silently down the steps to join Carlo, blade drawn and balanced. It was tempting. Five against six, seven if one counted the grieving father who was old – forty at least – but whose rage seemed barely contained, quivering up and down, wiry, powerful.

But no. He was here to save the face of his father. He needed to focus. Hold the interviews, collate the testimonies, summarise the verdict, witness the sow's execution, ride back to Rome. A simple remit. No distractions. Focus.

'My lords …' He gave a sardonic little bow of respect which fooled no one, 'On behalf of the seat of St Peter and the Magisterium, I need to hear the witness of this good friar. I shall speak to him in the cloister because it is not becoming for any man here present to breath the fumes of another man's piss. When we have spoken, the good Dominican here will return to this inadequate shit-hole just long enough for your lawyer to speak to him also. We shall then confer with my Lord Bishop for judgement. And then I shall consider this business at an end.'

There was a hanging pause. Drip, drip of some leaking pipe. St Zeno lay still and quiet beneath his silver mask. Drip, drip. At last the grieving father nodded, barely, grudgingly, every muscle in his neck taut.

'My man is arriving this evening. He will speak to this monk tomorrow morning. And be sure that he will also speak to the woman involved. I know your intention. That she will bear the weight of all the malice and intrigue and inept miscalculations which led to the tragedies which have torn my family asunder. Clean hands for your man, clean hands for you, Bishop, for you my Lord of Gandia, clean hands for the Papal Father. Clean hands. And yet such a stench of excrement from beneath all of your nails. My man will get the truth of this out into the open, your damned priest will hang from a rope and my daughter will rest in her tomb.'

'As Captain General of the Universal Catholic Church I am sad to tell you, good lord, that your precious daughter is even now writhing in the seventh circle of Hell, her pretty little face torn by the harpies who feed upon her flesh as she slowly withers, gnarled, sapless, twisted, a dead tree in a forest of dead trees. Hah! *Now, now, my lord, step yourself back or my man will have your throat.* I speak only orthodoxy, only what is true in gospel and scripture and holy council. A deviant view – even from a grieving father – is heresy. Are you a heretic, my lord? Do you deny that your little chit of a daughter is even now in Hell? Are you like the Cathars who denied Hell and punishment and went their own merry way until the flames caught them up? Are you a Bogomil, Lord Quaesemper? Are you a follower of Hus who denied Purgatory and Hell and thought that the common peasant in the field should be able to read the word of God and debate on equal terms with their betters? Are you a secret Converso, Lord *Whatever*? A filthy Jew pretending True Faith only to corrupt the Mother Church from within? *Be careful, my lord. I can see your desire to strike me, I can see your fingers itching.* But let me tell you now, a strike against me is a strike against the Holy Father of Rome. Denying Purgatory and Hell is heresy. Heretics burn upon the pyre. I can see in your eyes you'd die for your little bitch, your feisty whelp but you think they'll give you the clean swipe of the executioner's axe. You'd almost welcome it as a blessing, wouldn't you? But I tell you now, you strike me, sir, Lord Quaesemper, and I'll have you on the Inquisition's fire.'

Silence. Drip, drip, drip. Zeno himself, secure beneath marble, holds his lifeless breath beneath his silver face. Every man in the crypt has seen a burning. Witches, Hussites, converso Jews; Torquemada the Grand Inquisitor is even now burning hundreds and hundreds in the *auto-da-fe* of Madrid and Seville and Castile. Even men who confess and take the sacrament and are re-baptised, even these men he ties to the stake anyway and roasts until their skin pops and their fatty grease runs into the mud of the streets for the dogs to lick. *Burn them all for God will know his own!* Borgia knows his man. This grieving father would quite happily face the axe, the blade, even the rope for the pleasure and privilege of breaking Juan Borgia's face but nothing, nothing is worth the pain of burning.

'Now, Cousin Lorenzo, we shall sit awhile in the cloister above ground, you can explain your part in the piddling little events of this summer gone and tomorrow you can do the same with the Penny-A-Go lawyer this lord has hired to waste his money. Come, Raf, clear the way and let us get some air.'

------------- ∞∞∞∞ -------------

It had only been four days, perhaps five, but still the bright early autumn air was at once a glory and a sharp flash of pain, his retinas seared as if by needles. The Bishop helped the old monk up the crypt steps, through an archway to the side of the basilica's nave and soon he could smell, much earlier than he could see, that he was almost back home. Pink, warm stone, weathered soft by three centuries of sun and clement winter wind. High protective walls surrounding them, a long, rectangle filled with bushes and small fruit trees in the sunken garden in front. Four sides of paved walkway, opening out between arches into the garden on one side, the walls of the many Benedictine abbey buildings on the other. The muffled conversations of consecrated monks and lay brothers walking around the rectangle, hands deep in the folds of their tunics and cloaks, heads bowed and nodding.

Slivers of conversations snatched by the light breeze and wafting like the tempting offer of hot roast dinner beneath his nose. Two old men arguing in Latin about Petrarch. A young novice asking ignorant questions about the Council of Chalcedon and being told in no uncertain terms that he had mistaken it for the Council of Ephesus and should prepare himself better before wasting the time of his elders. A solitary Franciscan – a guest clearly, for this Abbey was dedicated to following the Order of Saint Benedict – recited, as he paced, the letter of Saint Clare of Assisi to Pope Gregory. The old monk – Father Lorenzo – breathed in deeply. This was like his home. Just a mile to the east, tucked snug into the loop of the river, his beloved Dominican abbey of Santa Anastasia. But this place – a different rule, a different name, a different colour for the monks to wear – this abbey felt so very like home. The uneducated novice was just like a young Dominican called Hugo. He was the fifth son of a farming family and impatient rather than stupid, the older man who looked a little like Brother Joseph should be more gentle! The two arguing about Petrarch were just like Brothers Malachi and Xavier. They had been having the same conversation, round and round and round, for twenty years. Once they had refused to speak to each other for a full six months. Father Lorenzo did not know the Franciscan and neither was he reminded of a friend but he knew the letter the muttering man was attempting to learn. An incredible thing, how a weak, sinful woman – Clare of Assisi – could understand and subsume so much of the Holy Spirit that she was able to gently persuade the hand of Gregory IX himself. He wished he had but a small portion of her fortitude.

Their small group – Bishop, monk, henchmen and Duke – had drawn attention. Monks, laymen, servants stopped their contemplative pacings and stared. All knew the Bishop of course and some knew Father Lorenzo for he had been the Dominican herbalist for nigh on twenty years now, since the passing of Old Guillaume, the foul-tempered Frenchman. The Dominican friars were often seen in town, preaching in the piazzi and this

Lorenzo sometimes held a stall on festival Fridays, selling herbs in the Arena market. But the presence of armed youths, by their attire of uncertain birth and class, was unsettling. As the Bishop and Monk sat themselves upon a stone bench in the shadows of the eastern cloister, the ripples of disquiet had clearly skimmed across the usually placid surface of the abbey floors to alert the Abbot himself who appeared at an archway. At first making his way towards the little group, the tubby little man stopped, started again and then stopped. His fellow monks gathered around, equally unsure of their feet. The Bishop waved vaguely in their general direction.

'Do not concern yourself, Abo. We are simply allowing the good Dominican Father some air and allowing him to pour clear light upon the sad events of the summer for the benefit of our esteemed visitor of Gandia.'

The Abbot seemed about to have some kind of apoplexy. Goldfish eyes bulging. 'My Lord of Gandia? We did not know . . . we received no word from the Holy See. My lodgings here in the abbey are yours to use. You will dine with us of course . . .'

'No, not of course, and no, not at all. You Benedictines live even worse than the Cistercians. For all the vicious complaints about how luxurious these establishments are and how they all need a good Augean clean, I am ever disappointed in the food, in the mattresses, in the wine and in the quality of cunt! Now, leave us alone and take your fellow rabbits with you.'

Stunned, the Abbot and his rabbits – all gathered around, and in truth more like twitching pigeons – at first seemed unable to find their feet.

'Shoo! Go pray and fondle each other's cajones. Or Raf of Salamanca will cook rabbit pie for me tonight. Be gone.'

The cloisters were soon empty. Even the midday sun seemed a little chastised and slipped herself quietly behind a stubborn cloud. Gandia yawned.

'So, Cousin Lorenzo, what part did you play in this sorry little *fabula*? It seems to us in Rome that a tawdry band of third-rate players came to this town and could not decide whether to perform a tragedy or comedy. But whichever genre, they performed it cack-handed. Talentless amateurs. My most reverent father enjoys the theatre,–did you know, Lord Bishop?–we all took parts in *Sofonisba* just a few months ago. My sister Lucrezia is but fourteen years old but already very... talented, precocious even and my father–loving parent that he is–indulged her a part. Lots of wailing, the wars in Carthage you know? Lots of bereaved fathers and ravaged dead daughters... is this what happened, Brother Dominican? You and the crazed inmates of this filthy little town were enacting some version of Roman tragedy? Did you fancy yourself Livy or Euripides even? Whilst the rest of the world was tearing itself in real tragedy and ejecting the French Monster from our hallowed peninsula, did you think to liven up this backwater with a piece of self-indulgent theatre?'

Was it time to speak? Neither the Bishop nor the hapless brother-monk could tell. The Bishop coughed into his hand but too late.

'You see it seems to me, *amicis honesta,* that this summer was simply a caponata of young men being hot-headed as young men have always and will always be. And a girl clearly in the midst of her *mensis insanire*, looking for attention, clearly overtaken by pubescent lusts–come now, we are all men here, you are educated in Aristotle, Hippocrates, you have a great library back at the abbey, yes? Not so good as ours in St Peter's clearly but I digress... Brother Lorenzo, you are a weak parasite suckered to the vigorous Borgia tree, let us not pretend that you are capable of great deeds. The first two deaths, they cannot be laid at your door, no?'

This was a clearer indication, invitation even, to speak. Even so, the Dominican was overcome almost by his nerves...

'I knew the young men, I knew that there was trouble brewing. It had been such a hot summer and they had not been allowed to fight the French at Fornovo, the older men, their brothers and cousins had fought, some of their fathers, the city was full of men who bore scars and were full of braggadocio in the taverns ... those who had not been allowed to fight were frustrated, angry, angry at their fathers and at themselves ...'

'Yes, yes, but you did not know they were about to kill each other? You did not instigate the butchery?'

'No, of course not. But if I had been there, I could have ...'

Gandia waved a flashing hand. An emerald? A turquoise? A flash of light across the shadowed wall. 'But you did not know. You are not blessed with the gift of prophecy, you are not Cassandra, no?'

'I did know. I felt the fury in the air. And you are wrong, my Lord of Gandia ...' This was a mistake but the monk's head was down and he did not see. 'I am in the confidences – small, insignificant, mean confidences to be sure – but I am sometimes consulted by certain Heads of the Great Houses ... I am sure I do not know why ...'

'Do you not? Are you such a fool as to be blind as to your blood?'

'But ... but ... who was there to know? I myself ... I have been in ignorance my whole life ...'

'Tchah,' the young Duke dismissed this with another flash of blinding brilliance, 'An abbot does not take on a bastard Borgia without very carefully inscribing this lineage in the abbey records. Your Abbo has always known and the Abbo before him. So the Lords who adopted you as their little pet, their bastard Borgia monkey on a chain, they were playing a bigger game than simply admiring the sage words of advice given them by a nobody. Hah! And you thought yourself so admired! You thought your little words of admonition, of encouragement, of wisdom, you thought these were valued in themselves? Because you have a little learning and can crush a concoction to stop the shits? Unbelievable. Is that not unbelievable, Lord Bishop?'

'I myself, Lord Juan, was unaware of this man's parentage until recently. I knew him only as a talented herbalist and tutor in Latin to many of the noble boys of the city. Perhaps the Abbo before this one knew. Or the one before him. But for his lifetime, Brother Lorenzo has been a child of Saint Zeno and Dominic, a child of Santa Anastasia's abbey. If he has a family, it is his family of Saint Dominic.'

'Tchah! Your willful ignorance of such things is beyond credence. But we digress and I am getting bored. You knew these young men, the ones who died but you were not there when they died?'

'No, I was not there. I was here in the herb garden, finishing an inventory of...'

'I do not care. Two killings. And then a few days later a third. And you were not there.'

'Not there, no. But that third murder... I am responsible, my Lord Gandia, because my careless negligence, my stupidity in trusting another to do what I should have done myself...'

'So you were there?'

'No. I came across the dead man soon after, in the cloisters at Santa Maria, and knew immediately what had happened but...'

'But you were not there and you did not strike the blow?'

'No.'

'And you did not incite the murderer to attack his innocent victim? Not by exhortation, by threat, by bribery, by malicious falsehoods?'

'No. But my negligence...'

'We have a dead man and another with a bloody blade. And two witnesses. I think that is enough for the Podesta. Now...' The lovely pale Borgia eyes became predatory, watchful, loving even. 'The girl. Did you poison her, Cousin Lorenzo? Was her young flesh too much temptation for your Dominican vows, did you transgress into the realm of Luxuria, did she entrap you, *lavish in her ruined fame, loose-haired, wild-eyed, her voice like a dying fall*, were you lost in her delight?'

'No! No!' the monk, clearly horrified, eyes wide, thin lips pulled away in grimace. Juan Borgia laughed.

'And you my cousin? Now I do doubt your parentage. Old Callixtus was a goat of the first order, a rutting stag. His copy of the *Pyschomachia* was so stuck together with the sticky effluvia of his dirty ejaculations that my brother, Cesare, and I had to prize the pages apart! Are you sure you do not have a well-thumbed version of *Le Roman de la Rose* here in your library, Bishop? Does the maiden not get deflowered in a herb garden, Brother Lorenzo? Did this young girl get under your habit to so torment you that you had no choice but to slip her a quick dose of *atropo belladonna*? Of wolfsbane? What is the other vernacular name for wolfsbane, I forget . . .'

'Monkshood, my lord.'

'Ha! So! Did this girl get too rough with the hood of this monk, do we think, Lord Bishop? Did she find your grey and grizzled hair, your liverspots, your rotten teeth just too much to resist?' And at each, he roughly caressed hair, skin, mouth with bruising gemstones. Brother Lorenzo winced.

'No, my lord. I have never been tempted away from my call to chastity . . .' *A lie. Another lie, God help his wretched soul!*

'Again, evidence that you are not Uncle Alfonso, Pope Callixtus' spawn . . .'

'And never would I dream of using God's gracious bounty to harm rather than heal.'

'And again, interrupting your betters.' A nasty pause. 'But here we have the nub of our problem, Brother Bastard. Lord Quaesemper seems convinced that you poisoned his daughter. What did you give her if not belladonna, if not monkshood?'

'It was a sleeping draught! A concoction of *cypridedium parviflorum*—you would call it Yellow Lady's Slipper—with *Melissa officialis* and henna. The *nigella sativa* would no doubt have lowered her blood pressure and reduced her heart rate . . .'

'But she recovered? She took your sleeping draught, she slept and she woke up?'

'Yes. Of course the tragedy was that . . .'

'But your disgusting little concoction which I would not, my lords, trust to the bowels of my horse or my dog or even to Raf Salamanca here, your concoction did not kill her?'

'No. I know my trade. God has in his infinite wisdom blessed us with herbs that cure and herbs that kill but he has also blessed us with the intelligence to determine . . . '

'And the other poison? The one that killed the boy?'

The monk shook his head, agitated. 'That was not from here. I do not know any herbalist brother or lay apothecary who would concoct or sell such a *venenum atrox*, such a terrible thing. It was not created or purchased here in this city, I would stake my life on it.'

'Hah!' the Duke of Gandia slapped the old man not gently around the ear. 'But that is precisely what we are doing! We are staking your life on these things! Not my life, I have another sixty years to drink and eat and shit and fuck tight cunni. Not my lord Bishop's life, he has another . . . ten years perhaps to – what is it that you do, Lord Bishop? – to recite Latin that none of his sheep understand, to give the flesh and blood of our Lord to unrepentant sinners soon to burn in Hell, to collect tithes from angry rustics who would prefer the Fraticelli or even the fucking Franciscans. But you, Brother Lorenzo, if you do not do a more heroic job of persuading me of your utter innocence, then yes, we may well be staking your life on these things. Now, Cousin . . . ' he leant in, close enough to bite. 'I personally do not give an *asinus asinum* whether you live or die. But you are a Borgia. Not a Borgia I would claim, not a Borgia I would piss on in a burning street but you are kin to the Holy Father and that it is enough. Did you poison anyone?'

'No, my lord.'

'Did you concoct poison that led to any person's death?'

'No, my lord.'

'Hah. Then there we have it. My innocent, harshly traduced cousin. I need hardly have made the journey, eh Bishop?'

'My thoughts exactly, my Lord Duke.'

The young Duke straightened up and stretched. The sun was high, he had broken his fast a good few hours past. The Bishop put a tentative, hopefully comforting hand on the brother's shoulder. 'It is nearly over, Brother Lorenzo. You will be back in your cell at Santa Anastasia's by Vespers tomorrow, ready to return to your life.'

'Yes. Thank you, my Lord Bishop. But I still . . . '

'No, no more.' Brushing imaginary dirt from his doublet, the Duke yawned. 'Back to your pisspot, Cousin. You can return to your no doubt equally disgusting monastic cell tomorrow. It never fails to confuse and amaze me that good Christians of some learning can actually believe that the Good Lord Jesus Christ Himself, King of Heaven, Prince of Peace would actually be flattered by grown men living like *rustici*, like plebeians, scourging themselves with iron-tipped whips, breaking their backs on hard pallets and scratching their God-given skin with horsehair shirts. You should come to Rome, Cousin Lorenzo, parade your name for all to see and you will be eating off goldenware with an army of servants to wipe your arse before you have time to take off that sorry habit. My brother, Cesare the Cardinal Cunt, was Bishop of Pamplona by the time he was fifteen, you know. Now, one more thing . . . '

The pale eyes narrowed. The sun was still behind the cloud. A cold damp finger running itself down the monk's spine. The emerald was like a cat's eye . . .

'Poison is a woman's weapon, is it not? My sister uses arsenica on the cats and dogs in and around the palace. She enjoys watching them froth and twitch. I think it is likely that this woman, the woman who belongs to Lord Quaesemper, is it not likely that she concocted this poison that killed the boy? It is just the sort of thing a bitter old spinster would do. Jealous of the tight cunni and high teats of her young lady, having to hear as the pair rutted well until dawn, her own parts dry and miserable. I would not be surprised if you had heard this, Cousin Lorenzo. Heard that some serving woman in Quaesemper's household had been seen buying sandarach resin to roast. Had been seen with a small bag of greyish ash. I would not be surprised to hear this. Would you be surprised to hear this, Lord Bishop?'

'Not...greatly surprised, Lord Juan.'

'Then perhaps I will hear this very soon. Right...Raf! Vincenzo! Get Carlo and Matteo, we need to eat and eat well. Lord Bishop, I shall return to the palace tonight to speak to the miserable creature, my lord father will expect it. Make sure she understands that a confession will allow us to go easy on her.'

'Yes, my Lord Gonfalonier.'

'And Bishop...I heard aright? The lawyer working for Lord Quaesemper arrives here tonight? Do we know this fool's name?'

'No. I have had no word.'

'No matter, no matter. But the Porta Palio closes at dusk?'

'Of course.'

Soon there was a little cloud of dust, some unsettled gravel and the Bishop and the monk were alone in the shaded cloisters, looking out onto the gardens. A common bird, perhaps a thrush, began to trill nervously at first and then with some vigour.

'We can stay here awhile, my lord?'

'Yes.'

Bright autumn sunlight. Leaves, flowers, soft brown bark, the thrush.

'He is really a Gonfalonier and Captain General of the Blessed Mother Church?'

'Yes.'

'*Deus prudens et incomprehensibilis.*'

Sigh. 'Yes.'

CHAPTER EIGHT

In which the miserable woman is rather roughly told the Duke's Deal and Raf of Salamanca comes to an insalubrious end

The five Spaniards find a half-decent drinking house which also has food which probably won't poison them and willing women who probably won't either. Juan of Gandia never eats very much at the best of times – and this sojourn north is not by definition the best of any times – but he drinks this afternoon an impressive quantity of Spanish Red. The mistress of the house has recently lost her husband at Fornovo and wishes to express her desolation and loss in person. Bereavement becomes her – her cheeks are flush, her teeth strong and white, her hair good for pulling – and the Duke takes her three times in the dead husband's bed. She is a little too willing for his tastes, all giggles and welcoming flesh, all eager fingers and wet lips. She whimpers a little when he forces her onto her front and pulls hard on the chestnut tresses so that her throat and chin are forced up and back, away from the bolster. Forcing her glistening thighs apart with his knee, he wonders if he could pull her head back so hard that her neck would break or would her windpipe crack first? She was keen enough to have him inside her the first two times – all breathy moans and shivers and scratching at his buttocks – but now the aperture is tight and unwilling and dry . . . he feels himself squeezed hard and glorious, breaking her, bleeding her, each thrust wetter and wetter. He comes again – no excess emotion, just a short grunt of animal satisfaction – and lies atop her for a while, annoyed by her little sobs but too drunk and tired to push her face into the pillow. He sleeps a while and when he wakes, she has gone, leaving dirty sheets. By the feel and angle of the sun, it seems to be mid afternoon.

He shouts for Raf.

'Sir?'

His boys don't bother with *my lords* and *your graces* and *my holy captains*. They would mix them up, the subtle distinctions would confuse them; he hardly understands himself what it is to be Papal Gonfalonier except that everyone salutes him for it and he can get into any part of the Holy City without explaining what he is doing there. He has a huge wardrobe back in Rome full of ceremonial robes and brightly coloured silk doublets, all covered with St Peter's keys, he remembers his predecessor Niccolo Orsini, bald bastard that he was, strutting around in armour – gold keys, brass keys, silver keys – but never to be seen on the actual field of battle. This little excursion however necessitates circumspection. He has the seal of the Holy Father for emergencies, he has his ducal signet on his finger, a silken coat of arms on his shirt and the papal banner, cloak and part-armour in a pannier but speed and a degree of anonymity is paramount.

'Sir?' Raf again. Looking a little disheveled. From what Gandia could hear earlier, the serving girl had not been as keen as her mistress. Raf has a long scratch down his cheek.

'My head feels like a Frenchman has shat in it. Go to the Bishop's Palatum. Get some kind of confession from the old witch he keeps in the cellars. Then before the gates close, get yourself to the Porta Palio. I want to know which Firenzi *advocatus cimex* Lord Quaesemper has hired to fuck me around.'

'How do you know he's a Firenzi?'

Juan of Gandia winces, hold his forehead. The Spanish Red is clearly some kind of local piss dyed scarlet. 'All arsehole lawyers are Firenzi. Just keep in the shadows and let me know where he's staying. Then you and the boys can pay him a visit in the early hours.'

Raf nods. He is a thug of limited vocabulary. An escapee of some Spanish misadventure, a noose with his name upon it waiting for him back in the land of the pomegranate. He is obedient without being subservient which Gandia likes. Unimaginative and unambitious certainly but Gandia has imagination and ambition to sink a papal ship.

'I'm going to sleep here for a few hours. Then I'll be back at the Podesta Tower. Join me there after you've followed him.'

Raf is soon out in the streets, missing the respect and wide berth he always gets when with his master the Duke. But he is sly and quick, slipping and snaking his way through the thronging masses, keeping the river to his left, and he makes fast time to the horseshoe bend where the cathedra and the episcopal palatum del Vescovado sit to the north of the piazza. There is a fuss of course. The Bishop's stewards do not want to let him in, they look down their long northern noses as if he has shit on his shoe. They call for the senior steward who calls for the *dominus villicum* who calls for the episcopal *privata scriba* who finally in fear of the imprint upon red wax Raf Salamanca holds in his dirty hands, call for his Grace himself. The Bishop fortunately understands the way things are. It is not proper or right to allow this *sceleratus,* this ruffian of the streets, to question a protected witness but the seal he bears is that of a holy Captain of the Mother Church on papal business. And it is only a woman already breathing the last of a very finite number of breaths . . .

She is brought yet again to the cellar with the single chair and the damp stone walls. She has lost some weight but then she had ample to lose. No tears, this time, a kind of stunned half-awareness, as if all she can hear are cicadas, as if her world is just a little bit out of focus. Raf Salamanca is not a tall man, he is stocky, wide about the shoulders, he smells of beef and does not shave. Interestingly, the Bishop notes, she does not seem afraid, just dazed. No doubt, a working class woman in a large highborn household meets rough men as a matter of course. No doubt they deliver the meat in the morning, they collect the rubbish, they argue about fees and payments and who owes who how much. They flirt with the girls who peel and cut the vegetables, women like this one defend their girls with a '*get out of here, you dirty beast*', '*I'll tell his lordship who'll tell your master and then where will you sleep tonight?*' '*No finger on her ring til there's a ring on her finger, my good man!*'

Raf is not charming like his lord. His does not delight in words, he has no education or erudition to savour and show off. He does not like the fact that this old woman is marginally taller than him so he calls for a stool. When she is perched, somewhat unsteady -

'*Where would I go in this town to buy charms? If I was going on a long journey across the sea?*

Where would I buy a poultice for my lord's headache?

If I had a goitre of the neck, as big as this, who would tell me what prayers to say and to which saint?

If my wife is with child, who can tell me whether it is a boy or girl?

If my sister had an unwelcome child growing in her belly, who would I go to to send the child back to God? (The Bishop winces a little at this but does not interrupt. He can see where this is going and does not completely disapprove.)

The answers come, unsteady at first and then trip trip tripping out of her, so eager is she to please.

There is a priest, my lords, a priest called Michele although I do think he is defrocked, he lives in the little chapel in the walls of the church of San Lorenzo on the Corsa Castelvecchio, he will give you a charm to be worn around the neck and this charm has been rubbed by a scarf worn by Saint Christopher himself. If you pay an extra three gold ducats, he will tie three threads of the scarf around the charm. For headache, you should go to Signora Bianchi in the Piazza d'Erbe, she will give you a cool damp cloth soaked in feverfew and willow infusion. I would use the same for the goitre and pay for the Sisters of St Clare to say ten Hail Marys for me. For a boy in the belly, a hanging black stone will swing around to the left and for a girl it will swing right. But it has to be a black stone, my lords, be careful the peddlers from Mantua do not sell you painted stones, they will do so and care nothing for their lie. If your belly is with child and it is not yet showing, then drink hot pennywort and fill a sheep's bladder with warm soapwort and cyperus and squirt it as high up inside you as you can. That has worked for many a girl and even high lady that I know tell. But if you have had your quickening, then you must add hellebore and catnip to the mixture.

And if I wished to cause my enemy a stomach ache, where would I buy such a thing?

If I wished to make my enemy see visions?

And if I wished my enemy to become blind for just one week as punishment for looking at young girls whilst naked?

And if I wished to rid myself of a husband, if he beat me? Where would I go for help in such a thing?

Her eyes seem to be fixed upon some mark upon the wall, high above their heads and behind.

Well my good lords, a mild poison to bring about stomach ache is easy enough, my poor dead husband, he would say that I gave him the bellyache when I would know that it was the liver they put inside the porcetta at the corner stall. He was so greedy, he would wolf it down so! But if you wanted to bring about a real bellyache, then put tomato leaves in any meal, that'll do it every time. Visions? Well, there's the little brown mushroom of course—all the boys go looking for it by the edges of the woods this time of year—and there's the amanita mushroom, ever so pretty with little flecks of red and white but that's a hard one to judge, that one. Nutmeg is good for visions but you have to use an awful lot and it takes a while to take effect... To cause loss of sight, my lords, well I would use drops of hellebore or belladonna but how to administer without the wretch knowing? When he is sleeping, I would think, my lords, when he is sleeping. And if my husband beat me, well, I would beat him back and I did, I tell you, on occasion I did! But if I was afeared for my life or the lives of my little ones, then I could use the amanita but he would most likely see that and not eat it so I would go to the Egypsi Roma, far out of the city walls towards the mountains to the west, they have concoctions that they harvest from the fangs of snakes, snakes they catch and hold tight until the poison comes gushing out and they gather it up in little glass bottles and you only need a tiny bit . . .

Breath. Breathe. Breathe. Breath. Raf is pleased.

'Woman, you know where to obtain every wicked poison under the sun. You know how to cause every misfortune a person could suffer. No one would believe that you have not done these things yourself. No jury. No Bishop's court. No Podesta. No *Santo Oficio de la Inquisición.* No one.'

He grins triumphantly over towards the Bishop who sits upon his plain wooden throne, with Lucius the scribe on another stool writing notes. His grin says *See! We have her! Her own foolish mouth condemns her with its every spew. Death will be doing her a favour, only death will shut her up.*

He has one more task to perform for the Duke and the gate will close soon so he swings his cloak around himself and prepares to leave.

The woman is still chattering to herself. Remedies for toothache, poultices for lockjaw, creams for sunburn. The Bishop is tired. His shoulders sag a little.

A cantrip to stop spirits. A medallion to make your lover faithful. A medallion to make your lover potent. A combination of herbs to fade wrinkles around the eye.

Last birdsong of the afternoon, imagined, dimly carried down perhaps through the very stone. Muffled laughter in the adjoining cellar rooms. His steward and some girl . . . he really must put a stop to it . . .

And if you wanted someone to sleep like the dead, to stop the pulse, a rare potion this one. For this, you must go to Brother Lorenzo at the Abbey of Santa Anastasia. He can make you a drink that will make your enemy sleep and when they wake they will be so heavy of heart, they will see angels and devils and be in such a torment that they can do nothing but throw themselves from high towers or drive sharp daggers into their breasts.

The Bishop sits up. 'What say you? Sharp daggers? Stop talking, woman. A drug that makes you want to throw yourself from a high tower? Who would sell you this demoniacal thing?'

Raf scowls. 'She said it was a defrocked priest at the basilica of San Lorenzo, a Michele ...'

'No,' says the Bishop although his head is screaming for him to drop this thing, to stop the scribe's hand and go and find his dinner. 'No, she said it was Father Lorenzo. Of Santa Anastasia. Our friend, I think.'

The Spaniard purses his lips and shrugs. 'So? He admits to giving the girl a sleeping draft. This is nothing new.'

The Bishop raises his eyebrows. 'It may well be nothing new. But my scribe has noted it anyway. *High towers and sharp daggers.* For the Church records. Your master is after all the Gonfalonier. He will want to present the most accurate detailed account to the Holy Father.'

Raf doesn't quite understand why he feels uneasy. As if something that felt right and in tune, now seems to have shifted a fraction and is now out of focus, discordant. He cannot see the outside world but it feels as though the sun is almost below the western hills. He needs to be at the old western gate, he needs to hide in the shadows and observe which stranger comes in. *Some penny-a-go lawyer, a damned Firenzi, some advocatus cimex.* Shrugging, he addresses the woman who is still muttering.

'Do you understand, woman, that your knowledge is an evil thing? That the good Bishop here and the good lord of Gandia need to empty it from your big ugly head? That you will never get into Heaven, you will not enter the Kingdom of God with a head full of such shit? Do you understand what happens to witches like you? Have you seen a burning, old woman? Have you smelt a person burn? Such a stench you cannot get it out of your nose for weeks.' He pushes her roughly, she falls to the hard stone floor, crying out as her hip hits the flags. He pulls her back up to the stool.

'No one here wants you to burn. It's nasty, fucking nasty. And God cannot collect up all the ashes on the Day of Judgement, you're scattered all over the world for ever and you won't get your body back come Judgement so you won't walk in the Kingdom of God. You'll be scattered forever on the four winds. You'll never meet Jesus. But if you accept that you're a bad old cunt of a woman, that you knew where to get poison, that the boy who died drank poison you gave to him, that you made the little girl drink whatever shit she drank . . . it was you, you bought the filthy potions, but it all went wrong and you're sorry and you want to make amends. A quick little hanging and it's all over, you get to make your confession, the Bishop himself will give you the Eucharist, he'll be there at the end to bless your dead body. And on the Day of Judgement, Jesus Christ himself will see into your soul and know that you are bloody sorry. Eh?'

He pushes her shoulder, she gives a little start and cringes. He slaps her lightly across the face.

'Just tell the Bishop's man here that it was you, tell him you're sorry, tell the families you're sorry. The Duke of Gandia is a fine young man, you know who he is? He is the Papal Father's own son. So you can trust him. Better than burning, eh? We wouldn't have a choice with a poisoning witch who won't repent, we'd have to get Torquemada over from Spain. Have you heard of Torquemada, old woman? He has special skills, he makes a burning last all day, sometimes into the night and all the time, it's screaming, screaming, screaming. I have a grandmother just like you, I wouldn't want her to burn, I'd do anything to stop that, anything.'

Eyes glazed, a slight trickle of blood from reddened lips. Does she nod? The sun is surely heading towards the hills, he is late and needs to hurry. Raf nods to the Bishop. 'She admits it. She knows what's good for her. Make sure your man gets it down that she nodded.'

'I saw her nod,' the Bishop is even more tired. This conclusion was the aim all along–ever since his conversation with the Podesta–but he feels drained, spread out, diluted. 'I saw it. You can tell the Duke.'

The swarthy Spaniard is gone, the scribe reads out his notes, the Bishop listens, nods, attaches his seal. On the three-legged stool, the fat woman with the uncombed hair licks her lips and mutters. He could have sworn that her eyes were cloudy, indistinct. But he sees now that they are clear.

---------- ∞∞∞∞ ----------

Not much traffic on the roads still, the whole peninsula is recovering from the French feet, tramp tramp tramp, *bouge de la, bouge de la,* tramp tramp. A Venetian glassblower and a cart well padded with wares, an excitable gaggle of piglets, shiny, pink, like little children off to slaughter. Field workers, goatgirls, shepherds, not a word of Latin to one of them, not an inch set foot outside the Veneto or beyond the Adige. Raf's eyes are getting tired. The southern road towards Mantua and then further on towards Bologna where the lawyer would no doubt have passed a night is quiet. Travelers are returning to the thoroughfares linking the northern city-states now but still footsteps are cautious, taken carefully, trodden with precision. Just half a day's ride due East of Bologna is Mordano. He has not been there himself but they passed a pathetic column of returnees just a few days before. Sacked and raped to its last breath, the city paid the price for French avarice and Sforza stupidity. From a distance it does not apparently look particularly ravaged but there are still corpses piled up awaiting Christian burial, eleven months on.

Raf is bored. It is an accustomed state and scarcely bothers him. He uses it to envisage food, drink, a woman's shining body. Waves of bored lust and well-thumbed desire wash half-heartedly over him. Fornovo would at least have been a change, he thinks, like opening a window on a cold night of storm, *whoosh,* the charge, the collision, the hot sticky breath and blood, warm piss suddenly down his inner thigh, feeling alive, feeling dead, feeling something. But Borgia had been forbidden to fight, Gonfalonier or not and so his men had stood with him on the hillside and observed at his side. And not much of a battle, to be honest, both sides claiming victory which is never a good sign . . . The French at least had fought like vicious bastards, he had almost found himself cheering them on, the *furia francese* they were calling it. But then a man always would fight like a mad dog at the thought of dying on a dirty foreigner's soil. He picks at his teeth. Long time since breaking fast. The City Watch are packing up, shepherding in the stragglers. He is in the shadows of the porta and can see the empty bridge, watches as the portcullis gate comes crashing down.

No more? He mouths to the Watch. They shake their heads. No Firenzi? They laugh and shake their heads again. Why would one of the Firenzi come here? It was miracle enough that the Duke of Gandia had honoured them with his august papal presence . . . He watches as they exchange pikes, helmets, swords with the Night Watch. Not soldiers, these men, lads, fathers, farmers, blacksmiths. The rape of Mordano a long way away. He flicks a bronze chit to the lad who had fetched him water, the boy sends a cheerful thumbs-up and disappears into the shadows of the town. The Spaniard in the shadows feels a sudden chill and pulls his cloak more tightly round.

---------- ∞∞∞ ----------

Raf Salamanca's dismembered body is not found until dawn and not identified for three hours after that. Indeed, one of his arms is never found at all. The River Adige is fast-flowing, it has a long way to go and it cannot stop for the interests of street urchins and *scelerati*. His eyes might have told the excited crowd of fisherboys the last sight he saw and then they could have run through the streets playing 'He!' and earning a ducat for bringing a mad murderer to justice. But the eyes have gone and even if they had known the face of the man who took them out, it is too late now.

CHAPTER NINE

In which John Oldcastle writes a letter to his old friend, Girolamo Savonarola

My best beloved cousin Samuel, I am very glad to hear from you, that you are well, and I would have you think that it is one of the greatest comforts I have in this world to hear of your well fare; I am very sorry to hear that your Father is still in that humour of offering you more wives; but as for this; she, this lady the third, has a great portion of wealth; which I think if I had; he would not so much mislike me as he does; and besides she is honorable which does go far with most men nowadays; but I protest I write not this out of any mistrust I have of your love; for I have ever found it more than I have deserved; yet I know not what I shall deserve; and thus with my best wishes; for your good fortune; and happiness in all your business I rest ever – your truly loving friend while I breathe, Jane Skipwith

A game between students, more lately a necessity of their survival. A lonely number – this time 3 – in a page of innocuous text (poor Jane! Would she never persuade Cousin Samuel's father to see her as a worthy wife?) and then the shifting of the alphabet just three paces from A to C and another letter written in lemon and balsamic tucked invisibly between the layers of the first. As a subterfuge, it was a little crude but John Oldcastle was not under so many wary papal eyes that his letters were habitually seized and read. Not yet.

To My Most Esteemed and Well-beloved Giramo and hoping to the Risen Christ that you are well, And so I found the city the eve of the second day in a mood of bountiful salvation, most of the youthful men being cheered by virtue of their being at the battle of Fornovo and, by logical necessity of course, survivors of it. I have been given rooms by our most generous host, patron and employer and feel somewhat a fraud given their sumptuous nature. You, my good friend Giramo, would no doubt pull the arras from the walls, the feathers from the bolsters and make yourself a godly nest worthy of Francis himself upon the floor. Here perhaps I should parade my Latin and make some jest about you being but one of the Lord's dogs, you *domine canis* but I shall refrain. And so I retired too late to further our good cause in any way but not too late to drop you this missive and put it into the hands of a trusted member of the noble household who will leave at first light.

Although arriving late as I say, I was welcomed into the small chamber to speak and break bread with my host. And here I must confess, my friend, that my usual calm, the ability of my nature you have mocked so often to hide deep down the unnecessary passions, humours and vitriol of the human frailty, this calm façade tonight almost betrayed the turmoil beneath. For my Lord Nobleman was in the most terrible of humours, so ill had our friend – yes, the devil's own spawn is here, in this city – the Papal Son, the Esteemed Gonfalonier, the Holy Captain of the Vatican Guard treated him. I felt my breath stifle in my throat as the good lord was talking. I had thought Gandia with you in Firenze. But we should have predicted this perhaps. The Papal Father is not going to allow his cousin to pay any price for his misdemeanors but he is not going to trust local podestas and bishops to acquit

him either. And who does Rodrigo Borgia trust more than his favourite son? No man living.

The boy we encountered three years ago, Giramo, was arrogant and cruel in his *prima facie* nature–who knows this better than we? Despite our experience of him being so brief–but he was constrained by bastardy and by youth. I regret to say that now, old friend, he is demonstrably restrained by neither. He is clearly determined to pressure the Bishop into exonerating the monk, regardless of the truth. And it seems clear that our host is correct in his suspicions regarding the duplicitous nature of this city's bishop who may represent the justice of Heaven in the lives of the poor and dispossessed but who seems determined to deny it in reality. From the choleric summation given me at late hour by our host–who still as a father, sheds unmanly tears that touch my heart even as a brother–it appears clear that the Dominican, the bastard of Callixtus, he is within a dog's whisker of walking *liberum et beatus* from the whole tragic business. With no hint of a satisfactory inquiry. And how ironic is it, my good and dear friend, that I–for so long the bitter enemy of the Inquisition in all its terrible forms, of the iniquitous laws against *dicitur* heretics, the cruel inquiries that sent my grandsire to burn in righteous agony of the pyre whilst the credulous cheered–how ironic is it that I should be calling for deeper questioning, for heavy hands, for less brotherly *amicitia* towards this particular brother? But the law of the land and the good Emperor still holds fast in these city-states for which we thank God, the League and the Emperor himself. And so, at first light I shall exercise the right of the accused–and damn it Giramo, we must learn this foolish woman's name, if she is to represent *Libertas et Justitia*, the good nobleman himself did not seem to know it although he has employed the woman in his household for nigh on fifteen years–and I shall visit her in the episcopal Palatum. And then I shall ensure that before I lose the sun of

the same day, I have also spoken to the Borgia bastard who seems so content to let another pay for his deeds and misdeeds. I am unsure as to how I will speak to him . . .

And as for Gandia himself . . . I am unsure as to how to proceed. My instinct – you know my instinct, Giramo, but I have no desire to suffer the penalty of acting rashly. I must think of Eleanor.

O Giramo, I hope you still share our more youthful and naïve passion for the Poet of Arezzo and will recognize my despair when I write; '*Greed and sleep and slothful beds have banished every virtue from the world, so that, overcome by habit, our nature has almost lost its way. And all the benign lights of Heaven, that inform human life, are so spent, that he who wishes to bring down a stream from Helicon is pointed out as a wonder.*' When I think of this foul young aberration being awarded such honours and dignitary titles and powers, I too with Petrarch wonder how the good Lord can have allowed greed to have banished every virtue from the world and allowed him to prosper. But I also know – yea, even in the darkest hours – that the Lord our God is just and patient and so we must be also. But it is hard, Giramo, it is hard!

And so I must retire and give some resuscitation to my tired and aching limbs and humour.

I am, as ever, your devoted friend in the True Gospel, John Oldcastle, Bastard.

Saturday

CHAPTER TEN

In which John Oldcastle (Bastard) has breakfast with a lord

Three years now and John Oldcastle had not slept past the hour before dawn. His good lady back in Spitalfields could lie on her back, red mouth open, and snore until shaken mid-morning – and sometimes out of a rare kindness he let her – but John himself stirred early and disturbed. His dreams were often cruel. Images denied him in daylight hours and by conscious thought, came bounding in like hounds with tongues a-lolling, rubbing him wet and sore, stinking memories given foul odour by the *oculta animi*. This night he had found himself drowning in a sea of smoke. Tentacles, grey and thick and as soft as kitten fur, wrapped themselves around him. Squeezing tight and tight, in his dream he gasps for air but inhales only the smoke. And then the smell becomes taste and substance upon his tongue, in his mouth, down his throat, pushing out his chest, greedy, angry, all-consuming. He can taste not just ash and smoke and Sulphur but burnt flesh, salty like tears, like pig meat in October when the air is full of screaming beasts as the time for slaughter comes. But it isn't All Hallows, when the pigs die, it is December. Light flakes of early snow stick gently on his eyelids and mingle with the smoke, hissing and popping quietly as snowflakes meet roasting meat.

He wonders why he is so hot when the dull slate sky is so full of coming cold.

But then the flames rise up, dancing, dancing and the air is filled with screaming. His mouth is full now, full of roasting flesh and melting muddy flakes, bloody flakes and now he cannot swallow, it is too much, he begins to choke . . . who is screaming? It is not him, he is Young John, he is a boy, he is a child, he is an infant, he is not yet born. Still the screaming. Another John, an older John, a better John . . . burnt flesh and mud and dirty snow. A dirty smell. A wet, dark taste in his mouth. He wakes, wet and warm. Takes breaths to clear the smoke. Swallows to rid his mouth of the taste. A familiar dream. The *vera somnia* of the unsettled internal soul, his was an *anima perturbator*. And yet not as bad as the other dream that often came. His dream of Eleanor.

---------- ∞∞∞ -----------

And so this autumn morning, as with so many others, he was up and pacing around the spacious chambers of the Italian palazzo in which he – so strangely – found himself that morning. The bed chamber had three enormous arched windows, ten feet high at least and he pushed aside the heavy plum drapes to look down three floors to greet the back streets of the New Town, already filling with citizens about their business. This great house was in prime location, of course. Well away from the river with his temperamental floodings in spring and malarial stench in the hot summer, it was directly opposite the fine piazza of San Zeno's basilica and abbey where even now he could hear Benedictine chant wafting across the square and down the narrow street over which his chamber looked. Directly on the level with his own window was another fine, tall building of pale rose-gold stone, with an identical arch he felt he could almost reach across and touch. It was cooling now, this northern Italian air and yet still warm to his Southwark-born skin. A life in Italy would, could, still be a possibility for him. All the great houses needed their *utile hominibus*, especially those well trained in not just common Italian law but ecclesiastical law and even Justinian. The Colonna of Rome, the Sforza and Visconti of Milan, the Medici of Firenze, any and all of these great familia would have taken him in and accorded him good living and respect. But . . . no. The Oldcastles belonged in wet, grey Albion. Their bones and blood and very viscera lay beneath the surface of her roads, her fields, her stones and her cloisters. The roasting flesh of Old John had flown, free, onto her winds and settled on briar and bramble and babbling brook alike. His words were carved upon the landscape, his dream was the English man's dream, his death was the English man's despair, his legacy the whispered word of the dispossessed who dare to hope. This John, this forty-something man with the greying temples and kind eyes, this man was not his grandsire, this he knew, (although admittedly *we* have yet to make up our minds) but something of the old man's blood ran hot and angry through his chilled English veins.

Early it was but there was always someone earlier. Did he wish to break his fast with the lord? Did he wish to eat in his chamber, a goodly selection could be brought to that table, sir, that table there, tis surely wide enough. Or if the English lordship pleased, the Lord of the House was in the Small Chamber, despite the hour. The lord had not really slept since the loss of his child, pacing, pacing, pacing. The lady slept well enough, too well perhaps for one so unexpectedly bereaved. One might kindly put the ease at which she fell asleep to exhaustion for surely she had cried all of Lake Garda's waters these past six weeks. But the lord rarely cried or if he did then the household never saw it, just stone and marble and sleet-grey eyes.

Yes. Yes, if it were not too much trouble, breaking his fast with the waking, pacing, grieving lord would serve his purpose. The bereaved father had information about this tortuous little case, information not yet accorded in letter to Savonarola, his friend. (And that was a mystery yet to be unraveled and one most interesting too. A stiff-as-starch Italian Catholic nobleman with obedient orthodoxy flooding his very veins, cold as they were, friends with the revolutionary firebrand of Firenze? It seems as unlikely as any friendship. And yet ... Savonarola had not always been thus. Once a good and solemn Dominican lay brother, he had been calm and ordered in his rationale, content to just pick at the edges of what they all considered frivolous and self-seeking mutations of the *veritas dei*; extortionate chantry prayers for the souls of the dead, pig bones sold for princely sums as the toe bones of saints, Purgatory itself perhaps if they had been drinking and it was late on those Oxford eaves .... Yes, Giramo had been a steady if not a stalwart defender of most of what was determined by the Magisterium, and such a man – with such a mind! – could well have befriended a minor Italian lord. Now of course the thunderous divine voice roaring and demanding such terrible things in the Dominican's ear would shock even Old John. And yet the friendship with this lord had somehow survived ...) Yes, he would break his fast with this man. And he could already smell – as he was led down the cool corridors, too fast to admire the heavy arras – something hot and good.

The girl at his side – up so early to sweep floors and knead dough and all the other things his own girls did under his feet and in his way – was the garrulous sort.

No, she was not usually allowed on the second floor where the chambers were, no, she would not ever ever be allowed down the great stairs. But the *familia* was still in such an upset. Six weeks now and still there was crying from the lady and black temper from the lord, no one to take over the duties of the three who had upped and left.

Why had they gone?

The second groom had gone because he had been heard laughing. Yes, just laughing, not laughing at all at the dead but just laughing at some jest, some silly nothing, but the lord heard him and that was that, he was gone. And one of the ladies who served the mistress had taken another position because she was scared.

Scared?

Yes, scared! The family in this palazzo has almost lost its wits. The two heirs gone, both of them, snuffed out. The girls who serve the lady never know if they'll be scratched or slapped or embraced! You'd need the patience of Saint Monica to put up with all that.

And the third? To give notice?

Ah, wait here at the foot of the stairs, my English lord . . . the third was the pastries cook, Helena. She had been in this *familia* for her whole life long but when she saw the Master kicking old Susanna out into the street, her skirts all up around her bare fat legs, she was so upset that she dusted down her hands, filled a bag and went to work in the Valmarana house.

She was popular then? This Susanna. Well-loved?

Hmmm, I'm not so sure we all loved her . . . she could talk and talk and talk. And such a rude tongue on her! Such dirty filthy jokes she would tell. I have to say I didn't even understand half of them. But she had been in the *familia* such a long time and looked after all the babies. And you think, well, you hope that when you've looked after the babies, that the family will look after you when you are old. I mean, I know that most of the babies died, God rest their souls, but even so . . .

And yet now Lord Cyprian is supporting her innocence?

Well yes of course. If she is guilty then it looks terrible bad on him. And if he can get the other one, the monk, done for it all then that's another blow against the rest of them, isn't it? It isn't really about us, you know, it's all about the Magna Familias.

I understand. What do you think of her? Could she have given the girl poison?

We're here now, sir. There's meats and fruits and cheese, my lord is within.

Alone in the hallway, a cavernous corridor stretching out into darkness ahead of him. The whole palazzo – the biggest, most opulent house he had ever been in and that included Cousin Cobham's town house – was very quiet. There was a heaviness in the air, an uncomfortable weight as if the family's terrible grief had taken form and was sinking slowly from the rafters to the flags, like mud in water. He had stopped outside the arched door. The smells of cooking had led him and his vanished companion here like Ariadne. The room within was dark, he could sense rather than see that the drapes were still closed. There was a long heavy table, the kind that needed eight good men to shift and was not shifted very often. At its head sat his employer, the friend of Savonarola, terse and tight-lipped, fair hair, pale eyes, he looked more Low Countries or even Viking than Italian. Another table, not so wide but looking even heavier and more permanent lined the wall to his left.

There were silver–yes, by the four apostles, it was silver and not pewter–silver platters with different kinds of fish, some with heads, all nicely filleted. There were bowls of some local specialty of meaty broth, bread and soft cheeses, grapes, oranges, slices of ham. All clearly untouched. And although this was his first morning, John sensed a recurrent theme here, in this rich yet cheerless chamber. He imagined for a moment Eurylochus, peering through the ruined arches of Aeaea at the banquet laid by Circe for men who were destined never to eat. Was that his destiny here then, to be made a fool of, to play some divine game and return home, porcine with shame and failure? But Eurylochus and his captain had eaten and had not become pigs, and his captain had–at the end of it all–returned at last to Ithaca, triumphant. John Oldcastle took a small breath and stepped over the threshold.

---------- ∞∞∞ ----------

'And of course, the woman is a prattling fool, I'll not defend her as some innocent Trojan woman lying prostrate at the boots of cruel oppressors, she is a meddling old sow and I wish her an aeon of torment in Hell,' The lord–and John had just lately, this very last minute indeed, been told to address him as *my Lord*

Cyprian, honour indeed – was curt in word, stiff of neck, he had an unnerving way of staring and not blinking as if his eyes were holding their breath in deep water.

'She has been a member of this household, a trusted member of my household, for as long as I have been the Paterfamilias. I never had much to do with her until this summer, the female servants are the business of my wife and the steward of course.'

John nodded as if he too had such a plethora of servants back in Spitalfields that he could firstly, delegate their care and oversight to a steward and secondly not even know their names.

'Her part in this terrible business, the death of my beloved girl, my daughter, my . . . and all the others is deserving of the most resolute reproach, I have already thrown her out of my house, of course, to beg, starve, I care not what, on the streets. But when I heard that the real meddler, the man with his poisonous fingers in every maleficent pie that led us to this pass . . .' He seemed to lose his way for just one second, then recovered. 'When I heard that he was to be exonerated of all blame, that the woman under my Paterfamilias was to be the . . . the . . .'

'Aaron's Goat?'

'Yes, yes, the Aaron's Goat of the whole most terrible affair . . . and then! By the saints, when then I heard of who this monk, this herbalist, this Dominican friar really was! To have been here under our noses all these years. Blood runs true, Signor Oldcastle, and Borgia blood runs most foul and true to its own perverse nature more than any other. Well, as you appreciate, Signor Oldcastle, I could not let that stand. No. That would not do, not at all. And so I wrote word of this injustice to Savonarola whom I have known longtimes and who I also know has a fine mind and a tenacious tooth for digging down hard to the plain ugly truth of a thing. And I knew that he had many friends of the same ilk, from his travels across Italy and indeed Oxford. I was hoping for Savonarola himself but he is occupied in Firenze. But he has sent me you. Signor Oldcastle. He has sent me you.'

To be appraised coldly, almost hungrily by a man with no hunger and yet ravenous still... John let it pass over him, met the pale blue-grey stare, brown on grey, ochre upon slate, let it stand, let it hold. There. The eye moved on, back to the cold anonymity of middle distance and yet he felt quite sure that he had passed.

'Tell me a little, Lord Cyprian, of this summer. Of all that passed between the young people who died, your own involvement, the woman in your household, Lorenzo Borgia the monk, the attitude of both Podesta and Bishop. Tell me all that you can. Please.'

The sun rose steady and unseen because as he had sensed, the great curtains of the paterfamilias' dining chamber had not been drawn. Their lines fell determined, full and settled as if they had not had cause to stir these long weeks past. Motes of dust floated upon the few rays of morning sunlight sneaking, uninvited, in. John half-filled his plate and listened as the great man unburdened himself. The middle distance – somewhere between table and door – lay heavy with the story. John did not interrupt, except with an occasional and quiet 'And he was related to you, how, my lord?' 'And the anger of this young man, you thought it diffused at this point?' 'And for how long, did you say, the monk had been associated with this other young man?' 'Could you tell me, my lord, the nature of the relationship between the monk and this boy?' At no point did he ask 'And so how did your young girl know these violent, intemperate youths?' 'Tell me, when did you know her involvement?' 'Tell me, my lord, what was your daughter *like*?' and neither did the great lord vouchsafe; 'And my daughter of course was like this and like this but not like that... ' 'And my little girl, you understand, did this and this but not this... ' and yet how subtlely and strangely was she there. She floated with the motes upon the dawn rays as they hovered and tentatively crept closer. Joyous childlike laughter seemed to cling to the heavy drapes of Indian cotton, disappearing as he cautiously turned his head to hear. The half-woman smell of her, lingering and yet fleeting, a soft pre-pubescent innocence tempering the fresh bread, the hams, the carefully filleted fish.

John found himself imagining this girl's face. Cheekbones just emerging from childish fat, lips full and practicing a lady's pout, the moue never held for long, giggles overpowering. Was she dark like the girls of the south or lighter like most others of this northern plain? Eyes? Brown perhaps but he saw them now and they were green. And her hair curled when it was allowed to fall as a child's should, it shone like honey because this girl was fair. *Eleanor*. The smell of wet hair newly washed and a young girl's warm, innocent skin . . . His little Eleanor. He shook himself away and awake.

The lord had asked a question.

'No, my Lord Cyprian, no children. My common-law wife has a son, nearly a grown man now, an apprentice maker of cabinets and suchlike, a good boy and I have treated him as my own. But no, the good Lord has not blessed us with children of our own.'

The lips were thin, a little vicious perhaps. 'Children are not a blessing but a curse. I had three boys, perhaps four, the women would not say, curse them for fools, but such small sickly things . . . One lad . . . ' Here the lips softened a little perhaps although the tone remained harsh, 'One lad grew to his fourth year, his naming day came and went, the sweetmeats still left over and the third morning after . . . cold. In the night they said. Nothing to be done. Father Athanasius came to give extreme unction, the Bishop charged somesuch for the funeral rites, twenty ducats to the chantry, enough prayers commissioned for one hundred years, put him under the stone, start again, there we have it. But after so many years, just one daughter. My house is great and ancient, we can trace our line back to the Etruscans, you know, my ancestors fought with the Romans against the Cimbri and the Teutones. The first Ciprianus fought beside Marius himself at the Battle of Vercellae, how many hundreds, thousands of years ago now? I don't know. So you understand . . . the pain of having no son.'

'And yet you welcomed your nephew into your paterfamilias, your brother's . . . '

'No, my wife's brother's son. A good enough young man in many ways, hot-tempered of course, arrogant even although that is not always a bad thing in one who must eventually lead a house.'

'There could have been a marriage. Cousin to cousin. Your line secure if a boy had been born in this next generation?'

There was a contemptuous flick of the hand. 'Perhaps. But they were too close. No doubt a papal dispensation could have been bought, the good Lord knows that these Papal Fathers we have now can be persuaded upon payment to grant many things beyond their natural remit . . . But I was uneasy about such a match.'

'Naturally. And it is said that oftentimes the children . . . well, the children of such unions are not the strongest.'

There was a silence, deeply mired in viscous pain. Then . . .

'My wife and I are cousins. A dispensation from Rome was given . . . we thought that was enough to cleanse any potential obstacles. The Bishop at that time – it was Bishop Barbaro, not the treacherous fool we have now – the Bishop said it was enough. It came from Rome and he looked at it long and hard. He promised our fathers – my father, my lady wife's father – the dispensation was good with Man and God. But I have thought a long time now that the dispensation should not have been given . . . '

'And yet the Papal Father is said to know best of these things.'

A short hawking from the back of a dry throat. 'This was Callixtus, Alfonso Borgia as was. He gave out dispensations as though they were honeyed treats thrown out at the Paschal carnival. And now we know what else he was giving out. His wild oats, his *semen feram*, to any loose slattern who opened her legs to the papal instrument – May God forgive me my intemperate words, Signor Oldcastle – but it is true.'

'It is true. And his untampered, ungodly ways have a long reach. Nearly forty years ago now, I think, this Pope died. And yet his bastard is at the heart of your family's great troubles today.'

The tightly clenched fist. The oak table. The silverware jumping upwards and clattering back down.

'Yes! *Yes!* The father through unwise dispensation denies me my living sons, his bastard takes away my only daughter. You see now why I am so filled with . . . I know not what . . . I cannot sleep, I cannot think of anything but this monstrous tragedy. And to have my way blocked yesterday by this damned Spaniard, this arrogant young pup, how the Bishop dares to let him share counsel in this case . . . '

Oldcastle felt a frisson of warning, a wordless voice, something pulling at the bones in his spine. But the lord would not stop.

"I will not let my family be trod in the shit and mud of the street, I will not let her memory be unavenged. And all the world seems against me! The whole of Christendom. It was not in anger or hope or righteous justice that I had word sent to Savonarola but . . . in . . . desperation.'

There. It was out. The truest and yet most painful admission. This was indeed a desperate man. The veil came crashing back down, the eyes steel grey and cold again, lips thin.

'Savonarola sent me word of your name and a little of your record in Oxford and London. But in truth his personal recommendation was enough.'

John nodded. False modesty had no place at this table.

'Nearly enough. This is my family name after all. And so of course I made enquiries of my own. Yours is an interesting name, John Oldcastle. And your lineage too . . . interesting.'

'And did you find anything of concern, my lord? Anything to cast doubt upon my ability to serve you in this matter?'

At last, a grim smile. A Death's Head grimace. But was that a girl's laughter too, floating out from beyond the doorways, down the corridors, through the dusty, murky air of two men talking?

'I found only what I needed, John Oldcastle, grandson of Sir John Oldcastle, Lord of–how do you say?–Corban?'

'Cobham.'

'A knight no less, a member of your esteemed English Parliament. A great warrior. Friend to king Henry Plantagenet, Fifth of his name, hero of Agincourt. Your grandsire also, hero of Agincourt. Scourge of the French.'

John nodded.

'But also . . . '

John did not reply. This proud Italian lord already knew what there was to know, he was not going to do his job for him.

'Ah yes, Sir John Oldcastle. Heretic. Lollard. Rebel. Traitor. He tried to kill his own King, I believe, the king who was once his bosom friend, his brother-at-arms?'

'Some things are more essential to eternal salvation than brotherly friendship.'

'And sacred vows to monarchs? More important than these?'

'Indeed.'

'Hmmm.' The girl had gone, leaving just a little wisp of the smell of half-eaten apple. 'I think you admire this grandsire of yours, John Oldcastle. I think perhaps you even share some of his heresies. What were they now? We have our own in Italy of course–the Poor Spirituals, the Apostolic Brethren, the Fraticelli, the Joachimites–mostly now either burned and reduced to the ashes of their desire or subsumed into the Franciscan order after the Council of Basel. Now, France! France has of course the greatest and most malevolently irascible of heretics–Albigensians, the followers of that madman Henry of Lausanne, the equally demented Waldensians–just as France has the most monstrous of kings, the most rapacious of armies, the most brutal of soldiers, so their heretics are also the most misguided, the most rabid, the most desirous of unholy martyrdom.'

John was still. He knew how to pass this test, had passed it often, strange how each examiner thought himself the first. This great lord was no different.

'So. So John Oldcastle, grandson of Sir John the Lollard. A follower of the heretic Wyclif, I think. You understand, as young scholars here in the northern plains, we get a good grounding in all the ways to Hell we must avoid, our Dominican teachers are zealous in describing to us not just how these men erred but what eternal torments are now inflicted upon them in Hell. We are taught the error of the otherwise blessed Clement of Alexandria. Clement taught, you may know, that all good Christian men must *naturalitas* break the rules and codes of their societies to embrace the life of the ascite. But he was misguided in this. Or perhaps mis-quoted over the years, such things happen. And so we are now taught most clearly that the life of extreme poverty is a choice, not obligatory for the good Christian man and that it is heresy to enforce it upon others, even churches and monasteries. And it is not just a matter of poverty, John, but of doctrine. There are some beliefs we may not deny. And yet your Lollard grandsire did deny them. He spoke against the holy rite of transubstantiation, I think even though Christ Himself said, *hoc est meum corpus.* He said it, John Oldcastle, said it clear to the Twelve. And your grandsire, along with all those others who thought they knew better than the Four Fathers, published a denial of purgatory even though in Corinthians we hear of a purifying fire and Christ himself talks in Matthew of forgiveness in the age to come. Not now, John Oldcastle, and not never. But in the age to come.'

'You are well-informed, my lord.' And this must be a welcome distraction for you, my poor man, a meaningless theological debate after so many weeks of breathing in the scent of her hair.

'So. The beliefs which led your grandsire to burn on the pyre at . . . where do you English execute your heretics and traitors – Smithfield.'

'St Giles Field, my lord.'

'Ah, is it so? So these beliefs, there are twelve I think.'

Again, what answer was needed here? Of course twelve, what other number would they have chosen?

'And most of these do not interest or concern me, I am a good Catholic, you understand? *Hoc est meum corpus*, John of Oldcastle, *hoc est meum corpus.* But I think your grandsire the Lollard believed that the Holy Mother Church of Rome should not get her hands dirty by involving herself in the temporal world? That she should not allow her bishops and cardinals to hold temporal offices and own temporal lands and have temporal powers over the citizens? This is also in accordance with my own beliefs and those of the northern states who chose many years ago to ally themselves with the Emperor rather than with the Bishop of Rome. The Holy Mother Church is here to safeguard our eternal souls, to administer the sacraments, to sing chantry prayers for our dead, to be the repository of holy knowledge and of powerful relics. But not to administer temporal justice. Not to sit on imperial councils. Not to raise rents as well as tithes. We have our podestas for this. And men such as myself of course.'

'Of course, Lord Cyprian.'

'And so, Mister John Oldcastle . . . this is all I need to know. Are you enough of your grandsire to be able to serve me in this capacity? Are you enemy enough of the so-called Holy Mother Church of Rome to help me against this perfidious priest and his maleficent papal backers? But orthodox enough to not taint me with the slightest stain of your grandsire's heresy?'

Yes. This was the nub of it. The stench of heresy clung to noble doublets for millennia and was never truly extinguished. One could scrub and scrub and scrub. Look at his cousin, Lord of Cobham; for how long had he and his long-nosed wife scrubbed bleach into the dirty stain of their infamous antecedence? Near on eighty years now and still the noble Cobham laundry was a grimy grey.

'I understand, Lord Cyprian.'

'And are you the man I need?'

'I am the man you need.'

CHAPTER ELEVEN

In which Rosa and Livia discover that they are not the only guests in the Podesta's house.

It is time to leave John Oldcastle and the grieving lord and see how fare our little bird and her comely sister. It is yet quiet in the tall, solid Podesta tower – many of its household, you will remember, went with its master to equip him to meet the Emperor – but a few swift shadows dart from grate to grate, from hall to hall; their feet are light and deft, there is hardly a tap heard. Which is why if we lean our heads just so, we can hear the faint song of Rosa whose heart has been torn asunder these six weeks past. She is not really singing, it is a poem, you understand, but her voice has that lilt and timbre that makes everything she says seem just a little like a song.

'My passion's folly is so led astray,
By following that which turns and flees
I fly from love's light supple noose
Hangs before my slow sad pace.
The more that I recall my steps
To that safe road, the less I hear
Nor helped am I by speed nor spur
To resist what love does naturally.'

'Don't stop! Your voice is so pretty. It goes up and then down like sliding down the grassy hill when it is all icy in winter. Like the Paschal mystery players we had in the hall at Easter. It is all soft and flowy.'

'Flowy? I'm not sure that's a word, Livia.'

'Of course it is. It means flowing nice and gentle like the River Adige when it hasn't rained for days. Flowy.'

'Well, perhaps.'

'What were you reading? Where's the poem?'

Rosa turned away from the window, holding out both hands empty. 'No poem.'

'But that was a poem. You have learnt it by the heart. You weren't just talking to yourself.'

The elder sister laughed, just a little. 'No. Well, yes, I was talking to myself but in recitation. You know your Petrarch, little sister, you began his poems last year.'

'Yes but I don't know that one.' A pause. 'It is a sad one, isn't it?'

'Most of Petrarch's poems are sad. You know how he loved the Lady Laura and she did not return his affections.'

'But that's silly. Why didn't he just love someone else who did *return his affections*.' And she said this with a twirl, her mouth a parody.

'Well, little Livia. You can't choose who you love. Cupid sends his sharp little arrows and sometimes they pierce the hearts of two people who should always have been and will always be together.'

'Like Mama and Papa.'

Livia had only very dim memories of her mother but had created a tableau of domestic bliss in her mind. Rosa felt an internal grimace but smiled softly. 'Yes, little bird, like Mama and Papa. Who are together again now in Heaven with Clare and Teresa and all the saints.'

'But you said sometimes. Sometimes Cupid send his arrows into the right hearts. Does he sometimes miss?'

Rosa sat back against the bolster and pulled the little girl onto her lap, smoothing her hair. 'People say that he misses and gets the wrong people accidentally and so all our troubles begin but I think that he is a little imp, a *puer impius* with a desire for revelry and he shoots his arrows at the wrong people quite deliberately.'

'Rosa! That's mean! Why would he do that?'

'Why indeed.'

'It's like in *Orlando Innamorato*, when Angelica loved Rinaldo because she drank at the Stream of Love but he hated her because he had drunk water from the Well of Hate. And Orlando loved Angelica but she kept loving Rinaldo even though he hated her. And then it all got turned around when they drank from the other streams and then Rinaldo loved Angelica but this time she didn't love him back. How did it end, Rosa, I can't remember?'

'It doesn't end, honey-hair, the poet Boiardo died, just these few months back. He stopped writing the poem because the French came and he wrote that he would complete the romance when the French had gone and peace returned but he died before that happened.'

'So what about Angelica and Rinaldo? And poor Orlando who was chasing them all over the world?'

'Well, I suppose they're still loving the wrong people and chasing each other all over the world and will be for all time. Lost in love for all time. No end to it all, not ever.' *Not ever.*

The little girl arched her neck back, her chin up like a cat being stroked. Rosa leaned forwards and down to kiss her forehead. 'You have hair like honey, little Livia. Shall I keep stroking?'

The golden head nodded.

'Were you saying the poem for him, Rosa? Do you still love him? Even though . . .'

Even though. How many silent hours in the heavy sleepless nights can 'even though . . .' count? How many tears? How many nails split dragging them down the rough stone of his hasty tomb? Even though . . .

I still love him . . . even though I should not.

I still love him . . . even though he is not.

I still love him . . . even though he lies cold.
I'll still love him . . . even though I grow old.

The young woman sighed. She could almost sense him laughing at her terrible rhyming. He of course, could pull the most startling verse straight out of the sky, like catching a thread of gossamer with his fingers and coaxing it gently down. She had never met anyone with such a tongue. It was like quicksilver. Smooth, silky, sharp, poisonous. And nothing on earth as beautiful.

She realized that Livia had twisted her head around to look up at her, two hazel brown eyes were waiting. She gently pinched her nose. 'How do you know such things, Mouse? You are so little, you hardly come up to my shoulder even when you are on your tall toes and I swear by Saint Clare that you still think your dolls come alive at night. How do your eyes see what Papa and Nurse Annamaria and the Cousins did not?'

'I watch you all the time, Rosa. You are my sister. I know everything you do.'

'Hmm. A very agreeable thing then that you love me best of all and keep my secrets.'

'Forever.' Another long companionable silence. Stroke and stroke some more. 'But Rosa, why did you keep it a secret? Isn't love a good thing? Why didn't you get married? Was it like Angelica and Rinaldo, did he not love you back? It seems like he did.'

'Hah, little spy, you were hiding in corners like a little mouse. I knew it! Do I need to blush for shame at what you saw, sneaky paula musa?'

The little girl shrugged. 'I am only ten years, I don't know what needs a blush and what does not. But he made you laugh. I've never seen you laugh the way he made you.'

Fingers tight, almost cruel on her arms, the stubble of a lazy yesterday-shave in her ear, his tongue flicking out to tease and then caress her ear lobe. Almost losing sight, sound, sense with the bliss of it – who would think, just the flick of a tongue on the ear? – then the quick nip of his teeth and a filthy word, some corrupted Latin, a dirty metaphor and she is laughing, head against his chest, shaking in pretended outrage.

'Yes. He made me laugh.'

'And now he's gone, you're reading sad poems.'

'Yes. Now he's gone.'

'How does the poem end?'

'Well, Livia, this is Petrarch so you know it is not going to end well.'

'I'm not a baby. You can tell me sad things and I can still choose to be happy if I wish. I say 'Livia, be sad today' and I am sad and then the next day I say 'Livia, be happy' and that day I am so happy I sing all day.'

'I have heard you. Sometimes I truly think the whole city hears you!'

'Hey, Rosa, that tickles, not my tummy, don't squeeze so tight! That's better. So how does your sad poem end? I promise not to get sad but I don't like stories that have no endings. I shall be awake all night, this night and tomorrow, thinking about Angelica and Rilando and Orlando and trying to think if I was Boiardo how I should have ended it. Please!'

The young woman took a deep breath. *Here I go again, diving deep in the dark green sea of my grief. But so much better to drink hard and harsh of its salt and bile than swim to the surface and breath air that is not him.*

'Very well, Paula Musa.

'*Like a horse under bit I am to him by force*
And in his sovereign power I remain
My loving states carries me sad t'wards death
I sip bitter juice whose taste is no solace
And fruit whose taste is a wound.'

There was the sound of men's voices in the Castelvecchio courtyard beneath their window for their room faced inwards. Horses' hooves, something heavy dropping but not smashing, more voices shouting. Deliveries perhaps, although Paulo

Steward had gone west with the Podesta. Livia squirmed a little. It had become very quiet.

'Is that it? Is it finished?'

'It ends in death. Do you wish to follow the broken hearts into Heaven or Hell like Orpheus?'

'Are you cross with me, Rosa? Your voice has gone funny.'

'Of course not. I was just sad. I was thinking of the last time we were all together. Do you remember? The *commedia dell' arte* at the Cousins' palazzo. It was the first evening we came out after Father died, a celebration of our victory over the French. That was the last time all the Cousins were together, all eleven of us.'

And now two of my cousins are dead but instead of weeping for them, I have a heart frozen over the image of you, ***mea dulci amor****. Your face alone.*

Livia put her head to one side. 'I didn't see the Cousins, I was sent to bed before the *commedia* began and they were all getting dressed up in their costumes. But Uncle Cyprian let me watch the players rehearse in the great hall and I sang with them. There was a song about Arlecchino loving Columbina and Pantaloni trying to stop their wedding but he turned her into a dove and she hopped down the tree outside her balcony.'

'Could she not have flown?'

'But it was woman, silly, dressed in white feathers and so she had to hop down a little step instead. Uncle said it was unseemly for there to be a woman in the Players, he would not have hired them if he had known but it was too late now. And when she heard me singing from the doorway, Columbina, had me come to the stage and sing it with her.'

'I know. You have told me a thousand times.'

'But Rosa, it was the most wonderful moment of my life.' Her voice, although small and childlike, was also full of an age-less wistfulness. Rosa felt her breath catch a little. Oh but she was so selfish. So consumed with her own pain. She woke puff-faced in the morning, she blundered blindly through the day, she cried herself to heavy sodden sleep, all the while never really asking herself how her little sister was feeling. She had lost the Cousins too, one so close in age to be almost as child-like. How much Livia had been told, how gross and brutal the details of how they had died, she was not sure and did not want to ask. Six weeks and they had never really talked about it. Six weeks assuming her pain was all that mattered.

'Sing it to me now, Little Livia. The song you shared with Columbina. It will remind me of happy times, the last time we were all together. And although you were not there in the hall, you were just upstairs in the nurse's bed and you were there in the song too.'

A simple little song about two lovers and cruel fathers, wings and feathers and clouds and flight. She had Livia, still on her lap, sing it three times in a row and then for the fourth, she added her own harmony.

Quiet. The men with their dawn deliveries were gone from outside, the bells had rung for Prime and were still.

One last squeeze, two pairs of legs swung over the edge of the bed, the ten-year-old deposited – not ungently – upon her own two feet. It was well beyond dawn. They ate in the kitchens now that the Podesta was away but if too late the fires would be assigned to cooking for the evening and the morning porridge and bread cooled to hard. For some reason, Adela, the serving girl who turned down their bolster, laundered their clothes and lit their little fire had brought their evening meal to the room yesterday. She seemed flustered, upset even, pretty yellow hair escaping the pulled cap when usually she was a portrait of decorum. No doubt the absence of the Podesta's wife was encouraging some standards to slip. She had not appeared this morning though and Rosa saw no reason to expect such especial treatment – their presence in this house was an imposition after all. The Podesta had been kind enough. They were not going to act like ingrates.

At the door, she felt a pull on her skirt.

'You are still sad. Tell me a nice poem. Do you know one about a mouse?'

'No, but I know one about a bird. If you stop pulling at me…

Little wandering bird goes singing
Your time is come, with soaring notes
Seeing the dawn, the summer near
The night and all the fearful months behind.'

This clearly found its mark. The little girl clapped her hands and then did a little pirouette with her arms flapping like wings as they made their way to the stairs.

'I am the little wandering bird, am I not, Rosa? I am going to flap my wings and soar over the clouds and the mountains and over the rivers and all the valleys and the fields that grow grapes and the great city of Paris and I shall keep flying until I land with a bump and I shall be in England. And when I marry Prince Arthur the Tudor I shall teach him to fly and we shall fly round and round the little House of the Poor Clares and you will see us from your saint's cell and wave.'

'Little wandering bird indeed.'

There was a man, suddenly appeared at the threshold of the Podesta's suite of rooms. Fair hair worn fashionably long and waved, wispy curls of reddish beard, Rosa took in a cut of doublet and a silk sheen rarely seen in the north, there was a smell of soap, a courtly bow but all she remembered later was that he had a polish on his nails. He crossed the landing and stood at the head of the stairs.

'I am sorry, my lord, if we disturbed you.' She bent her head and stepped to move past. He hadn't moved and yet he was now in their way. Rosa sighed. She was used to such men. Narrow eyes looking long and hard, the swell of her breasts, stays pulling tight at her waist, taking the slow insulting journey south to imagine her legs, the space between, measuring the level of her willingness, the charm or force it might take to have her open up. It had all been so easy, just six weeks now. Family, name, history, honour, brawny cousins ready for a fight, angry father with a dozen men at his finger's click. She could pull her waist in tight, flick her eyes up behind the long lashes, whisper words of soft encouragement. But then Annamaria would come and whisk her away. One of the many male cousins. A servant. Her father even. All scowling, tight palms beneath her elbow, ushering her away to safer waters. And so all the while, whatever their rank, the sheen of their hose, the cut of their cloth, they could only dare touch her after sweet permission. And that she had only given once.

'I name it not disturbance when the poet's voice is so dulcet. I name it the Angel of the Dawn, whispering me out of my repose.'

'No angel, sir. Just a house guest and her sister. Staying at my Lord Podesta's charity.'

She saw then her terrible mistake. Dressed in shabby, unfashionable robes – although alas not the habit of Poor Clare, if only she had thought to throw it over but why should she have? – she thought herself safe, safe, sexless, not worth a man's time. But now she saw she had given him the opposite impression. Now she was without name, without family, without household, without brawny cousins quick with their fists. For the first time in her privileged, sheltered life she knew what it was to be vulnerable. Livia was too young, the undercurrents of lust, desire and sudden fear washed over and above her golden head.

'I am Livia,' she said perkily and flushed red with delight when the young man bowed and reached out to take and then kiss her little hand.

'Encantada, pequina Livia. Encantada. I am Juan.'

She wrinkled her nose as Rosa tried to shift her skirts so that they hung looser over her hips. If she brought her chin down to double, if she slouched her shoulders . . . she knew this man. Juan, Giovanni, Alexandro, Piero, it didn't matter, all they cared for was the chase, the hunt, the kill, the feast and the discard.

'That's a funny sounding tongue, Signor Juan. Is it from the Kingdom?'

'From Napoli, little Livia? No, no, no, I am from Spain. From across the Mare Nostrum. Watch the sun go down tonight and that is where my homeland is. Where the sun kisses the earth.' Lazy eyes flickered up and over to Rosa's. Too late she darted her own downwards.

'Then I shall travel to Spain when I have my wings. Perhaps on my way to England.'

To be fair, he was very good with her. Most men paid scant attention to a fanciful ten-year-old acting as chaperone to her older sister. Asking where her nurse was usually came predictably fast. This huntsman was smoother though.

'So you are Petrarca's little wandering bird then? I have often wondered of whom he was thinking when he wrote his lines. Although I think your sister here has changed them a little.'

He sent Rosa a knowing look. As if they were already co-conspirators, already friends bound by a silly little secret.

Livia looked up, a little suspicious. 'Did you, Rosa? Did you change them?'

'A little.'

Juan Borgia, Duke of Gandia straightened up. 'She did the impossible, little bird, she improved upon the poet of Arezzo's great work. Your sister turned winter to summer, night to dawn, grief to joy. And all for you.'

Appeased, Livia tiptoed on one foot and then the other. 'She is clever, isn't she? And very pretty.'

'Enough, Livia. We must go down to the kitchens. There will be neither broth nor bread if we tarry here any longer. Good morning, sir.'

It was impossible to reach the top step without brushing past him. She knew this script, she had seen this play a dozen times, she had played her part, sometimes happily, sometimes with reluctance, occasionally with disgust but always against the backdrop of absolute protection. Now she had no choice but to brush her shoulder against his own.

His shoulder resisted, just for one insolent second. His breath was on her neck and fear ran like burning ice down her spine. She suddenly knew now why the girl Adela – bless her! God bless her for trying – had brought their meal to the room, had tried to keep her away from this dreadful man. A second, perhaps a lifetime, her shoulder pressing against his, hot desire like summer wind upon her clavicle. At last he gave way but she knew it was not her victory. There was no victory against a man like this, there was only flight or defeat.

As they both passed him, Livia tried to do a little curtsey on the top stair, Rosa pulled her down so roughly she unbalanced and nearly fell.

'Hey there little bird,' his arm had reached out to steady them both, 'Would you like to hear what Petrarca wrote about you as a girl? He knew you, you know, before you were a bird.'

'Oh did he? Please!'

She pulled Rosa to stop. They balanced precariously, both on the third step down. Rosa determinedly facing down towards the hall, Livia twisting upwards, her face shining.

His voice was low, a player's voice, a voice used to adoration and audience. The words rolled like slow waves of sweet honey towards them, down the steps, swirling around their feet.

'*She let her golden hair scatter in the breeze,*
Which twined it into a thousand sweet knots,
A wavering light, beauty beyond measure, burned,
In those lustrous eyes, now so dim.'

Rosa managed to pull hard enough on Livia's hand for her to turn and reluctantly begin her descent. But she took the steps almost backwards, beaming up to the young man who now was leaning over the balustrade and speaking down towards them. Rosa could feel his eyes on the nape of her neck.

The sticky slick of honey followed them down the marble steps.

'It seemed to me that her face wore the colour of pity,
I did not know whether false or true,
I who had the lure of love in my heart,
And wondered if I might sudden catch fire.
She was a sprite, no mortal thing,
But of angelic form and her lovely speech,
Rang higher than a human voice.
A celestial spirit, a living sun . . .'

The wide entrance hall, a cool corridor, an open door, a small flight of steps, another passageway, the smell of bread and frying onions and radicchio. Juan Borgia's voice faded as the young woman dragged her sister along. Finally, at the doorway to the Podesta House kitchens, Rosa stopped and took a ragged breath. Livia snatched her hand away, annoyed but still full of delight.

'I am a sprite, Rosa, a.. a *celestial spirit.* Does that mean I'm like an angel?'

'Yes, it does, darling. But wouldn't you prefer to be my little wandering bird? If you flew to Albion as an angel or a celestial spirit, Arthur might not be able to see you. You would blind him with your shining skin and your eyes would be like torches. You could appear on his balcony like a golden ghost and send him running for his guards to see you off. Or for his priests to cover you in bronze and make a statue of you!' Livia was laughing now, her hand back in Rosa's. 'But as a little bird you will whisper in his ear and perch upon his shoulder. You will become his confidante and his friend and then when you finally reveal yourself, he will fall in love with you too.'

'Like the frog prince and the spoilt princess who sat by the pool?'

The pastry cook, now in charge, was bustling in their direction. There was a little cloud of flour, a gabble of nonsense in a rough city dialect, warm hands pushing bowls of porridge towards them, two stools by the open fire. Livia started to sing a little ditty, something about cats and mice and a disappearing round of cheese. Rosa warmed her palms stretched out flat to the flames, alternating the bowl, this hand, to this hand, to this again, to this again. Ten minutes, twenty. Still she felt cold.

CHAPTER TWELVE

In which John Oldcastle talks to the Bishop about natural law, and finally meets the unfortunate serving woman.

From the noble Lord Cyprian's fine palazzo one had to walk through the New Town into the Old to find the episcopal palatum. Ordinarily, John Oldcastle would have taken his time, breathed in the various airs, tried to decipher the accents and tones upon the breeze. A felony rarely took place in a vacuum, it was a response to a situation, to a mood, to a zeitgeist. The murder, the blackmail, the theft, it happened in a small, private place but its echoes rippled outwards and its causes rippled in. Sometimes those ripples bubbled backwards in time to harsh words said a year back, to misunderstandings in a very former time, to jealousies and desires of people now dead. Sometimes those ripples spread out to the family next door, to the woman who served at the tavern, to the farmer in the next village who kept moving his fence boundaries in the middle of the night. So many affected, so many affecting, so many with snippets of information they themselves perhaps knew little of. And he, John Oldcastle, his fingers found loose threads and followed them back to something important. Like Theseus with Ariadne's homespun line wrapped around his hand, he pulled gently on the line until it tugged tight and then he made his way towards the other end. A chance comment, a gossipy indiscretion, a bitchy remark, all of these he noted, weighed, catalogued and collated until the labyrinth of information began to look like a clear pattern. A grid which had him see *this* man as the one who embezzled the guild levies, *this* man who faked the land certificate and forged the abbey seal, *this* woman as the one with two husbands and the beneficiary of both.

His success as lawyer and preliminary investigator to three borough sheriffs had brought him a modest income, the house he shared with his little family in Spitalfields was comfortable and clean. He had enough set by in gold and investments to not fear an overly painful old age. He had a small but gentle circle of friends whom he was able to help financially when times were dark. But in truth it was not the money he made from his clients and from the civil delictual law that was his specialty that gave him pleasure; no, it was the pursuit of truth when she hid in a very dark pottage of lies, the discovery of justice at the bottom of a stinking midden. And if he got his fingers dirty whilst searching, then so be it. He was used to the smell of bleach upon his hands.

And so on an ordinary morning in a new town following a fresh thread, he would tarry in the environs, hear the gossip of the watersellers, the particularity of the insults, the subject matter of the complainers. Sniffing the air, he would weigh up whether this was a happy place, a contented community, a mass of humanity cursed by discontent and envy, a place saddened by some as yet un-named social sore. This morning however, his lord and employer had assigned to him a young lad so swift of foot and silent of tongue that they virtually flew through the narrow streets. Oldcastle tried to send his ears out as far from his head as they would hover but still he was unable to truly get a picture beyond hazy hints of an ordinary regret that the summer was over, of tired joy that the French had gone, of personal ire that their loved ones did not understand or appreciate them. He did not sense any overt pain. No layer of injustice. No community calling out for revenge. Frustrated, all too soon he was delivered to the imposing *latus ostium* of the palatum and taken within.

This Bishop was not quite what he was expecting.

'And so – Mr Oldcastle, you say – yes, I was warned by the noble lord that you would be coming. Your papers here, yes, I recognize the seal of Merton College, we had a lay preacher visiting here a year or so ago – perhaps you know him, William of Sheriff Hutton? – he too had received his degree from Merton. A very wise and catholic preacher, he was popular with the congregation here. Young, perhaps a little younger than yourself. Full of zeal. But fully orthodox you understand.'

'I understand, Lord Bishop. But no, I do not know this man. It is twenty years since I studied for my degree at Merton.' *But do you know who I am, Lord Bishop, as the good Lord Cyprian knew?* John Oldcastle was unusually unsettled. He could always tell if someone knew about Old John, there was a wary tension at the corner of the eye, a flickering away, a stiff shoulder. Sometimes the other man would be cold and hostile, looking for the door. But other times there would be a fake camaraderie as if John was some kind of rabid dog that could be appeased by false kindness. But whichever reaction, it was always clear if a man knew his story. This man however, this Bishop come newly from early Mass and still in his white diamatic tunic and gloves, this man's mind was opaque, his body language, still, calm, even cautiously welcoming. But over the white gloves, the episcopal ruby ring blinked like a slow, lazy cat, measuring him up, pound for pound.

'So. So.' An intelligent face, thin, smooth, wide-lipped. John Oldcastle thought fleetingly of his own bishop, Richard Hill of London. Petty, spiteful, always seeking opportunity to undermine and denigrate John Morton, Canterbury's Archbishop and Cardinal. A foolish man. A discontented man. A man with elevated ideas of his own ability and importance. Of enormous learning but limited understanding. He had come up against him thrice now, and won each time. Issues of land boundaries and inheritance, bread and butter work. Hill was happy to concede if the concession was painted up as a lordly gift, a benevolent condescension, a blessing from the mighty episcopal hand upon the brow of the unworthy. Hill always took the plaudits of concession. Oldcastle took the win.

This bishop though . . .

They were seated in a pleasant inner courtyard, mid-morning sun reaching over the rooves, just caressing their elbows. Some kind of biscotti appeared, well-watered wine tasting more of honey than grape. There was the strong smell of cut grass although he had seen no lawn. Oldcastle waited. He was guest here after all but in truth he always found it best to let the opponent speak himself out. And he had never met a bishop who did not love the sound of his own voice.

They sat in companionable silence. Almost like old friends. It was very quiet in the courtyard, a distant sound of singing, high boys, perhaps even a castrato, God help them all if that Italian fashion reached England, there would be Hell to pay. The palatum was in the middle of the Old Town, the Roman city, built against the walls of the great Santa Maria Matricolore but the vague buzzing of civic life beyond its walls seemed almost dreamlike. At last the bishop spoke.

'This case, I think, Mr Oldcastle, has no winners. The losses are already tremendous on all sides. You have been apprised of the facts?'

'I have been given the viewpoint of my employer. I would not yet say that I am apprised of the facts.'

'Wise, wise. Yes, indeed, you will see this tragedy painted black from one side of our piazza and red from another. And you will look down upon it from the bell tower of San Michele and you will see that it has turned yellow. And then you turn away and it is blue, as blue as the Mare Nostra.'

'Perspective is what I seek, Lord Bishop.'

'But what you will find here, Mr Oldcastle, is all that is subjective. Nothing more. *He* is the villain because this, this, this.

He is the villain because this, this, this. *She* is at the heart of it all. *She* is but a useful, useless tool. *He* is the machinator, full of Satan's wiles, he is a well-intentioned public citizen. The facts do not change but our perspective is blighted by the subjective filter all have cast upon them. Your investigation, your interviews, your collation of times, speeches, relationships, these so-called facts – they will change nothing.'

'You do not believe in Law then, Lord Bishop? For the law sees through the subjective, it discards personal perspective. It deals in fact and applies most dispassionately, most objectively, without prejudice the justice dictated by those facts.'

The bishop smiled. 'I believe in God's Law, in natural law of course. How could I not? '*True law is right reason in agreement with nature; it is of universal application, unchanging and everlasting*'. If a pagan like Cicero can determine such a truth and if a saint like Thomas can then beautifully and with genius synthesize our well-loved pagan with the Word of God, well then. Of course there is the Law. But there is also law.'

Oldcastle bent his head slightly. 'I agree. But Aquinas tells us in *Summa Theologica* that a primary precept is to live communally in a just society. This is my province. My country. And to live in harmony with our neighbour, the guilty must be punished here and now and the innocent must be set free. For the ordinary sheep in the Lord's flock, that is the beginning and end of it. We may debate the Ancient and Thomistic natural law but that does not aid my seller of shoes who has been cheated of his guild-right by an embezzling clerk.'

Another smile. 'No, no, he must see the minutiae and be content with the minutiae. But that does not mean that the glorious arc of Natural Law does not provide the sky above our head and the ground beneath our feet, whether your seller of shoes sees it or not.'

'But this case, my Lord Bishop. It seems to me that what is expedient, what is political has blinded us to what is lawful, just and good. You would agree, of course, that this woman, this serving woman already exiled from her home, is as much God's creature as you or I. As much God's creature as Lorenzo Borgia the priest. '*And far more God's creature than the current Duke of Gandia,* he could have said but did not.

The Bishop shrugged, holding out his palms. Open palms held outright, untouching but as if to say *see how my hands are tied in this!*

Oldcastle continued. 'And when I speak to her – soon, I assume, this hour shall we say? – I am sure that I will hear that she played no culpable part in this series of deaths. That not only did she play no part but she had not the opportunity nor indeed the wit to play such a part.'

The episcopal hands were still outstretched but now the long slim fingers seemed to take on a more entreating mien. *See how we are fixed here! What can any of us do?*

'And we have also a man who is known not just to harbour and collect but to create poisons. A man who comes from a heritage well known as possessing the most unhealthy, perhaps I could say, *pathological* delight in poisons. And we have at least one, perhaps two deaths by poison. An attempted poisoning also.'

"I do not think you have the full story of this case. The brother of whom you speak is a herbalist and as such deals with Nature's bounty, both mild and fierce, but all to the benefit of our community here. To accuse him of maleficence would be akin to accusing all the herbalists in our world, all of whom do God's work.'

'And yet I know not of other Dominican herbalists who are so closely connected to three poisonings.'

'I think one, just one poisoning ...'

'Whoever saves one life, it is as if he has saved the world entire.'

'You know your Talmud.'

'So it follows that whoever ends one life has cursed the world entire.'

'Perhaps. Perhaps. But that is not our case here. Those who took lives–*prima facie*–have paid with their own. Those who took their own lives are no doubt paying as we speak. You believe in purgatory of course, Mr Oldcastle. I hear strange things of you Englishmen . . . .'

John Oldcastle inclined his head. Now was not the time nor the place nor the person.

'And so we have already punishment of the suicides and of the murderers. But we must still perform justice upon those who are the *sceleris facilitator*, you understand? Those who made possible these crimes. And your woman is far more closely connected to at least one of the poisonings than the Brother monk. Indeed, the Brother monk has no connection whatsoever to the poisons used. His hands are clean of it. He has no stain.'

'Then no harm can come of me speaking to the woman.'

The hands stretched out again. 'No harm at all. Come, I shall take you myself.'

---------- ∞∞∞ ----------

She was exactly as he had imagined. There was a cook in the Lord Mayor's kitchen, a slovenly type with questionable personal conduct but a great creator of rabbit and thyme pie–three dozen in a day she had boasted–and she could have been this wretched woman's sister. And the wife of the publican at *The Bell and Mitre*–give this poor woman a bushel of wild red hair and, yes sisters. He had insisted on her being given a stool and he pulled his own close so that their knees were almost touching. The good Lord Bishop had clearly wanted to stay but John waited patiently until with a swish of white robes, he left them alone.

'So,' he began gently, for it was obvious that this woman had been mis-used, 'You understand that I am here to speak for you. To give you a voice so that your part in these events may be fairly heard.' His Italian was good but the northern dialect and accent was strong and unfamiliar and so his words were slow and careful. Her eyes were on the floor but there was a slight nod.

'And so, I understand that you were for many years in the service of this great noble family. That you gave many years' good service. Never a cause for censure or complaint?'

'I . . . I . . . yes, my lord. Many years. Part of the family. And I was a good girl! My lady she trusted me with her little ones, it was not my fault that the little boy died! He had his own nurse, it was not me!'

'No, that is not the death we are investigating this day. There is no question that the boy died at God's good hands. But the other one. The child that came later. The girl.'

The eyes flickered upwards, red with weeping, the beginnings of an abscess in the corner of the left. 'Such a good little girl. I lost my girl. But then God gave me a second chance, didn't he my lord? She was like my own sweet Susanna.'

'I am sure you were like a mother. And yet she died. Just six weeks ago now.'

Confusion. 'No, my girl died fifteen years now, three times my fingers and thumbs. But it wasn't my fault, there was a terrible sweating fever in the town.'

'Yes. These things take the innocent and guilty alike but God will know his own. Now tell me, Mistress Susanna– is it acceptable that I call you by name? You have the same name as your daughter, God rest her soul.'

A bright flush swelled up the reddened cheeks. 'My . . . it's been a long time . . . I can't remember. Yes, I was Mistress Susanna, Signora Susanna, my husband was Giovanni but he died.'

'Ah. That is my own name. Giovanni in England we say John. I am John, John Oldcastle. That is to say Giovanni Vecchiocastello. Castelvecchio, like the great castle just a few streets from here which is now home to the Podesta. Oldcastle. And I am here to ensure fair hearing and justice for you. Do you understand?'

'Yes, my Lord Castelvecchio. I swear by Maria Mother of God and by Zeno himself to tell you everything I know of this.'

There was then a rambling account of the foolishness of boys, of the rashness of the men they thought they were, of girls who should have known better, of parents who cared not enough for their children, of secret assignations, of unsanctioned marriages, of threats and promises and lust.

'But the poison,' he tried to turn her gently back to the path, 'the poison used was not yours? You did not buy it, you did not commission its manufacture, you did not know of its existence?'

'Dear lord!' she fell clumsily to her knees, 'I swear I knew nothing of it! How could I? How could I gain admittance to a monastery herb garden? How would I know what filthy potions were in the little glass bottles?'

'So you have seen such things?'

She sobbed, huge breasts rising heavily, coming loose from their dirty stays. There was a large bruise on the flesh above the aureole, he averted his eyes.

'I confess, my lord . . . '

'No, you cannot confess to me.'

'But I have a grievous sin. If I am to die, I needs must confess. And who else but to you who means me so well?'

'But I am not a priest, there is no sacrament of reconciliation here, this can only be done by a priest who acts *in persona Christi* (But did they? He was sure they did not). I am not a priest, Signora Susanna, I cannot offer you absolution.'

She grabbed his knees with meaty hands. Yes, three dozen rabbit and thyme pies in a day would not be beyond her at all. 'I do not understand. But I need to tell you my most grievous sin.'

'And it involves . . . potion. In a glass bottle?'

The thinning hair bobbed up and down, miserably. He sighed. How ironic that of all the people she should confess her miserable sins to was the one man in this city-state who did not believe in either the sacrament itself or the Purgatory she was so desperate to avoid. How Savonarola would be laughing.

'You may tell me your sin. To unburden your conscience.'

A deeply held and gratefully released breath. She must have an abscess in her gums too, her breath was foul.

'I have never been to Father Lorenzo for any potions, he would never see the likes of me, he only deals with men. But there is a little shop in the vicola da palude, it sells soaps and unguents for sore feet, little brushes to rub away calluses. But if you wait for the woman to appear from the back . . . and you tell her that . . . that . . .' Her brow creased as she thought hard, 'Phoebe has not come. Phoebe has not come for three months and you need something to make her come again. Yes, that was it. My cousin told me what to say.'

'Phoebe? Ah,' he was momentarily embarrassed but shrugged it away, 'This concoction will bring back the monthly courses, it will restore a woman's cycle?'

'Yes,' she looked uncertain, one brownish eye looking up at him to check that he really understood. He sighed. He was not here to debate the moral standing of abortifacients or the nature of the unborn child.

'I understand, Mistress. Sometimes the time is not right for a child. Sometimes, Phoebe has to be encouraged to return and set things back to how they were before.'

She nodded enthusiastically, still on her knees. 'And they are so small, it is such a little thing and so must surely be such a little sin. I knew that it would be forgiven.'

You are probably going straight to Hell, was his immediate reaction but he kept his face neutral.

'Taking this concoction was wrong but you have admitted it now and your fate now lies with God.'

She jerked her head up, almost angry. 'Sir? Me? I would never do such a dreadful thing. To kill a little child, nesting in the belly? I would have a dozen, my lord, a dozen more of my little Susanna.'

'Then I am confused. For whom did you buy this concoction?'

'For my Lady of course, Lord Cyprian's wife!' hissed his new confidante, eyes darting towards the door, 'She cannot bear any more dead babies, after the last little boy died, she came to me all white and shaking, her eyes like glass, she said she was going to throw herself in the river, 'Let the Adige take me,' she said but I sat her down and I told her that there were ways; ginger and stoneseed root, mix them together and drink daily. And if perchance one unlucky time a little 'un caught on, well, that is when I went to the vicola da palude and asked for something to bring back Phoebe.'

'Now I understand. Thank you.' The air in the room was getting stuffy, her breath was faintly nauseating. He was nearly done. Leaning back, he stretched his back and shoulders as she clambered back onto her stool.

'Is there anything else you wish to tell me? About the monk, Brother Lorenzo? I understand you met with him two or three times over the summer.'

'A very clever man.'

'Yes he is. Did you know that he had prepared a sleeping draught for your charge? A sleeping draught which would have her wake in a torment, which would reduce her to madness?'

She had obviously been asked this before. 'No sir, I knew nothing of it. He would not confide in me, I am just a foolish woman to these high men.'

'But you knew of his scheme to bring the two together? In defiance of tradition and the Podesta's authority?'

'Yes, I knew. But I am a simple and stupid woman. I cannot read, I cannot understand Latin, I cannot count past twenty. I thought Father Lorenzo had authority in these things.'

'Yes. The blame lies with him, assuredly.' He got up and pushed the stool back against the wall. Despite the feast of Circe, he had not eaten much earlier in deference to his host's abstinence and now he found himself very hungry. She was mumbling something. Stretching, he gave quick roll of his head and neck. It was easy to get stiff in these damp rooms. The woman was still muttering on. He heard one word and stopped.

'What did you say? Repeat yourself, Mistress Susanna. Please.' Hairs were standing up on his forearms. 'Please. I did not hear.'

Her chin now raised, he could see mucus and dirt and blood in her nostrils.

'Father Lorenzo. He has a good heart, I said, my lord. He wanted only the good of the city. When I was waiting in the little chapel of the abbey, I heard him say it, I couldn't see to whom he spoke, he said that the Podesta and the city lords put themselves first always, never the ordinary people, never the young ones living in their shadow, only themselves. But that when the Scaligers returned, it would be put right.'

'The Scaligers. He used that word?'

'Yes, my lord. I think they are the magical fairy folk who live in the mountains west of here with the Egypsie. When I was young my mother used to threaten me with the Scaligers if I was naughty. *Wet your mattress again*, she would scream at me, *the Scaligers will come and they'll beat your little arse!* Begging your lordship's ears, but it was a common threat in all our houses in the Vicoli where I grew up.'

'I see.' His empty stomach was forgotten. 'And did you hear anything else, about these Scaligers? Were any here in the city? Did Brother Lorenzo welcome any into the abbey?'

She looked shocked. 'Fairy creatures in the abbey? The holy water would stop them entering, surely? No demons may cross over onto hallowed ground, I know that and I am only an ignorant old bitch, as my great lord said just three weeks ago now as he threw me to the ground.'

'No. No, you're right. They could not enter the abbey or its church. You are not so ignorant as the great lords think, Mistress.'

She beamed and he saw how few teeth she had. 'I am not! And my dear husband was wrong on that account too! God rest his soul. No, no, the Scaligers never came to the abbey to meet with Brother Lorenzo, no. He met with them outside of this city. In Mantua. That's what he said.'

'You heard him say this? That he was meeting with these Scaligers just fifty miles west of here, in Mantua? And you would swear this with your hand upon . . . ' He was going to say Holy Bible but knew better, 'With your hand upon the silver mask of San Zeno himself?'

It was as if the sun had burst out from behind dark clouds so great was her joy. 'The silver mask! I could put my hand upon it? Will it not burn my skin away?'

'Only if you lie, Mistress, only if you lie.'

And so she told John Oldcastle all she had heard about the bastard son of Pope Callixtus, his Scaliger demons from across the western hills and soon it all became so clear, he knew exactly what he had to do. And so great was his excitement that he had his case, he missed the lightning flash of amusement on her simple, well-bruised face.

CHAPTER THIRTEEN

In which John Oldcastle gets a shock and remembers a Roman hunt

The Old Roman City was ringed by the Wall to the south and the river to the north-west and north-east. The First Century amphitheatre was by far the most impressive remnant of a more illustrious age but there were still some fine piazzi and a multitude of splendid churches pressing themselves onto the suffocating bodies of the pagan temples below. The Roman wall was still in good shape and the main gate, the Porta San Zeno – even though it was nowhere near the basilica and tomb of the great man himself – was a still beautiful edifice. Oldcastle walked casually along the Via Postumia and looked up at the Porta. Three storeys high and double-arched at ground level with great Corinthian capitals in white limestone. Above the two wide thoroughfares, the two storeys above themselves boasted six arches apiece. People leaving the Old Town took the right arch, those entering, the other. Oldcastle liked the simple assumption that the populace would do as they were told. That they would leave by this arch. And they would enter by this one. And they did. No matter the thickness nor the paucity of the crowd, the citizens were obedient and conscious at all times of the public good. He would have liked to see London's mayor try such a thing in Lombard Street. Through the Porta he then found himself admiring the arena. Not as large as Rome's

Coliseum of course and in a shabby state of semi-neglect with stalls and half-built shops surrounding the entire circumference. But you could still see how many thousands of people it had once welcomed. How clever and industrious the people commissioning, designing and building such a thing must have been. How desirous that everyone should be able to hear the screams and see the blood.

Some of the more recent churches were fine buildings of course. Santa Maria was only a few centuries old – built anew after an earthquake destroyed the original – and work was still being done, adding chantries, cloisters, towers, columns. And of course there was the Castelvecchio itself, arrogantly new at just a century old. He could see its strange red-brick towers from where he now stood with the arena at his back. Oddly disproportionate merlons. They seemed at discordance with the gentle, white grace of the little basilica – San Lorenzo's? – next door. And rudely trying to compete with the amphitheatre itself, like an arrogant young man thumbing his finger at his elders, not realising how gauche and crude he appeared.

It was a fair walk from the episcopal palatum back to the New Town palazzo of his host but John Oldcastle liked to walk. A slight detour to the Castelvecchio would be interesting, although the street was now busy. And so he walked on, northwards, with the Old Wall to his right and the start of the New Town to his left. The street was a main thoroughfare and already busy. Italians here seemed very much like the citizens of Rome, of Firenze. They were not particularly rude, they were not overtly aggressive but they were also not going to get out of the way. But John Oldcastle liked cities, he liked crowds, he liked noise and fuss and humanity itself in all its stinking, sweating, heaving mass. But interestingly enough, he didn't particularly like people.

He thought on this as he walked, well aware that as his shallow upper mind contemplated unimportant casual thoughts, his deeper mind would be busy assimilating, filing, analyzing, arranging the more important aspects of the job at hand. In particular, how to trap a Dominican friar and perhaps even his close-lipped, long-nosed bishop into admitting a charge of treason. Yes, people. How many people did he actually like?

Oh, he liked a few well enough. Eliza, he was very fond of although if true be told it had taken him a good ten years to come to this very ordinary pass. And even if she didn't seem to like him very much at the moment. It had been Eliza herself–six years his elder and already a mother of a still-suckling babe–who had come across him clerking for some bad-tempered advocate in Lincoln's Inn and had decided that she could do a lot worse. It hadn't been a seduction of any kind, simply an arrangement put upon the table, very clear, very calm. And he had had his sister Eleanor to think of, herself a babe-in-arms and his mother getting drunker by the day. No, as an arrangement it had worked well. Both babies got a family and some kind of stability, he had himself a clean, fed household and a woman with a sharp tongue and warm arms to keep the wastrels away and the children safe.

Did he love her? He wasn't sure what that even meant. He had worked hard, too hard probably, taking on cases, winning most, slowly getting a reputation for being fair and thorough, not too pricey but reassuringly not cheap. A room above an apothecary's in Southwark and then after five years, a grand move north of the river, leaving his mother behind in a puddle of her own vomit. The house in Spitalfields, the serving girls, the cases for the Mayor, the deals with the Bishop–all these came and he took them as his due, still working until the wax grew too soft and low to sustain the wick and then tumbling, often still dressed, into their soft low bed. Occasionally, he would leave them all and take on cases in the Low Countries on behalf of English wool merchants suspecting foreign thievery in their books. He traveled to France on occasion to secure wine contracts, land purchases, even to chase down fraudsters fleeing prosecution. He learned French and Dutch and even some German to complement his Latin-Italian. He came home with toys and sweets wrapped in bright bolts of exotic cloth and his little family would race down the creaking, shaking staircase to throw themselves upon him. Teasing them with languages they did not understand, he understood vaguely that his excitement at coming home was all for Eleanor, that she was the only one he missed, that her safety was the only thing that mattered. But over the years a slow affection for Eliza and her sweet-natured boy had entwined itself gently into the love he felt for his sister.

They had never shared each other's bodies, he and Eliza. Dimly he remembered that this abstinence had been part of the deal she had offered him, the terms of which had been so precise and thought through that he had imagined, in another world, her life as an advocate or clerk. She had nearly died having Thomas, she explained, and she was not going to risk that again and leave him all alone. Her husband had been injured at Tewkesbury, fighting for Lancaster and, although he had escaped the subsequent Yorkist reprisals, had never recovered from the repeated infections in his wounds, dying horribly of gangrene five years later. Oldcastle had agreed. He had no desire to father children. He had experienced his mother's own miseries, his father's shame at being bastard-born, the cold indifference of his true-born Cobham cousins. No, it was as well his branch of the line ended with him. Oldcastle brought bad luck in barrel-loads, no matter how his many cousins twisted it into Ollcassel, Old-Castel, Oldencass. Everyone knew who they were. And no one in England was yet ready to forgive.

He found a spot opposite the Castelvecchio – the irony of its title not escaping him – and sat on a huge piece of masonry that had fallen many years since from the arena.

Yes, he did like Eliza and he liked Thomas too. But how much would he really mourn if they died? He added a quick prayer to the Almighty who he was convinced was always listening in some capacity or other. He would never wish them harm, no, of course not. But if the Almighty stretched out his hand and said that it was time... would he grieve? Probably not. There had been a very clean and good-humoured whore in Cheapside whom he had visited irregularly for years and when she died of some nameless fever, he had missed her more than he'd predicted. But he had replaced her very quickly and now her face and laugh had completely faded from his mind. He drank sometimes with fellow advocates and lawyers in the Drunken Duck and the Hole-in-the-Wall. Dick Halfpenny, Martin Brokenshire, Luuk van der Thijs; all good men. But if their time came . . . No, he would attend their funerals and then find new men to drink with.

Only Eleanor. Only Eleanor was real to him, only she lived bright and shining in his heart. Only the loss of her, the thought of it, took his breath away, sharp and jagged, raw. A terrible bout of sweating sickness when she was five. Suspected smallpox that – thank sweet Jesus – had turned out to be something else. A fall down the stairs to twist her ankle. But she had survived the London childhood that claimed so many other little lives, she survived and she was strong and she was kind and she was beautiful.

And now she was choosing death, all of her own accord.

Above his head, the clouds were high, allowing short spells of blue sky to peer disinterestedly through. There was a dampness in the air although it was yet to rain. Autumn came late by the Mare Nostra but when it did, it came in wet and cold.

He wondered where the nunneries were in this town. It was sure to house at least two given its population which was not inconsiderable, although perhaps not quite deserving of the word 'city'. There were at least seven in London, this he knew having visited them all with his sister over the past year. Eleanor had finally chosen to give her life to the Benedictines of St Helen's Bishopsgate. They had stood together, just ten months ago now, marveling at the strange double nave of the church, one side for the nuns, the other for the laymen, divided by high arches hung with dividing tapestries and embroidered banners. The church and abbey with all its rambling outbuildings and patches of land was tucked into the old Roman wall, just by the great Gate for which the ward was named. He had felt her breathing deepen. Had felt her relax. She had not smiled – she had not smiled for three years now – but she had pursed up her sweet mouth in approval, giving him a little nod. His heart had broken yet again at that moment. And how many times would he have to endure the splintering inside his chest, the deep lurch of his stomach? He had hoped, right up until that little nod, that she would change her mind, that she would choose life instead. But the Prioress had been kind and strong, she had taken Eleanor by the hand and called her 'my daughter', she had listened calm, cold and furious to their halting, censored story.

'There are forty-three of us here,' she had then said, not commenting on their circumstances for what was there to say? 'We have our gossips and our discontents, we have those who squabble and speak ill but most of the days, we are a kind family and we love each other. We follow the Rule, we sew and we garden. We teach some of the children of the parish who can afford no other schooling. There is no dancing or music or revelry here save on the Feast of St Nicholas when we allow revelry for the children and novices. You may keep a little dog as long as he is well governed and you do not bring him into the quire or nave. We divide ourselves into four familia, named of course for the Gospels. In time, you may be the Head of one of these Houses. And then you will have an office of your own and a small budget to balance. Do you count? And perhaps read?'

Eleanor had nodded. He had resisted the urge to tell this woman how clever his sister was, how lucky they were to have a girl who read Latin and could do arithmetic and accounting but he knew that this was not now his life to lead. Her life was slipping away from him and if he reached out and grabbed its tail, he would only cause her pain.

'Can I be silent?' her little voice, every word wrenched from an unwilling throat. Where was the voice that had sung so light and high every morning? How could such a voice be lost forever, sent down into the dark, silent void? It had come to him then – fast and true and deadly – that he would never hear his sister sing again, that her voice had been torn from her throat as surely as if a wild beast had attacked her. Which of course it had.

The Prioress had nodded. 'We have silent meals and silent Hours. If you wish, you may renounce speech altogether – we have three sisters with us now who have not spoken for many years – but this is never a lifetime vow and may be rescinded.'

She had looked at him then, beseeching him to let her go. And so he had walked home to Spitalfields alone, had stood silent as Eliza had cursed him for being weak, for letting her little girl become lost to them all. He had let her rant and rave at him because she did not know the truth of Rome, she thought Eleanor's silent misery a passing phase of puberty, unhappy but common and soon lifted. The distance between them had grown after that day. They tolerated each other from habit and need but he realized that she no longer even liked him very much and he also realized now that he did not care.

Ten months and he received little letters, beautifully embroidered samples, thank you notes for the generous allowance he sent every first of the month and which he worried did not go to her but which he sent anyway. He had her last little letter in his inside pocket, next to his heart. She thanked him for the money, for the biscuits which she had shared amongst the children. For the new collar and leash for her dog, Caesar, so that he might be more easily chastised. For his thoughts and prayers. And then she had written;

In the twilight hours after Vespers, we pray in silence in the quire. It is my favourite time of all these blessed times. The younger sisters are tired and sometimes sleep. There is no disquiet, no rancour, no remembering of grudges. The light begins to fade and our habits, our hair, our skin, the walls, the floor, the colour bleeds out of all around us and a common greyness silvers everything. We are fading into the very world.

To distract himself from tears but not yet ready to focus on the case that had brought him to city, he began to count the Castelvecchio merlons. Truly it was an ugly building. He knew that most of it now was used as storerooms or guest housing, the tower right ahead on the south-east corner having been converted into the Podesta house some decades ago now. He was not much interested. The current Podesta was away and the Bishop his main adversary. He gave up counting merlons; their multitude had not made them any less ugly or any more in proportion. Cleary Cangrande della Scala had had issues with protesting his ego. And an obsession with size. About to get up and make his way back to the New Town, he realized that the smaller door–still a hefty height and weight–was opening.

Four men stood in the morning light, one yawning large and wide. The main street which ran parallel to the river lay between Oldcastle and the four but he could see them well, the passersby giving them wide berth. Dimly aware that there were sounds all around–birds, children playing on the fallen stones, a woman shouting at her friend–Oldcastle felt it all go quiet as a cold hand squeeze his whole world into a narrow tunnel of light which stretched from him to the tall young man in the middle of the group. A man he had only seen once. A man he had seen as a callow youth and from a distance of at least one hundred feet. It should not be possible to feel no doubt. It was foolish, ludicrous, illogical, impossible to feel such certainly. And yet he knew, without a doubt, that here was Juan Borgia.

---------- ∞∞∞ ----------

Three years ago–in Rome–he had run in a blind fury from a cheap tavern in the poor district of Celio, trying to hunt this man down. Like a rabid dog, he had raced up this street and that one, pushing men, women, children aside, shouting at anyone in his way, not knowing where he was going or what he was thinking, only knowing what he would do when he found him. It was pure madness, a *caeca furore*, eventually he had collapsed in the ruins of the Forum, heart screaming against his ribs, mouth full of froth, eyes red and streaming. Back at the tavern, no one could help him. They shook their heads in dumb sympathy, shrugged their shoulders, sent for a doctor and a kind nurse who stayed for three days. But they would not offer their witness. No one would go and fetch the *vigiles* cohorts or city magistrates. No one would tell him where this monster lived, they laughed grimly when he demanded they tell him. *Find the House of God*, they shook their heads sadly at the shame of the world, *cross the river and find Saint Michael the Angel. Knock on the door of St Peter's basilica and demand that the Papal Captains give up their favourite boy, go and tell the new pope that he must needs surrender his golden bastard son.*

And so the next morning, before dawn, he had gone. He had dragged Savonarola across the river to the Castel Sant'Angelo, prowled around the Parco Adriano, looked up impotently at the huge thick walls of the circular mausoleum. He had paced alternatively calm and white-cold with fury and then wrenched apart with an almost unbearable desire to scream, to hurt, to tear apart, to vomit. They had found themselves a priest in the small crowd queuing for supplication and patronage by the Papal Captains lodged in the Castel. This priest knew Juan Borgia by sight, he claimed, his fellow Franciscan had had the unfortunate honour of tutoring the boy and his brother in Greek. Foul beasts, both of the boys. Spoilt, indulged, encouraged, flattered, his friend had been relieved when Rodrigo Borgia became Alexander VI and a more expensive tutor was hired. They'll appear up on the battlements when the sun rises over the hills, their new friend explained. The Papal Captains show their faces, they let us cheer the boys and then the boys go to bed. They have been whoring all night so they need to go to bed.

And there he had been. In blue, yawning, red-gold hair slightly wild, just the touch of fuzz on his chin. A beautiful boy.

An angel surely waving arrogantly down from the castel battlements. Just as Lucifer too had been an angel.

There was no way into the mausoleum, no way to know where or when Juan Borgia would venture back into the Celio or anywhere else. And so after a week, at her own mute and broken request, Oldcastle had taken his little sister back to London. But the image of the golden angel waving in derision to the minions below him in the Parco had not faded. He could not now picture the face of the whore he had fucked for fifteen years but this face, this face he remembered.

And here he was. Three years on, one life destroyed, another life gliding on into privilege, untouched and oblivious. Of the three guards with Borgia, one was the biggest man Oldcastle had ever seen, one had red hair, the other had his hood up and his face covered. So he was here. He had been in Firenze and now he was here just as his Dominican cousin faced accusations of poisoning. A deep, warm glow spread out from John Oldcastle's belly, almost sexual in its urging. So be it. They would play out this piece of theatre, they would argue over the guilt or innocence of monks and beggar-women. And then, then they would see.

CHAPTER FOURTEEN

In which Juan Borgia, Duke of Gandia (ex-bastard) mourns his friend

'I didn't see no one! Not a penny-fart. I swear, I was on the bastard bridge all night and I never saw no gang of thieves, no bloody *teppisti*, no one, I swear.'

The lad was doing well. His nose was broken and one arm certainly dislocated from the way it was swinging, loose and limp. Covered in mud and stinking now of the shit he had voided in his terror, give the boy his due. He was still crawling away, denying anything and everything and all in between.

Juan Borgia affected a languid yawn although his fingers were quivering with barely suppressed rage. He had kept his Spanish leather boots out of the piss and shit, he was on the outskirts of their little ring but still the boy knew whom to beg for his life. Carlo swung back his leg and directed another heavy kick into the boy's chest. They all heard the thin, spindly crack as another rib snapped clean apart.

This time his voice was harsh and bubbly. 'I didn't seen no one. There wasn't any gang coming over . . . bridge, no one came up from the south. I was there . . . Porta Palio . . . ' he sobbed like a small child, 'I was there from fourth bell, the sun was already past the middle. There til night time. Aaagh, Mama . . . please don't kill me, I don't know what you want me to say. Mama please.'

'Tell us the fucking truth, *ratto italiano*,' Matteo was poor to the point of embarrassing with words but he was a hefty weight, a weight he delivered now by launching his full body to crush the lad's hips, pelvis snapped, femoral artery severed and bleeding out. He picked himself up and laughed as the boy started to twitch.

'Idiot. What can he tell us now?' Borgia sighed and deftly picked his way across the lightest of the blood and shit. Gracefully he hunkered down, head slightly to one side as if vaguely interested by some unusual phenomenon.

'You don't have much time left, boy. You won't see your mama again so you can stop blubbering for her. If you tell me who came over the southern bridge to the Porta Palio from Firenze towards the end of the day, now, now, stop breathing like that, I can hardly hear what I'm saying, now just lie still, soon be over. My good friend Raf Salamanca was fished out of your stinking river not six hours ago. Roughly handled I would say. No arm. No eyes. Now Raf – lie still, you stupid lad, if you move the blood will flow out more quickly – Raf Salamanca was a hard bastard. He could hold his head up and take down three, maybe four and still walk away. So we're looking for a group of five or more. Not hard to spot. Now, if you tell me which way they went and the lodging house they declared with the Porta Watch, I'll get Carlo here to call a priest and you can say your sad little confessions. But if you don't tell us – and I really don't understand, boy, why you would not at this parlous state of your soon-to-be-ending life – if you don't, then I shall let Matteo kick you to death and you'll die unshriven. Is that clear?'

This boy dies twenty heartbeats or so later and our story moves on. But it is to his great credit, that – and of course we do not and will never know his name – this boy uses up the very last breath God gave him to spit a little dribble of blood and stomach lining onto the Duke of Gandia's Spanish leather boot.

Sunday

CHAPTER FIFTEEN

In which all of our characters spend the Lord's Day of Rest thinking and finding purpose in their lives

John Oldcastle, Bastard

It has been a long time since this has happened, he thinks. To have such single-minded purpose, to have a clear aim, the means, the support, the . . . dare I say it, dare I think it? . . . the God-given *sanctus permissione*? I think I know the way ahead now. No, I do not think, I am sure. The woman has given me the means to achieve one goal and the other will be given me in God's good time.

I had purpose as a child, he considers. I was quite renowned in our parish, in the stews of Southwark. The bastard grandson of Sir John Oldcastle, heretic and man of ash. Even as a boy. *How dares he hold his head up, take his lessons, do his sums, score his scores? He lives in drafty Shitwell Lane like the rest of us south of the City, his high and mighty kin don't care that much to raise him up out of it, to take him north of the river. Where are they? Even the Bishop's summoner don't dare come here, not to the Bankside stews, not to preach to the whores and the drunks of Gropecuntstreet. You might drag yourself out of the stews to the grand glories of Long Southwark road and live to thirty-five but you're still heading for the common pit at St Mary Overie along with the rest of us. And you, missus, you his mother that should've known better. Best apprentice him to the brewers, get him a trade, keep him home.*

He tries to remember the woman's name. She had lived on the floor above with Edmund Crouchback and woke him every night when she fell drunk out of bed. *And where now is the cocky little bastard,* they asked his tearful mother ten years later, *gone to Oxford, we hear, with the proper boys, the young men of families, the upright, the quick and the good, the ones who make and shake? Find out who he is and there'll be Hell to pay. They'll sodomise him senseless and send him home to Shitwell, ruined and fit for nothing, not fish, not fowl, just a sore and used arse.* He's still my boy, she would smile tightly, it doesn't matter, what is past is past, a new king now, the old king long gone. All's forgotten. And then more kings came and went and the world turned red and white as roses flew against Percy lions and Warwick bears fought rampant stags until a king bled out on a muddy field.

In the warm Italian sun, he feels an old and familiar shiver of revulsion. He had fought alongside his Brooke cousins under the banner of Baron Cobham for the usurper Henry ap Tudor; ten years ago now but still the stench of shit, mud, manure sometimes grows back in the hairs of his nose.

He doesn't remember much of his one and only battle. Commissioned by some Cobham steward on behalf of the lord who didn't want to soil his boots in Southwark mud by coming himself. Meeting up with yet more Brooke and Oldcastle cousins in Herefordshire with a small group of friends either eager for a fight or, like him, dragged there by obligation of a quasi-noble blood people now chose to remember. Walking half way to Milford Haven, back again out of Wales as they caught up with Tudor going north, walking more, camping, waiting, walking again, all the time cursing the Cobhams who had horses. Two days, three days. Trying to avoid Philbert de Chandee's French mercenary contingent who were universally acknowledged to be obnoxious cunni, avoiding too the Welsh under Rhys ap Thomas who refused to speak English, the Cobhams had finally settled themselves in with Talbot of Shrewsbury's men. Finding their higher ground, waiting, scrounging food, playing cards, trying not to fall into the makeshift latrines, more walking, scrapping, more waiting. Four days, five days. Finally, back into lines to the edge of the Cobham position, his feet sinking into the Leicestershire mud of Ambion Hill. Still waiting. The dim noise and dust and splattered chaos of men fighting some way ahead. Only really conscious of the breath of the man behind, the stitching on the leather jerkin of the man in front, the twitching of one neighbour, the smell of urine on the boots of the other. The whole world condensed into something very small, very intimate. Soldier-gossip running like waves of water up and down the messy ranks of men-at-arms. Tudor's forces had engaged, the King was fighting in the thick of it, *murdering cripple's got some balls then*, they agreed, *not like Tudor, watching in the third ranks*, most men not really caring who won as long as they didn't die. Then *That bastard Northumberland isn't committing. Percy lion-rampant just sat there, look, over to the hills right ahead of us, not so rampant now . . . what's he playing at?* He had tried to see, rose up on tiptoes but it was just the backs of heads and a bit of rain. *What's the Stanleys doing*, the soldier-voice became a roar, *what the fuck are the Stanleys doing, look at them both, up to the right, Christ Crucified if they ride down that hill now we're all fucked, boys.* Then *we're in, we're in* and the mass of men stumbled forward. Feet faster and faster, spaces opening up, the Cobham banner veering slightly to his right, three drunken lions on a golden chevron, the sounds of horses screaming, men shouting. To this day he does not know how many men he killed or whether those he struck at died there and then, died later in the stench of their own guts, blood and vomit or whether they limped home to their wives and were alive still. He remembers the cut across his forearm, the scream of one of Talbot's boys on his knees, cut short suddenly by the hooves of a rearing horse, the sudden groundswell roar of *Stanley's turned! Stanley's turned for Tudor!* and then it was a heavy stomp forward, the retreating backs of bastard men and boys just like him, running off home to change their colours and unpick the Whyte Boars from their sleeves.

Ten years later now and John Oldcastle, bastard hero of Ambion Hill,–bastard hero because if he ran around hacking aimlessly at least he was on the winning side and didn't die–sits in a fine Italian palazzo at a desk he could not even fit into his petitioning rooms in Spitalfields. He thinks idly whether it would fit if his scribing-boys removed the legs. No, still the wide expanse of whatever fine wood this was was too broad for the height of his doorways. Perhaps, if he removed the front window that gave out onto St Mary's Spital Lane, left up towards the hospital, right down towards the fields. Maybe. He smoothed his hand across the surface. Fine work. He'd not seen anything better. And yet presumably this was only Lord Cyprian's second best desk...

His mind turns back to its calm, measured appreciation of its current purpose. The obedient, frightened man at Ambion Hill was the aberration, he reminded himself more now of the tough, single-minded ten-year-old he had been, the lad who had walked through the wet lanes of Bankside, had crossed the Bridge to the City and had stood outside the tall townhouse of the Cobhams until one of the Brooke household had taken exasperated pity on him and sent him away with a promissory note to some third-rate tutor of grammar. Someone in the big house must finally have said to someone else–*he is an Oldcastle after all. Not a Brooke of course but we share a grandsire, God curse the old man. If the little bastard has a brain, send him into Chancery or to Lincoln's Inn if we think he can make it. And he'll owe us for life.* And so at nineteen, off he went to Merton College with a fair stipend from Thomas Brooke, the fifth Baron Cobham himself.

And there to sit upon the eaves and drink cheap red wine with Giramo Savonarola.

The bells of San Michele, of San Zeno, of numerous other little churches, chapels and chantries begin to peal out for Terce and second Mass. Oldcastle has already risen just before dawn and attended at Santa Maria Matricolore with his lord, a rather grim affair with his companion wearing his furious grief like a cloak of feathers, flowing around him as the congregation halted their steps so as not to touch it. The Bishop himself held out the wafers and chalice for the city's English guest, a knowing and somewhat resigned look in his eyes accompanying the *hoc est meum corpus*. As he ever did when receiving the so-called Host, Oldcastle held in his head the precious words that allowed his conscience peace; *I say the truth through true understanding: His flesh and blood, through his subtle works, is there in the form of bread. In what manner it is present need not be debated, whether as subject or accident, but as Christ was when he was alive, so He is truly there.*

Back now at the shining brown ocean of polished wood upon which lies a few sheaves of beautifully white, smooth Spanish vellum covered by his scribbled notes, he allows himself to relax. He knows what is to be done. There is a road ahead. Not an easy road but **she** is worth any pain and endeavour.

She had loved to sing once. Dawn to the dying sun and beyond to welcome Phoebe, ditties, rhymes, nonsense, even snippets of Chaucer he had her recite. It was over now. Now in her dark, cool cloister Eleanor prayed in the silent world of those of her fellow sisters who had chosen to listen only, never speak. He likes to think though that she sings to her little dog, that Caesar hears what he, John Oldcastle, once took so much for granted.

He hums, half speaking, half along the tune he still remembers. More father than big brother, he had brought her into his household as the unexpected, unwelcomed late child their mother could not love. Such a tiny little mite. Such a pair of lungs. How many sleepless nights had he sat by her cot, wondering where she had come from, this tiny pull upon a heart he had not known he had? But he had loved her enough for the world.

'*Of every kind of tree, Of every kind of tree,*

The hawthorn blowëth sweetest, Of every kind of tree.
My sweetheart she shall be, My sweetheart she shall be,
Fairest of every kind, The rose she bloweth sweet and mild
My sweetheart she shall be.'

Tears are well beyond him. But clear purpose rises up and leads him along the road.

Lorenzo Borgia, Bastard

It has been a long time since this happened, thinks the priest in horror. Those momentary lapses in concentration, when he allowed his foolish old mind to wander away from contemplation. But it has been years now. An old temptation thought fully vanquished. And as he sits back on his heels in holy repose after an hour on his knees, as he prays to be clean enough, full enough, empty enough, good enough; *Soul of Christ, sanctify me. Body of Christ, save me. Blood of Christ, inebriate me. Water from the side of Christ, wash me. Passion of Christ, strengthen me. O good Jesus, hear me. Within Thy wounds hide me. Suffer me not to be separated from Thee. From the malignant enemy, defend me. In the hour of my death, call me. And bid me come to Thee. That with Thy saints I may praise Thee.*

But as he kneels there on the cold stone, his old knees starting to ache, the old so-familiar warm swelling, the rush of blood downwards, the slowly purring, growing, spreading pleasure of the flesh. And he cannot help himself. He remembers. He does not resist or combat the memory, oh God in heaven he welcomes it. *Deus in caelo, Deus in caelo*, the smell of his hair, honeysuckle and sweet fresh milk and crushed powdered paint, how is it that he smells it now in this dank, airless cell? Honeysuckle and sweet fresh milk. And mint. Mint from the leaves they would chew in the herbarium. Breath like mint leaves and his lips, his lips . . .

He has no penitent's whip, only a shirt of rough horsetail hair to rub against his skin. It is not enough. And so he draws his ragged dirty nails across the skin of his forearm, again and again until slowly and then more and then more the blood wells up the long riverbed of his wound.

'O God, who willest not the death of a sinner, protect with Thy heavenly aid those persons who may now be exposed to special temptations; and grant that in the fulfilment of Thy commandments they may be strengthened by the assistance of Thy grace; through Jesus Christ our Lord. Amen.'

Still the lips, soft, soft, warm, the smell, the taste of mint.

'O Lord, O King, resplendent on the citadel of heaven, all hail continually; and of Thy clemency upon Thy people still do Thou have mercy. Lord, Whom the hosts of cherubim in songs and hymns with praise continually proclaim, do Thou upon us eternally have mercy. The armies aloft, O Lord, do sing high praise to Thee, even they to whom the seraphim reply, "do Thou have mercy." O Christ, enthroned as King above, whom the nine orders of angels in their beauty praise without ceasing, deign Thou upon me, Thy servants, ever to have mercy. O Christ, whom Thy one only Church throughout the world doth hymn, O Thou to whom the sun, the moon, and stars, the land and sea, do service ever, do Thou have mercy. O Christ, those holy ones, the heirs of the eternal country, one and all with utter joy proclaim Thee in a most worthy strain: do Thou have mercy upon me. Please, please, on me, on me.'

The old man was crying now. So long ago and yet that white dazzling light that had seemed to explode inside, outside, carrying him upwards. Resting in each other's arms after the angelic glory, blissful and yet fearful, hearts uplifted by the utter incandescent beauty of what they had done, and yet weighed down with the black terror of their sin.

'O Lord, O gentle Son of Mary free, O King of Kings, blessed Redeemer, upon those who have been ransomed from the power of death, by Thine own blood, ever have mercy. O noblest unbegotten, yet begotten Son, having no beginning of age, yet without effort (in the weakness of God) excelling all things, upon this Thy congregation in Thy pity, Lord have mercy. O Sun of Righteousness, in all unclouded glory, supreme dispenser of justice, in that great day when

Thou shalt strictly judge all nations, I earnestly beseech Thee, I, who here stand before Thy presence, in Thy pity, Lord, then have mercy upon me.'

Lorenzo Borgia reaches out to the bedstead and pulls himself heavily up, knees creaking as they straighten. So many years. So many years to forget, so much to repent and regret. And yet has he? The Lord Jesus Christ sacrificed himself upon the cross for the forgiveness of all sins past and yet all sins from that time forward . . . how many times has he knelt at confession? How many brothers have heard him within the seal? And five abbots now, these past thirty years. And four bishops for he can just remember old Bishop Guido Memo, dead these fifty years now but he had taken his very first Confession and Holy Communion as a young boy. And to not one of these fine, kind, wise and venerable men has he spoken the truth. Perhaps now it is the time.

Father Lorenzo takes a deep breath and wipes his wet cheeks. Gently clearing his throat, limps a little to the door of his cell.

'Please.' It is quiet and cold down in the crypt with San Zeno but no one hears. 'Please.' He gives a timid little knock against the wood.

'Father?' A rough voice but not unkind. If it is Francisco, son of Old Barbo the Vintner then he has many times applied a poultice to a swelling on his calf. It keeps re-infecting, he is not sure why. He changes the prayers every time, has added a little feverfew and perhaps that has done the trick, at least Francisco has not returned for a while.

'I . . . thank you . . . I would like to see the Lord Bishop. I know on this most holy *requiem die* he is busy but could you send word? That in his own time . . . Father Lorenzo would like him to . . . to . . . hear his confession.'

'I'll send word, Father.'

'Thank you, thank you. *Benedicat tibi Dominus.*'

The old man sits down on his pallet. He is not sure of the time but he heard Sext called a while ago. He tries to imagine the sun as high in the sky as it can be. Tries to imagine how it feels to be young. To welcome sun on unlined skin. To feel strong fingers run their way down his arm. To feel the glow of a love so huge, so terrible, so all-consuming it can be nothing else but a gift and a curse.

'Holy Father Aquinas, will you listen to me? If I beseech you with your own words? Give me, O Lord, a steadfast heart, which no unworthy affection may drag downwards; give me an unconquered heart, which no tribulation can wear out; give me an upright heart, which no unworthy purpose may tempt aside.' He pauses. *'But most of all Father Aquinas, give me a penitent heart.'*

Juan Borgia, Duke of Gandia

It has been a long time since this has happened, thinks the young Duke of Gandia as he pushes the girl away and lies back with his hands behind his head. Her waves of relief are almost palpable, he is inclined to slap her but is too distracted, a little confused it must be said and yes, curious. Soon she is gone. Reaching down to caress himself, long clever fingers soon bring back the pulse, the blood, the stiff column. But he lets it fade and die. There is nothing wrong with the flesh, the flesh is willing as the holy celibate said to his boys in the Garden. But the Spirit is decidedly fucking weak.

There are worrying rumours in the streets of Rome that the Spanish explorers under Columbus have brought back something truly of the devil to Christendom. Some dread disease which causes the male member to itch and twitch, then swell grotesquely. A disease which causes the skin to blister, which raises up purple swellings on the throat and face. Borgia visits prostitutes – which rich noblemen with a functioning cock doesn't? – but he also likes to take advantage of those who have not chosen to make it their living. He likes serving girls, flower-sellers, begging girls on the streets. Firm young flesh, innocent eyes sharpening too late with terror; girls who have no idea what or who is coming their way are far more pleasing than whores who have made it their tawdry profession. He feels relatively safe. His brother Cesare roams the whore-alleys of Rome and has a different one every night. Any foul disease sailing back over the western ocean with Spanish gold will surely find Cesare, sooner or later but hopefully sooner. But he, Juan ... the young man looks up to the plain ceiling, thinking with derision of how poorly it compares to the gilded plastering of his Vatican apartments. No, he, Juan, is more careful than his brother, he will not risk his beautiful body by sharing it too hastily with dirty whores come straight from hungry sailors. No. No whores for a while. But worth finding an apothecary with a good supply of mercury when he returns to the Eternal City.

What time was it? Certainly past midday, his stomach was bubbling slightly with the effects of over-indulgence the night before and then abstinence since. He, Matteo and Carlo had been toasting Raf's shade, helping its way towards Hades with red wine and some local sloe ginever, a bottle of which was coaxed none too gently from the landlord who at first denied his possession of any such thing. Vincenzo, he had sent out to prowl the taverns for word of Raf's killer, for gossiping men in their cups letting loose the stray word. Of his three companions, Vincenzo was the quiet one, the one with the unremarkable face, the nondescript aura, the one most likely to blend in unnoticed. He was also the most obedient. Matteo and Carlo did what they were told but could not control their emotions playing out like theatrics upon their face, their eyes, their very skin. Asked to haunt the taverns whilst staying sober – they would have done it but they would have exuded petty resentment. Vincenzo however simply nodded and was gone.

And so the three of them had drank and sung and drank and toasted and Matteo had got into a fight with the landlord's son, breaking his nose. Eventually they had been given their own little room and unlimited food and drink. Carlo kept forgetting that Raf was dead and repeatedly asked where he was. Matteo told exaggerated stories of how many women Raf had had, how many men he had killed, how savagely he had fought at this battle and that. His two companions had advocated sending the body–grim thing that it was–back to Salamanca but Borgia had eventually vetoed this with a heavy slam of his fist. It wasn't that he didn't appreciate Raf's many skills and the loyal service he had given him over the years but dead was dead, a body was a body and the flesh would wither and fade as well in the communal lime-pit as any marble tomb. Matteo did not understand even the basics of Catholic tenets and had nodded his inebriated agreement. Carlo was slightly better educated than his meat-headed friend and almost made the huge mistake of asking why then did the Borgias have such great and expensive marble tombs? Something stopped him and the next morning he would wake with a heavy head, a bolster covered in vomit, a snoring whore but also a vague sense of relief that he kept his tongue in its place.

The three all had their own theories as to why Raf had been killed the way he had. Carlo thought it was local *brigadia* boys, the local city-state gangs who ran undisciplined through the streets at carnival time and whose excesses were marshalled by their elders into city versus city brawls out in the countryside between. These semi-organised mass fights had been cancelled this year because of the French invasion but the boys were still congregating after dark, harassing foreigners and itching for blood. If enough of them had rounded on Raf, then even he would have stood little chance in the dark. And as for the gouging out of the eyes, the amputation of the poor fucker's arm–well, this is what the *brigadia* did, they all had their individual ways of identifying their kills. Matteo had disagreed. Raf had taken a fancy to a very young whore down by the river and her *mezzano* pimp had claimed her as virginal, trying to up the price. Raf had taken her then and there and refused afterwards to pay anything over the standard rate. *Mezzani* were known to be unforgiving, mean-spirited bastards, Carlo concluded, almost thoughtfully. Poor Raf doubtless fell foul of a *mezzani* guild and they came after him in the dark.

The Duke of Gandia had not put forward his own theory, shrugging at those of his companions, seemingly touched by neither grief nor curiosity. This morning, however, he is thinking as the door opens and the girl leaves. He tends to agree with Carlo that Raf fell foul of some *brigadia* group, young men trying to make a name for themselves, trying to carve out a place on the shady sides of city society by committing not just a murder but a shocking and memorable murder. There will no doubt be another eyeless corpse within the month by which time, the little gang will have made a small name for themselves. He will have gone back south by then so it won't matter. But even so . . . There is some quiet but insistent voice petulantly nagging at him that this was no random killing, that good as Raf of Salamanca had been at making enemies, it is just too much of a coincidence that he should die here and now, in this city and at this time.

The Duke of Gandia rolls over onto his side. The girl now gone had brought him a tray of something but it was all over the floor, the plates broken and some kind of egg concoction smeared on the rug. The smell was starting to annoy him. It would get cleared up obviously but perhaps a different room . . . There would after all be a *stain.*

He stands, as naked as Adam, in the open doorway. The chamber next door to the left is the Lady's Room, now occupied by Matteo and some rather noisy whore he picked up by the Pool of Hetaira. To his right, some kind working space, big table, no bed, lots of marble busts of Greek gods and Roman emperors, copies of originals his holy father actually owns. Tiresome how unoriginal these provincials are. Order a bust of Marcus Aurelius and suddenly you think you can write letters and philosophize . . . Ahead of him over the deep well of the staircase down to the entrance hall, a landing mirroring his own with a series of doors, all closed and in shadow. No doubt she had come from one of those. A house guest she had said. Guests of the Podesta. But the Podesta was gone, sticking his tongue up the hairy Germanic anus of the Habsburg emperor. And he would have to wait in line. So for the time being, the Podesta's house was the Duke of Gandia, Papal Gonfalonier's house.

Still naked he walks round, past the top of the staircase and a quick snatched flash of their meeting at the stairs comes to grab him by the balls. He rubs himself hard and long. Yes, there it is. He would have no problem with **her**, of that he was sure. He tries to recall the fleeting, hardly-there scent of her, the wide eyes, that beautiful hair scarcely contained. Lust fills him up. He can feel it roar through his veins like a tidal surge.

Gandia passes the staircase, veers right and stares hungrily down the landing, three, no four doors. She is hiding behind one of them. Smaller rooms these, looking out onto the huge inner courtyard of the castle, not the Roman arena and Old City. He wonders whether she sleeps naked. Below there is a gasp, a scurry, a patter of feet as someone looks up, catches sight of him and runs back to whichever dark domestic hole they emerged from. Sighing, he pulls at himself strong, long and hard until he comes, spurting out his pleasure onto the polished floorboards. It is enough for now. For now. And the chase of hungry cat and helpless mouse can now begin.

He stretches, exhales a loud belch and walks slowly back to his room. Eyes in the shadows below watch up at him both fearfully and in awe because in truth, he is very beautiful. His adoring and indulgent father often has him stand next to the statue of Hermes that graces the corridor leading to the Papal suite and declares his body infinitely superior to that of the young god. Juan Borgia wrestles and rides, he swims with young men of questionable virtue in the Tiber and her tributaries, he is an expert at throwing the javelin and no one can defeat him at Maglio. Not one *pulgada* of fat pollutes the taut lines of his body and his skin is hairless and as smooth as one of Myron's *discobuli.* The beautiful body prowls along the landing and stops. The egg is congealing on the fine Arabian rug. A dim anger rises up, anger at the stupid girl who failed to arouse him and who is such a slattern she leaves his room like a midden. He considers calling her back, taking her hard from behind, wrapping her hair around his fist as he hits the back of her head. No. He is Papal Gonfalonier, he is Juan Borgia, he is his father's son. Perfecting the virtue of patience will be a most delicious agony. A day, perhaps two of sweet pain as he seeks this house guest out, hears her voice, touches her skin and walks away unsatisfied. And then. And then he will have her.

Rosa the House Guest

It has been a long time since this has happened. Rosa wakes in the early evening and her first thought is not '*He is dead! He is never coming home. I shall never ever see him again in this world.*' Instead her first thought is a wordless, creeping smoke of fear that rises up and takes form, the form of the beautiful young man with the long red-blonde hair who stood on the top step and ripped her clothes away from her back with his tongue and his eyes and his mocking gentility.

Livia is still asleep, the afternoon siesta proper for a young lady having crossed almost seamlessly from the afternoon nap of the small child. She is curled up, rounded belly hugged tight against some patched velvet doll, tiny little snorts of rhythmic contentment, mouth slightly open, eyelids twitching. She cries less and less now for their father and in truth has been crying more for the idea of him as her father than for the actual man they had rarely seen. Rosa scarcely thinks of him at all.. He had been uncomfortable in the company of women, he was a man who thrived in the stables, in the tiltyard, the tavern, on campaign. Bleeding out on the field of battle as the French turned tail and jogged away would have been the end he most likely would have chosen. And besides, she has no grief left for her father, no spare tears not already assigned.

She stares up to the ceiling. It is not as grand a set of chambers as she has at home, the tall solid House Marin where her father and his father and going back to how ever many fathers it took to get to Aeneas, had lived. Her suite of rooms there had beautiful ceilings. As a child, she spent hours counting cherubs, assigning them names and personalities, spotting every hidden wren, every tiny bee drinking from the depths of the roses. There had been roses painted on the walls too, red for love, white for purity, yellow for jealousy and pink for her, for Rosa. An uneven number of roses, Annamaria had told her once, an uneven number for luck. But Rosa had counted them once and again and again and she was sure that she counted seventy-six. Nonsense, Annamaria had scolded, your good mother, she would never have given orders for seventy-six, there must be seventy-seven, you silly girl, you have missed one, count again! But Rosa counted again and again and still she found seventy-six and eventually she stopped counting but wondered privately if that was why her mother had died.

There are no roses on these guest room walls, nothing painted at all although there is a pleasant hanging depicting a summer hunt with harts fleeing hounds and ladies with their hair all unbound. Above them, the ceiling boasts a few delicate plaster flourishes and she counts the curls she thinks are supposed to be leaves. One bunch in the very centre, four others at the corners. Fifteen delicate little plaster leaves in each. So altogether … she taps her fingertips together … sixty. Sixty little leaves. An even number again. Perhaps Annamaria was wrong, perhaps it is uneven numbers that bring *infortunii.*

The heavy weight of fear and revulsion sits still in her belly. In her eighteen years she has probably known more men that most young women about to enter the cloistered life of a Poor Clare but for the most part they have been boisterous cousins, respectful even bashful friends of cousins, courtly older men come to see her father. That one of these was mostly likely already picked out as a future husband she has always known. Most probably one of the older men – the minor dukes, the army captains, the more prosperous merchants even – but the death of her mother, who in ordinary times would have organized such things, meant that her bridal pathway had been left unclear. And then this summer . . .

She had known him for most of her life, she thinks. Since she has memories of anything, she remembers his face in her mind's eye of childhood. And always fighting, scrapping, mocking, teasing, every boy's favourite co-conspirator, beaten God knew how many times for this rudeness, that cheek, this misdemeanor, that lack of courtesy. She had watched him in the tilting yard, somehow hanging on to the mane of a horse denied him by the grooms and yet somehow now careering around the space, knocking over stands, frothing across its flanks, baring back pink wet gums. She had not seen the thrashing but she had heard her father shouting furiously, pulling the little pissmire down from the saddle, throwing him to the sawdust. Always, always the same. But who else knew the names of all the constellations – Cassiopeia, Ursa Major, Orion – who else could tell her about Dido of Carthage and how she had lain herself down so carefully upon the pyre as Aeneas's ship left her harbour? When had her exasperated admiration turned to passion? It had crept up so slowly and yet had also felt like the sudden flare of a great bright torch. One day she had enjoyed his company, the next she could not eat nor sleep for love of him.

Why had they kept it so secret, this passion of theirs? He was a flirt, a terrible romancer, boasted to his friends of the many women low and high born, free and married that he had seduced. He taught his little gang of boys about the thrill of the chase, the passion of the battle, the sweet fruit of victory and then the next chase, women were deer to be hunted, castles to besiege. Perhaps he taught them too well. The more callow of his friends had chosen her as his first conquest, had written poor sonnets, had declared a self-pitying undying love. In a bid to pour ice upon his fire, she had declared herself bound for the Poor Clares – and how ironic does that little lie seem now, oh be wary those who mock the saints, *cave superbium* indeed – but this had only increased his childish posturing. In truth she had hardly noticed.

Sleepy half-thoughts as she woke, the bright sharp alertness of the fresh day, the drowsy last moments at night; every waking moment was of him, her mad, unpredictable Hermes, protector of thieves, inventor of lies, singer of songs.

How he had laughed on hearing the lie, that she was to enter a nunnery and live as a chaste sister. In the high grasses of the apple orchard beyond the eastern bank of the river, he had insisted on taking her there and there, bright daylight, no shame, no shame at all! And then after, as they lay exhausted with her messy head upon his shoulder, he had sung her a foolish little rhyme. There and then, he had made up a song to mock her and it had been more wonderful to her ears than any lovelorn nonsense his friends could compose in a thousand sleepless nights.

You shall ring your sacring bell,
Keep your hours and tell your knell,
Rise at midnight to your matins,
Read your psalter, sing your Latins;
And when your blood shall kindle pleasure,
Scourge yourself in plenteous measure.
You must read the morning mass,
You must creep unto the cross,
Put cold ashes on your head,
Have a hair cloth for your bed,
Bind your beads, and tell your needs,
Your holy Aves and your Creeds;
Holy maid, this must be done,
If you mean to live a nun.

Despite the pain of what had happened after, she could not help but smile. He had been the most wonderful, gifted, wickedly terrible man. But she had loved him so much. And was it so foolish to think they could have married? Her father would have discouraged it, of course. Blood and wealth were important and her Hermes was cousin to the Podesta himself but he was also a comet racing across the sky, a fireball scorching everything it touched. He would have made a most dreadful husband, a negligent father, a careless *paterfamilias*. She knew this. Still, lying bloated and empty with grief, she still knows this. But she had also known a different man. Strong brown fingers tracing their path down her cheekbone, her body fitting against his, it does not, even now, seem possible that she will never feel him again.

Livia twisted a little and Rosa moved herself slightly to give her sister room. It was late afternoon. By rights, they should be at San Zeno for Mass, how strange it felt not to have been for what? two weeks now. She closed her eyes and tried to smell, taste, hear, see and feel her dead lover. That very last time.

Two days before he died, at the Cousins' *commedia dell'arte,* that had been the last time. They had hidden behind the most inadequate of masks, he the Little Skirmisher, Scaramuccia, sly fool, conniving servant and she of course had been Isabella. But perhaps the more lustful Columbina would have been more fitting. Smiling despite herself, she remembered that he had suggested that the scandalous La Ruffiana would have been appropriate–*Am I so old?* She had pretended outrage, *Am I nothing but an aged whore creased dry by wrinkles and disappointment? Do I look like some tart who has said yes, yes, yes to a thousand men?*–but after what she had let him do to her later that night in the gardens...

'Why does love hurt?' she had asked him afterwards, still flushed with pleasure. Expecting a caustic reply, clever, rude, a euphemism mocking her, mocking her sex, mocking himself, mocking God, he had instead caught her breath with mere words.

'*It is fitting that I burn for you, and breathe for you, since I am yours and you are mine: and if I am parted from you, well then, I suffer less from all my other griefs. It is fitting that I burn for you, and breathe for you, since I am yours and you are mine: and if I am taken from you, You shall suffer less from all your future griefs.*'

And it was true. From the very second, she had learned that he had died in the hot sandy dust of the road, that he had died cursing them all to Hell, she had stopped feeling pain. Stopping feeling fear. And yet…she rolls over to her side and puts her arm around her sister, still deeply sleeping. This day she feels fear again.

The Bishop of this small city-state

It has been a long time since this has happened, thinks the Bishop sadly as he places his hand on the back of the sobbing man's head. He has accepted the man's confession of course and under the holy seal of the confessional, this man's fate is now in the hands of the Almighty. From the disconsolate shaking of the old Dominican's shoulders though, it does not seem as though he has resolute hopes of the Good Lord's compassion. Yes, a long time since a monk under the charge of the Abbot, firstly had come to the Bishop rather than Abo for the sacrament of penitence but secondly a long time since a confession of full sodomy was declared.

Laymen imagined that those under holy orders were the most consistent and unrepentant of sodomisers. These were the furious complaints of the Bogomils, the Cathars, the Waldensians, even the Franciscans, that the less ascetic of monks – The Benedictines, Cluniacs, Cistericans, even the silent Carthusians – not only spent their days drunk and gluttonous but also in lustful perversions of the most hateful kind. What had John Chrystostom said? *Only the insane lust after other males. They do an insult to nature itself.* And Chrystostom had advocated death by stoning for those who took the passive role and allowed themselves to be sodomised because they had renounced their manhood and chosen to become women, against God's express purpose for them. Yes, '*driven out and stoned*' that was it. The Bishop withdraws his hand. But whatever the hysterical fears of the heretics, those monks having physical relationships with their brothers were not common, at least not in his experience both inside and outside of the Seal. Most confessions involved unconsummated passions, usually young novices for each other or foolish old pederasts for the prettiest of the boys. Unfortunately, Father

Lorenzo was guilty of everything so it seemed. Allowing himself without complaint to be sodomised, unnaturally caressing the private parts of another man, allowing precious seed, the unique homunculus, to be spilled without possibility of issue . . . it was all familiar and horrible but not beyond what he had heard before.

Well, it is done now. Confession made in full, penitence seemingly clear and sincere.

It is getting late. A busy day of rest, a full congregation all finding new impetus to worship from the horror of the last few months. He had not seen the young Duke of Gandia in his cathedra congregation, no doubt the Gonfalonier had a private arrangement with one of the smaller chapels. Our Bishop stifles a yawn and hopes that his stomach does not embarrass him in the stillness of this cell.

'My Lord Bishop,' a hardly audible whisper, the Bishop leans in. 'My gracious lord, what now? What shall I do now?'

He is a little confused. What more is there? The sin is an old one, thirty years now and not repeated. Contrition is full, the rest up to the infinite mercies of God.

'Brother Lorenzo, you are the Abbey of San Zeno herbalist. You are a stalwart and valued member of this town community. You are respected as both venerable and compassionate by your brothers. This matter now confessed is with God and therefore no longer concerns this earthly world unless repeated. And this other matter which has tormented and vexed us all these past few weeks will soon be over. You simply must speak to the Englishman sent over from London – and what a farce, my brother! To trouble a foreigner from such a distant and irrelevant land to investigate our affairs, I do not know what the Lord Cyprian was thinking – but needs must you speak to him, explain your ignorance of the murderous intent of the young men, your benevolence in the matter of the sleeping draft, your innocence in the matter of the poison. He will see the truth, inform the lord that he is to be disappointed in his irrational vendetta – brought on no doubt by tremendous grief – and you will leave this dark place of the soul and return to the sunlight of your garden and your *fratrum in deum*. All will return to how it was before this summer.'

And when the Podesta returns, it will be but a distant dream, a tragedy performed by players who have long since moved on to a different town. I will have done my job. We can hand the woman over to whichever captain-at-arms the Podesta has left in charge and the secular authorities can reduce her to nothing.

Shuffles his feet, re-arranges his heavy white tunic, stretches his back as if to rise. The monk is still on the floor but now looks fully up, grizzled chin giving him a wild look. For a second, the Bishop thinks of St Hilarion '*so wasted that his bones scarcely held together,*' '*so various were the temptations and so many the demonic snares that a volume would not suffice to relate them.*' But this is no Desert Father and saint, this is a Borgia bastard and he is best not giving the poor man pretensions.

'Return to the abbey? As *Dominus Herbarius*? But . . . my Lord Bishop, I have sinned, I have most grievously sinned.'

'But the sin is now long done. You have repented, made full confession under the seal and there is no possibility of repetition. Is there not?'

'Of course not. He is dead.'

'Brother Lorenzo. There is to be no repetition because you have repented of your actions, not because this . . . other is now deceased.'

'Oh . . . yes, of course. But I was not talking of the . . . actions that occurred between us which were abominable, yes, abominable, '*despised by the world, we were more unclean than animals*'. Pope Gregory, I think. Yes, Gregory, ninth of his name, blessed be his works. But I speak now of the . . . . love. The love that bound the two of us.'

'It was not love, Brother Lorenzo.'

'It was a love as I have heard Solomon speak of Sheba, of Sarah to her child Isaac, of Christ even to his apostles, did he not say he loved them, was not John the apostle who Christ loved best? Are we not told by Paul that love is the greatest of the three holy virtues, greater than hope and of even of faith, the greatest of these is love, he told us, the greatest of these is love. Love is patient, love is kind – and my lord, we two we were patient with each other's weaknesses, we were so kind, so kind to each other, there was no cruelty in it, no harshness – it does not envy, it does not boast, it is not proud – and I did not envy him his easy way with the other brothers, I was proud at how popular and well-thought of he was, and we were not proud, no, no, we did not think our love better than the love of other men …'

'Brother, this is not seemly …'

'It is not rude, it is not self-seeking, it is not easily angered – we never had a disagreement, we concurred on all things in such sweet harmony, never have I known a mind that so mirrored my own in matters of theology, of *de ratione dei*, of the significance of our *Dominicus vota*.'

'Brother Lorenzo.'

'It keeps no record of wrongs, in does not delight in evil but rejoices in the truth. We … we …' Here he falters a little, there is spittle on his lower lip. 'We did not rejoice in evil. Our actions were evil, we knew it and it tormented both us but the love, it was pure …'

'Only Christ was pure.'

'It was almost transcendent, Lord Bishop, ineffable, just as at the Transfiguration, the three were lit by a light that blinded them, their clothes cleaned whiter than any bleach could whiten, they came down the mountain and not one of them could describe what they had seen, what they had felt …'

'Stop. This is getting close to blasphemy. Do not push me into censure, Brother Lorenzo, we do not need to walk down this road. Fortunately for you, we are still under the Confessional Seal so I am not duty bound to report your words to Venezia, indeed I may not. But do not think that this sudden loosening of your tongue will be greeted with anything other than horror and swift punishment on the outside of the Seal.'

A quick light of hope flashed. 'I think that is what I need, my Lord. I know a great punishment awaits my eternal soul but my earthly body cries out for just penalty.'

A flicker of alarm, of premonition even as the Bishop feels a growing sense of disquiet. This little serpent of false guilt needing extirpation must be crushed beneath the heel.

'You know your conciliar edicts, Brother, you have acted as Confessor yourself. You know that sins of the mind, thoughts, lusts, envies, these are all to be forgiven within the Seal as venial sins **not** as mortal. You have already confessed the unnatural deeds you committed. They are now with God. The corrupted perversion you call love has also now been confessed and is with God as a venial sin, most likely to accord just a momentary time in Purgatory.'

'I am going to Hell.'

'Brother, Brother, these are not our decisions to make. Now you must steady yourself. At first light tomorrow the Englishman is coming and you must be rested and calm. Think of your return to the herb garden, think of your fellow brothers who miss you and await your return. Think of the reputation of your abbey.' And is this last exhortation the most important? Shame upon him as a Shepherd but this is the compromise of rule in the earthly kingdom.

'I need to make public penance I think. I think that if I make public confession with my hand upon the tomb of San Zeno himself…'

Holy Mother of God, this was certainly not going to happen! The Bishop feels sick and cold and hot all at the same time at the very thought of it. He reaches down and takes both thin, sharp shoulders by the hand, ruby-red episcopal ring glinting against the dirty brown homespun.

'Listen to me, Brother Lorenzo. If you make public confession, it is outside of the Seal and the ecclesiastical and secular authorities will make you their prey. In the past, our learned Fathers and Council all condemned what you have done but many advocated exile or the monastic life as punishment. Pope Alexander the Third at the Lateran decreed 'if they are clerics they must be expelled from the clergy or confined in monasteries' and the good Bernardino of Sienna in his compassion decreed that such unnatural offenders must be ostracized. A few, it is true, advocated castration but it was within the compassionate authority of the Holy Magisterium. But at the Fourth Lateran it was agreed that punishment of sodomites should be shared with the secular authorities. Do you understand, Brother, the secular authorities? And just forty years ago, Nicholas V, Papal Father, gave permission to investigate sodomites to the Inquisition. The Inquisition. You know what your brother under Dominic is doing at this very moment in Spain? Torquemada is burning not just Jews and heretics but sodomites. And he does not care how old the sin, he does not care if it has been confessed, he does not care if it was only in thought but not deed. He is burning men by the hundred.'

Ragged breaths, a deep sigh. The wild eyes have fallen back to the floor. The Bishop tries to regain his composure.

'So there we have it, Fra Lorenzo. I am leaving the cell and as I close the door, the Seal is broken and no more. You will not speak of this to anyone, you will dismiss it from your mind. You have confessed the great and unnatural sin that was weighing heavy upon your soul these past forty years and you will sleep tonight, the blissful rest of the man with so little sin it is as if the angels are lifting him up. Fra Lorenzo?'

'Yes, my Lord Bishop. Thank you for hearing my most grievous errors. You have truly been the face of Christ for me in this dark place.'

Somewhat appeased, the Bishop helps the old man rise and gives him a companionable squeeze of the arm. Dusting off his skirts, he leaves the cell, the door closes shut and the Seal is gone.

Monday

CHAPTER SIXTEEN

In which another letter flies south to Firenze and the English lawyer finally meets the Dominican monk

My best beloved cousin Samuel, Forgive any impetuosity on my part for writing this so soon after the last but my concern for our future wellbeing blossoms like the bitterness of buds upon the hawthorn bough. I hear tidings that your father has approached the Master Guildsman of the Toledan leather curers, resident many years now in your city, a prosperous man with no fewer than five daughters, the eldest of whom is considered most comely.

We can leave the fictitious romantic quandaries of the equally fictitious Lucy Skipwell and her cousin Samuel. Suffice to know that the code was of course the number five and the slip of paper hidden within the first was winging its way south to Savonarola in Firenze just after dawn.

My Most Esteemed and Well-Beloved Giramo and hoping to the Risen Christ that you are well. I have now been resident with CC for three days now and have spoken at length to the Bishop in charge –*soi-disant*– of this case. It seems very clear that your instincts in detecting the foul odour of papal interference and corruption have yet again served you true. The woman is being used to divert the eye away from

the guilty party so as to minimize stain against the most heinous name of Borgia. And as I wrote you before, he is here, Giramo, HE IS HERE. Staying in the Podesta's house with a small retinue–too many for me to overcome by myself of course–and now he has appointed himself *defensionis.* The arrogance knows no bounds. I know we must have faith in the words of Proverbs that pride comes before destruction and haughty spirits before a fall but sometimes it is so hard to have enough patience to let the Lord's will be done. Gandia–as he is now–thinks he can corrupt the Council of Ten and his tame Bishop and have this disreputable scandal swept away with the autumn leaves. Observers of the rise of this *familia horribilis* might wonder that they should even care about their reputation when they do daily cause the Queen of Heaven herself to turn her face away in shame but the peculiarities of the immoral and the insane are not for us to rationalize. Suffice to combat their unholy subterfuges as and when we come across them.

The woman naturally knows nothing of the poisons used to excite suicide and madness, she did not and could not have prevented the killings, she had neither the motive nor the opportunity. Do they not teach Cicero to these bishops and podestas in this, the end of days, my old friend? I found myself saying over and over in the heat of my exasperated mind; *cui bono?* Lord Bishop, *cui bono*? The woman, her name is Susanna something, she has no connection to the six deaths aside from her position in the familia which accorded her a gossip's inkling of what the young men and the girl were up to. However–and this, my good friend, you need to especially note with the incredulous joy with which I myself heard her mutterings–the Borgia monk has been in communication with the Scaglieri themselves. Yes, the Scaglieri. More properly known as the Familia della Scala. And here, my old friend, I imagine you sitting down heavily upon your simple three-legged stool, your rooms bare of all furnishing, arras, gewgaws and paintings and yet now lit up by the wondrous incredulity upon your dear face. Yes, the Scaglieri. So, now we have a deeper plot, one now of politics, intrigue and treason. As you know far better than this poor Englishman, the Familia della Scala have long desired their return from imperial exile to this city. I hear Benedetto Scaglieri has a son named Julius Caesar who is page to Maximilian himself! What a farcical conceit. Julius Caesar indeed. The Podesta of this town is even now travelling to the Emperor's council at Milan – he should have already arrived – and is no doubt expecting an awkward kiss of peace with Benedotto but a kiss threatening no more than mere awkwardness. He, after all, holds the office Benedotto craves. But now there may be more danger to our Podesta than mere social inconvenience. If these killings have been orchestrated deliberately to cause civil unrest in this town and to undermine the Podesta's position, perhaps even to the point of unseating him and encouraging a popular demand for Scaglieri return and if a Borgia bastard has been recruited to cause this unrest . . . my dear and good Giramo, I shall speak with this Dominican Borgia tomorrow morning and send you immediate report. If he admits under holy oath any part in such an intrigue, then Juan Borgia and the so-called Papal Father will have failed in their attempt to protect him. And we shall ensure that the Dominican's true identity is made clear for the whole of the North to see. And make clear, more importantly, the incessantly meddling papal finger in all the secular affairs of the Italian city states and beyond. The Emperor himself will want a report if this is true.

Now My Dear Friend. I hear reports from travelers reaching us from Firenze that you are growing increasingly vocal in your condemnation of the excesses of the prelates and the populace. That you preach from dawn to dusk, that you have burned all of your possessions on a great fire in the Piazza della Signoria, that you are encouraging others to do the

same. We hear of paintings and furs and tapestries being dragged out of the palazza and thrown into the flames. We hear of women throwing their velvets and silks, children their toys, men their Spanish leathers and silk hose. And all of this I can agree might be pleasing in the eyes of the Lord for when we stand before Him we shall all be as naked as we were in the Garden and shall care nothing for such distractions. We should all wish to be Wailers, your own *piagnoni*, followers who shrive themselves with tears as the effluvia of our vanity is reduced to ashes in the piazza. But we also hear, Giramo, that you are burning books, Giramo, books! And that you are preaching loudly and without care for your personal safety that a New Cyrus will come from the North to establish a New Jerusalem in Firenze. Who is this Cyrus, my Friend? Is it the Emperor of whom you speak, certainly Maximilian is pleased to associate himself with your prophecies but all to his own secular gain, surely you know that? Oh be careful, my good brother, we also hear word that excommunication has been mentioned in the papal corridors. If a bull of *latae sententiae* is passed against you, then any man is free to abuse you at his will as an enemy of the holy Catholic Church. I fear that your many enemies will then be freed from their restraint and will attempt to end your work in Firenze. But I must say no more, for fear of tearing this fine vellum. When matters are settled here, I shall travel back south and stay with you awhile and we shall sit out on the eaves of your house, stare up at the constellations discussing Boethius and Jerome as once we did. Please do not consign the best Firenzi wine to the flames of your bonfires, good friend, save at least two bottles for my return. I remain your most honest and faithful friend in the Lord, *sole scriptura et dominus*, John.

Letter carefully slipped between the paper of Lucy Skipwell's emotional and no doubt unduly suspicious torment and sealed with wax, John Oldcastle entrusted the missive to the household steward who promised swift delivery to the courier.

He broke his fast alone in his rooms. The Borgia monk was not going to hand himself over to the secular authorities without being persuaded, cajoled, tricked and forced to do so. It may well be that the two roads most like to succeed would be 1) to appeal to Lorenzo Borgia's sense of self-preservation to name his accomplices for surely as a cloistered Dominican he had little access to the machinations of the Imperial court without a go-between carrying letters. It might be possible to paint a picture whereby the accomplices bore the brunt of the treason and conspiracy charges and the monk himself stepped back into the shadows as ignorant dupe. 2) If selfish self-preservation and lack of loyalty were not the keys to the man's tongue, then perhaps physical fear was. Any man found guilty of trying to encourage sedition against his Podesta and Bishop would without doubt be given the most horrendous death. A nobleman no doubt might appeal for decapitation first but a Borgia bastard, here in a northern state loyal to the Empire, was certainly not going to be accorded such a mercy. Oldcastle had seen disembowelings, castrations, blindings, they left the observers carrying the heavy stench of shit and blood for days. He had seen drunken boys laugh and jeer, their fathers curse and throw mud, their mothers cackle and point at the shrunken bleeding genitals but in truth, most quarterings were watched in a fascinated and appalled silence. But although it was probably subjective and only a matter of conjecture – fortunately for most people – no method of killing a man could be worse than burning.

He sat back and pursed his lips. His task was this day far easier than it had been when he arrived. Before the woman's stuttering evidence of 'Scaliger' involvement, Oldcastle's case against the monk had perforce to rely upon incitement, procurement of poisons, malpractice, intimidation and secondary manslaughter by proxy. But now there was a charge of treason to be made and defended, the issue of the six dead could be presented not as the primary charge but as the *adiuventia crimen*, just corroborating evidence of immoral character leading to the *prima crimen* of fermenting sedition. Far less contentious. Far easier to prove. The man no doubt would be expecting the interview to concentrate wholly on the six dead, he had no way of knowing that the foolish old woman, with her talk of demons and monsters, had inadvertently let slip the political. So, he would encourage this mistake, let the interview take the course the old man expected. And then Oldcastle would find the space, the chink, the tiny unnoticed side alley leading almost without thought to the main course. And hopefully by the time he realized that the menu had changed, that he was now mired in a completely different set of charges, the Bastard would already have incriminated himself.

The Bishop would be there of course. As this was a case of an ordained brother facing secular charges, the rivers were murky. Ordinarily it was a town's ruler who investigated such matters as murder, rape and arson and the ecclesiastical authorities watched, relatively impotent, from the sidelines. Although of course in reality, the secular and ecclesiastical authorities were usually from the same great families, brothers even, such were the cesspits of corruption that Italian city states had become. But as a technicality, it would be the Church handing over the responsibility and privilege of both trial and punishment to the secular. Executions of course had always been handed over, even executions of heretics and witches, the great Mother Church not wanting blood on her hands. But now the trial itself was very often not under Church control. Oldcastle however was not the Podesta of this city, indeed he was not even a citizen of the state, he had no official rights nor function whatsoever. Expecting Lord Cyprian to accompany him, he had been told at dawn that the lord was unwell but that he had signed and sealed a *note compromissi*, delegating Oldcastle as his executor in this matter and this matter alone. In the circumstances therefore it would be prudent to have the Bishop present too. Two against one. Oldcastle smiled. The Bishop was an intelligent man, weighed down by book-learning, skilled in canon law, the Borgia bastard also no doubt learned and potentially fighting for his life. But despite everything, Oldcastle still liked the odds.

----------∞∞∞----------

The Bishop had brought Father Lorenzo out of the cell in San Zeno's crypt and had welcomed the monk–under guard of four deacons for the mile or so walk–and the English lawyer into his private study, as if they were both honoured guests sharing a glass of wine and pleasant conversation. Bound books, both scribed and printed, and rolled manuscripts filled the shelves; here was a minor king's ransom in vellum, parchment and paper alone without even counting in the value of the heavy Turk tapestries and glass panes in the windows. It was reasonably clever psychology, thought Oldcastle as he took a comfortable seat–there were no three legged stools or wooden benches here–with his back to the windows and light. Talk to a man in a dark, stone-walled cell and not only does the interrogator make assumptions about the man's guilt–so as a man looks so as he does–but so also does the accused himself. Dirty, hungry, evidence of his own shit and urine still in a bucket in the corner, any man feels worthless, angry, defensive, hopeless, all manner of emotions that can do him no good when he starts to talk. But dress him in clean robes–as the good Bishop had clearly done–find someone to shave his whiskers and wash him, rub something sweet-smelling from no doubt his own herb garden onto his skin and here we have an obviously innocent and benevolent man of God, sat deep in a red damask settle to talk theology and the finer points of law.

The Bishop did not take his place behind the desk as he might have done to establish authority and precedence but instead drew up another comfortable reading chair so that the three of them sat as equals in a little circle. Another inch or two and their knees would be touching. *No investigation this*, thought Oldcastle enjoying the tableau as it was set out before him. *Just an exchange of pleasantries between comrades. I like this bishop. He is no fool.*

After making the requisite introductions and washing each guest's hands in a silver bowl of water, drying their skin himself with a linen cloth, the Bishop entwined his long fingers into an arch and rested his elbows upon his knees.

'This is of course highly irregular, Mr Oldcastle. Any investigation of suspicious deaths and death by malpractice in this city is the jurisdiction of the Podesta and the civil courts. And as I have already explained and shown you the Podesta civic seal left by that great lord on his departure for Milan, I have been given his authority to question those involved. As this is as yet simply *sub judice*, just a preliminary inquiry, I have the right to take on the Podesta role if he so chooses to delegate *in absentia*. And any suspicion of suicide is of course my jurisdiction anyway as a spiritual matter, clearly laid out in canon law. So your part in these proceedings is really superfluous to requirements.'

Oldcastle let the silence fall. He knew exactly what he was going to say but it did no harm to show deep consideration.

'This man here,' At last, he nodded politely, the monk had not yet met his eye and did not do so now, 'This Dominican priest has much representation. He has the worthy bishop, your good self, speaking his case, he has the Duke of Gandia, Papal Gonfalonier himself– unheard of for the Papal Father to involve himself in such matters. And yet the woman who is accused of incitement to murder, of incitement to suicide, of procuring poison, she seems utterly without a voice. Not one of the Abrogati to stand her case. Not even so much as a village notary. The cornerstone of justice is that all shall be represented. This is the view of the great lord who engaged my services. A fair view surely?'

The Bishop nodded. Lorenzo Borgia stared at the plush knotted rug as if unravelling its plaits.

'You are correct of course, Mr Oldcastle. Our common law is crucial to the harmony of our society. Much of what the

Ancients taught of legal representation was lost in what the estimable Petrarch calls the dark ages, that time when literature and art and justice lost their way in civic society. But common law, despite its secular nature, was preserved in the body of the Holy Mother Church.'

'Yes. Preserved in monastic libraries to which no one but ordained brothers might have access. Preserved in huge drafty mausoleums of abbeys where even the most well-intentioned and thirsty of scholars would be turned away if he was not of the Order. Preserved but unread and as unknown to the world that needed them as much as if they had burned in Alexandria with the Seat of the Muses itself.'

'Not unknown. Waiting. The great works of the Greeks and Romans and of the Early Fathers were kept safe so that we, closer to the end of days, might re-discover them. Aristotle was not lost. He was waiting, quiet and patient, for the great Aquinas to be born so that the Last Father might take the pagan's wisdom and show it the light of Christ, He who was both Man and Logos. Justinian was not lost, he was preserved. And all held together in the *Promissione Maleficarum*, our great codex of all the Italian laws. But we digress. You are of course welcome when we have concluded our business here this morning to visit the Santa Maria abbey library which, although not large, contains some interesting books. A *Commentary* on the Laws of Solon you might not have in Oxford. Plato's *Laws* of course and Aristotle's critique of them. An early version of the *Corpus Juris Civilis* which no doubt as a student you cut your teeth upon but this version has a *glossa* from Accursius you might wish to see. Not as sophisticated as later commentaries but an intriguing precursor to the discipline of commentary.'

And for how long will this gentle, tree-lined road take us around and around the town? thought Oldcastle, nodding politely. In truth, an invitation to spend a day or two at the Santa Maria Matricolore library would be something that ordinarily he would have eagerly seized. A week would hardly whet his appetite, in fact he would quite happily start here with the Bishop's own collection. But something was pressing upon him more urgently than his own desire to run his fingers across ancient vellum. The sketchy reports coming up from the southern road daily of Savonarola's excesses in Firenze filled him with alarm. Best he finish this business here and re-join his impetuous friend. The monk had still not raised his eyes from his deep contemplation of the carpet. Oldcastle wondered if he was even listening.

Again, he let the silence drift around them like smoke.

'You are most courteous, your Grace. I may well take up such a generous offer. The libraries of Lincoln's Inn and the Oxford Colleges are wonders to behold but there is no pursuit quite as satisfying as searching for a volume one has never seen before and then finding one's fingers land gently upon its leather cover.'

The two nodded in sympathetic memory. The Bishop smiled almost innocently as he played his best card.

'And of course our library of Santa Maria Matricolore has the only – forgive me, I think I am right – the *only* surviving copy of Cicero's *Epistulae ad Atticum, ad Quintum et ad Brutum*.'

He sat back and looked a little rueful as Oldcastle's eyes flickered, just a little. Dear Lord, that collection was here? He had assumed when Petrarch discovered the lost volume, it had been taken to Rome... To sit for just one day, an hour, to read the words of Cicero to his friends after the world had lost and forgotten them, to read them once more... But John Oldcastle had inherited more from his grandsire than just a name. *As stubborn as a hound looking for his bone* his mother had scolded repeatedly but it was true and it was no insult. Almost as if remembering something just at the edges of his memory, Oldcastle addressed the third man who had been almost forgotten.

'You understand, Brother Lorenzo, why I am here? That the woman Susanna of Lord Cyprian's *familia* has been accused of maleficent incitement to encourage suicide and murder, that she was the one to procure the poison which led to one, probably two of the deaths. And yet from the lord who has hired me's understanding as paterfamilias, you yourself are just as culpable, preliminary investigations might seem that you are more so . . .'

'There have been no preliminary investigations of my ordained brother, Mr Oldcastle, save those interviews by myself and the Duke of Gandia's man, all of which have pointed to complete exoneration . . .'

'And yet it seems far more likely that a respected member of the community with some influence over these young people should be our maleficent enticer, our *raptor malefici*. Surely a woman approaching old age and with no standing, no education, no Latin, and let us face it, Brother, no teeth! should have been able to influence these fine highborn men to fight and kill each other. And before we allow ourselves to think that if we ourselves did not actually unsheathe the blade, wield the blade, buy the poison, pour the poison, then our hands are as clean and spotless as a maid's, let us imagine instead the dirty stains upon Pilate's fingers. Our common law derives from the Code of Justinian, both *Codex* and *Digesta* but before you say to me that as an ordained member of the Order of St Dominic you are somehow exempt, let me remind you that *ecclesia vivit lege romana*, the Church lives by Roman Law.'

'No one here needs tutoring on the origins of common law, Mr Oldcastle, I have already told you that our *Promisssione Maleficarum* combines both church and civil laws, ancient and more recent. We simply need to examine the details of the events leading to the six civilian deaths and determine whether this man was culpable in any way.'

'Or whether indeed the woman was. We seem to have forgotten her part in this play. It is as if exoneration of the Brother here necessitates automatic conviction of the woman without any further evidence.'

'In this we may well concur, Mr Oldcastle. It has seemed to me these past few days, a great shame that the Podesta's original verdict six weeks ago no longer seems enough for your employer.'

Oldcastle was not to be caught out. 'Yes. The original verdict exonerating everyone. Save of course those who were already dead. A convenient decision from your Podesta.'

'It was wise. The feuding of the families had to be stopped, there were five families involved, all angry, all stricken with grief, all concerned with reputation and status. And when his verdict was given, there seemed to be an accord. The city needed to grieve but also to look at the wider world around it; French troops were skirting our borders, bodies were still being brought home from Fornovo, the Emperor wanted to seal the League of Venice with more than just an inconclusive battle. We are part of the wider world, small though we are. My Podesta was wise to demand a cessation to enmity from the five families.'

'Yes. Expedience ahead of justice, I can see that such a philosophy might have its adherents.'

The Bishop smiled sadly but refused to be drawn.

'But acceptance of the ruling, the turning of the collective cheek, did not seem to extend to this woman, Susanna. The paterfamilias of one of the more dominant families, the family of the last dead boy, found her on the street and decided to make an Aaron's Goat of her.'

'She was on the street of course because your Lord Cyprian threw her there.'

'As was his right. She had clearly transgressed in the matter of the marriage. But accusations of poison and witchcraft then seem excessive. They were clearly a thinly veiled attack on the house of which she had but recently been a member. No wonder my Lord Cyprian withdrew from the accord and looked again at the culpability of this man here.'

They both looked at the Dominican. Still he stared downwards, lips quivering a little as though he was saying something but to himself, no other.

'Father Lorenzo . . . ' the Bishop's tone was gentle; Oldcastle could not help but be a little touched by it. 'We need to hear your voice now. We may feel that it is an imposition and unnecessary burden for the great family in question to have commissioned an Englishman from London Town to act as counsel for a poor woman here in the smallest of the Italian city states. But he is here now and as a man of the law, he is only interested in the truth.'

Oldcastle inclined his head. The monk raised his a little. His eyes were surprisingly clear and focused, holding the Englishman's gaze steadily.

'The truth?'

'Yes,' Both men spoke at once, Oldcastle politely giving way to the older man. It was after all his study, his comfortable seats, his city.

'So Brother Lorenzo. You knew all four of the young men who died, I think. But except in the matter of the marriage, you did not have regular contact with them? You were not to know of the first two deaths which occurred in the street without your presence and you had no inkling that the third brutal murder in the cathedral cloisters would take place, nor of course the subsequent suicides.'

'That's right, my Lord Bishop. The heat of the summer . . . the young men who were not allowed to fight the French at Fornovo . . . there was much anger, much frustration . . . they felt that the atrocities carried out at Mordano were unavenged. They called out to Mary Mother of God as they died. Thousands dead. Despoiled and denied burial, children even, young girls ravaged before their slaughter. They called out to our Holy Mother . . . *Ave Maria, gratia plena, Dominus tecum, Benedicta tu in mulieribus et benedictus fructus ventris tui, Iesus, Sancta Maria, Mater dei, ora pro nobis peccatoribus nunc et in hora mortis nostrae*'.

The two witnesses felt unable to interrupt, both grateful when the old man paused for breath.

'We understand,' said Oldcastle taking advantage of the Bishop's distraction as he genuflected. 'We understand that tempers were high and that the blood of young men is rash and ill-considered. But this is not our concern. It is the matter of the poison that concerns us.'

The monk blinked. 'There was no poison at Mordano, just the sword and axe. No, the poisoned well, the muddied waters are here, here in this city...'

'A poisoned well?' Oldcastle leaned forward a little.

'*When a righteous man listens to an evil man it is as if a spring is muddied and a well poisoned.*'

'Proverbs 25, verse 26,' explained the Bishop, as if to a child. Oldcastle had to smile. He had revised his Justinian Code but had neglected to read through Old Testament poetry, more fool he.

'Brother, as an English lawyer trained at Merton College Oxford I have a little learning and a little more experience. And so I should like to establish not whether you were present at these terrible events for we are all in agreement that you were not. But the common law is clear. There are principals and there are accessories. Principals are person present at the scene of the crime who participate in its commission. Accessories are persons who were not present during the commission but who – and here we need to pay good ear – but who aided, counseled, procured, commanded, encouraged or protected the principals before or after the crime. You are clearly no principal actor in these crimes, Brother Lorenzo but my task is to determine whether you fit the *legum descriptionem* of accessory. Did you aid, did you counsel, did you procure, did you command, did you encourage, did you protect?'

The Bishop seemed about to intervene so Oldcastle moved on quickly.

'Accessories are of two sorts; before the fact and after the fact. Did you aid, encourage or assist a principal in planning and preparing a crime even though you were then absent during the commission of the crime? An accessory after the crime is one who knowingly provides assistance to the principals to avoid prosecution. Now, after the murders and suicides, the principals were dead so *de facto* you cannot be an accessory after the fact. But I am not yet convinced that you are not guilty of being *accessoriae ante factum*. The case for your guilt, it seems, revolves around the poison. Two poisons indeed, perhaps even three. One used to induce madness and suicidal thoughts, the other two to bring about immediate death. And all were used and three lie dead, one a grieving mother, one a young girl. Who else but yourself could either concoct or procure such diabolical potions?'

Here the Bishop visibly winced. 'Mr Oldcastle, you may not, here in this place, use the word *diabolical*. There is no question here of the presence of the Evil One unless of course we see his wickedness in all the corners of this temporal world.'

'I apologise.'

'And Brother Lorenzo has been most clear. The first was not a poison but a sleeping draft, used most efficaciously. The second we are told was bought elsewhere. By a young man now dead. And as for the third, it seems that the woman in question had a sleeping draft of her own, bought many years ago in her home city.'

'Valerian,' interrupted the old man, 'Valerian is very good for sleep. Mix with a little *hypericum perforatum* of the blessed St John. And I add *papaver somniferum*, the Chinese poppy – very rare and expensive but a traveller from Samarkand brought me some many years ago and I use it sparingly.'

'You know your botanics of course, Fra Lorenzo,' Oldcastle leaned back casually, 'and so of course you also know that the opium poppy causes delirium and hallucinations, that *hypericum* does the same, hallucinations, fast beating of the heart, morbid fancies, irrational thinking. A combination of the two plus whatever else you threw into your concoction …'

'I only meant to induce a deep sleep …'

'And yet you must also have known that the effects would also be madness, a desire to end such awful torment, to throw oneself off a high tower perhaps, to embrace drowning, to cut the veins in one's wrists, to embrace the sharp edge of the knife.'

'Please. Do not ... ' The eyes bent down again to the carpet, 'Do you not think that I lie awake every night and torment myself with these visions? With the *imago horribili* of the agony these young people went through, how they must have suffered as they died, how they must have thought themselves abandoned by God. The blood upon his white lips, how he must have shook and choked. The cleaving of flesh and muscle and heart as she drove the blade ... '

'Stop Fra Lorenzo!' / 'Do you torment yourself often with these thoughts?' Both men spoke together but Oldcastle was a rising wave. 'You torment yourself because of guilt? Because of the part you played as accessory in this tragedy? You would not the first villain to be acquitted in law but to then accuse himself via the *conscientia* placed in every human mind by Almighty God at the very Creation. How else did Adam know he sinned? A truly innocent man would not be plagued by these dreams, he would sleep sad but secure. You, Fra Lorenzo Borgia, sleep neither sadly nor securely but as if the guilt of the Iscariot himself lies on your breast.'

'Mr Oldcastle, I insist!'

'And so we must now ask ourselves the question most absent from recent interrogations of the woman. Why? *Cui bono*? Who benefits from these deaths? What outcome might be expected and who gains from it?'

'Mr Oldcastle, here you must admit defeat.' The Bishop had a high colour now, smudges of crimson on his aristocratic cheekbones. 'You have caught yourself in your own net for indeed there is no motive. The brother here has found himself in a dank underground cell with no light and the prospect of serious punishment. He has received no material gains from the deaths, he benefits in no way whatsoever ... '

'Perhaps, your Grace, we need to take a wider look and consider who else might benefit from this sorry state of affairs. A city with its leading families at war, its Podesta helpless to end discord and death in the streets. But let me take a different road for a while. Brother Lorenzo, I heard my employer's account of this tragic story and it seems that you were not the only Dominican brother involved in this conspiracy.'

Both men of God looked confused. Then the monk's eyes narrowed and Oldcastle was gratified to see a certain wariness.

'Can you tell me, please, and remember that if we have not sworn oaths upon the Holy Book or upon the numerous relics I am sure this city holds in its cathedral crypt *(and forgive me Old John for spouting such nonsense but it is that only language these ignorant and superstitious fools understand!)* but transporting such a relic for you to place your hands upon would not be difficult. The silver mask of Zeno himself perhaps?'

'Oldcastle!'

'So let us imagine that we have the silver mask here before us and you have already placed your hands upon it. You would be bound to speak the truth then, yes?'

'I have already spoken the truth. I am an ordained brother of St Dominic of Caleruega. How could I lie?'

Admiring the old man's spirit, clearly not quite extinguished even yet, Oldcastle nodded his head. 'And in such a spirit, then can you tell me of this Brother John, this Fra Johannes that seems to have acted as your messenger. Who is this Holy Hermes that does your bidding?'

'I don't understand. He is my brother, he is assistant librarian to Brother Athanasius, he travels sometimes to the other cities to gather manuscripts and rare books for the scribes and illuminators to copy. He came to us many years ago now from Berghof, old Vindobona after serving first at the abbey of . . . '

'Berghof? Which is also called Vienna, that troubled city and now the capital of the Holy Roman Empire?'

'I believe so. But I do not see . . . '

'So you are close comrades with a Dominican from Austria, a man who knows the lands between here and the Hapsburg domains. He must speak the Germanic languages too. And you use this man to take letters for you, you have already attested to the Podesta in front of witnesses that he was carrying a letter for you – a secret letter, with secret instructions – the day before the last four deaths.'

Both men of God were clearly confused now. The road the investigation had taken was not one they had predicted.

'It was simply a letter of reassurance to the young man, that the girl – whatever he might hear – was well.'

Oldcastle was in his stride. 'Whatever this might have meant in code we shall determine when we talk to Fra Johannes. But suffice to say that you have used this German monk often to take messages out of the city for you.'

'Perhaps. I needed some Kashmiri saffron, we only had Persian and I heard that some could be found in Genoa . . .'

'And to the Empire, have you sent him westwards to imperial cities?'

'I do not think . . . I cannot remember . . .'

'What is this, Oldcastle?' The Bishop stood and towered over them both, half blocking out the filtered sunlight. 'Messengers and secret letters and Kasmiri saffron? I think you have been reading the Romances of your Thomas Malory. There is no relevance in these things to the matter we investigate . . .'

Oldcastle leaned forward and touched the old man's shoulder. He flinched away, but whether frightened or revolted, Oldcastle could not say.

'Did you know, Brother Lorenzo, of the deeper purpose of these communications? Did you write the letters or did you merely pass them to Fra Johannes from someone else in the abbey? Just a few moments ago you quoted Proverbs to us; '*When a righteous man listens to an evil man, it is as if a spring is muddied and a well poisoned*'. Who is the evil man who has poisoned the well? Where did the letters given to Fra Johannes to take to Vienna originate? Are you a willing but innocent dupe in this tangled web?'

And here is your chance, old man, he thought grimly. *For the love of God, take it or all the others will surely run and leave you alone with the noose and the butcher's block.* Lorenzo Borgia, bastard son of a long-dead pope looked up and opened his mouth to speak.

The Bishop was by the door now, clearly about to end the meeting and call for someone to take the pair of them away. And so it was that when Juan Borgia, Duke of Gandia burst in with no announcement, no permission, no knock and no apology, the Bishop narrowly avoided a broken shoulder and was ten heartbeats spent composing himself again.

But ten heartbeats was all it took for the Papal Gonfalonier to cross the floor, pick the old monk up by the shoulders, shake him down like a wet dog, set him on his feet, bid them all 'On behalf of the Papal Father, I find this man innocent of all malice and hereby undertake to return him to God' and be gone. There was a strong smell of spice, sweat and calfskin. It lingered long after the two men left behind heard half a dozen boots upon stone, loud voices, the palatum side doors slam shut. Then it was very quiet in the study. The Bishop absently rubbed at his shoulder, then looked over to where the Englishman sat, clearly stunned into shock. But shock can only last so long. After cursing both inwardly and out loud, apologizing for the latter, making his curt excuses and stamping angrily out, John Oldcastle finally got to wondering what Gandia had meant by returning the old man to God.

CHAPTER SEVENTEEN

In which the bastard Dominican suddenly finds himself free but in the hands of a woman and Matteo makes short work of the unfortunate Brother Johannes

So where are we now in this *tragici fabula*? After days of late summer sun, it has finally started to rain. Gently and with no hint of much ferocity to come but you never know with Italian weather. Like its people, soft and warm and then there's a knife in your back. It has been a horribly hot and dry summer, the gravediggers sweating and cursing as they hew at ground as hard as stone to bury all the bodies. Even now, a few rotting, smiling corpses occasionally find their way home to their grieving–and let's admit it, disgusted and revolted–loved ones. The cemeteries are getting full, communal pits starting to spread outwards. Every time they have to open it up, the gravediggers hope that the dead already interred have sunk down a few feet but in this weather–there they are! Barely six feet deep, fingers stretching upwards, the lime still stinging, blistering, scorching, scarcely enough depth to safely dispose of the next lot. Even the nobles are having to make hard choices. Family tombs and ossaries are getting full after Fornovo, the bones of grandfathers and great-grandfathers not quite ready to strip and gather up into bundles for neat arrangement in a corner, skull cheerful and possessive on top. So noble lords are squeezed on top of their sires, sometimes pushed down so that ribs crack and bowels split and spill. A cursed employment, pushing noble corpses down onto and into their ancestors. Throwing the poor into communal pits is easier but don't even think of suggesting it to Lord This and Lady That, they'll have your tongue. The priest might talk of ashes to ashes and dust to dust, all appearing naked before Christ on Judgement Day but when it comes down to it, some people's dust belongs in clean marble tombs and other people's dust in the shit and stench of the pit. And a long dry summer has not changed a thing.

But now it is raining. Everyone rejoices; farmers, fishermen, vintners, even the whores who bathe in the Pool of Hetaira, a small circle of water getting dirtier and muddier by the day, now they look up to the skies and think of clean hair and skin and cunni.

It is Monday still, a busy day everywhere as stalls and shops and taverns open up again after their day of rest. The rain has brought a flowering of tongues, even the complaining has a joyful timbre. Brother Lorenzo is marched through the crowds and narrow streets by the Duke of Gandia and his three men, one huge and thick-necked, one slim with a low, unintelligent brow, the third bringing up the rear and watching their backs with cool eyes. The monk is clearly confused. These are not the streets that will take him back to his beloved Abbey of Santa Anastasia with its pink-gold stone and rose window. He does not know where he is being taken, so rarely has he ever left the cloisters.

If we were a soaring bird however – let's imagine the *falco peregrinus,* for peregrinus means the wanderer – we can imagine the graceful flight over raw and wounded Mordano, north-westwards over Mantua, swinging east and north again to this little city-state and the narrow streets through which the Duke and monk are now hurrying. And with our falcon's eye we can see what Brother Lorenzo cannot, that despite being a stranger to the town, the young Duke knows exactly where he is going and there they are, outside the Fourth Tower of the long, solid block that is Castelvecchio.

----------∞∞∞----------

'Find this man a room,' the second steward gawped as Gandia pushed past him, depositing the hapless Dominican on the threshold. 'On the first floor landing. Next to our other houseguests.'

There were muffled sounds and gestures of obeisance but Gandia and his three unpleasant *scagnozzi* had already headed towards the main suite of chambers on the ground floor. Various calls for wine, bread, oil, olives, cheese could be heard. Their wet, dirty boots brought mud in across the polished stone floors and before the second steward could protest, the rugs upon the Podesta's study floor were ruined.

The Dominican was stared at for a while by the second steward, by the pastry cook and scullery girl from the dark door beyond, by the boy who blacked the grates with his brush and tar in hand. Then finally, Celestina, wife to the chief steward came bustling in from the back of the house where she and her absent husband kept two small rooms.

'What's this then? Alms already? It's not any season for alms, is it? Saint Matthew's Day is gone and the Day of the Three Angels is not yet come. Are you collecting, good father?'

Fra Lorenzo had not been spoken to by more than five women – or indeed spoken to more than five women – in nigh on forty years. He looked at her in growing horror as he realized that she was indeed addressing him. It was as if St George saw the Great Worm, the basilisk for the first time. He was Perseus confronted by Medusa but with no shield, no sword, no courage and no idea where he was or what he was supposed to do. His voice was clearly not going to find words, not in her lifetime anyway and so she tutted, turning instead to the second steward.

'Horto, what in the name of Gabriel is this monk doing here? This is the Ostium Primum, alms-beggars go round the eastern side into the courtyard.'

Horto began to enjoy himself. The unpleasant young Duke with his equally unpleasant entourage was out of earshot.

'The Duke, he said we was to put him in one of the guestrooms, up on the first floor. Next to *tu sai chi.*'

'What?' Celestina sucked in breath, 'He said that? What does he know of... of the Podesta's guests?'

'Don't know, Mistress, but that's what he said. Put the Brother there, next to the girls.'

Celestina was universally considered to be a good woman. Not especially easy on the eye, not now she had passed her fortieth year and born five but she had a quick, efficient way about her that made her staff feel as though they were in safe hands. And with her husband, Paulo, they ran the household in such a way that there was no opportunity for laziness, theft or blasphemy but also that no unhappiness went unconsoled, no bereavement un-noted, no injury untreated. She gave alms when it was time and not before or after, she paid monies every month to chantries for the souls of her dead, she let the hungry mouths at the kitchen door have the scraps. She felt a maternal capacity towards the young and foolish girls in her care – for had she not promised their mothers that they would not only learn their trade but also be safe? – and had up to this point secured their good sense, their kitchen skills and their virginities. But today was Monday. The young bastard – for never in the secret corners of her mind would she ever call him Duke – had only arrived on the Thursday night. Four days, fewer, and already he had turned her household familia upside down.

Horto was waiting. She thought fast. After what had happened – was still happening – to poor Adela, abuse over which she Celestina had no control whatsoever, she had vowed to herself that young Rosa would not suffer the same fate. No mother, no father now, such a tragic mess over the summer, who else was there to look after the girl and that little songbird of a sister? You only had to look at them both to see broken hearts. The Podesta had done a kind and courteous thing, taking her in but who could have predicted the arrival of such a beast?

'Horto, I have been thinking of finding Lady Rosa, Lady Livia fresh lodgings, it is not suitable that they are here unchaperoned with four strange men in the house. And we do not know when the Lord Podesta is to return. Get your coat–it is raining–and go fast to the House of the Poor Clares. Ask if they could take the girls in. Today. See if you can talk to Sister Clement herself, she that was the Podesta's sister, Sophia. Lady Rosa is going to become a novice after all and little Livia is such a delight, she would cause the Sisters nothing but joy. Go now, now. I shall take this... Brother to the kitchens, we have minestrone still hot. He can sit by the fire and tell me his story if he dares. Go, Horto!'

The door swung and slammed, sending splashes of rain onto both cloak and skirt. Eyes still firmly on the floor, the Dominican had scarcely moved.

'Well now, Brother. You are welcome here. We are a quiet and Christian house...' she paused at the sound of laughter and shouting from along the corridor, 'and you will be treated as though you were St Paul himself, shipwrecked far from home and needing comfort.'

There might have been a little nod. She softened a little. 'Do you have a name, Father? I must needs write to the Podesta to let him know he has a guest in his house.'

The monk cleared his throat, rough and ragged but trying to be polite. 'Lorenzo, Fra Lorenzo *Ordo Praedicatorum.*'

'Well, I'm sure I have no idea what that means. Is that your family name?'

He was clearly confused and then astounded that anyone could not know. 'I am an ordained brother of the Order of Preachers. We follow the Rule of Saint Dominic.'

'Ah. Now that is different from the ones in grey, is it not?'

'In grey?' Then he looked down at the dark brown, almost black of his own cappa. 'Oh. Yes, I suppose . . . the Greyfriars, the Order of Saint Francis.'

'And the ones in black?'

'Ah, yes, the Benedictines. Their abbey is next to the great Basilica of San Zeno.'

'Oh, I know them, Brother, they're not hesitant in coming forward when they want something. And I am sure the Bishop is a very learned man but if I was that tall, I would not look down my long nose quite so.'

He looked at her quite horrified that a woman could dare talk so disparagingly of such a great prelate. But she was smiling kindly.

'So we have established your name, Brother Lorenzo Dominican. I am Celestina, wife to the Steward who is Paulo. He is with the Podesta in Milan. We have a smaller household here now my lord has gone but we shall feed you well and make you comfortable.'

'Thank you. I . . . ah . . . I do not eat very much.'

She laughed although he did not understand why. And then he was beside a big fire, on a warm wooden bench next to a couple of young potboys with gaping eyes and a steaming bowl of vegetable soup in his hands.

---------- ∞∞∞ ----------

Celestina watched him from the door. It was as if a man had dropped out of the sky and landed in a place of fairies and trolls. Never had she seen someone quite so confused at the prattling talk of young Musa and his little friend whose name she could never remember but who seemed to spend more time in her kitchen than ever she had given him permission for. The monk was hugging his bowl of minestrone as if it were protection against the two small boys and yet as she watched she saw him hesitantly smile and answer one of their incessant questions, wagging his finger at the one who had got the answer wrong. Oh dear, now they were demanding to see the full of his tonsure . . . well, they meant no harm. Her mind turned to the problem of the girls. Adela was coping as best she could with the abuse. Twice she had escaped from the bastard's clutches but twice more she had had to succumb. The Podesta would have put a stop to it, Pope's bastard or no, but his lordship was one hundred miles away at least and for all Adela might cry, he might as well be in China. The best Adela could hope for was that the young goat would leave her a fat purse and a thin belly. The vice versa would be a disaster.

Rain had set in now, dancing down and then up on the stone pavements outside the slitted windows, thudding in rhythm upon the roof of the kitchen which led out into the small potager garden fenced off from the huge central square. Celestina set herself to cleaning some silverware in the hall that led from the main staircases to the back rooms and kitchen. Here she could see the upper landing, the Side Door and the chambers where the Duke of Gandia was eating. If he and his fellows were grieving for their murdered companion, they were not showing it. *Come Horto, come*, she urged the boy to hurry. If she could hear from the Poor Clares now, then she could help the girls pack and they could be gone by the time Gandia finished his second bottle. She could go upstairs now and warn the girls to pack quickly but then she might miss Horto's return or fail to keep Gandia where he was. Almost running, she bustled through the kitchen, ruffling young Musa's head as she passed, made her way carefully down into the cellars and looked up and down the shelves filled with barrels and caskets. This was her husband's domain but she hadn't been married to the Chief Steward twenty-two years for nothing. There, that one. Sending a quick apology to Paulo and to the Podesta but feeling sure that the Podesta at least would understand, she took the dark and dusty wooden barrel, small but heavy, in both hands, and made her way even more carefully back up the steps.

'A Rioja? From the Alta?' Gandia looked at the small oak casket with a specialised and appreciative eye. He turned the wooden barrel towards the light, then stood and walked to the high window against which the rain was happily knocking. 'How came you by a barrel like this, Mistress? I have never seen one so small and well-sealed. And the mark upon the wax?'

Celestina kept her eyes down. 'The good Lord Podesta went on pilgrimage in his youth, he walked el Camino de Santiago and became friendly with a bodega collective in Calahorra. They have been sending him the finest of their wines ever since. This, I think, is one of the best. I know the Podesta could think of no greater recipient than a Papal Gonfalonier. He knows that you will no doubt have left this city before his return and so instructed me to make of it a gift. My lord.'

Gandia was still at the window. His pale eyes slowly looked up from the barrel with its red waxen seal and found hers. Resisting the urge to swallow, she looked down at her feet. 'A fine gift. Mistress Celestina.'

'My lord.'

The huge Spaniard, she thought his name was Matteo, knocked back the full cup of whatever he was already drinking and held it aloft. Gandia exhaled in derision.

'This is far too good for you, Matteo of the Midden. See, Carlo does not even bother to ask, he knows he cannot tell a Quintilian Rioja from a bowl of cat's piss. Mistress, get another casket, a bigger one for my two friends but nothing that would trouble your Podesta too acutely by its absence.'

'My lord.'

'Carlo, go and help her carry it up.'

When she had gone, the Duke of Gandia took out the small knife from his inner pocket and gently, reverently slid it deep and sharp across the seal. The heady burst of spice and honey rushed up to greet the air, he swilled it a little to dispel the oils, then breathed in long and deep.

'Good one, my lord?'

'You have no idea, Matteo, no idea. Pass me that clean glass, be careful, you have no idea how much that one you dropped yesterday was worth. Any glass in this house was made in Venezia, you ignorant mountain, you will never earn enough in your lifetime to buy a single decanter.'

Matteo grinned, throwing the handblown goblet over eight feet where it was deftly caught in Gandia's right hand as he balanced the oak barrel in the left.

'*Podex perfectus es*!' Gandia out the glass down carefully and dripped a very steady stream of crimson liquid into it. They sat back down as the Duke carefully savoured the Rioja and Matteo helped himself to a handful of black olives.

'So. So. What shall we do with our Cousin the Monk then? Sadly, we cannot simply throw him into the Adige, my papal father would be unhappy at the loss of Borgia blood even though this poor creature is unlikely to be passing any of it on. I think they sheared his cajones clean away when they tonsured his head. I think we need to take him back to Rome with us and the Family can decide what to do with him. We have another problem though.'

Matteo waited. He was not there to contribute, simply to act. It was a simple relationship, brutally simple but it suited them both. And now that Raf was gone, Matteo was the strongest and heaviest fighter the Duke had. Carlo and Vincenzo were quick but they did not have the weight.

'Yes. I have heard mention – how stupid Bishops are to not close their own doors properly – of a certain Fra Johannes, a *Hermano Juan*. Our foolish Cousin Lorenzo has apparently been passing messages to this Johannes. I am certain they are unimportant and fatuous, no doubt pederast monks in lust with novices or fucking local girls. But I have been in this northern *monton de mierda* for too long now, I need to get back to Rome. Christ Himself knows what my brother, Cesare, has been doing in my absence and my wife will have the child within the month. I need to be at home to make sure she delivers a live one. But this Brother Johannes, we cannot take two bloody Dominican monks with us. And this second one might not be as tractable as my dear cousin. No. He needs to be erased from the tabula. Today.'

---------- ∞∞∞ ----------

An extremely rare miniature casket of Calahorra Rioja later, the monk was safely locked into a guest room on the first floor landing and Juan Borgia was standing outside the second door further along, his smooth white fingers running themselves up and down the polished planks. Vague, muffled voices could be heard from the room within. A low soft timbre, a higher quicker one, it was like a little piece of music. Yet again, he found himself getting warm and hard. Leaning close until his nose, forehead, lips were pressed against the wood, he let out his tongue, slowly, hot breath onto the oak, he licked up, down and up again. The symphony of their voices within had stopped. She knew he was there. He was a damned cat on his feet but she knew. Good. They were starting to establish a bond. He liked that.

Taking one last taste of the door, he stepped back and walked back up the landing to the first room. Matteo was already towering over the old man who looked feebler and more helpless than ever. How old Uncle Alfonso had sired such a miserable creature, the good Lord only knew. Gandia sat down and bade the monk to do likewise on the single wooden bed.

'So. Cousin. We are tomorrow to ride for Rome to introduce you to my most beloved father, Alexander VI of that name. He no doubt will find some use for you.'

The growing horror was so apparent even Juan Borgia, used to inspiring horror, stopped short. 'What is it? Speak, you old fool.'

'I … I … thought … my lord, I have been found innocent of all wrongdoing. I thought I should be returned to the Abbey, Santa Anastasia. I am herbalist there.'

'I am sure they can find some other half-educated mud-scratcher to supply the town with aphrodisiacs. No, if you stay here the good Lord *Quaesemper* will find some other reason to harass and accuse you and then I shall be sent back here. I do not want to come back here. Matteo does not want to come back here. No one who was not *loco* would want to come back here. I have been here four days and that has already been too long for one lifetime. But before we go, we need to speak to a certain Brother Johannes. I understand from the Bishop that you have dealings with this man and that he leaves the abbey often.'

There was the distinct smell of threat and fear in the air now. Brother Lorenzo swallowed. 'I hardly know Brother John. That is, we are brothers together of course but he works in the library ...'

'But you pass messages to him. A message over the summer which went astray causing, I think, great distress and misunderstanding and led to at least one of the killings.'

'It was not ... he is a somewhat foolish man perhaps; he does not always listen to what is being asked. Sometimes he is sent to pick up a parcel from the farms outside of the city walls, they grow herbs in greater quantities than I can and he takes a whole day to travel just a mile or so and when he returns very often he will have chamomile when I asked for feverfew, most unfortunate. And in the matter of the letter, yes, he was delayed which was not his fault but he did not think to tell me. He does not always think ...'

The thin wavery voice trailed away. Gandia was staring hard.

'And the other letters? Why should the Englishman be asking you about letters sent via this Fra Johannes? What deeper plot does he think is hiding in this pissmire of a town?'

The Dominican shook his head, eyes flicking from Gandia to his smirking companion back to Gandia. 'I do not know. He seemed concerned about Brother John's travels to Berghof but I do not know why, they are journeys for manuscripts and books to augment our library stock, nothing more.'

'And still . . . ' Borgia pursed up his lips. 'I can spare no more time for this nonsense. I have done my duty, I have secured your exoneration and release and I needs must return home. My dear wife Maria is having our child, did you know? My Papal Father will no doubt want to reward me for making him a grandsire. The fat sow is now so big that the physics tell me it is twins! Twins! Like Romulus and Remus themselves. And born in Rome. It cannot be anything other than a good auger for the Family. So I must be there to ensure nothing unfortunate happens. My brother Cesare is the jealous sort. And we all fight for our father's love. I wonder how they will react to yet another Borgia living in the Vatican? Don't look so worried, dear Coz! I am sure they will welcome yet more competition for my father's love with open arms! Now,' he leaned forward, 'I do not wish to trouble the Abbot or your boring Bishop. How would we find this Brother Johannes – what is today, Monday, of course – how would we find him?'

It was not a fair contest of wills and the old man soon capitulated. The day after *dies ires*, the good brother was always entrusted between the hours of Sext and None to go to the apothecary close to the southern gate and refresh the abbey stocks of inks, powders, grits and pumice. In truth, he could have bought a month's supply and left the abbey only then but Brother John was a sociable, lazy man completely unsuited in Brother Lorenzo's mind to the monastic life but he was some kind of cousin to the abbot and so his jaunts and journeys were tolerated.

Matteo disappeared from the room which seemed to grow larger and lighter in his absence. Gandia got to his feet.

'We ride at first light, or at least by midday. Do you ride? Of course you don't. Well, you'll have to sit as best you can and we'll tie your mount to Carlo's, I cannot waste time with a carriage or litter. We shall find you a donkey! An ass for an ass! Not Easter for a good few months sadly but even so . . . Stay in this room. Go nowhere.'

On the landing outside the closed doors, he wondered if it was too early. She was definitely in there but her inconvenient sister was too and although he could order her out, lock her away somewhere, it would be noisy and cause too much attention. He was almost certain that if he actually wanted to he could take the girl there and then in the main piazza and the townspeople would let him but you never knew with the northerners. Their respect and fear for the Papal Father's authority was assuredly not what it once had been, not now they had thrown their collective lot in with the damned Emperor.

Down at the foot of the grand staircase Celestina looked up and cursed under her breath. Too late. Somehow, although she kept her face neutral and expressionless, somehow she felt he knew what she was trying to do, that he was looming down triumphant, some beautiful Lucifer laughing down on pitiful humanity.

'More excellent Rioja, Mistress? You will have your Podesta returning to an empty cellar. But–how did you put it?–*the Podesta could think of no greater recipient than a Papal Gonfalonier*? I am sure those were your exact words, Mistress. But you are right that we will be gone in the morning, at midday at the latest. I will need another horse, tell your steward to trade Raf's mount for a more gentle beast, a donkey or even better a mule. But a young one that can keep some pace. With the money made, tell him to buy a suitable saddle and some panniers, fill them with food for our journey.'

'My Lord Duke.'

'There should be a few ducats left. It's a good horse.' From far above her on the landing, Celestina could see him yawn, flashing down fine white teeth. 'Take a couple for yourself. And for–what is her name, the girl who brings my meals?'

'Adela, my Lord Duke.'

'Give a couple to Adela. If there's a bastard in her belly, do whatever she wants if it's a girl. But if it's a boy, tell her to send him to me when he's a lad. I can find a place for him in my familia.'

'My Lord Duke.'

His elbows were now upon the balustrade, he was leaning down, eye to eye. Staring at her, long and hard.

When she was very young, Celestina had often camped out in the forests of Cascare della Molina, helping her father and two brothers bring down game and snare rabbits in the shadow of the Pale Mountains. Her brothers were too close in age, just ten months apart, they were twins in all but name but possessed opposing temperaments, the one always too loud and fractious for their father's peace, the other too timid and obedient for his respect. Celestina the older by two years had always been the bridge without whom the little family fell apart. And besides, she could snare, catch, kill, skin and joint any beast smaller than a pig better than any man. She had been just ten years that summer, her brothers sat either side, her father gone away for the night, checking his snares. They had eaten, the fire was losing its flame, her brothers had stopped pushing and complaining at her and were becoming drowsy. It was as dark as only God's land beyond Man could be. She did not remember whether there was a moon, perhaps there had been a hopeful burgeoning sliver, nothing more. Behind them a high granite escarpment against which they leaned their tired backs. Ahead and to both sides, deep, wild bushes, taller trees looming up in the shadows, even taller thicker ones behind, then an impenetrable black. One brother leaned against her heavily and began to twitch, the other sank down to the side, she used one hand to cover him as best she could with the edges of the blanket they shared. There was no way to measure time. The gentle snoring of the younger boy might have served to set a pace and length but she was so immune to the sound that she could not hear it. So she was not sure, was never sure, how long she had sat and stared into the dark, wondering how soon she could gently ease the older brother to the ground without waking him, it might have been a few heartbeats, it might have been half the night. She became aware of the wolves in slow, creeping stages.

By the time each sense had finally caught up to its other, when she could taste her fear, hear their breaths, feel the skin crawling upon her arm, smell their rancid teeth and finally admit to herself that she was staring straight at half a dozen pairs of hard-as-gimlet eyes, her body had already decided to stiffen. A calm, quiet decision was then agreed between her mind and body; sit as still as the granite wall and stare back like the – what did her papa say about Carraresi of Padua? – the meanest son of a whore that ever lived. It was a fervent faith she never felt later for any god or saint, this faith that if she stared back at the wolf right in the centre of the hidden pack, then they would not attack. As the night skies drifted slow and cruel over her head, as every muscle in her neck, shoulders, back thighs screamed out in agony, as her eyes grew dry, as she took only the tiniest of blinks. She had won. Her brothers had slept miraculously still and her eyes had held. Red, raw, weeping, still she had held the stare of the beast who in its desperate hunger would have torn them apart. And as the slightest glow of not-quite-black began to appear over towards the east, she had taken an agonizing lightning-quick blink and when she reconnected, they had gone.

She never told her brothers or father – what would have been the point? The wolves went away harmless, didn't they? But for the rest of her life, Celestina would occasionally awake in the night with her eyes screaming out in rough, sore, dry pain, her shoulders aching, her neck stiff.

As she stared back up at the bastard Duke of Gandia, she felt the urge to empty her bladder. She dropped her eyes.

She knew at that moment what he was going to do. That some time soon – this hour, this night, this dawn but soon – he would demand she open up the door of the girls' chamber – or he would break it down with those perfectly honed legs – and he would discard little Livia into the corridor, slam the door and do what he wished with Rosa. And the knowledge he could see, plain on the creeping blush of her cheeks and forehead, was only serving to amuse him more.

---------- ∞∞∞ ----------

One last thing, this wet miserable Monday, we need to resume our flight as the falcon and use our newly-divine vision to focus down into the blurred streets to find the large, inelegant bulk of Matteo. He is hunting down the fat jovial scent of Fra Johannes so that he can either push him into the river and hold down that that round, tonsured head or slip a quick stiletto blade into his wobbling flesh. Matteo prefers to crush his victims with his not- inconsiderable weight – we have seen that already with the unfortunate bridge-boy – but such torture, although lacking all finesse and contemplation, necessitates time. And time is not something the young Duke has given Matteo. No, they must be gone at dawn, with one Dominican monk not two and this second one must not see another daybreak.

Perhaps we should educate ourselves a little about this tragic brother Dominican, we are after all about to see him die. But we need to get back to John Oldcastle who is pacing and fuming at the abrupt loss of Brother Lorenzo, to the Bishop who has already sent a fast horse to the Podesta in Milan and to poor Rosa who is sitting on her bed as her sister clumsily sews a pretty sample, waiting for the monster she knows is coming. And Lorenzo Borgia (bastard) has already told us all we need to know. That this Johannes is a cousin to the Abbot without the true disposition suitable to the monastic life of sacrifice. He is good at obedience – he is too stupid to relish making his own decisions – but not much good at celibacy and poverty. So now we watch as he shuffles along the narrow alleys and streets with unbrotherly haste. It is not excitement at viewing paints and pigments and boarhair brushes exercising his delight but the thought of the buxom merchant's wife who will serve him in more ways than one in the little room behind the counter. Alas, he will not feel that wet, impudent tongue ever again. A huge, bearish *teppista* is on his heels, blocking out the little light the rain is allowing into the alleyway behind the apothecary. Johannes is too caught up in his own expectant lust to notice the shadow behind him loom larger. The light disappears, the fat monk half turns, he notices the man, the smile, the blade and the sharp pain in his chest all at the same time. As Italian city-states go, it is not a bad death. Certainly the bridge-boy suffered more. And our not-much-lamented Raf Salamanca – well, suffice to say he suffered most of all. But all of this might not have been much consolation to Fra Johannes *Ordo Praedicatorum* who was expecting a long life and a comfortable death. But very few of us are going to get what we want in this little story.

CHAPTER EIGHTEEN

In which John Oldcastle (bastard, Lollard) goes in fury to confront the Duke of Gandia (ex-bastard, Papal Captain) but instead finds himself swept away by an inconvenient passion

'I have asked Sister Clement – Sophia that was – to take you in as soon as possible and she has agreed.'

'And Livia?'

'Yes, of course.'

'But . . . he is still here? In the house?'

Celestina took the young woman's hand. She expected it to be trembling as a good noblewoman's should at the thought of what they both envisaged but it was calm, calm and cool and steady. Good, thought Celestina, she is going to need her wits about her.

'So we can go now?' The girl with the darkest chestnut eyes had not even raised them yet. Her luscious glowing hair was severely tied back, uncombed, greasy even and her fingernails were ragged. Clever girl. Celestina squeezed the cool hand.

'It is not quite that simple, Lady Rosa. The Duke . . . he is still downstairs, drinking. I think he and the other one, the thin mean-looking one, are waiting for the big fellow to return. He was sent on some errand. They are . . . drinking very heavily. And playing some kind of a game. The side stairs at the end of this landing, the one the girls use, we could take you both that way but it twists down into the potager garden and the castle courtyard. And the courtyard is overlooked by the Podesta's study. If we could wait until it is a little darker, I can find an excuse to close the study curtains.'

'I heard shouting earlier, people running in the streets outside...'

Celestina shook her head. 'Horto says there's been a killing, a stabbing, I don't know. Only a day since they found the Duke's man dead and then all those killings in the summer... Oh Lord, I'm sorry, my dear, I clean forgot. They were your friends, weren't they? And the little girl was your cousin?'

'Yes. She was.' The young man's name hung in burning letters between them, too hot, too painful for either to touch for hadn't Celstina known him too, hadn't the Podesta's wife fallen to the very hearthstone in a faint when she heard? His name hung bright and beautiful, just as he had been so very bright, so very beautiful. Rosa ran her hand to tame a wild curl escaping from Livia's scrappy chignon. 'I knew them all. Every one of them. Since I was a child. And now there's just me and Livia.'

'Well, you'll soon have a new family, you'll have a dozen sisters and a mother too. And Livia will be so well loved here. Five years now since Sophia left to become Sister Clement and this house has been so quiet, too quiet. The Lady Podesta is still young and the Podesta not yet so old, they will be good to her and she will sing so loudly! You will hear her in your little cell, every morning her sweet little voice will wake you up.'

'I pray it is so.'

'Well then.' There seemed nothing else to say, 'Well then.'

It took no time at all to pack their few possessions, two trunks to be sent on after them, a bag each with a change of linens and one extra shift for Livia. Some basic toiletries – an earscoop, some salvia for under her arms, her last piece of precious olive oil soap, a tight pack of sanitary rags – but they seemed such a small sorry pile compared to what she had enjoyed at home. Would she be allowed salvia as a Poor Clare or must her armpits smell of dirty hairs and sweat? Did Poor Clares have their monthly cycles or did God stop the bleeding when they took their vows? He must surely...she could hardly imagine Saint Anastasia having to fold laundered rags into her underclothes every month. And what about her teeth, she could not bear it when her teeth got fuzzy and her tongue sprung its coat of white fur. She had the salvia but she had run out of salt crystals. Did nuns rub their teeth? Was toothache and stinking breath a sign of godliness? She tried to remember Sister Clement. The young woman had emitted no unpleasant smell as far as she could remember, her teeth all seemed to be present, Rosa could remember no gaping black holes but all the same...

'Mistress Celestina, do you think we could have...buy from you some salt crystals? For Livia's teeth. I have salvia but no salt.'

'I have some paste mixed up from the garden, mint, salvia and a little salt, you can have a pot, I have more. I'll go and get it now. You are right to be thinking of such things, she is still your sister right up until you take your vows.'

As she made her way quickly down the main stairs – a luxury she would have to curtail once the Podesta was back – Celestina could hear sounds of bad temper. To her growing dismay, she recognized Horto's high voice – pathetic and defensive – trying to find its way between the strong southern accents, the loud privileged tones of Spain and Rome. Almost slipping on the flagstones, she made her way to stand outside the study door which was wide open.

Horto had brought back the money from trading Raf Salamanca's horse but clearly the Spaniards felt he had been cheated in some way or was trying to make fools of them. He was attempting to explain that horse prices had fallen since the French marched through and no one wished to be on the roads, that the saddlemakers got their leather from Mordano and so since the massacre those prices were also high...

A careless slap or two and Horto was being pushed rudely past her and out of the Porta Secundi by the kitchens. It seemed that all three Spaniards and whatever the quiet one was, were going to encourage the unfortunate horsetrader to reconsider his prices in the light of new information. He clearly had not believed an idiot like Horto when he explained that the customer was ducal, no *papal* and had been treated and cheated like a babe. Celestina waited for a count of fifty. In the kitchens, there was some cursing, the sound of a crash and water spilling, a girl crying out. And so it was another ten minutes before she came out again to the foot of the staircase. Rosa and Livia were, she could see, at their door, peering anxiously down over the balustrade.

'One minute! Stay up there! We'll take the back stairs down into the courtyard.'

She was not going to entrust this to one of her girls but good Lord knew what panic they would fall into if they thought her missing.

'Adela! Francesca! Musa, sit down for the love of God. All of you, leave that alone, just put it down, no, just for a moment, it won't boil over, just push it to the side a little, now listen. Horto is gone for I do not know how long but he will be back with the young Duke. I am going on an errand to ... to ... the House of Silks over by Porta Palio ...' Somewhere far to the west, somewhere very much away from the little house of the Poor Clares, tucked into the eastern bend of the river's loop. 'I should not be later than the bells of Vespers. Make sure the bread is rising under the cloth, Francesca, when it is so high separate into small rounds the size of your fist like so. Musa, scrub those pans and you can tell your little friend to take the rest of the minestrone with him but he must bring back the bowl. Right. Right.'

But already she had tarried too long. If she had not gone to the kitchen, had not worried about Francesca and the bread, had not offered her customary harsh generosity to the lad with no name ... there was a knocking, an authoritative knocking on the side door.

'Damnation,' she cursed under her breath, breaking one of the most stringent house rules. Normally it was not her place to open any door but the kitchen stable gate to the potager garden. But with half the men away and Horto off the Lord knew where with the Devil Himself…

The Porta Prima was the great arched double door with iron studs and the feel of a real castle, rather than just a stumpy tower. It was very rarely used and needed three men to push it wide. Further towards the castle wall, away from the tower was the smaller entrance used by the Podesta, the Porta Secunda, eight feet high and solid, but she was a strong woman and it was well greased and oft used. Outside in the rain, half hidden by the early onset of evening was a man in a long cloak. There was something odd about his clothes beneath but she couldn't quite work out what. His skin was very pale but his smile was a good and honest one although there was something about the eyes that made her realise that he was angry.

'I am sorry, sir but we are not receiving guests or visitors. The Podesta is away. All matters of importance must go to the Bishop.'

'I have just come from the Bishop, good lady,' a thick accent, although his northern dialect was not bad. The inflection on 'lady' was very Lombardi, most gave it the Roma lilt and couldn't hear the difference. 'He would have come with me but the weather…he did not want to walk and I did not want to wait.' Again that decent honest smile but his eyes darted over her head to the hall and stairs beyond. She was confused.

'There is no one here, my lord, to deal with any enquiry. We are simply a skeleton household, the clerks have either gone to Milan or are lodging at the palatum with the Bishop.'

'But you have guests?' His impatience was almost tangible; he was edging himself closer towards the threshold. Damn but he did not sound Spanish. Or from Lazio either. She racked her memory for his accent. He had given a little half bow. Greyish temples and lines around the eyes but not old. A strong nose and firm mouth, this was a man of some position but what was that accent . . . ?

'Lady . . . Mistress . . . I am a stranger in this city, I have come a long way on a mission for a noble lord of this town. It is raining and although as a Londoner I am well used to rain much heavier and colder than this, still it would be good to get out of it.'

She was a good judge of character; this man was no wolf. Stepping aside slightly, she gave a little curtsey as he passed within and returned a bow.

'Thank you, Mistress. By the saints, this has set in!' He shook his cloak a little, one of the older hounds not gone running to Milan sloped out from some warm corner and sniffed approvingly at the stranger's shoes. He ruffled the dog's ears. She was appeased a little. Ajax was grey around the gizzles now and half blinded by cataracts but he was an even better judge of men than she. For four days she had had to keep him well away from Juan Borgia; he bared his gums and rose his hackles every time the evil bastard walked by. One growl and there would have been a slit throat, a dead dog and puddle of blood for her to clean up. And despite the old boy's age and occasional incontinence, he was a dear old fellow.

The Londoner stamped his feet sending droplets everywhere.

'Thank you again. This is a hard night coming, not one to be abroad alone. You have heard the news? A murder in the alleyways down by the eastern bend of the river. A monk, would you believe? The devil himself is walking these streets if a tonsured man of vows cannot walk his way without facing a blade in the heart.'

Biting at her lip, she drew in her breath. 'I did not know, sir. I did not know it was a monk.' A coincidence of course, that she herself had a monk resting in one of the guest rooms of this very house, a man who had no business whatsoever to be anywhere but Santa Anastasia's, a coincidence of course but even so . . .

'Mistress. My name is John Oldcastle and as I say I am from London. I am a lawyer, an advocate. I am here to investigate – with the Bishop – the tragic events of this summer past. I am here to talk to your house guest.'

'So you are here to see Lady Rosa? I am not sure what more she knows. She told her story to the Podesta when the last two died.'

'Rosa? Ah, no. No I have not heard this name.'

'Oh,' Celestina was furious with herself. 'I am sorry, my lord. No, she is not important to your enquiry, she told all she knew to the Podesta as I say and he has not questioned her since. It is Brother Lorenzo you have come to see.'

The Englishman's eyes opened up. Ajax whimpered excitedly.

'Brother Lorenzo is here? Then I am not too late. And the . . . the Duke of Gandia, I trust he is here too then? The Bishop told me that this is where he was staying. I have many words, not all of them kind or courteous, to share with the great and illustrious Duke of Gandia.' She had been right; he was bristling with a simmering fury but controlling it well. 'So Mistress, if you could direct me to firstly the Duke and then to the Brother Dominican, I can discharge my duty for this night at least and ensure no further miscarriages of justice.'

'I am sure that is well and good but I am going to disappoint you both times over, Mr Oldcastle.'

'You insist that I return with the Lord Bishop?'

'Return with the Bishop, the King of England and the Trojan Horse if you wish, my lord, but you'll still find the Duke at the horsetraders beyond the wall and the Brother Dominican locked in his room.' She surprised herself at the temerity in her voice – how her husband would scold her if he heard! And to a guest! – but she was aware, more than anything now, of the two girls on the landing and of how short a journey it was to the horsetraders just beyond the wall. The Englishman frowned.

'You have locked the monk in his room? I approve, good lady, he is not to be trusted. He may appear benign and innocent from his appearance but I am yet to be convinced that beneath the exterior he is not a conspirator of some significance. So you have done well by . . .'

She gave him a gentle push towards the stairs. 'Sir, I run the household, I oversee the cooking of meals, I train the kitchen staff, I oversee the cleaning and the supplies, I write lists and count coppers and chase out mice, what I do not do is lock Dominican monks in my guest rooms. The Duke of Gandia locked him before he left and before you ask, he took the key with him. And there is a strong lock on the window which is very high and nothing heavy within the room with which a man might break down a door. And again, before you ask, if you want my opinion, the poor old thing has not the spirit to squash a spider let alone break down a door.'

By this time, they were at the top of the stairs and she marching him around to the right, stopping outside the first door. Oldcastle had a vague impression that the second door further along had just swung shut.

The steward's wife had her arms folded over her ample chest. She reminded Oldcastle very much of his wife – or whatever Eliza was – back in Spitalfields. And so in consequence, he warmed to her; to her courage, to her temper, to her exasperation at the foolishness of men, to her spirit.

'Here, Mr Oldcastle, is your monk. If you wish to speak to him, you will have to do so through three fingers of wood. Unless you wish to wait until the Duke of Gandia returns?'

'I do not think that I do.'

'No, I should imagine not. Most people of sense would be of the same mind. Now speak to the poor brother if you will. I have an errand to run and am running late for it so if you would give me leave . . . ?'

'Of course, of course,' he watched her broad back as she made her way along to the second door. Curious, he stood still as it opened. A young woman in an odd, ugly dress, then suddenly as if from nowhere a child with wild honey-blond hair appearing at her side, trying to smother a smile and copy the serious faces of the other two. A rushed conversation, low, strained, the little one looking up from one to the other like an excited marmoset, a raggedy doll tucked into her elbow. Suddenly, the young woman's eyes met his. Just a lightning flash, a link soon severed, a flash of something he knew not what. Then he remembered the name. Rosa. Lord Cyprian had mentioned her. She had played some periphery role in the young people's discords, had not acted a major part, had not a perceivable hand in the deaths. But perhaps...

The door shut, all three were gone. He could hear a hurried conservation, urgent voices, the sound of footsteps. Turning back to his own, he rapped sharply, one, two three. And again. Harder. A distinct shuffle getting closer, a slightly tremulous voice.

'Yes? My Lord Duke?'

'No, Brother Lorenzo, this is John Oldcastle. We were talking just this afternoon, a few hours ago in the Bishop's palatum with His Grace the Bishop. Before you were so rudely exited from that company.'

'Oh. Yes. The Englishman.'

'So, Brother Lorenzo...' He knows how important it is to be calm. He has seen inexperienced advocates and notaries lose cases because they could not control their emotions. Coming here on the crest of such an anger was not wise, it was anything but wise. And hearing of the murder of Brother Johannes, his only other witness, hearing of what that bastard had done to secure the release of this pathetic little monk...why had he come here, straight on hearing of such a thing? The Bishop had urged him to stay, to share a meal, to discuss their options but he had raced out into the wet night. To do what exactly? Oldcastle had no idea. All he knew was that he was more angry than he could ever remember being. It was as if a great heavy tide of acrid bile was pushing up from his stomach, up to his gullet, to sting the back of his throat and coat his teeth. He tried to keep his voice low and measured.

'You think you can escape to Rome and leave your part in this half-hidden? You think it is the Christian path to avoid the light of honest exposition, to bury truth in shadows? *Veritas liberabit vos*, Brother, do you no longer believe that truth shall make you free? What will you say when you meet our Maker at the Throne of Judgement, when the Blessed Christ divides us into sheep and goats? Will you say that your part in six deaths was of no import to the state of your soul?'

The enforced calm was dissipating, bursting like bubbles in salt. He was thumping on the door now, aware that this no doubt rendered his words inaudible but the frustration that had been simmering, brewing, rising since Gandia had snatched this man from under his nose, since he had heard of the new stabbing...

'Are you a hypocrite, Brother Lorenzo? Is your Borgia blood finally running true? You men under vows are not the only ones to know your scriptures. Listen to Matthew, yes and in Italian, my friend, not Latin, will your ears burn away to hear the Word of God in your own vernacular tongue? *'Woe unto you, scribes and Pharisees, hypocrites! For you are like unto whitened sepulchers, which indeed appear beautiful outward but are, within, full of dead men's bones and of all uncleanliness. Even so, you also outwardly appear righteous unto men, but within, you are full of hypocrisy and iniquity.'*

He took another breath, well aware that he was being foolish, shouting at a door. 'You have an innocent façade, Brother, the good housekeeper here tells me you have not the nerve nor inclination to squash a spider. What would she think if I told her the truth? That you connived with Brother Johannes and parties as yet unknown to send seditious letters to Berghof, to incite Scaglieri insurrection here in this peaceful city-state, that you were the key to treason which would have left the Podesta of this very house dead and hanging from a scaffold.'

He could sense at his right that the door had opened again and the housekeeper standing very still, listening. He knew he was speaking out of turn, knew that his usual taciturn reticence, always serving him so well, was draining away and he regretted its loss even as he took a breath to continue.

'You thought to escape justice by running to Rome and the so-called sanctuary of your blood family? You value your vows so lightly that you cast off your family-in-God, your Dominican brothers, to hide in the rotting, leprous arms of the Borgia Bishop of Rome? Was that the plan? That for your connivance in carrying letters encouraging sedition and riot, the *soi-disant* holy father would grant you some kind of poisonous sinecure? What are you of tomorrow, Brother Lorenzo? Are you the Bishop of Napoli? Are you Archbishop of Nimes? Cardinal? If Juan Borgia can be Duke of Gandia and Papal Gonfalonier then I am sure that I can be heir to the English throne and you the Holy Roman Emperor. Where shall we stop, Brother Lorenzo? Shall we make this good housekeeper here Empress of Byzantium? And the dog Pharaoh of the Sands?'

There was a firm but gentle hand on his own, stopping the incessant knocking. Celestina shook her head. He had not even sensed her coming so close. The young woman was at the door again. He daren't look, she was a distraction . . . but those eyes . . . .

'Mr Oldcastle, I doubt the Brother can hear you. Although it is certain that my old father now in Venezia can. And perhaps even my grandfather on the Plutonian shore.'

Nodding, he forced himself calm. He was being a fool, a childish fool but the deep, primeval instinct to hurt Juan Borgia long and hard was something he had carried with him three years now.

A brief memory, sometimes this was the one to flash in front of him, always at the worst of times. His little sister, scarcely sixteen, pushing him away, clutching at herself, blood on the sheets of the cheap Roman guesthouse. Shaking his head, he waited three heartbeats. He tried again.

'Brother Lorenzo, Saint Matthew tells us of dead men's bones, the hypocrites who stand before righteousness but carry pestilential lies in their bellies hoping that the light of truth cannot penetrate so deep. You know–Lord help me, you know better than me–when you appear for Judgement, our Blessed Lord will want not just truth but contrition. And that contrition must start here on earth. Now, I . . . ' he stopped, wondering what in Hell's fires he was saying but unable to stop, 'I do not believe in purgatory, Brother Lorenzo, my grandsire was burned for denying it, I believe that when we die we pass immediately to Heaven or Hell and there is nothing in the power of a priest or a chantry prayer than can make a difference to my soul's eternal fate which in truth was decided by God at Creation.'

Could he vaguely make out an '*angelis sanctis*' as the old man on the other side clearly genuflected in horror? No doubt.

'No, Brother, I do not believe in Purgatory and chantry prayers and the bones of saints curing scrofula and migraine . . . '

'*Sancte Michael Archangele, defende nos in proelio; contra nequitiam et insidias diaboli esto praesidium . . .* '

'It is all a nonsense. And if the people could but read the Scriptures in their own tongue, then they too would see that there are no popes, no bishops, no sacraments, no pig bones masquerading as the tibia of Saint Catherine . . . '

'*Princeps militiae caelestis, Satanam aliosque spiritus malignos, qui ad perditionem animarum pervagantur in mundo,divina virtute, in infernum detrude . . .* '

'I do not believe that a sinful priest can change bread and wine into the body and blood of Christ . . . '

'Mr Oldcastle, please! Keep down your voice!' the housekeeper shook his shoulder. She could see that he was nearly in tears. The young woman called Rosa came and stood at her side, both looking worriedly down the staircase.

'I do not believe in such things, Brother Lorenzo. But I know that you do.' He paused for breath. 'I know that you do. And you must know that if you wish to lessen your time in the grey misery of Purgatory, then your contrition must start in this life. Admit your part in this sedition. Make full and free confession to the Bishop or Abbot. Full and free confession.'

A low but surprisingly strong voice came from the other side of the door.

'I have already made full and free confession of my sins. I was absolved. *Te ego absolvo*. He said it, he said the words.'

The Englishman cursed under his breath. 'I know, I know, Brother. But we also live in the temporal City of Man, justice must also be seen to be done here on earth. The temporal law must also be respected just as Christ himself taught us to render what was Caesar's unto Caesar. You must make full confession outside of the seal. To the Podesta as well as the Bishop.'

There was a deep silence. The two women seemed even closer now. The housekeeper smelt of yeast and herbs, the younger woman of soap and . . . something else, something that tugged at the memory of his heart.

The monk was quiet. Then; 'I know.'

'You will confess? Make full declaration of your part in this sorry affair?'

'No. I do not know what you are talking about. I sent no letters to Berghof, I have never met the Scaglieri, I gave a letter to Fra Johannes to warn a boy not to believe rumours about the death of his beloved but that went wrong and they all died. I need punishment, Mr Oldcastle, for old sins and for more recent ones.'

Oldcastle leaned his forehead against the cool wood, both palms stretched flat either side of his head.

'That is not enough. I need you to confess outside of the seal, *extra sigillum,* that you and Johannes worked with others unknown to bring discord to this city, to encourage insurrection. I need you to admit these things and sign with your own name, your proper name . . . You know what that is.'

'You do not want me at all, Mr Oldcastle, you want him.'

The voice had not raised its volume and yet it seemed to echo. Both women looked at the Englishman expectantly. John Oldcastle swallowed.

'The name of Borgia cannot be allowed free reign, there must be checks and balances to power…'

The voice through the door was quiet but determined. 'Mr Oldcastle, you know your scriptures so you also know that we are told in Hebrews; '*Obey your leaders and submit to them, for they are keeping watch over your souls, as those who will have to give an account.*'

'Yes, yes, if those who are our leaders are indeed interested in keeping a shepherd's watch over our souls. Do you really consider Rodrigo Borgia a good shepherd of souls? You know the crimes of which he is accused. And you must surely know that this son of his… *Now the works of the flesh are evident: sexual immorality, impurity, sensuality, idolatry, sorcery, enmity, strife, jealousy, fits of anger, rivalries, dissensions, divisions, envy, drunkenness, orgies… I warn you, as I warned you before, that those who do such things will not inherit the kingdom of God.*'

Oldcastle pulled away from the door, realizing that he had been gently thudding his forehead against it.

Lorenzo Borgia sounded tired. 'It is not always the man we venerate and obey but the office. Are your kings of England always the best of men? Are they not sometimes weak, imperfect, sat upon the throne because they were the eldest but not because they were the best. The mind of God is unfathomable, his plan mysterious, our duty simply to follow not to understand and most certainly not to oppose.'

Oldcastle had a sudden vision of his grandfather burning, burning on the orders of his King, the king who was also his dear friend, the friend he had tried to overthrow for the love of the gospel. He shook it away.

'Brother. When James and John questioned Christ about who would sit either side of him in Heaven, you know – I know that you know – what he told them. '*Those who are recognized as rulers of the Heathen lord it over them; and their great men exercise authority over them. But it is not this way among you. Whoever wishes to become great among you, shall be your servant; and whoever wishes to be first among you shall be slave of all.*' Is Rodrigo Borgia a servant to mankind? Is Juan Borgia slave to all? Or slave to his most vile and base passions?'

There was a quick intake of breath from the girl who turned her head away. He felt rather than saw the older woman reach down to take her hand.

'I . . . I do not know. I am a herbalist. I cultivate the garden so that we might have simple medicines. I do not know what you want from me.'

'Admit that you used Fra Johannes to send letters to the Imperial Court. Admit that as a Borgia you used your name to encourage the exile Scaglieri to anticipate a return and that you used your influence to ferment unrest in the streets so that six prominent citizens died. Your papal cousin is renowned the world over for such unholy machinations. And his son, the Duke of Gandia, well I cannot begin to describe . . . '

There was a tugging at his sleeve, it was the housekeeper. 'Sir, you cannot use an old man like this, to besmirch the Duke and his kin. He is a beast, this young man, true enough, but an old monk telling tales no one will believe is not enough to bring him down.'

Oldcastle shook off her hand. 'Brother Lorenzo, do you know where good Brother Johannes is now?'

'Mr Oldcastle, do not tell him, not like this . . . '

'Brother Johannes? He is in the library, I should think. Or the kitchens.'

'He is back at Santa Anastasia, Brother Lorenzo, yes he is, but on the mortuary slab. The wound that pierced his heart no doubt being cleaned up with olive oil and something to make him smell less bad as the Abbot prepares to bury him. Your new friend, your beloved cousin Juan Borgia had him slaughtered just a few hours ago. Slaughtered like a pig in the street. How did the assassin know where the good brother would be? The Watch are calling it a robbery; the gold crucifix he wore around his neck has gone. But I think we know differently, do we not? Do we not, Brother Lorenzo?'

There was a muffled sound of a heavy body slowly sliding down the other side of the door, he could make out the shadow through the gap at the bottom. More prayers, this time too indistinct to perceive. Oldcastle hit his knuckles hard against the wood. Celestina took his elbow.

'This is no good, come, come quickly, we need to calm you down or the young bastard will be back with his three animals and with you in this state, they will set upon you and poor Fra Whoever-He-Is will not be the only corpse being washed down tonight.'

Too frustrated to focus, he found himself sitting on the edge of a low bed, one woman either side of him and the strange little girl, sat cross legged on the floor, and staring at him intently. Very quickly calm and no little ashamed of himself, he flexed his fingers as if by concentrating on one simple task he might all the sooner control the rest of him. The housekeeper however was now the agitated one.

'Englishman, you will stay here until you are more composed. Lady Rosa, I must check ... you know, I must check that all is clear in the study, I will draw the curtains in any case ... and I have a little bag packed in the kitchen with things you and Livia might need ... I shall bring it up with me when I return. Can I leave you alone with this ... gentleman for a short while?'

There was silence as the three of them remaining listened to her footsteps hurrying down the stone steps. The little girl – Livia – started to hum something under her breath, Oldcastle could make out a few words.

'Zephyr returns and brings fair weather, And the flowers and the herbs and his sweet family, And Procne singing and Philomela weeping, and the white springtime, and the trees.'

Big, light-brown eyes looked up at him. She repeated the verse, this time adding a different tune to the end line which he recognized would be a harmony to the first. He smiled. 'I know those words but not the tune. Very pretty. Whose words are they?'

'Petrarch, sir. But the tune is mine. I like to make up songs. And then I make up another one, which is like but not the same, and Rosa then sings it on top.'

'Clever.' His pulse was slowing now, the little vein just under the skin on his forehead slipping back down. The girl tilted her head slightly to the side.

'You are English? You speak Italian very well. Doesn't he, Rosa?'

'Thank you, Lady. I have a very close friend from Firenze, what we call Florence. We were at Oxford University together for a while. And I think I have a good ear for languages. Italian is Latin after all.'

'I speak some French. But I need to learn English because I am going to live in England.'

'Livia . . .' The older sister half-smiled, almost painfully.

'But I am. After I finish living here, I am going to England to marry Prince Arthur.'

'Livia . . .'

Oldcastle leaned forward, elbows on knees. 'Prince Arthur, Duke of Cornwall? That would be a fine match. He is the hope of our nation, the fulfilment of prophecy, the once and future king. We have suffered a lifetime of wars, family against family, red rose against white rose, he is the bringing together of old foes. Do you know the story of his parents, the good king and queen?'

'No.' She was entranced and leaned forward too, her doll drooping to the floor.

'The King his father is a Tudor, heir to the House of Lancaster. And Elizabeth the Queen is of York. York and Lancaster have fought bitterly since before I was born. Battle after battle, brother against brother, father against son, they called it the War of Cousins because every man was pitted against his own kin. Castles fell and farms burned, young men were killed upon the field and hanged from trees, even slaughtered as they sought sanctuary in holy churches and upon the steps of market crosses.'

The woman shifted awkwardly, he could feel her leg against his own. The strange and beautiful child leaned closer.

'Did you? I mean, fight, sir?'

'Livia! You must not . . .'

'Yes, little one, ten years ago now, I fought for my house. My family name is Oldcastle, Castelvecchio like this great fort, my cousins are the Brookes of Cobham, Baron Cobham is both my cousin and my liege lord.'

Her eyes – such an amber-on-brown, so much lighter than her sister's which seemed so dark to be almost black – her eyes were wide, her mouth half open. He gesticulated with his hands.

'The field was called Ambion Hill, near a small town called Bosworth. The armies were arraigned like this and like that, with this a slope and this a hill. And I was stood ***here,*** shaking and quaking like this and like that!' She laughed at his gesticulating. 'And charging down the slope came the Yorkist king, Richard Plantagenet, and up on the hill his captain Lord Stanley. And here the Lord of the North, Lord Percy the Lion Rampant. And here am I . . .'

'Shaking and quaking?'

'Shaking and quaking! And off we went, right in the middle, bish bash bosh, mud in my eyes, mud in my ears, mud up my nose. And the king in the middle of it all, waiting for his great Lords, Stanley and Percy to ride down and come to his aid.'

She gasped. 'And they did not! They betrayed their king.'

'They betrayed their king. They sat upon their fine steeds and watched, to cast their lot in with the victor of the day. And here is the king in the middle of it all. And the king sees my noble lord, Henry Tudor of House Lancaster, sees his chance, he rears his horse around and leads just a half dozen men to take on the Tudor . . .'

'He must have been brave . . .'

'Livia, hush . . .'

'He was brave, no man denies the Plantagenet that. But the half dozen are surrounded, the King falls from his horse, the end comes quickly for him.' And we need not describe the cries of despair as the doomed man looked for his horse, the many blows raining upon him, the gleeful despoiling of the naked body afterwards, the humiliation.

'And you were there? As the King fell?'

'Now you know, little lady, that I was ***here*** . . .'

'Quaking and shaking.'

'Quaking and shaking. But I was close enough to see the new king ride by with the gold of the old king's crown sat slightly askew upon his helmet.' Slightly askew and still covered with mud and gore.

'And the Queen, Prince Arthur's mother?'

'Well then, so we had a new king, the Tudor Dragon. But still men hated men, brothers brothers, cousins cousins, white rose red rose, Lancaster York. But the fallen king had had a sister – Elizabeth – a young beauty of the white rose . . .'

'And she married the new king, the red rose, and the two houses came together!'

'Indeed. The two roses became one which was both red and white. And ten years ago now . . .'

'I am ten!'

'The good queen had a son, Arthur. The once and future king.' *And let us pray that this is the prince we have long waited for, the prince who will take us away from Rome and the abuse of men such as these Borgias, who will shine light upon the dark superstitions of their nonsense, who will open the windows and allow the fresh air of common sense to rush in to our English homes. Pray that my grandsire did not burn in vain.*

'Thank you, sir. For indulging an imaginative child.' He knew her smell now, knew that it was olive oil with cedarwood and sweetpea, a summer scent. Their eyes met and it was as if he had never seen a woman, never felt passion, never made love to a woman in an English bed, never felt the sudden tightening of his stomach, the pain in his balls. He was forty and one, he was a damned bloody fool, he had a good woman at home, he could not move his thigh or his shoulder or his eye.

'Lady,' There was the sound of the housekeeper running back up the stairs. Oldcastle spoke quickly, not knowing what he was going to say before it was said but said it anyway. 'Lady Rosa. Forgive me, this is not my place, we are strangers. But I do not feel you should be here in this house. I cannot, out of the love I bear another, give you the story but believe me when I say that this young Duke is not a nobleman of chivalrous honour, no matter what his coat of arms might herald. He is a dangerous young man, a greedy and ... lustful young man. I think you must leave.'

'She is leaving. And now.' Celestina was out of breath. There was a small bag hanging from her wrist. Rosa jumped up, pulling her sister to her feet roughly as she squeaked in mock protest. Oldcastle touched her arm.

'Do you need escort? I am but one man but I am better than no one.'

Celestina looked quickly from Rosa to Oldcastle and back. Something too fast and sharp for him to decipher flashed between the two women.

'Yes, yes, Rosa knows the way. I shall take you to the garden at the back and from there you cross the courtyard and on your right is an archway leading through the walls, out of the castel, turn right and into the streets close by the Duomo piazza. Keep the Roman Arena on your right and head towards the eastern side of the river's loop, the House of the Poor Clares is in one of the alleys leading down to the riverbank. You'll see Santa Anastasia's two streets up. If you get to her, you've gone too far. It is raining, I am sorry, you have only thin cloaks. But the rain will make it harder for him to find you. Cover your faces, you too, sir, he knows you too I think and this will anger him.'

She took his hand. 'I know you came for the old monk and it may well be a greater tragedy for the world if he is allowed to escape to Rome with whatever sins he has committed. But if you keep this girl safe, a small tragedy will be averted. Small to the world perhaps but …'

'I understand.'

And he does. He was not there to save Eleanor but if he can save this Rosa of the deep-as-black eyes then some small redemption is possible, some small reconciliation with the unfathomable plan of God that allows such things. For small does not mean unimportant. And he holds both their hands as he hurries them out.

---------- ∞∞∞ ----------

If we could stop here and like Boiardo, stop writing until the French go, and leave poor Angelica and Rinaldo running around the countryside, chasing the wrong loves, we could pick up the story and make our own ending. John Oldcastle and the three women rush down the back stairs. We could imagine a tense scene as the foul and pestilential duke comes in from the rain as they slip down the castle steps. We could imagine him shaking off the water, cursing the weather as he stomps angry into the Podesta's study, just as Oldcastle, Rosa and Livia run, drenched, through the courtyard. He is but five feet away from them but the walls are thick and the curtains have been drawn – *bravo Celestina* – and they slip away into the night. The streets are wet and dark, their breath comes harsh and frightened but they find their way to the House of the Poor Clares and then … then, we are all free to assign the ending we wish.

But we are not Boiardo, this is not *Orlando Innamorato* and we are not staring at a blank canvass with missing words to add ourselves. See how many words and pages are written still in this little book and none for us to devise according to our own taste.

And so here we have the truth of it.

Juan Borgia is already returned from the horsetraders, he is standing at the foot of the stairs as our four little birds try to get to the end of the landing. Who makes the noise? Is it Livia giggling because she does not understand? Is it the footfall of four against creaking wooden floor boards? Is it the sharp senses of the Duke who is already turning his feral attention towards the chambers where his girls are hiding? Whichever the guilty party, he hears, he sees, he orders. They stop. What else can they do? He is Papal Gonfalonier, he is an anointed Duke, he is Juan Borgia. He strides up the grand staircase, two steps at a time. And he has Matteo and Carlo just behind him, sweaty, meaty, hungry for a fight. Oldcastle tries to turn the attention away from the girls, tries to argue that the monk must be returned to the palatum and the Bishop. He stands as tall as he can, he tries to spread his cloak so as to hide the women. Pointing towards the locked door, he is valiant and brave and clever and hopeless.

Borgia laughs. 'My houseguests are my houseguests,' he smirks, 'I will not have them stolen away from me. Monk or . . . '

Another smirk, 'Lady. Here they are. Here they stay.'

I think – and I am sure you agree – that Oldcastle would have made a stand here. He has no weapon, but he is very good with his fists, he grew up in Southwark, you remember and he fought – none too shabbily – at Ambion Hill. But his certain death is written upon the air which stinks now of testosterone. And so it is Rosa who saves him. She pushes past his tense, wide back, allows herself a small squeeze of sorrow? gratitude? regret? upon his arm. And she is pulling Livia back into the chamber, slamming the door behind them both.

CHAPTER NINETEEN

In which.

He came for her that night.

They were both on the narrow bed, turned to face the window like spoons so he took her on the wooden floor, not caring much whether the sister woke or heard. What was there to be done, after all? There was a brief struggle, the usual crying stifled by his hand, a bit of *no-no-no* pleading, the spasm of pain as he forced himself past and through her innocence. Then a rigidity of disbelief, a slackening as he thrust himself into her so she became wet. And like all beasts he fooled himself as ever that she was good for it, that she–or at least her body–acquiesced in some way which not only lessened his culpability but even allowed him some base rationale. That it was blood and not delight did not occur to him. She was a vessel, a recipient, a conduit for his pleasure and it was as good as he had hoped. Afterwards, he left her crying soundlessly on the floor, knees bought up to her chin. He dimly recognised that through her terrible silence she was trying to save her sister, that her shattered mind still registered in some undamaged part that if she awoke there could be terrible consequences, that even in her agony and shock, she was thinking of the one she loved. Part of him probably should have realized at this point that even a broken bleeding girl upon the floor was a better creature than he. But he didn't.

Tuesday

CHAPTER TWENTY

In which the Bishop is told to hang a fat, old woman and a horse called Dido saves the day

If the Bishop could wish for anything this miserable autumn Tuesday–apart from the end to suffering, the End of Days, the end of sin, the return of Christ Jesus of course–then he would wish for the speedy return of the Podesta. Gone not even a week and already the work is piling up. Two murders of course, two corpses needing justice and one of them disfigured quite horribly in such a way to have the common people already talking of demons. And the second murder that of a monk, no less. The Dominican abbot's own nephew. It could be passed off as a robbery although that, he knew, would be a lie. But to question the Pope's own son over such a thing...? And the two dead bodies were not the only matters calling for attention. There had been a drunken brawl outside The Leaping Fish (and one of the brawlers still halfway to Hades in San Zeno's infirmary), some petty dispute over a boundary line, a heavy-handed husband who beat his wife so hard she lost an eye, four lads caught poaching on Santa Anastasia land who needed their hands branding, a bondsman deserting his land and caught half way to Venezia...The Bishop puts his head in his hands. As Shepherd of this particular flock, he is already under the heavy weight of a case of sacrilegious oathbreaking, two dozen long term offenders who were not attending Mass quite regularly enough, an old rascal of a heretic living out towards the woods who has not been to Mass in a decade but who is steadfastly refusing to be found when called. He also has three deacons who need chastising for drunkenness, fifteen other novice deacons who need their weekly briefing now postponed twice, two abbots who need counselling, especially now that one of them has a dead monk in his infirmary...

He looks up as if to beseech the Lord but all he sees is a damp patch on the plaster which has annoyed him now for a decade. How in the name of all that is holy have they come to this? Six weeks ago the Podesta made his judgement – none to blame, he said, none to blame and all of us suffering so let us share the kiss of peace – they had kissed in peace and buried their dead (even the woman he is absolutely sure had been a suicide, he allowed burial in her family tomb under the pretext of *per obitum cor contritum* when he was quite certain that death from broken heart did not actually exist as a diagnosis.) A quiet period of perhaps a month. The right words said loudly, still the kiss of peace holding. And then a few angry words from servant to servant in the lesser taverns and darker alleys. A fight or two harshly dealt with. Badly disguised hostility at the council meetings the Podesta shared with the lords of the town. Some arguing about petty matters; this landright, that fishing license, all normal noble quibbling but with an atmosphere polluted by six dead bodies. And then came the demand that the meddling old woman be punished. A demand that could have been assuaged by a quick flogging, a shaved head, a crawl of penitence to the steps of the cathedral. But no, once the woman had been accused so then had the damned monk been. Battle lines re-drawn anew but in familiar old places. And with the monk came the Duke and then the Englishman and now the city has one dead Spaniard with one arm and no eyes and one dead Dominican with a stab wound to the heart.

Salve Regina, Mater misericordiae, vita, dulcedo, et spes nostra, salve. Oh Mary Mother of God, help this little city over which you gaze. He is not quite sure where to direct his thoughts, they race and clash and separate and come together again; they are like hares in a field racing the hounds.

Deodamnatus, to Hades with that arrogant young pup! To interrupt an episcopal interrogation, to burst into a bishop's own private study, to drag a confused and terrified old man out of the door even as a Prelate of the Holy Mother Church protested. Flaunting those papal keys as if he had somehow earned the right to bear the signs of Peter. *Filius canis*! He remembers old Cardinal Barbo, Marco Barbo, cousin to Pope Paul II who had stayed in this very house twenty years ago now on his way to Venezia. A huge man, choleric and greedy, generous too when it suited him, quick to eat, quick to argue, quick to laugh – he had taken a most precious copy of Boccaccio's *Decameron* when he left, promising to return it, a promise broken of course. But even Marco Barbo – so nearly pope, an appointment blocked by Rodrigo Borgia himself who even then had been paving his own path – even Marco Barbo would never have disrespected a fellow prelate. And his own predecessor, Ermolao Barbaro, a foolish prattling old woman, worrying himself into an early grave, picking nits and finding fault even as he lay dying, even Ermolao would never have presumed to abscond with a crucial witness, a tonsured brother no less.

He rolls the twist of paper around with his finger and thumb. The broken seal had a jagged edge but the crossed keys can still be seen. The command had arrived just an hour or so just after he celebrated Matins. It is still dark outside, yesterday's rain now today's.

And yet he has of course won. The Podesta wanted the woman out of the way and the monk exonerated and thanks to the rather brutal intervention of the Duke of Gandia, this is now a certainty. This ducal missive he twirls in his fingers is quite clear. ***We hang the old sow today. The monk goes with me. Materia finitur. Gandia.***

Where he sits he has the tall window behind him, both so that he can see best what he writes but also so that his own features are in shadow, in silhouette even on a very sunny day, all the better to impress and intimidate his audience. To his right is a full bookcase, the one so admired just yesterday by John Oldcastle. A volume sits a little proud. It is a volume he looks at often; he never quite pushes it back in properly. Fifty years ago now in another city, he remembers himself as a boy, a novice being tutored for the holy orders of priesthood. Bright, innocent, full of questions, keen to learn for the glory of God. He had an enlightened tutor, a man who loved the ancients and saw them as holy precursors to Christ, the Gospels and the Church Fathers. Cicero, Pliny, Marcus Aurelius, the little boy voraciously swallowed them down whole. Some ancients of course were forbidden to the novices, considered too scandalous, disrespectful, vindictive, unchristian. Especially this one. The leather spine was dark and well worn, the gilt rubbed almost away. *Vitam impendere vero.* He had never considered taking the law, all he had ever wanted was to take his priestly vows and dedicate himself to God and to a flock of sheep as their shepherd. But a priest must needs search for the truth too, spiritual truths and sometimes more earthly ones, uncomfortable truths that even Juvenal himself–satirist though he was–would recognize. *Vitam impendere vero. Had* he dedicated his life to the truth? A suicide disguised as a natural death. Poison disguised as sleeping drafts. Heretics as lawyers. Wolves as sheep. Bastards as papal messengers. Monks as spies. *Sic et non. Sic et non. Sic et non.* But now he is no better than Abelard! The clear waters of truth get muddied so easily when an arrogant man dares to elevate human reason so that it sits alongside faith.

And this of course is the vice of poor John Oldcastle, Englishman, and all of his ilk. They dare to put such a value upon their God-given reason that they extricate it from the far greater gift of faith, extricate it, polish it up, put it on some plinth in the piazza and then cry to heaven when it gets wet in the next hailstorm. They read their secret vernacular copies of scripture, dare to interpret the word of God themselves, excite the populace into believing falsehoods and to reject truths. And then they are surprised, always surprised, when the populace turns into a mob and burns down the church. Why allow them to read what they cannot understand? Why allow them to hear divine words in coarse common tongues? How is that best serving the flock? Oh but he has become the cynic. How right they were to lock away Juvenal and the others. Perhaps he should stop reading Roman essays. Perhaps he should stick to the Lives of the Saints. Perhaps he should be the politic prelate who obeys his holy father without question and rises to the top of the Christian tree. How much better could he serve his flock then?

He looks back at the three short sentences. He is not actually able to hang the old woman himself, only the Inquisition has the right to take life, in all other cases, the Church hands over final execution of judgement to the secular arm. The Podesta has left one of his noblemen as his *in loco* of course and this deed can easily, legally, quickly, expediently be done by him.

As the light in the room becomes slightly brighter, diffused by long lines of rain sloping almost but not quite vertically, he looks again at the spine. *Vitam impendere vero.* What did Juvenal know of the truth? He spent his life writing childish poems, mocking his betters. He thought so little of the people, he thought them content with bread and circuses, the very circuses awash with the blood of Christian martyrs …

And yet '*Quis custodiet ipsos custodies*?'

'Who will watch the watchers?'

Lucius is at the door with John Oldcastle. The Bishop feels a flicker of annoyance at being seen unmasked and vulnerable. Lucius knows and bows, red-faced. But this John Oldcastle is a persistent and unusual man. He, the Bishop will not be too hard on his servant this time.

'I apologise for the early hour, *Domine mi*, but it seems to me that there is much to discuss after yesterday. You were quoting Juvenal, I think.'

The long, lean face affects a disinterested mien. 'Perhaps. The Ancients sometimes become one in my mind. I remember them from my boyhood of course . . .'

'But fascinating and no doubt the work of God that this is the line you remember today. Of all the verses you must have learned as a boy, that this is the line. *Who will watch the watchers*?'

'Perhaps. As I say, I was distracted. It is early. I have only just returned from the cathedral. Please come in and sit down. Lucius, some well-watered wine, some biscotti.'

They sit. John Oldcastle, he thinks, is like one of those little digging dogs they call terriers, dogs of the earth. They are used to dig out rats and to fight each other so that drunken men can win money. They deal with dirt and mud, with holes and warrens, they scratch out and kill vermin, they exist alongside the pestilential scum of the natural world. But they are loyal and fierce and passionate. He allows his eye to appear glazed but in truth it sharpens as he looks down his long nose. Yes, Oldcastle is a passionate man. And angry. Like the little terrier dog, he quivers. He has had no sleep, concludes the Bishop who always slept soundly.

'You asked yourself, Lord Bishop, who will watch the watchers? Who will ensure that the powerful do not become tyrants? What better example do we have before us this dawn of a man in power who needs checking?

The Bishop takes a slow considered draught. Sets the glass down slowly. There is much at stake here. A terrible balance to be won.

'You are my adversary in this matter, John Oldcastle. You have been employed as advocate to the woman, I am ecclesiastical advocate to the Dominican. As is the Duke of Gandia. I admit that the abrupt and rude manner of Brother Lorenzo's exit yesterday was not perhaps ideal but the Duke of Gandia has papal *auctoritas* to pass judgement. And the woman admitted having knowledge of many poisons and certainly had means. The Dominican however admitted only to sleeping draughts. There is no evidence against him whatsoever.'

'And the other? Brother Johannes, so conveniently murdered just yesterday afternoon, a few hours after I made it clear to Brother Lorenzo of my suspicions concerning their trading of letters?'

'I trust you are not accusing Brother Lorenzo of being involved? He has been in custody the entire time.'

'You know exactly what I am saying. The Borgia bastard knew Johannes had something that would incriminate his cousin and sent one of his Spanish assassins to stop his mouth.'

Long, thin fingers tightened around the thick stem of the glass. It was a soft spring green, lightening to an almost clear transparency at the bowl, the glass twisting like thick ivy stems around a tree. A beautiful piece of craftsmanship. He puts it down slowly.

'Be careful, Mr Oldcastle. You are accusing the Papal Gonfalonier, the legitimized son of the Holy Father of complicity in murder.'

'He is a . . . ' Oldcastle searches for his roughest Italian, almost spitting out the word, 'A *cacafuego*! A man not worthy to sit in judgement on any matter, let alone one where his family is so bemired in the stench of complicity and conspiracy.'

The Bishop holds up his hand, the ruby glowing as it catches the spark of the dying fire. 'You have an admirable touch with our language, the dialect too and a passable accent. *Cacafuego.* Yes, I hear some of our youngest novices sometimes call their little enemies this, *he who shits fire* . . . How convenient that you speak Italian so well. I understand from my sources that you learnt it as a student. From a resident of Firenze?'

The Englishman has the good sense to drop his eyes at this. The Bishop continues.

'Be careful, Oldcastle. Girolamo Savonarola is rushing head first into fire and I do not think that I mean that as a metaphor. He is a dangerous man, an extremist so close to heresy that he must be able to smell her breath and pick the shit off her teeth. Excuse my language. Your own... close connection to a man who is at this very moment defying the Pope and the Emperor too, the man who is inciting the populace of Firenze – I think you would say Florence – to rise up and declare themselves a free republic, a New Jerusalem even, under his own auspices, a man who is burning books and statues and urging the gullible Firenzi to throw paintings and tapestries onto the fire, your connection to this madman would not garner you sympathy here. Not with the noblemen who already dislike the lord you serve and not with the people of this town. Who are, on the whole, a conservative flock. But – please hear me out – it may surprise you to know that whilst I would never allow the word '*cacafuego*' to pass my lips, I agree wholeheartedly with your use of this insult to describe our papal friend. Yes. But papal friend he sadly is. What would you have me do? I am but a Bishop, not a cardinal, not Papal Gonfalonier, and only the Holy Father takes precedence over the Duke of Gandia – one more thing, if you would be so good as to indulge me – As you know, we have had a summer of war, unrest and death. If one small act of... sacrifice might bring us to peace, well then. *The noblest motive is the public good.*'

'There are things you do not yet know, *Domine mi*, things told me by this woman about the content of the letters passed from Brother Lorenzo to Brother Johannes. Quoting Virgil at me is all well and good but another more pertinent verse might be that '*it is expedient that one man dies for the people*'.

'Now who is the impudent one?! I may well bear the burden that is your comparison of me to Caiaphas – I have broad shoulders and thick skin – but by the same token you then compare a toothless, witless serving woman to Our Lord.'

'Christ Himself said that when you care for the homeless, the prisoners, the naked, you are doing it for him. *The least of my brothers*. And she is the least of all, this wretched woman.'

'Come now, do not be so disingenuous, Mr Oldcastle! Your interest – and that of Girolamo Savonarola – is not some nameless kitchen wench – can you name her even? – but Borgia himself! All three of them indeed, the monk, the Duke and the Holy Father. You cannot bring them down no matter what happens here. They are unassailable. Is London Town so far away at the edges of the world that you do not know the power of this family? You, whose grandfather sat and ate with kings? Who tried to rise up against the men in power and found himself burning at the stake for his foolishness?'

'You know a great deal, Lord Bishop.'

'This is my city! It is my place to know who comes amongst my sheep to sow discontent . . .'

'Not discontent. To prevent an injustice. You cannot believe that she is guilty.'

'And I cannot believe that he is.'

'But I have not yet told you . . .'

'My Lord Bishop!' Both men turn towards the door where Lucius looms awkwardly. 'My Lord Bishop, the Duke of Gandia has sent his two men for the woman. The witness we have in the lower rooms. I asked them to wait but they had his seal and a missive, stamped also with the papal signet. They have taken her.'

'Where?' Both men are now standing, Oldcastle's cup falls and there is sound of a deep painful crack as the glass breaks.

'To be hanged in front of Santa Maria, just outside. There's a crowd already.'

'*Deodamnatus*, he has not the authority! I have sent to Milan for further instruction . . . This foolish boy . . .' They are both in the hallway of the palatum now, it is just a short walk through the hallway, under the fine archway, across the piazza to the cathedral steps. The Bishop stops.

'Mr Oldcastle. I cannot be seen with you. If it becomes known . . . your connection with Savonarola, the heresy of your grandfather, I can do nothing here if I am touched by the stain of heresy. It is one thing to have you in the privacy of the episcopal palatum but walking together in the piazza . . .'

The Englishman gives a short, tight smile. 'As you say, *Domine mi*, the stain is hard to expunge. I myself scrub hard every day and yet still . . .'

'Go with Lucius through the back quarters and he will show you the cathedral steps he means – there are three sets but I can imagine the Duke means to choose the most prominent, the Western Portico – although I should imagine by now you will only have to follow the crowd. There is nothing the plebeians like more than a dawn lynching. I shall do what I can for her but I cannot lay hands upon a Papal Emissary. Even one so unworthy. If he hangs her himself, all I can do is give last rites and write a letter of protest. That is the length, the breadth, the height and the whole of it.'

---------- ∞∞∞ ----------

Despite the rain, there was a crowd of perhaps a hundred or so in the Piazza Duomo. Oldcastle stood a few feet from the back stepping up onto a mounting block so that he had an uninterrupted view. Santa Maria Matricolare, the city cathedral, was ahead, just to his right, built of the pale pink stone that graced so many of the buildings here. The same architect – Nicholaus – had built San Zeno too with its Briolato rose window but the identical rose window gracing the cathedra was now partly obscured by the huge two-story portico sheltering its dark double doors, the second story of which served as a balcony from which the Bishop addressed the populace on saints' days. The two sides of the portico rested upon two giant stone griffins lying down, front paws stretched out away from the building and towards the paved square. Oldcastle could see the Spaniard called Matteo sitting on the top step and leaning back against the griffin on the right, shouting up to someone or something above his head. Just behind the Spaniard, the Angel Gabriel in bas-relief delivered the Annunciation to the shepherds and then on the other side of the door, again to the Magi. Oldcastle twisted his body over to his left to make out what Matteo was looking at.

The other Spaniard, the thin one with narrow eyes and low brow, Carlo, had somehow shimmied up to the second story and was swinging himself over the balustrade. The fourth man, the Italian Vincenzo, was standing below him gently swinging a loop of rope.

The crowd around Oldcastle was murmuring quietly. He tried to lean forward to hear without unbalancing himself. There was a rumour that the murderer of Brother Johannes the dead Dominican had been found and was to be executed. But surely, came back the crowd, there would be a trial, the Podesta would return from Milan? It was the leader of the Egypsies who camped out in the western hills, said another voice. They were the ones who supplied the poison, they keep venomous snakes in their caravans, they worship a goddess in the form of a cobra. But worshippers of Satan were burnt not hanged, came back more knowledgeable voices. And if we were burning devil worshippers today there would be a pyre and the Inquisition would be here. The Inquisition does not creep quietly into a town, they come in their hundreds and stay for months. We would know! We would be hiding under our beds, you, Mistress Caravezzo, you would be hiding your sachets! And you, Julia Megora di Salazzio, you would have killed your black cats, all six of them! And you, retorted the women, you *podex perfectus es,* you would be hiding that little potion you take to put the bone into your *salsiccia.* Hush, said the people at the front, the Bishop is here. Shut your mouths, we want to hear, look how angry he is!

And there was the Bishop in his long black cassock with its red piping, now also with a red over-cloak, shining out like a bird of paradise in the dim wet light. Oldcastle watched him stride over towards the steps, Lucius hurrying behind, impotently carrying another, presumably more waterproofed garment. Matteo against the griffin was shrugging, getting—at last and with insolent slowness—to his feet. Carlo peered down from the portico balcony above. Vincenzo was still swinging the looped rope although its velocity had lost its vigour.

'Who dares this thing?' the Bishop was not shouting but long years of projecting his voice across huge spaces had won him a great and natural boom. 'The Cattedrale Santa Maria Matricolare is a holy place, the sepulcher of saints, the martyrs Firmus and Ruminus lie just yards from your misbegotten feet. Get down from there, Spaniard! Unless you intend to speak to this good congregation on the mercies and wisdom of the Gospels and Fathers, I suggest you leave that balcony where so many good men of God have spoken the Word, and get back into the mud of the gutter where you were no doubt born and bred and where you will doubtless take your final breath.'

An episcopal breath. Then, 'And you, *muta bove*, can get your fat backside off my griffin!'

Faex, his Grace is going to slap the dumb son of a bitch! The crowd as one shuffled forward, leaving Oldcastle on his mounting block. Carlo was still up on the portico balcony, showing no intention whatsoever of climbing down. The huge bulk of Matteo leaned casually against the first column, his backside returning momentarily to its position on the griffin's smooth head. Then hovering. Where's the Duke, asked the crowd of everyone and no one in particular, where's Gandia, those are his men, do you recognize that big one? Spanish *irrumator*, drinks like a bloody bull. Look at the size of him!

As crowds move, so this one too moved as one and turned its collective head back towards the tall man in black and scarlet who was standing at the foot of the small flight of steps. He had been their shepherd for twenty-five years now, cousin to Pope Pius of late memory, offered a cardinal-priesthood whilst in Rome, one-time candidate for the bishopric of Venezia, but now their own. He had returned to their city when the French invaded and he had kept them strong. When the French massacred thousands of civilians just one hundred miles south in Mordano, he had preached to them three times a day from that very balcony that God and Saint Zeno would protect them, that he would lead them in prayer. And when their young men had marched out to join the League at the Battle of Fornovo, he had stood upon the battlement walls with the Podesta. He had led the Benedictines in song as their men marched away and he had welcomed the wounded back five days later. He was their Bishop. He was their father. He was their conduit to God. And now he was angry.

'Who dares this thing?' Oldcastle could not help but admire the man who could project so calmly, and with such focus, his obvious and outraged fury. The Bishop moved up to the second step. Matteo was still slouching but Vincenzo had the good sense to back away and let the heavy coils of rope rest still against his thigh. But as the Bishop turned to face the crowd and opened up his arms, the people could see what he could not; that the great double doors of Santa Maria Matricolore were opening, that Juan Borgia was Duke of Gandia no longer but Papal Gonfalonier. Dressed in full ceremonial robes with the Crossed Keys of Peter long and black against the bright blue of his cloak, his steel breastplate also had keys embossed in what could only be gold. A gorget hid his throat and in one gauntleted hand he held two poles with banners dragging. Once in the hands of Matteo who was now standing erect, they were wedged between the griffins and the columns and as if by design a light wind came up from nowhere, flickering the images of the red bull on the gold background, the black and gold stripes, the crown of Castile, and again and again, the golden crossed keys. Borgia had a light helm covering his hair and there was the shine of more steel and gold at his knees as his cloak moved. In his other hand was a rope, the end of which looped itself around the neck of a short, squat figure, dressed in shapeless tunic and blinking

myopically as she was pulled out of the church and into the grey-green light. The Bishop was almost the tallest man in the city but he had chosen to make his stand on the second step. Gandia towered above him.

'Welcome at last, Lord Bishop! We had long awaited your presence and had almost forsaken hope of it. But here you are at last. A little wet perhaps. Please share this stage with me. Under the portico and in the presence of the Angel's Annunciation, we are quite dry.'

Clever bastard, thought Oldcastle, holding down the waves of fury and nausea as he looked for just the fourth time in his life at Juan Borgia, once bastard, now Duke. An unbidden, long-repressed memory of Eleanor crying wordlessly into her bolster rose up to assault him. On the steps, the Bishop was momentarily wrong-footed. He had no intention of sharing any stage with this man. He was only too conscious of what such a joint image would imply to the crowd. And so he stayed where he was, on the second step and in the rain.

Gandia laughed and gave an insulting little half-bow. Pulled on the rope, the woman lurched forward again and almost fell. Her hands were clearly tied behind her back. As she straightened, Gandia pulled harder and this time her knee hit the heavy marble and the crowd heard the crack.

'Good people!' Gandia did not have the Bishop's deep, commanding tone but he had a vicious arrogance that they all recognised and feared. He was at the same time, a boy-man who needed a good kicking and a slap around the ears but also an omnipotent demi-god who could raise his finger and have any one of them flogged or worse. The men in the crowd restrained their frustration, their boiling need to kick this little shit down the steps into the river. Wives next to husbands reached out to hold their hands. They looked up, twice, thrice to make sure their husband's eyes were down. Oldcastle felt no such restraint and fixed his glare as if it could burn a hole in the bastard's pretty forehead.

'Good people, you have suffered calamity upon calamity this summer. You have seen war and French atrocity, you have buried your soldiers, you have been hungry. You have seen young men kill each other in your streets, you have seen a brutal murder here, in the cloisters of this very basilica where rules this very Bishop as one of your finest young lords was cut down by another. And then, there were those that were poisoned, two to death and one to madness and then death by dagger. And you have rightly called for justice in these things. Your Podesta – far away, breaking his fast now with the German King who impudently calls himself Holy Roman Emperor – he was too concerned with his own reputation in Vienna-Berghof than in caring for you, his people here. An expedient peace, all sides innocent! Where is the justice in that?'

Oldcastle could hear murmurs of agreement. Clearly the Podesta had misjudged the populace.

'And so the Holy Father in Rome sent me to supervise your good Bishop here as he investigated and we dared to walk where your Podesta did not dare. We interrogated the monk falsely accused by one of your noble *paterfamilias* and there was no hint of anything but benevolent innocence, perhaps naivety in his story. And then we spoke long and hard to this woman – a woman employed for many many years in the household of this same noble *paterfamilias!* – and there! there we found our answers! If you wish to blind your neighbour! This woman here is your source! If you wish to curse your husband with impotence! This woman will have the potion to slip into his beer! If you wish to murder in the womb an innocent child of God, then this is your woman, she will wield the stiletto. And if you wish to poison to death your master or your wife, come to this woman. This woman here!' And he jerked the rope so that her neck and head were brought sharply upwards and she gave a little cry.

By the light, you'll break her damned neck, thought Oldcastle, realising that he was looking at the last few minutes of his client's life and that he had forgotten her completely, forgotten that she was supposed to be at the centre of his work here in Italy. He had got distracted by so many other things and he had failed her.

At last the tall man on the steps regained his composure and took control.

'My Lord Gandia, Lord Gonfalonier, I do not dispute your right to investigate this matter and I am grateful on behalf of this smallest of cities and Zeno himself that the good monk Lorenzo *Ordo Praedicatorum* has been cleared of all charges. It may well be that this wretched woman has confessed to procuring, handling and passing on pernicious poisons, yes, it may well be true,' He paused and the crowd were very quiet. 'But if the penalty for poison – even as accessory – is death, then you know as well as I that the Holy Mother Church may not dirty her hands with blood. That we must pass over the onerous task of delivering sinners to the secular arm, to the state. The Podesta has left secular matters in the hands of the good Lord Valmarana and the City Council of Ten but I am certain that did not include executions, not when the Podesta now intends to return within the week. And anyway, I do not see Lord Valmarana here.'

There was a low but perfectly perceptible groan of disappointment from some in the crowd. A hanging was not much to see but it was something. And if nothing else, a decent excuse to be late for work. Borgia held out his arms.

'Your Papal Father wants you to have justice! His reach is long. His body may reside in the great Vatican palace in the south but his eyes and mind are everywhere, they see everything.'

This was not going down so well. There were murmurs Oldcastle could make out along the lines of 'the lecherous old goat had better stay there then,' and 'where was the bloody Pope when the French marched through?'

'My Lord Duke,' finally the Bishop turned and consented to acknowledge the young man's glittering presence but still he stayed on the second step. 'The Council of Ten may well meet today and pronounce judgement on this wretched woman but in my view they would still vote to wait until the Podesta's return.'

'Are they mice? Are they old women hiding behind the skirts of their betters?'

This got a bit of a laugh especially as at least four of the Council lords were small, old and grey and one in particular–Valmarana–known as Lord Rodent. Borgia gave a little flourish.

'But it matters not. Come now, Lord Bishop, we all wish for a new beginning. Doesn't Seneca tell us that every new beginning comes from some other's end? End this one miserable worthless life and look forward. Vincenzo, my good servant, throw up the rope to Carlo. Carlo, trusted papal servant!' The thin foxy face appeared through the balustrade. 'Tie it fast for she is a fat old sow!'

The Bishop dropped his voice to protest personally to the Duke but before he could finish whatever he was saying, the coil of rope was thrown twelve feet skywards, caught and quickly fastened. The remaining length was then dropped back down so that it dangled above the right hand griffin.

'Your Lord Bishop is telling me that even as Papal Gonfalonier, I cannot carry out execution. He may be right, he is a learned man. But Cicero tells us that *veritas odit moras* and I would tend to agree with even that miserable old coward. So as to ensure an end to all delay, we need to look no further than our own Bishop!'

The crowd and Bishop himself were clearly confused. Borgia grinned, enjoying the tableau.

'You were away from this fine city, were you not? For eighteen months at least, during the reign of Innocent VIII, you went south to the Holy City for the papal inauguration but you did not return for almost two years. A normal thing for many a bishop to neglect his flock but you so conscientious! I think you were on papal business, I think you had been offered the fine episcopal seat of Venezia if you completed your task. Alas, you came home early and have had to make do with this little place ever since.'

The crowd were quiet now, most of them not liking the turn of tone but not understanding it either.

Oldcastle realized from his vantage point that the Bishop knew exactly what Gandia was taunting him with.

'My mission for Innocent VIII, may he rest in peace, has nothing to do with the matter at hand on this very miserable and, may I say, wet morning. We have established that you cannot execute this woman so if we could get . . . '

'No but you can.' Gandia's gauntleted finger extended so that it was almost touching the taller man's forehead. 'You spent eighteen months with the Holy Inquisition. You took vows as Sanctus Inquisitur and as such are permitted to oversee the taking of human life.'

'In cases of witchcraft and heresy!'

Gandia turned back to address the crowd. 'And who uses poison but a witch! What greater heresy is there than thinking yourself above Moses' commandments?' Turning back to the Bishop, his shining gold and steel helm bowed a little in mock sympathy. 'Come now, Bishop. You wanted Venezia once and lost her. Do this little thing for me and I'll make sure you get it as soon as Tommaso Dona is dead. You'll be a Patriarch! With precedence over all the other bishops.'

The two men separated by two feet and forty years stared at each other . . . Oldcastle could almost see the torn duties play themselves over and across the tall man's face. One command and it would all be over. Gandia made a gesture behind and the end of the rope was hastily, roughly tied around the woman's neck. Matteo lifted her up to balance precariously upon the griffin's head and held her there as she started to cry out. *Mercy*, he thought she saying but it was rough and indistinct. Above her the slack was taken off and she began to be pulled upwards, her chin unnaturally high, her cries now squeals of terror, then just grunts.

'This one's going to be a strangle not a snap,' muttered the woman in front of Oldcastle. 'The shame of it. Never good to strangle, always better to have a long drop and a snap.'

Her companion disagreed. 'You get a real mess with a snap. All the innards come out, sometimes the head pulls right off if the rope's too long. With a strangle, they piss and shit themselves but even so, there's less of a mess.'

Oldcastle wanted to lean forward, touch each woman on the shoulder and tell them that however awful a hanging, nothing was worse than a burning but this was Italy, they would already know. On the steps, Matteo was holding the woman's body with one huge arm and sliding the rope above their heads over away from the column with the other so that when he let her fall, she would not be able to reach out and touch the griffin's head with her feet.

'Best tie the feet together,' observed Oldcastle's neighbour, 'She'll go all over the place if she can kick. Bishop's not happy. Don't think I've seen him lost for words. Usually got a lot to say, our bishop.'

Oldcastle found himself agreeing with her observation. The Bishop was indeed in a clear quandary; this was after all the conclusion he had wished for, the monk exonerated and the woman blamed. But Oldcastle could not believe that the prelate would have wanted it quite like this. He himself was trying hard not to look at Juan Borgia, the triumph on the young man's face was making him physically sick.

'So, for the crime of procuring and administering poison ...' Borgia raised his voice, beside him Matteo held on tighter as the heavy woman began to twist and squirm, all the while calling out wordlessly, *'In nomine patri et filius et ...'*

'No! No, I shall not be used in this way.' Finally, the Bishop took the top step and towered furiously over the young man. 'I do not give permission for this execution, I find my authority *as Sanctus Inquisitur* inadequate to the circumstances. This is not what the Holy Inquisition was established to do.'

Realisation dawned like a vicious wave. '*You dare?*' Borgia had kept his voice low but there was not a person in the cathedral square not following exactly what was going on. Oldcastle found himself shouting silent, speechless, wordless encouragement to the tall, grey haired man, soaked now to the very bones of him but standing straight in the face of a boy who had never been told 'no'.

'I dare. I do not want to be Patriarch of Venezia. This is my home.'

There was a moment caught in the eternal eye of God himself, a moment when the woman struggled, when the brutish thug holding her nearly let go his burden, when Juan Borgia, Duke of Gandia turned to the crowd to gauge his chances. And he nearly won. Oldcastle could feel it. The division, the indecision, the collective torn mind of a crowd prevaricating between duty to a respected but distant prelate and the crude joy of watching a woman hang. Of duty to a distant deity and of pleasing a god stood flesh before them and covered in golden keys. Who would not want permission and a clear conscience to allow the basest of all instincts its freedom? Oldcastle could feel a grumble of acquiescence and Borgia raised his golden hands for them to cheer him on.

The horse that came clattering down the Via Santa Maria was a mare, a black-as-coal Friesian at seventeen hands and twelve years. Her iron shoes slid and skittered on the wet paving and she complained loudly as she careered towards the steps but she held her gait. The crowd in her way scattered like autumn leaves. At the Battle of Ambion Hill, Oldcastle had walked and stumbled and run behind horses like this one. He had gazed up the arseholes of these magnificent beasts, had waded through their shit, had wished to high heaven that he earned enough to own one. She was wheeled around a full ninety degrees with effortless precision and slowed as she stepped almost daintily towards the marble flight. Her black satin skin gleamed with rain and sweat, small flecks of white ran across her flanks like little crests of froth upon waves in a storm.

'It's Luca Carraresi,' swept the crowd's single voice, 'Luca Carraresi and Dido. Ridden all the way from Milan.'

The rider carried the arms of San Zeno on his cloak–sword, cross and three black eagles aflight–his light armour plain and steel. As the rain intensified, the gold and bright blue of Gandia began to appear gaudy, he shone like a little boy's toy soldier. Oldcastle had no way of knowing if this really was the fabled Luca Carraresi, heroic scion of the immensely powerful da Carrera clan of Padua but he was in no doubt that the crowd believed it. Keeping his visor down, the knight stepped his horse carefully to the bottom step and then to the delight of the crowd, some of whom gave up a little cheer, rode her daintily up the first two. The visor flicked up.

'My Lord Bishop. From the Podesta.' If the young man noticed the meaty arms of the thug to his right wrapped around the moaning, wriggling woman, he was too well-bred to show surprise. Dido was also extremely well-bred but she was also an honest creature and bared her sharpened teeth, snorting furiously through flared nostrils. Matteo had the good sense to back off at speed and in so doing lost his hold on the heavy weight which swung forwards and sank down sharply, feet flailing twenty inches above the top step. There was a collective gasp. The crowd moved forward but did not dare to be within striking distance of the honed hooves so a small group found themselves half way up the steps. The Bishop was shouting for Borgia to cut the woman down, Borgia was standing in his way, arms outstretched, the woman's eyes began to bulge, her skin was red, then scarlet, her tongue began to protrude and by Saint Zeno did her legs kick.

'From the Podesta,' shouted the Bishop, 'He is to return on the morrow at dawn and will resume his command of all matters civil and criminal. The Council is to reserve judgement on all capital cases until then. Now, for the love of God, let the poor woman down.'

She had stopped wriggling and bucking her sagging body to and fro, her chin was pointing almost to the ceiling of the portico, her neck stretched and taut, her swollen tongue flapping like a fat fish upon the bank. Juan Borgia took a quick look behind him and stepped forward to block the Bishop's path. Arms outstretched, it was a costly error. Dido had been pushed to her limits from well before dawn, covering the one hundred leagues in less than three hours and although she was exhilarated and could have run some more, she also didn't much like the slippery steps beneath her hooves and the gurgling sounds from the hanging lump of rags to her right. And so when the gauntleted hand came within range, she reached out and took a mighty chunk out of the unprotected upper arm.

The Podesta's command meant something, in truth, to the populace because he was well thought of despite the chaos of the summer. But Dido was a beast of legend, daughter of the vicious nineteen-hander Hannibal himself. The little group on the steps ran up as one and as three held the strangulated woman aloft, the others took out pocket knives to gently cut the rope from the woman's swollen red neck. If she made any sound, it was blocked out by the furious screaming of the Duke, as deep red began to flow fast and dark through the white of his tunic and onto the blue of his cloak.

'Oldcastle!' The Bishop was staring directly at him, across the heads of the growing crowd for this was now better than any travelling mystery play. 'Secure the monk! I shall come! But get to him now!'

The last thing Oldcastle saw as he jumped down from the mounting block and turned to run back to the Podesta's Tower some ten blocks south was a tall grey haired man, a black biting mare, a huge Spaniard flailing his meaty fists and a blue cloak covered with bloody red keys.

CHAPTER TWENTY ONE

In which the Lollard and the monk come to a heroic understanding and the Bishop and the Duke come to an understanding that is minus heroico sed magis pragmaticam

It has rained all night. Steady, incessant, caring nothing, it is at the same time a remorseless repetition but also at some point a strange comfort too. Her pain seems to gather to itself the rhythm of the weather, a rhythm which gives her a measure of control over its extremity. Pit pat wait wait pit pat wait wait pain pain breathe breathe pain pain breathe breathe. There is a damp sour taste in her mouth, her breath she knows is foul. Livia sleeps deeply, curled up against her sister's back, tiny noises, bubbles and gentle gasps, are the only noises in the room. Rosa has a terrible ache in her belly, between her legs, in her stomach, her very guts heave and groan. A wild green serpent thrashes in her very self, it is thick and heavy, it rolls itself around, under her skin, she feels bloated, tight, stretched, as if the taut skin across her hipbones would at any moment split and tear. She lies still but the serpent mocks her by curling itself around her lungs and her heart, squeezing, releasing, squeezing, releasing. She keeps her breath tight, short, shallow, controlled. If she moves, Livia might wake. And it is very important that Livia does not wake. Every other thought, formless wave of rage, mute roar of shredded-nerve pain, she focuses them all into a single, narrow beam of light–keep still, keep quiet, let Livia sleep.

And she will never share this night with her sister, never let her know how Rosa lay so still that night that every muscle screamed in pain until she felt at one point that she rose above her poor shattered heart and saw her body lying, helpless upon the bed.

Celestina comes at dawn and gives her poppy. And for Livia too, she insists, and they both obediently nod, grateful for the strange kind woman who has taken charge now that they cannot. The poppy is cold and cool upon her tongue, dissolved into something sweet and cloying, hard to pass down her throat but then she burns, burns with shame, with fury, with dry tears that will not come. She burns with vengeance, with mortification, with a desire to kill and a desire to die.

The poppy is very strong. They sleep through biting horses and hanging women, they sleep through bleeding dukes and laughing crowds, they sleep as John Oldcastle comes clattering up the staircase in his ugly English boots. They sleep even as he, Lucius and Horto, break down the door of the next room along.

---------- ∞∞∞ ----------

Brother Lorenzo was cowering in the corner as the bottom door hinges finally splintered away from their casing. Trying to stand, the elderly man leaned against the wall, reaching out towards the bed with thin fingers. Oldcastle helped him over and he sat heavily, head and shoulders down.

Celestina looked at the mess. Ordinarily she would have been furious and ears would have rung with the boxing of her tight little fists. But this morning held other cares.

Even so, she glared at Oldcastle. 'You are only back in the Podesta's house because you are with Master Lucius here. I don't let any English heathen break down my doors. Even if they are rescuing monks.'

'I appreciate your generosity and understanding.'

'Hmm . . . well. The dog likes you,' she added somewhat to his confusion before turning her attention to the Dominican. Almost gentle; 'Some wine, Brother Lorenzo? Let me send Horto here. And I do not think you have eaten since that soup yesterday. Horto, some bread as well. Now, breathe. Englishman, don't crowd him so, let him breathe.'

There was quiet in the room although Oldcastle's impatience to speak was but barely contained and almost visible. Celestina looked towards the partition wall beyond which she hoped the girls were sleeping.

Finally. 'Is he coming back for me?'

The housekeeper quickly caught the Englishman's eye. No point in lying. Oldcastle nodded. 'Yes, Brother. He will be back soon. He sustained . . . an injury,' Celestina looked up at this, 'but he will be back as soon as the Benedictine physic has bandaged it up.'

'And he is taking me to Rome?'

'Yes. He is planning to take you to Rome.'

Silence. Then; 'I do not think that I wish to go to Rome.'

'It is the Eternal City. And you are a new-found Borgia. You could spend your remaining years in luxury and with some influence. You could read books you do not have here at San Zeno's or the Santa Maria library. You could be in charge of your own gardens and train novices to be herbalists.'

'I do not think that any of those things are going to happen if I go to Rome.'

'No. No, Brother Lorenzo, I don't suppose that they will.'

A deep sigh. 'The young man, the Duke of wherever it is, he has declared me innocent of all charges?'

'Yes. And I suppose he has that right. Especially as the Bishop is also of the opinion that you are innocent.'

'I see. But that is a great foolishness, isn't it? Because none of us are truly innocent. Why would Christ have come otherwise? Why would we need the great Mother Church now?'

Oldcastle had his own very firm ideas about how much the children of God needed the Holy Mother Church but now was not the time, the place nor the person. Lorenzo touched the Englishman's arm.

'Do you remember yesterday? You spoke to me through the door, that door, of hypocrisy, of hiding away secrets, you quoted from Matthew; *'Woe unto you, scribes and Pharisees, hypocrites! For you are like unto whitened sepulchres, which indeed appear beautiful outward but are, within, full of dead men's bones and of all uncleanliness. Even so, you also outwardly appear righteous unto men, but within, you are full of hypocrisy and iniquity.*'

'Yes, I remember. I must apologise for my stridency, I was angry and frustrated.'

'No matter, no matter. It is at the heart of all things, you see. To be true to one's self. Aristotle was right, all those years ago. What else is *arête*, virtue, but being true to the creator who molded us into form with his mighty hands? Thomas Aquinas knew, he knew all else was froth and foam if we did not remain true to our selves. Because how else can we be true to God? If we do not know ourselves at Judgement, how are we to find the way? And I have been a hypocrite all these years. I have absolved brothers and laymen of all kinds of venial sins, I have sent them away with how many thousand *ego te absolvos*? And yet at the same time I have carried a terrible secret and allowed another to pay the price whilst I stood in the shadows.'

Celestina was moved to speak. 'Be careful, Father. This man is a paid advocate to speak against you, he has been hired to speak for the woman they nearly hanged today.'

The tonsured head looked up. 'Nearly hanged her? What evil is this? She is a foolish old thing, not a jot of sense in her head, I met her twice I think and there was no cunning, no vice, no cleverness in her. And she loved that girl, loved her as though she were her own.'

'She admitted to knowing where to procure poisons . . .'

'Hah! So could every woman in this city! And every monk. Since when was knowing the position of a knife, evidence that you have used it to kill? Ah but . . . I see . . . if she is guilty then I need not be. It is a most terrible fulcrum and balance, a dreadful set of scales. For one to be innocent, the other must be guilty.'

'Nonsense,' huffed the housekeeper. 'it is perfectly possible for two people to be innocent. Why can the Podesta not find for you both again as he did before? No hangings then, I remember, just kisses of peace and golden statues.'

'It has become so. The great lords have made it so. So my innocence has been bought with her guilt. That must please you, Englishman.'

'I am finding it hard to find pleasure in any of this, Brother Lorenzo. But I cannot let my client hang.' His client? What was her name again? He had spent longer with Lord Cyprian, longer with this monk of the opposing side, longer with the Bishop. He was a disgrace to his training and to his vocation. It was Borgia, always always Borgia.

Here was an uncomfortable truth to be said. 'The Podesta is returning tomorrow.' He housekeeper started and looked horrified but he held his hand to stop her interrupting. 'He has delayed the execution but I think that he will be forced to agree with the judgement of the Papal Gonfalonier. His priority is civic peace after all and I do not think there has been real peace here since the summer, despite the pretense. There is something in human nature that seems to desire blame and punishment. It is almost as if a people cannot come together without casting one of their own out first. But the Podesta will agree with the Gonfalonier eventually because there is nothing else to be done.'

'How long will this all take?' The housekeeper seemed strangely anxious. Oldcastle was confused.

'I have no idea, a week I should imagine, one could hardly expect him to call the Council of Ten the day he rides back and the law would expect the woman to recover a little from her injuries before she was questioned again for one last time.'

'He cannot stay here another week.' She was biting at her lip, eyes not meeting his but restless. He wasn't sure who she meant... 'That young bastard, the vicious evil monster, he cannot be in this town for another week, I'll not have it.'

By the holy mercies of Christ, what has he done now? Oldcastle felt his skin itch as the hairs on his arms rose. He caught her eyes flicking towards the wall. He almost lost control of his bladder. No. No, not that, not Rosa with the brown-as-black eyes. He knew without hesitation that it was true. But still he demanded confirmation and held the housekeeper's stare until she flushed and nodded, clearly horrified that he had guessed. The monk had no inkling of what was passing above his head. And yet...

'He is an evil young man although he is apparently my cousin. I did not think there could be so much evil in one so young. It is not what he says... but there is a miasma around his head, a cloud of something truly awful... Like dead bees.'

'The dog can see it.' Celestina's quiet certainty seemed fitting. 'They are the best of beasts, dogs, and they can sense when there's something bad about a man.'

I cannot ask this of him, thought Oldcastle, *it is too much. The penalty for treason is to be hanged, drawn and quartered, and it is not just pain long drawn out but public degradation. I cannot ask it of this decent old man.* But when he dared to look sideways, fearing the desperate grey eyes of a frightened man, he saw something very different. Lorenzo Borgia was smiling. A sweet, gentle deeply-felt smile. It radiated something scarcely definable but it was impossible not to believe as genuine. The Dominican monk had found something deep inside that lit up his skin, his eyes, his mouth turned upwards and tentatively reached up to meet the corners of his eyes.

'If he thinks I am guilty of something, or at least planning to admit something, he will abandon me, will he not? The Borgias are not a family to succor a liability. He will go if I become an embarrassment.'

There was no disagreement, how could there be.

Celestina shook her head. 'No, Father. This is too great a price.'

Again that almost beatific smile. Radiant. Radiating. 'Too great a price? When Christ Himself hung upon the cross for the sins of the most wretched of us all?'

'But... but Father. The Lord was God Incarnate! I know I am an ignorant housekeeper who can scarcely read and write enough to order meat and pay the pennies but even I know that He was sent to die for us, He had strength given to him by God himself whereas...'

'Whereas I do not?' A slightly quizzical furrow, an almost... yes, he was almost laughing at her, gently, with fond love as she floundered in confusion. Lorenzo Borgia looked sideways to John Oldcastle.

'I think you understand, Mr Oldcastle. To save a single life is to save the world entire, is it not? To be given such an opportunity... to emulate in such a small and base but priceless way the supreme act of sacrifice made by our Lord... what an honour! Can you see, dear lady? There is a bright, glowing path straight ahead of me. It is paved with warm, soft stone and lined with every herb and flower and they wave and bow as my feet pass them by. The hem of my cassock brushes their leaves – can you smell? Rosemary and lavender, good salvia the best of all herbs... such a pleasant path. My feet cry out to cast off these sandals and walk barefoot all the way until the end where he waits for me with his soft loving arms outstretched and I will hold him again! How can any man deny me such a journey with such joy at its end?'

He was now the master of the room, the housekeeper and the Englishman mute, staring. Outside, the afternoon was rolling on towards evening, gentle, inexorable, impossible to reason away. Soon it would be dusk. Although it felt that time had gently slowed within their four walls, the Castelvecchio street which ran along the castle's walls and ditch, buzzed with people. Their own window looked out upon the castle courtyard within the great compound but even so, the hum of humanity rising up from the living breathing heart of the little city hovered outside the narrow open slit which served as a window. It seemed to gaze in, politely but firmly reminding them to stop their indulgence and rejoin the world. The Dominican patted Oldcastle's knee, sending then an almost boyish wink up towards the woman who was swallowing hard.

'An easy decision. With one short confession, I free this city of a pestilential pox and secure the life of a sad daughter of Eve who deserves more than she has thus far been accorded. And this city may then truly return to peace. Only the Bishop, I think, is harmed by this turn. And he may be tall and thin with a Roman's nose but he has shoulders stronger than you think.'

'It is too much ...' Oldcastle shook his head.

'Nonsense. And I atone for the death of poor Brother Johannes who died not at my hand, command or will but through my cowardice. Yes, I am ashamed at my base cowardice yesterday. I was no man but *imitation hominem.*'

There was no doubting the old man's sincerity and the uncanny peace in his eyes. The monk spoke again.

'Let me atone. You cannot, you will not, deny me this. It is a gift.'

Horto reappeared at the shattered doorway.

'The Bishop is here. I have shown him and Lucius to the study. I did not think that this room ...' He looked at the two men on the narrow bed, the door leaning dejectedly and at a painful angle against the wall, the splinters of wood upon the floor.

Celestina came back to life. 'Downstairs then, my lords. I'll break into yet another cask of the Podesta's finest Rioja. I think the Bishop may need some fortification ...'

'I think we all do,' And it was as if the old monk had lost thirty years and gained an insight to which they could only scratch at the edges. And as he led the way down the grand staircase, it was as if they were children. The heavy folds of the dark cassock swept the steps, the housekeeping slippers and the ugly English boots followed. And at the bottom was the old blind dog who heaving himself up, with a groan and whimper, led them all into the study.

---------- ∞∞∞ ----------

A wide dark puddle spread out from beneath the Bishop's robes, even the red lining of his prelate's pride was dark and dejected. The episcopal grey hair was now slate and Lucius tried to dap ineffectually at this arm and that shoulder and this neck. But the Bishop was impatient and too wet to care to be simply damp. On such a day of extremes, to be half anything was to do the day a disservice. No, he did not want wine, no, Horto could take away the damned biscotti, no he was not going to sit down, no he did not want to remove his cloak. But he was relieved that Brother Lorenzo was safe and well. He was reassured by the precipitous return of the Podesta and he was astounded – although why he did not know – by the wisdom and courage of Friesian mares.

'Amen to that,' added Oldcastle somewhat sacrilegiously. Celestina, Horto and Lucius had disappeared – although Lucius had disobeyed orders and made sure Horto left the wine. The monk had sunk deep into a long settle seat and seemed very far away.

'Well,' said the Bishop, unable to stop pacing. It was as if he had run the fastest race of his life but although it was now all over, could not stop still. His sodden skirts left a wide swathe of damp, dark upon the fine polished floor. He walked over the path leaving footprints, his skirts followed and smoothed them away, he made more, they patiently followed, wiping them clean again and again. 'Well . . .'

'You did well, Lord Bishop,' said Oldcastle simply, because it was true. The Bishop nodded. Stopped momentarily. Began pacing again.

'I shall pay some price, no doubt. The Borgias do not react with humility to public displays of disobedience. I fear, they have the terrible family trait of bearing grudges.'

'The people of the city, the Emperor himself, will not allow you to suffer.'

'It does not matter. I have thin bony shoulders but they are surprisingly broad. And anyway, the bastard will get what he wants. The Podesta and Council will have no option but to hang her at some point. She has admitted to procuring poisons and the people seem to need someone to pay for the summer madness we all allowed.'

'Father,' the soft-grey eyes were steady, 'I must needs confess to you, as my spiritual head, and to the City Council as the secular arm governing this smallest but best of all city-states. My testimony may well change the course of the Podesta's justice.'

'Brother Lorenzo, you have confessed under the seal, there is now no sin, you were absolved, it has been wiped away by the blood and tears of Christ Himself. Say no more.'

'There is something else.'

The pacing stopped. The Bishop looked out towards the middle distance as if there was something crucially compelling in the tapestry that lined the outer wall. What was that? A kneeling unicorn by…oh yes, a fountain but it was a little unclear. There were green bushes all around filled with brightly liveried huntsmen. Were they to observe the unicorn or capture it? There should be some white-clad virgin somewhere…there she was. But was she an innocent penitent or had the huntsmen been using her as bait? He could feel a small but growing wave of confusion followed by what might have been horror, then resignation as he saw all they had tried to work towards flowing down into the gutter and disappearing.

'Sit down,' advised the Englishman. The Bishop considered refusing but what the hell…The Rioja left behind by Lucius, who knew him well, was strong and sweet, it slid down his throat as thick and smooth as blood.

'Come on then, Brother Lorenzo of Santa Anastasia. What have you done that determines such drama? This *tragici fabula* of ours is in danger of becoming a *mimica in comedia.* Today I saw a giant horse bite the arm of a Papal Gonfalonier. I saw papal keys covered in blood. You can imagine the augers. Crowds are such a superstitious and ignorant collection ...'

The Brother then spoke for a long time. He spoke of being recruited by an unnamed visitor-monk – a German – many years gone, a monk now dead but who had been resident of the Dominican House in Bergof. How this monk persuaded him of the legitimacy, both moral and legal, of the Scaglieri case. How the great della Scala family who had ruled the city for one hundred years were the key to its future greatness. How their current servitude to Venezia was unseemly. How a Scaglieri return would ensure the commune's independence, how the Emperor would recognise them as an ally independent of the Patriarchy. And then there were letters sent from members of the most noble families to the son of Cangrande Scaglieri, known as the Great Scaliger, *Dominus della Scalla* and the last to rule the city before their imperial exile. Letters were followed by instructions and so he had begun to ferment discord by encouraging the stupidity and foolish lusts of young men of opposing noble families, of encouraging unwise relationships, of conducting secret, unholy marriages. And then, most horribly of all, he had procured and given poison to two children, both of whom had then died. The plan had been to so excite discord that the city would erupt into chaos and blood, the Podesta would be overthrown and the Scaglieri welcomed back as the bringers of *justitia et pax, lex et ordo.* Brother Johannes had been at first the carrier of letters but had had a change of heart when he saw the pain their endeavours had brought to innocent people. He had been silenced by a Scaglieri assassin when bravely threatening to go to the Podesta with all he knew.

'Dear God,' breathed the tall man with the wet hair, 'Dear God.'

He looked at Oldcastle who shrugged his shoulders. 'Dear God indeed.'

'Am I expected to believe this nonsense?'

'Which part is so impossible?'

The Bishop jumped to his feet. 'I shall not allow this, Brother Lorenzo, you are not the Aaron's Goat of this town, it is not your place to bear the sins of others upon your shoulders to then be torn apart by the wolves of unfair vengeance. I did not take my vows forty-five years ago to stand silently by and let a monstrosity like this go unchallenged.'

'It is not your decision, my lord.'

'I know what this is! Do not think I do not know what you are doing. Just because it was told under the seal, does not mean that I don't know.' And the thin episcopal finger which so terrified his deacons pointed straight and furious.

'You cannot speak of it.'

'So you will put your hand on the bones of San Zeno and swear this . . . this *child's* tale of plots and letters and mystery monks? On the very bones of Zeno?'

'Please do not make me.'

'No! Because you cannot!'

'You would prefer the woman to hang? And for Borgia to leave in triumph and take me to Rome?'

The blow struck home. 'No. No, I would not have any of those things.'

'And so we are in sweet accord, my Lord Bishop.'

There was nothing to do but accept defeat. Oh, the Bishop fulminated and objected and again, threatened to bring the bones of Zeno into the council meeting to prove the Brother lying but they all knew that he would not do it. He paced a little bit more, his skirts and boots now almost dry. Oldcastle and the monk sat quietly and let the little storm blow itself out. Outside, the weak autumn sun began to disappear behind the western city walls and Porta Palio. Finally, he stopped his pacing and sat upon the bench meant for city supplicants and let his head and shoulders hang. The three men sat in silence until Lorenzo Borgia stretched out his hands and took Oldcastle's in one and the Bishop's in the other.

'*Deus meus, ex toto corde poenitet me omnium meorum peccatorum, eaque detestor, quia peccando, non solum poenas a Te iuste statutas promeritus sum, sed praesertim quia offendi Te, summum bonum, ac dignum qui super omnia diligaris. Ideo firmiter propono, adiuvante gratia Tua, de cetero me non peccaturum peccandique occasiones proximas fugiturum. Amen.*'

Finally. 'Let me take you back to the palatum, Brother Lorenzo. You can stay in some comfort with me before you speak to the Podesta and City Council tomorrow.'

Getting to his feet, knees creaking slightly, the monk shook his head. 'I think I would like to go back to my old cell in the crypt beneath the church of San Zeno. Zeno himself is there and that would be a comfort. I shall not now see my old cell at Santa Anastasia again now nor my beloved herb garden but I think in the presence of Zeno I could imagine them one last time.'

---------- ∞∞∞ ----------

If we now swap the fine feathers of the *falco peregrinus*–not much use where we are going–and instead take upon ourselves the soft, downy fur of the common house mouse, *mus musculus*, then we shall eavesdrop upon the conversation occurring a few hours later. The good Bishop has changed his damp vestments, deputised his least useless deacon to take evening Mass at Vespers and is now back at the episcopal palatum. Brother Lorenzo has had his wish and is lying–half a mile away–upon the hard wooden pallet in the cell along from the tomb of Zeno himself and although it is only early evening, he is sleeping at last. His dream is a warm, soft one, it smells of fresh linen and warm milk and mint, the arms holding him are strong and young and brave. Our little mouse cannot go into the dreams of monks and this one in particular is not for us to witness.

In the episcopal palace, Juan Borgia, Duke of Gandia is a mighty tower of fury. He is a tall candle, a column of righteous wrath. In scattered pieces on the floor are pages from some of the priceless books he has swept upon the floor, their words on the paper are like the veins of leaves brought down by a sudden autumn storm. He forgets the wound in his arm and howls in furious pain as it bites. More books fly like wild birds in a terrible storm. The Bishop looks down upon the wreckage of so much loving labour, so much study, so much dedication in the pursuit of wisdom and God's glory. He can almost see the inky words, the very letters twitching and moving, flying up from the torn pages of captivity and leaving them forever. He is desperate to kneel down and gather the letters, the words, the pages to him, to soothe them back into compliance upon the parchment but if he attempts to pick them up, the Duke will no doubt find another shelf.

At first, it is angry disbelief that such nonsense could be even considered to be true ((and here of course the good Bishop has to keep his face neutral because here at least they are in accordance). Then the Duke rages on to blame; he will kill the mendacious old fool, he will tear out his ungrateful tongue. Does he not know how the Family has succoured him all these years, paid his slut of a mother not to drown him at birth, paid the abbey to take him in, feed him, educate him, succor his petty pretensions of scholarship? Would anyone have done these things had he not been Borgia? How dared this sniveling, *error vilissimus* of a man throw back the generosity of Pope Callixtus, his father? Or Alexander VI? Of Juan Borgia, Duke of Gandia, Papal Gonfalonier? Did he have a wish of death, this *fragmen stercore*? The Bishop merely waits this out. Our tower of fury moves on; it is the Bishop's fault, he has not kept control of his sheep, he has allowed the Dominican dogs to play around his feet with no thought of chastising or bringing them to heel. He is a sorry excuse for a prelate. He will be on his knees before the Holy Father begging for his life. He is fortunate that he too does not find himself without a tongue here and now for dragging the Papal Gonfalonier into this *horrendum pulmentum*. And then he moves on to the pissmire of a town he has been forced to come to. Their boring, parochial unimaginative little squabblings, the fuss made over the deaths of six unimportant nobodies. Who cares? Who cares that this lad killed this lad and this other lad killed the first and the first lad thought his *vacca stulta* of a wife was dead and killed himself like some *podex perfectus* and his mother—yet another *moecha pudita*—killed herself. Who the fuck gave a faex about any of them?

The Bishop stands—for Gandia is pacing and has not given him leave to sit—throughout all of this and more. He is asked to repeat, twice, thrice, the details of the supposed confession. When he demands to know the whereabouts of his treacherous rodent of a cousin, the Bishop sends a mental prayer up to the Almighty and lies;

'He is back at the monastery of Santa Anastasia. They have him held fast in one of the penitentiary cells. The Podesta's men along with the Abbot's, are guarding him close until the Podesta returns tomorrow.'

We can see—from our position perched upon the back of the wooden settle where just a few hours before, the Brother in question sat to tell this tale—that Gandia is considering storming into the abbey and seizing the object of his fury. The chances of Brother Lorenzo surviving this experience are probably small. But we can also see—for mice have sharp eyes and sensitive olfactory nerves, picking up all kinds of emotional responses only dimly perceived by humans—that the Duke is dismissing this idea as soon as it rolls like a wave upon the shore. He has only three men with him—and Matteo is nowhere to be found, that fat lump of an ox—and although the Papal seal can intimidate most people at most times, he might have stretched its influence a little too far this week. We can see as we shuffle along the carved settle back that he is torn between two wild horses—he has the overwhelming desire to stay, to shout down the nonsense of his cousin being some Scaligieri spy, some traitor conspiring revolt, to take on the Council and rip apart the ancient Dominican's fairytale story... But the other side of him – for the Duke of Gandia is many things but he is not a fool – knows that anyone west of China and east of the setting sun will have no trouble believing a Borgia conspiracy. *Blood will show itself true*, they will think to themselves. *Bloody Borgias, how dare they meddle with the affairs of city-states, how dare they plot beneath the very eyes of communes, podestas, councils and even emperors?* The monk will perjure himself, the Council and Bishop will believe him, the foolish old cunt will die and Borgia will go home to his father looking like an absolute fool. How Cesare will laugh...

A deep fear of looking foolish in front of his older brother is always going to win out. The little clan of children, all bastard-born of Rodrigo Borgia and his paramour Vannozza dei Cattanei, lives in a perpetual state of conflict and faction. The four of them – Cesare, Juan, Lucrezia and Gioffre – make pacts, form alliances, break promises, doubledeal every day of their young lives. They fight each other for their father's approval, for their mother's vague affection, for the luxuries and positions raining down upon them or dangled and then snatched away by parental whim. They have their every need granted but still feel dissatisfied. They are flattered and idolized but still they feel wretched and inadequate against the tawdry golden glow of their siblings. They are cruel to their servants, cruel to their wives and husband, cruel to each other. Rapacious in appetite, they vie to outdo each other not simply in the acquisition of earthly powers and wealth but in the excesses of their behaviours. No serving girl is safe from Cesare and Juan, and when she runs sobbing to the sanctuary of their sister Lucrezia, she finds that this noble lady is worse than her brothers. Certainly her unfortunate husband Giovanni Sforza is currently finding her so. At twelve, Juan Borgia beat a stableboy with a whip and flicked out his eye. At thirteen, he impregnated his first tavern girl. That same year he had three tutors sent to the papal dungeons for daring to criticize his work, had the Bishop of Ruffina dismissed for laughing at a flush of acne despoiling his youthful skin and so often reduced his father's new mistress, Guilia Farnese, to tears that she was forced to move her suite. And so when at the age of sixteen, he raped Eleanor Oldcastle – a young English guest sleeping in a tavern in the Celio area of Rome as her brother and his friend chatted downstairs – it was an incident he could not even remember three hours later.

The fire eventually burns itself out.

'This is not forgotten,' he spits at the prelate who nods companionably.

'No, my Lord Duke, please be assured that nothing that has occurred here will be forgotten. Indeed.'

'Vincenzo? Carlo?' His two henchmen appear at the doorway. Carlo looks sly, Vincenzo – the only Italian in the group – blank. He has a perpetually blank face, as if there is nothing passing between his ears at all.

'We are leaving. Go back to the Podesta's hovel and get the housekeeper bitch to pack my luggage.'

'Sir. And,' This is Carlo with the fox-face, 'Where shall we meet you?'

'With the horses. Find that dumb bastard, Matteo. I'll be in the Tavern-Within-The-Wall next to the stable.'

'Will we be needing the ass, my lord?'

One last sweep of the bejeweled ducal fingers and Boethius, Jerome and Marcus Aurelius go flying across the room, to scatter themselves in a pile of wisdom on the floor. Our little brown house mouse nearly gets hit with the *Decameron* and scampers down the scrolled sides of the settle to the safety of the skirting. As we scurry along trying to find a convenient hole, we hear the parting words of Juan Borgia, Duke of Gandia, Grand Duke of Napoli, Governor of St Peter's and Papal Gonfalonier of the Holy Mother Church.

'And you, Bishop, can go fuck yourself. Right up the podex.'

CHAPTER TWENTY TWO

In which Saint Zeno himself makes his feelings very clear. And in which, by the end of the day, John Oldcastle finds a new love and Brother Lorenzo remembers an old.

As Juan Borgia drinks too much cheap wine in the Tavern-in-the Wall and Carlo and Vincenzo search fruitlessly for Matteo, Saint Zeno himself – dead since 371 AD – comes alive. He has lain, bones and crumbling cloth and shrinking sinews, for one thousand, one hundred and twenty-four years. His bones lay first in the church of the cathedra, now called Santa Maria Matricolore, then five hundred years later he was carefully moved to rest in the new basilica, built especially to house his mortal remains by Charlemagne himself. Two hermits, Carus and Benignus, were chosen to carry his light-as-dust cadaver from Santa Maria to his new home where King Pepin of Italy, son of Charlemagne, waited with an enormous crowd to welcome him to his final resting place. And – with one clumsy short-term removal back to the Old City and Santa Maria's to avoid a tenth century Magyar invasion – final it was to be. Other invaders – French, Vikings, Swiss mercenaries – came and went but still Zeno lay still and fading. Around him however, the little church built of rose-cream volcanic tuff grew and breathed and bulged with a greedy, beating heart of its own. Portico and extensions, bell tower, Romanesque arches, great bronze doors, all crowned by Brioloto's rose window, looking down like a wheel of fortune upon them all. Here Zeno lies, deep beneath the fine floor with the nave, the aisles and the transept above, deep in the crypt. The crypt itself has a nave with eight aisles, the arches of which are supported by forty-nine columns, each topped by a unique capitol. The entrance columns and bas-reliefs show terrifying creatures – griffins, cynocephali, serpents, manticores – all the better to encourage a suitable frisson of horror in the heart of those who venture down to be with the dead. Zeno is not alone down here – there are numerous bishops moldering away in solid stone sarcophagi – but he is the first, the foremost, the famed. He is Zeno and today he comes alive.

---------- ∞∞∞ ----------

The man to discover the miracle is an old deacon called Justin. Justin has been a deacon at San Zeno's basilica for thirty years, he has seen three bishops in his time and will see a fourth before God calls him in. In the Book of Timothy the ideal deacon is described as grave, not double-tongued, not given to much wine and not greedy of filthy lucre. If this is so, then Justin is most assuredly a good deacon for he fulfills all of these most worthy criteria. As he sweeps the crypt floor – a ceremonial duty rather than one of necessity as there are servants to do the actual cleaning – he goes over the sermon and Mass over which he has just presided. The Bishop is otherwise occupied apparently and Justin was given very little notice but fortunately he has many sermons stored up in his head, just waiting to be allowed the fresh air of exposition and one about Esther, wife of Xerxes, had sprung easy and fresh out of its stable. He is deep in thought, trying to remember whether he has remembered every detail, for Justin likes to look at his congregation on the very few occasions he has to speak to them and so he does not rely on written notes. The Bishop has a definite stern style and booming voice but Justin has a quiet pride in his ability to tell a story well. He stops. Oh dear. He mixed up the order of events slightly; Esther had not known about the massacre until Mordecai told her but in this afternoon's sermon...did he have her telling Mordecai instead of the other way around? Now that would not make sense, no surely he would not...

He stops. He is quite old but in good health, all five senses, thanks be to God, working almost as well as when he had been a boy. There is a smell. Where is it coming from? And he knows it...what is it? Light, slightly acrid, just floating away as his nose follows its thread, the scent of...iron. That is it. But of course the scent of iron means...blood. It is as if someone has left behind a freshly slaughtered leg of lamb or side of beef. Not unpleasant exactly...Something in the periphery of his vision is wrong. Every tomb, every niche, every plinth, every plaque upon the wall, every alcove, he knows this place as well as any man living. Something is wrong. Something out of its place. And yet this cannot be because everything down here in the main nave is fixed, part of the structure, cemented into the stone floor. It is simply blocks of marble sarcophagi, some in the centre of the nave, others snug against the walls in alcoves. There are cells ahead of him towards the end of the nave – one occupied by a Dominican monk who seems to have returned after disappearing – but the doors are firmly shut. He swings around slowly, full circle, narrowing his eyes. No, nothing. No buckets of dirty water left behind, no votive candles, no flowers. His heart slows. Ahead of him in pride of place is the tomb of Zeno himself, a plaster and wood simulacrum of the saint lying with its feet pointing towards him. The mask has moved. Zeno's silver mask has always sat upon the simulacrum's face; it is periodically polished but never moved. Not for centuries. But now it sits upon the folded hands. It seems untarnished. It has been moved carefully and placed exactly over the joining of both sets of fingers. Justin walks closer.

'Holy Mother of God.' Stops. Walks closer still. '*Mater misericordiae. Vita, dulcedo et spes nostra, salve.*' He cannot believe what he is seeing. And yet seeing it, he is. Genuflecting, he drops the broom, the noise echoes around the empty nave, candles dip and bend. His breath comes out in one great painful gasp. He reaches out. Touches. Snatches his hand back and runs for the steps.

---------- ∞∞∞ ----------

'Tell me again, Justin! Calm yourself, man! Stop crying. I cannot hear what you are saying. Take a breath and tell me again.' They were walking fast from the palatum to the basilica of Saint Zeno, Lucius trailing in their wake. The Bishop was at least a foot taller than the deacon, his strides double the length and Justin was having to run to keep up.

'The blessed saint!' he exhaled wheezily, they passed women with full bags, carts of rotting vegetables, stallholders encroaching the thoroughfare. Above them, the high buildings loomed over towards each other like heavily laden trees bending with their own weight. The dusk sky was still grey and rose not black but the walls above them blocked out much of the light.

'What of him?' the Bishop impatiently lifted a boy from his path, set him down on the side and continued on his way without losing so much as a stride. They came out of the alleyway and broke out into the wide space of San Zeno square. Here the light was still golden, the Basilica glowing pink and cream. Lucius, who was portly, had been long left behind. Justin caught up.

'He is alive, my Lord Bishop! Alive!'

'How so? Did you speak to him?'

'My Lord! I would not dare!'

'But he was sitting up? Breathing? Broken out from his sarcophagus?'

'No, no, he has come alive in the form of the wooden figure of his holy image. Just as . . . ah ah . . . God made Adam from clay and Adam was no more than lifeless mud, just as a statue and a wooden image are the . . . ah . . . simulacrum of life but no more than shadows . . . ah ah . . . upon the wall. But then through his most miraculous grace, the Lord breathed life into the inanimate clay and it became flesh, flesh! My Lord, can we slow down?'

'And this . . . wooden figure is now flesh?'

'Yes, my Lord! There is no doubt. He even smells of blood!'

'What?' the Bishop stopped so suddenly that Justin fell into the prelate's black and red cloak. 'He smells of blood?'

'Yes. Most assuredly. It is an unmistakable smell.'

'It is.' They strode up the steps and through the great double doors, down the crypt steps and Justin was once against standing beside the great tomb with its painted figure atop. Everything was as it had been. The still silent figure, paint now faded and peeling in places. The mask moved away from its proper abode, the face of the wooden figure covered anew with the flesh of a living man.

'*Pie deus*. Oh most merciful God.' The Bishop had believed it for all of four heartbeats even as he knew in the sly corners of his mind that it was not so. Saints would come alive at Judgement and they would burn and glow and be fiery beacons of light and glory. They would not lie still with the freshly sliced face of Matteo the Spaniard, slippery and wet upon their faces.

'Mother of God, *mater misericordiae, vita, dulcedo, et spes nostra*.'

'See! See, my Lord Bishop, see!" Justin was almost jumping from one foot to the other in excitement. This was truly the most glorious day of his little life. 'His face has skin and lips and brows and beard. Just as we were told in the *Zeno Vitam Sanctum*, this is his own visage, his own likeness.'

'Other men also have skin and lips and brows and beards, you fool! And one unhappy individual has sacrificed his own this grim day.'

'I don't understand, my Lord. Are you saying that this is not a miracle? How can a statue grow the skin of a saint and it not be accounted the most incredible miracle? This is better than the image of Madonna and Child in the Basilica del Santa Maria dei Miracoli. What do the Venetians have? A small dull picture of Mother and Holy Child which has cured a few headaches! And the donors have given thousands and thousands of ducats to build a whole new church around her. And you yourself have venerated the blessed Anthony's tongue in Padua – the rest of the great man's jaw all rotted away as is right but the tongue still pink and glistening! How is this miracle any different? Indeed, an entire face must surely be greater evidence of God's good favour upon this town than a simple tongue? I think that only the arm of Saint Thomas Aquinas could better this . . .'

'Shall we go to San Domenico and bring it here?'

'My lord, it is all the way south in Naples.'

'And what about the dragon's bones hanging in the basilica of Santa Maria e San Donato?'

'I . . . I don't know, my lord. I think Venezia is very fortunate to have such incredible objects but this . . . this Face of Zeno, my lord, it would rival any arms or images or dragon bones. This town will be the greatest city in the North when news of this reaches the populace. How the bells will ring! How people will flock to our walls!'

The Bishop felt a drawn-out longing. For supremacy over Venezia, for the right to patriarchy which would surely come, for the gold which would flow in with the pilgrims, their purses fat with coin. He would be the prelate who welcomed a resurrected saint back into the world. His own beatification would not be impossible. There would be another basilica, this time built for him . . .

He was tired, so tired. This nonsense had gone on too long. Angry boys had killed each other in a street just two buildings away from this church. A foolish monk had married two children in this very crypt against the orders of family and Podesta alike. In the cloisters of Santa Maria Matricolore the finest nobleman in the city had been cut down for no reason than simply being in the wrong place. And in Santa Maria's nave the same two children had killed themselves with poison and blade. It was a damnable mess. A damnable mess and he was not going to glorify or make memorable such a terrible summer with another lie.

'Justin. Go and lock the main doors. Keep Lucius outside on watch. We cannot have the ignorant and clumsy come trooping in.'

Bowing, Justin the Deacon took the steps two at a time, quite some feat for a man of fifty and one. The huge bronze doors were heavy and had to be pushed closed one at a time, the solid wooden length of polished oak swinging down to fit into the latch so that they could not be swung open again. He ignored the shouts and then banging of Lucius who had caught them up. Sweat shone on his forehead and he glowed pink with exertion and excitement. But by the time he raced back down the stairs, the Bishop was on his knees in prayer and the flesh face of Saint Zeno a silver mask once more.

---------- ∞∞∞ ----------

John Oldcastle did not witness the miracle of Saint Zeno's Face and would not have believed it a miracle even if he had. He had no use for holy images, saint's arms or even dragon's bones and would have helped his friend Savonarola put them all upon the fire. Neither did he witness the rather unceremonious and certainly hasty departure of Juan Borgia from the city walls. With his two remaining men, the Papal Gonfalonier clasped the reins of his horse with one hand, as the other arm hung swollen by his side, and kicked the stallion into canter as they crossed through the Porta Palio and over the bridge. Boys scattered, a cart turned over, a wooden cage of geese split open and chaos ensued. By the time order was restored and the geese recaptured, it was almost time for the gate to come down and the Night Watch take their places. The three horsemen were by this time long gone. None of them would return.

John himself was preparing his client for the next day's confession. Understandably delighted, Lord Cyprian pressed upon him wine and fine food but the Englishman ate enough to be courteous and accepted his fee in ducats before taking his leave. Firenze was calling and after Firenze, London and his old life. The little house in Spitalfields, his wide and hard-working common-law wife, her dutiful son, the comfortable existence they led there together. He had no intention of staying overlong. Gandia had gone but he would keep for another time. Lorenzo Borgia had made up his mind and the die was cast but Oldcastle had no stomach to witness what *Justicia* would do to the old man. It was getting late. His room upstairs was well warmed and Cyprian had sent up more food, there was a huge tub of fresh hot water waiting by the fire, fresh linens, a fur stole for his neck, books, paper, sleep. But instead he slipped out the side door and made his way through the quiet streets towards the Podesta's solid, square tower with its crenellated fringe and sullen merlons for one last time. Celestina had known he was coming, the door swung open even as his knuckles rose for a second knock. The old blind dog sniffed at his hand and approved him.

'She seems better,' the housekeeper said softly. 'but she'll be dizzy so don't talk too fast or too long. I'd sing a song if I were you. Rosa likes poetry and Livia likes music. So you won't go wrong with a song.'

'I'll just tell them he's gone, gone for good.'

'You'll give them a bloody song, Englishman. A song about kings that were and are and will be, somesuch nonsense about swords in stones and ladies in lakes. They'll like that.'

'I'll do my best.' And he stepped lightly up the stone, turned right upon the landing and the dog laid down to wait.

---------- ∞∞∞ ----------

That night, Saint Zeno wiped Matteo's foul stench from his wooden face and slipped down the nave to slide himself carefully under the door of the little cell where the elderly monk was sleeping. He hovered at the end of the hard wooden pallet for a long while and then slipped even more carefully into his mind.

---------- ∞∞∞ ----------

It is 1454 and northern Italy is about to enter a period of relative peace, hope and prosperity. The wars between the northern Lombard city-states and the Empire have momentarily come to an end with their victory over Frederik I at Legnano and the fractious families all vying for dominance in the vacuum left behind have been squashed by the Peace of Lodi. The Scaglieri have been forced out to skulk in the skirts of the emperor and his successors. The north is now ruled by the four Duchies and the two Republics. And in this peace, the North blooms. Art, philosophy, music, theatre, architecture, mathematics, poetry; for fifty years a re-birth of all culture demonstrates itself in celebration, innovation and adventure in every field. In Firenze, Cosimo de Medici the banker is transforming all that can be seen, read, touched, heard and walked upon. His new Michelozzi -designed library at San Marco is free to use for all those interested in bettering themselves, those now called the literati. To fill the shelves, he is sending out archivists and librarians by the dozen, men like Bracciolini, the eagle-eyed book scout, who have been set free to fly to every city in Europe, to Syria, to Egypt, to Greece, all with the one task; to bring back books. And those precious volumes that then find themselves in Firenze, he has copied by his forty-five strong team of copyists. The very first complete collection in Latin of Plato, Herodotus, precious Aristotle–at the same time, he is patronizing Donatello and filling the city with his statues. Further north in Venezia, that cradle of trade with eyes looking both west and east, wealth creates wealth until the one hundred and eighteen islands seem to sink beneath the weight of their own unending success. What was not possible in Venezia? What was not available to eat, to wear, to drink, to smell, to sell on at twice the price?

Just a few dozen miles to the west of Venezia, a smaller city-state accepts her fate as subject vassal and makes the best of it. Churches grow, gardens bloom, children thrive, the markets become increasingly full of the most wonderful and strange of goods. Famous through Europe, the great Basilica of San Zeno glows and breathes, the little church of Santa Anastasia in the Roman Old Town extends its tower, its arches, its statuary, the number of columns, of funerary plaques, of alcoves. And next door, the Dominican abbey of Santa Anastasia grows too, buying land beyond and building cloisters, refectory, herb gardens, infirmary and novice dormitory. It would never rival the great Benedictine abbey adjacent to San Zeno of course but the Dominican Order had never set itself up to rival the men of Saint Benedict but to offer an alternative.

And here in 1454 are two boys, one seven and the other one eight. Lorenzo is the older of the two but he is quite small, often ill. Uffizi is seven but tall, robust, direct of eye. They are like brothers because neither can really remember brothers of their own. They arrived at the abbey on almost the same day, both scared, both sniffing back salty shame, both traumatized by the betrayals of their mothers who, they felt, had abandoned them. And so they find each other very quickly. Their futures are mapped out. Or to a certain degree. If they are found to be quick of mind, obedient to instruction, clever of eye, deft of finger then they will be trained as illustrators or translators or copyists. And what a time to work with books! To find God in Platonic forms. To find God also in the true world of Aristotle. To have in your hands, books and rolls and papers which have been reverently brought all the way from Persia. As boys they yearn to be initiated into the sacred mysteries of paint and ink and ideas which line the multi-hued path to God himself. How these two boys try at their letters, at the skill of transferring ink to paper, at their copying. For if they do not appear to have the aptitude or skill, then they will face the ignominy of menial work–kitchens, cleaning, animals, cooking–or the slightly less shameful life of infirmary assistant.

The months and years pass by with a gentle rhythm. And Saint Zeno be praised, both Lorenzo and Uffizi are as bright as dawn crickets.

They are not encouraged to discuss their former lives for it is understood without being explained, that they will never return home. But as they whisper to each other after Compline as the older novices snuff out the candles in the novice dormitory, they trade precious memories. These memories are like shiny stones fished from the bottom of rivers on sunny days and they are all the more precious for being finite. Uffizi has a smooth grey stone which is his father's last sad smile as he slipped into unconsciousness and death. Lorenzo has a bright ochre-red one which is, he thinks, the birth of a little sister and the proud smiles of a man who is not his father but hers. They have stones for food they miss and stones for friends with whom they used to play, names now guessed at as much as remembered. And the boys trade stones just as Venezia trades cinnamon and silk and coin. They swap and gift and trust their tiny pile of memories until the two piles become one and Uffizi cannot remember which lost friends are his and which are Lorenzo's and Lorenzo almost remembers holding his own father's hand as he dies. One of Lorenzo's most precious stones is the rich brown one with the golden flecks. This is the stone of the first Monday of the month. He asks Uffizi in a whisper one night which day of the month the little purse of money came for his mother? Uffizi does not understand. No money came, his mother went to work each day cleaning the kitchens of highborn families. She would come home with the pennies, no one sent them. And when her fingers ached too much and she could not work any more, he was sent to Santa Anastasia as a gift. Lorenzo is confused and re-examines the yellow flecks of the stone. No, he remembers right. The money came on the first Monday and it meant that they had meat and sometimes slabs of honeycomb which made his mother laugh and scold at the same time. He had never been told but he knew that the money came from his father's family. How strange that Uffizi's father's family did not do the same. The very last stone to be shared, a smooth black pebble that was always cold, was not added to the pile until the boys were almost young men. It was Lorenzo's final memory of his mother, screaming and crying, reaching out to him as three men in some kind of armoured livery came to take him away from her. By this time, he has perhaps fortuitously lost the stones that represent the two hours on the horse, the vomit on the mare's mane, the childish attempt to run away whilst peeing. But the cold touch of black stone never fails to bring back his mother's face. When he adds it to the pile, Uffizi touches it gently and reaches out to trace his cool finger down Lorenzo's cheek. This is perhaps the start of the sin.

Earlier on in their lives together, both boys knew they were bastards. They were not clear until slightly older what that meant in terms of the Church but they were aware from the tone in which the word was said that it was not a good thing. But both boys observed from very early on that the Abbot protected Lorenzo from the majority of these slurs whilst ignoring everything said to Uffizi, no matter how cruel. And as they grew out of childhood it became accepted and never analysed that Lorenzo was in some way special whereas Uffizi–who did not even have a proper name, just a description of a great building where his father sometimes had laboured–was simply the bastard son of two nobodies who, for reasons abhorrent although unknown, had chosen to bring him into the world whilst unwed. Fortunately for Uffizi, he was clever. Even brighter and quicker than Lorenzo who studied hard and made good progress. Uffizi though was more than bright. He held whole poems in his mouth and let them drift out from between his teeth, stanza by stanza. He could name the constellations even on cloudy nights. He added up figures and stopped using his fingers to count, he could recite huge giant slabs of scripture without a pause or mistake, he was so deft with a brush he was eventually allowed to use sable not goat.

They both took their vows on the same day with five other novices. They took their vows of obedience to the abbot, to the Order, to Saint Dominic himself, to God, the Blessed Mother and to the will of the community. They swore to seek to do the will of God in their vocation as Friars and members of the Order, they promised to preach the Gospel and endeavour to grow in perfection. They vowed to follow Jesus on his path by renouncing worldly gain through the spirit of poverty.

'We seek to purify our minds and hearts through God's gift of chastity,' they said together and they meant it fervently for the gift of chastity kept them safe from women who filled them with dread. The sin of lust was something they associated wholly with the weaker sex, no one had warned these boys that what they might also feel for each other was also sinful. Their passions – Lorenzo and Uffizi – were for ideas and illustrations, Uffizi in particular was clever with shading and smoothing different hues of the same colour together, just as he saw in nature. Lorenzo was the reader, he devoured all that he was allowed; Aristotle, Theothrastus, Pliny's Natural History, he followed the garrulous Greek and then the grumpy Frenchman who oversaw the infirmary and herb garden, determined to become the *secondo discipulo*. And as the boys passed into adolescence, so their responsibilities increased, as did their devotion to their order and as did their devotion to each other.

It did not just become physical and therefore sinful on one particular day. They did not stand on the edge of a river and then one day jump in. They were not *here* – good in the eyes of God – and then one day they were *here* – damnable sinners destined for Hell. No, they grew up and grew together and shared touch each and every day of that growing. An arm around the shoulder, a playful punch of the arm, a hug of solace, a reassuring squeeze. This is how life is. This is how love is. This is how they were.

The other Brothers had no inkling that the bastard brothers–which had now become a most affectionate monika for both boys were well loved–sometimes found themselves gently rubbing each other's shoulders, backs, thighs. When the gentle reassurances became mouths upon mouths, curious tongues, probing fingers, there was no one to warn or fulminate or punish. Perhaps it was a particularly innocent set of brothers at that time, perhaps an abbot too interested in other things, perhaps the small community was just too used to see the pair together and thought they were brothers in blood as well as in God.

Zeno pushes the dreaming on a little. He is not really interested in the expression of physicality–it being such a long time since he himself had such a thing–but he knows what is coming and he wishes to give old Brother Lorenzo something that will strengthen his resolve. He gently manoevres the dream towards a deep vermillion sunset back in 1467, both young men are twenty or thereabouts and they have found a space up on the roof above the cloisters which cannot be overlooked. They have finished their duties in the herbarium and library and are not due to attend Vespers until sunset. There is the smell of honeysuckle and olive oil and paint powders. Uffizi has not washed the hues off his hands properly and the powder clogs up his fingernails, leaving little traces as he runs his fingers along Lorenzo's forearm. He is a favourite of the steward and has a goatskin of fresh milk to share. The smaller boy–for they are still boys really–leans his head against his friend's shoulder. Uffizi has grown broad with his father's physique. He could have been a blacksmith or a labourer, it never ceases to amaze Lorenzo that those strong hands hold brushes and feather quills so gently.

'I'll sleep in your cell tonight,' said Uffizi ruffling Lorenzo's dark hair with an absent-minded affection, 'Brother Stephen has a terrible cold and he is snoring so loudly through the walls that I hardly slept at all last night.' Lorenzo turned his face inwards a little so that it rested closely against Uffizi's ear and cheek.

'Good,' he said happy with the simple expectation of pleasure, 'Augustin is doing his rounds a little earlier tonight, wait for the candle in the window.' They could have lasted a long time, those moments taken upon the roof half hidden by the kind and generous honeysuckle. But in all likelihood these times together were short and snatched. In memory however they were extended and sweet and lasted until both were utterly sated with the completeness of it all.

Zeno lets the dream linger. He allows the memory of the times spent, flesh to flesh, upon the roof, upon the narrow bunk, outstretched in the meadow amongst the corn flowers on the occasions they left the abbey to preach the Word; he allows these memories to stretch into eternity. The old man is prepared to do a brave and generous thing. He will bring shame upon his name and he will die a horrible death. A small thing for him to dream of strong, brown arms around his shoulder, gentle fingers running themselves down his cheek, his throat, between his rough wool habit and down the skin upon his chest.

No need now for his mind to take that old familiar and dreadful path towards the end of the story. The grumbling pain in Uffizi's lower belly, the grumble which became sharp agonizing pain. The raging temperature, the incomprehensible raving, the crying out for his brother to help him. A short respite when Lorenzo held his friend's hand in relief and agreed that the worst was surely over, both missing the look of resigned sadness upon the brother physic's face. The return of burning pain, all over the belly now, a quick steep slide into unconsciousness, breathing slowing and coming to a gurgling halt sometime between Lauds and Prime. No need to remind Lorenzo of the feeling that he had stepped off a high cliff into a pitch-black hole, that he had woken every morning for thirty years and fallen anew every single day.

Zeno observed the slow sweet dreaming for a while, tinkered around the edges so that the sunset was a little deeper, the scent of fresh milk a little stronger, the feel of flesh upon flesh a little warmer. His ghostly fingers reached out beyond the shadows of Plato's cave and snatched small piece of the Form of sunset, the Form of flesh, the Form of scent and drew them slowly and carefully into old Lorenzo Borgia's subconscious mind.

Let him sleep another few hours, let him smell olive oil, paint powders, milk and fresh sweat. Let him smell honeysuckle. Let him be fortified and let him not be alone.

Wednesday

CHAPTER TWENTY THREE

In which Brother Lorenzo tells his story and the woman at the heart of this tragici fabula is released to start again.

By mid-morning, there was a column of men, horses and carts trudging, prancing and rolling their way through the western gate. The Podesta led the procession on his chestnut Andalusian stallion but it was Dido the Friesian who drew the most applause from the waiting populace who lined the narrow streets and plazas. Word of her audacious bravery in the face of Papal tyranny was already becoming the stuff of legend. She was no longer a foul-mooded mare with a barely controllable temper, she was the embodiment of the city itself, kept docile and impotent for too long under Papal–or was it Venezian?–dictatorship and now breaking free to a bright new dawn. Accepting with some bad grace the mood of the crowd, the Podesta drew in his own mount as they approached the main cathedral piazza and allowed Dido and Luca Carraresi to lead the column. Flowers were strewn, sweet bunches of herbs and tall grasses, even apples and carrots which caused the horses to pull at their reins and the riders to flinch as they rained down. The cathedral bells rang in both the hour of Sext and the return of their lords. There was some bowing and cheering from the marble steps where only the day before Dido had apparently seized the Papal bastard and shook him down the stairs, trampling him with her sharp shiny hooves. The young Duke had then run crying from the scene, pursued by Dido who bit his papal arse so deep he shat blood. Carraresi accepted the adoring cheers with a slight grimace. As the heir and scion of a great Paduan house, he was not overjoyed at being linked to the humiliation of the Pope's own son but it was a long way to Rome and he would have his pick of pretty girls that night.

The Podesta stood on the steps with the Bishop and they exchanged brief, curt summaries. Anyone noticing would have seen the Lord of the City scowl, grimace, scowl again and then sigh, shoulders shrugging. He then left the scene early, letting the young men have their fun without bothering the populace with any speeches. After all, it was not as if they were returning from a great battle. A three-day council between the Emperor and the Lombard cities was important but it did not necessitate an Imperial Triumph. His wife was already back at the house with Paulo the Steward, both of them having been given a slightly censored version of what had occurred in their week's absence from a calm but relieved Celestina. The house was clean enough but Paulo narrowed his eyes and gave his wife one of his 'we shall discuss this later' looks as he noticed the missing rugs. Quite what he would say when he noticed the missing Calahorra red was a problem for another day.

Giving Paulo orders to strip all the beds and burn the sheets, the Podesta left the Fourth Tower and made his way with a small entourage back to Santa Maria. Ordinarily a Council meeting would be held in his study but this trial – if that is what it was – involved the interrogation of a monk and so the raised dais in the apse, behind the cathedra throne and altar, was right and proper. As the four deacons and the sacristan scurried around getting the table, chairs, refreshment ready, the Podesta sat next to the Bishop on the front bench. Both men put their heads in their hands.

Finally. The Podesta. 'I leave you in charge for one week.'

There was the low sound of men fussing on the dais. The hum of Benedictine chant from next door in the abbey. Slightly off key. The novices rehearsing for Saint Bernard of Clairvaux whose Day it was the morrow. The Bishop counted to ten.

'I do not think, Lord Podesta, that you had the pleasure of meeting Juan Borgia, Duke of Gandia, Papal Gonfalonier?'

'He's a boy isn't he? Nineteen? Twenty? What of it? I'd have thought papal support would have made our case all the more solid.'

'Hmmm.'

'Lord Bishop! What is 'hhhmmmm' supposed to mean? How is it that I left you with an innocent monk to exonerate and a guilty woman to hang and somehow we seem to be on the verge of accomplishing the opposite? And what is this about Saint Zeno? Men are whispering in the ranks that he has come alive! But when we enter the city, I see no banners, no celebrations, no monks chanting in the streets.'

'A misunderstanding by my deacon, best left to fade.'

'I see,' Clearly the great man did not. 'We could do with a good miracle. Are you sure it was a mistake?'

'Absolutely.'

'A shame. And the damned horse? How is it we managed to physically attack a Vatican Captain? You could be excommunicated, you know.' There might have been a slight glint of lordly humour in his eye. The older man with the slate-grey hair shrugged.

'I shall bear the weight of papal displeasure. But I somehow think that the young Duke will not want the world and his father to know the details of his brief sojourn with us here in the North.'

'Just as well.'

'*Deus sit ut.*'

They bent forward to pray awhile. The Podesta cannot last more than ten beats.

'Will he truly tell this tale of treachery tomorrow?' The Podesta had pretensions to poetry as a boy which had sadly never met with critical or commercial success. He gave occasional recitals which the Bishop dutifully attended but the man had a real tendency to overdo alliteration.

'I think he will. Yes, I do.'

The Podesta was incredulous and who could blame him? 'But he will die. The Council will have no choice at all but to sentence him to death as a traitor to the Republic.'

'I know. But he has made up his mind.'

'Then damn well unmake it for him!'

'He wants this, I think. I cannot say why.'

'You can bloody well... oh, I see. *Ego te absolvo*?'

'*Ego te absolvo*.'

'So he has been forgiven for one sin but still wants to be punished for it?'

'It is easier for us all if we accept that he has been a Scaglieri spy for twenty years and has passed treasonous messages inciting rebellion amongst the younger members of the populace.'

'Hah. If that is the easiest option, I do not want to know the more difficult ones you discarded first. I shall despair of our Council if they accept such a fairy tale, you know.'

'Quite.'

Another pause. 'One lord will be happy.'

'He will.'

'And the other?'

'Has come down with a severe cold on the chest. He has never really got over the shock of losing both son and wife in one day, poor man. I should imagine he is concentrating on his prayers today, not the fate of the Dominican monk who gave his boy such bad advice. I am not convinced that he was ever particularly interested in seeing the foolish old woman suffer, I think he was directing his grief outwards in all directions so as to not feel it inwardly. But one can only put off these things for so long. There is always an accounting for unexpressed grief.'

'By Zeno, Bishop, what a sensitive soul you possess! With such a heart, you could do great good to those in need of pastoral care. You would have made a great … aah …'

'Priest, Lord Podesta? Thank you. I do my best. Ah, now here are the Greybeards – Stefano dei Casale can hardly walk without a stick and yet he is ten years my junior, such are the legacies of over-indulgence and indolence. And the younger Bertoli of the Master Guildsmen. Younger of course a rather subjective appellation, he was old when I first arrived here I am sure … I can hear Cyprian Capulet laughing with someone – Abbot Horace I think – on the steps. Yes, I should imagine our Lord Capulet is happy today. You and I. That's six. We shall wait until we are eight – I suppose we must include Valmarana, he was left *in loco* after all – and then I shall have the Dominican brought over. The Council of Ten can be the Council of Eight just this once. And may God forgive us all for what we are about to do.'

---------- ∞∞∞ ----------

Eighty years earlier and a thousand miles west, a thirty-nine-year-old heretic called Sir John Oldcastle, Lord Cobham, also faced a trial. He was – thanks to his third marriage to Joan, heiress to Cobham – a peer of the realm, master of Cooling Castle. He was also closest of friends to the young King Henry V of England himself. And so unlike Lorenzo Borgia, John Oldcastle Senior got a full St Paul's Cathedral of lords and bishops, presided over by Thomas Arundell, Archbishop of Canterbury himself. Lorenzo Borgia will walk down the nave to the apse with his head bowed, he will not need manacles, he has a gentle smile on his face. Oldcastle however was a raging lion.

Oldcastle had been betrayed by friends in the Welsh hills and wounded upon capture. A veteran of Henry's French campaigns, a hero of Agincourt, he was as tough and wily as an eel. As clever and amusing as he was stubborn and recalcitrant, he somehow managed to charm his way into the young King's friendship again and again and again. Whispering his heresies into the young Plantagenet's royal ear, he was feared and hated by the other lords but loved by the common soldiery who would have followed him anywhere, yea to the gates of Hell. Which was exactly where the Church pronounced him heading.

'There is nought in the Holy Book of priests nor bishops!' He would shout whilst raising tankard after tankard as his men cheered him on. 'Where does it say that we must confess our sins to priests? A lecherous drunken priest forgiving the lechery and drunkenness of John Oldcastle! What farce is this? Only God . . . God alone can forgive my sins!'

Finally, his heresy – Lollardy they called it after Lolhard the heretic burnt somewhere in France – alienated him even from sweet Harry himself and Oldcastle was arrested. The young King's vigilance was perhaps not all it should have been for Oldcastle escaped Windsor and headed for Castle Cooling, his wife's great seat in Kent.

'Come John, appear before Convocation, tell them what they wish to hear!' had been Harry's royal begging. And so, before Convocation then John Oldcastle had appeared. *No, to the transubstantiation of bread into flesh and wine into blood*, he declared. *Heretic!* the Bishops called him. *No to priests hearing confession. No to the worship of statues. Heretic! Heretic!* They had screamed, eyes popping. The Lollard Knight was thrown in the Tower. But the power of the Church was despised and the passion of Oldcastle admired. And the young king still, still, still had hopes of his friend seeing sense and bending the knee to Rome's behemoth. *Give me forty days with him,* said the King to Convocation, *forty days to make him see Truth.* ***But the Truth shall set you free***, says Scripture and so a daring plot hatched him out of the Tower's iron jaws and flew him westwards into the arms of the Celts. Another plot, a worse one this time, a traitor's plot, an unforgiveable plot. To surprise the King himself at his Twelfth Night Mummers Ball, to lay hands upon an anointed king's person – his own friend! – to hold hostage king and princeling brothers, to force him to Lollard will. Had he lost his mind, this hero of French conquests, had heresy addled his wits like canker in the brain? Betrayed by a spy, the plot revealed, Harry beyond fury in his humiliation. Four years on the run, more plots, more spies and turncoats, uprisings, deals with the Scots, with Germans, with soldiery, with Lollards. Unwise but lusty visits to his much-loved wife and their six, – or was it seven? – children, midnight escapes on sweating horses. One more betrayal and desperate retreat to the Black Mountains – when they caught him, he fought to such a wound that he had to be carried to London in a litter.

'*No! To temporal power in the hands of ambitious priests*! He shouted at his second time before Convocation. *No! To lascivious priests turning bread and wine into flesh and blood. God as Flesh is everywhere at all time, yes in the bread, yes in the wine but not because a incelibate bishop has made them so. No*!'

'*Heretic*' the Bishops said again, '*De Heretica Comburendo*!'

'*No!*' he shouted even as they dragged him, torn legs and all, down the nave. '*No, to the Word of God being hidden from God's people in Greek and Latin.*'

'*Burn!*' they pronounced as the great doors opened and he was surrounded by the December sleet of his last earthly day. If he thought he had another forty days' reprieve, another softening of the royal heart, he was much mistaken. The bishops were not going to make the same error twice and there and then he was carted south-west to St Giles' Fields and there and then hanged, brought down alive and burnt, gallows and all.

---------- ∞∞∞ ----------

Eighty years later, the Bishop of a small Italian city-state had his own experience of burning heretics, heretics not unlike Sir John Oldcastle. His time in Spain with Torquemada had seared furrows and scars upon his memory and he did not want to return to them. Here before him though is no bleeding, shouting Lollard.

Lorenzo Borgia is quiet and reserved, he bows meekly to the assembled City Council of Ten, he does not demand ecclesiastical privilege as might be his right, he does not demand advocacy. He seems to hover slightly, so smooth and gentle are his steps to the transept where he stands. Looking down upon him from the dais, not the full Convocation of angry English prelates but eight old men; Greybeards and Mice. He does not return questions with insults or orthodoxies with heresy. Lorenzo Borgia is a devout Catholic. *Yes, the priest has the right to receive confession. Yes, the spiritual must involve itself in the temporal. Yes, the bread and wine becomes flesh and blood. Yes, yes, yes, it is all true, it is all right and it must all be told in Greek and Latin to protect it from men just like John Oldcastle.*

But Lorenzo Borgia is not on trial for heresy. And neither is he facing the charge of unnatural lust. This is a civil charge and thus he faces the civil Council and trial beneath the *Promissione Maleficarum* (for all the good it has ever done them). The *Promissione* is a cobbling together of the law codes from Rome to Justinian to church canon. It has little coherence and delights in contradiction, it is largely ignored and yet must be respected. This Council of Ten could not recite more than five points from it but they know they must be seen to bow beneath its heavy, ponderous weight.

How must they begin as they take their seats?

'*We hold that justice demands our unceasing vigil and diligent concern in order to correct excess and to punish crime.*'

Simple enough. They recite and they sit. But what is a crime? What constitutes an excess? Who decides guilt and what is appropriate punishment? That is where the clerks tiptoe in, like nervous mice, to flick through the pages and find lines that make sense.

This morning however there is no need for clever clerks and the nimble fingers of learned deacons. There is no defense from the accused and so the *Sex Essentialia* – the six essential stages of any trial – can be sped through. The *accusare*, the *intromissione*, the *placatare*, the *voto majoris*–all four already agreed. Accusation, investigation, case put to the Council, the vote. What is there to dispute when the accused stands before them to testify to his own guilt? After the accused's testimony, there would simply be the proposal of penalty and its vote. And so after the eight have agreed that in the sight of God and Man they are Ten, the Podesta beckons for Lorenzo Borgia, *Ordo Praedicatorum* to step forward and speak.

And so the small man with the straggly grey hair tells his little tale of letters carried in the secret pockets of Dominican habits, of encouraging intemperate youths to become even angrier as the summer grew hot. Of performing marriages designed to cause uproar, of fermenting disorder, disarray and disgust. The eight men were at first stunned, then angry, then confused.

'Why do this to the city that has nurtured you, to the abbey that has been your home, to the great Zeno himself who is your father?'

'I was promised great power,' said the monk meekly, 'I was promised the abbey as my own, I was promised the books of this great cathedral's chapter library, I was promised ...' and here perhaps he might have overreached himself, 'I was promised the mask of Zeno to wear upon my face.'

This excited general dismay and much genuflecting.

'He is surely mad,' agreed the Master Guildsman and the Abbot of the Benedictines. 'Only a madman would even imagine such terrible things.'

'Not mad but corrupted!' spluttered the Captain of the Watch, now so ancient the title was purely honorary. 'Corrupted and incomprehensible. The Scaglieri! God forbid the return of such a destructive and tyrannical family. And to plot the death of our esteemed Podesta here, safely returned from the Emperor himself only this morning!'

The Podesta grimaced. He seemed quite unlike his usual ebullient self; clearly the journey from Milan, the series of long diplomatic meetings, trying to avoid whoever was representing the Doge, clearly these things had exhausted him. His words were as tired as his shoulders.

'Your plan, I am sure, did not involve my death, Brother Lorenzo? Perhaps I was to be persuaded to accept Scaglieri patriarchy? To bend the knee?'

A single tired hand of mercy stretching out towards a drowning man. The Bishop looked over to where the old monk in the now tattered grubby habit stood. The mild eyes were half closed, the wrinkled old hands like papery leaves folded one over the other. Surely he might take the offer even now . . . ?

'No, Lord Podesta, your death was at the heart of this enterprise.' Whether the subdued gasps and curses from the table were for his words or for the contrast between the words and the soft kind voice that issued them was not clear. But there was more.

'The higher lords would all have to die, the Scaglieri have retainers to whom they owe a lot of money, they would be given your patrimonies. There would be a new bishop too, no doubt one of my cousins, I forget which one . . . '

'Zeno, stop this nonsense,' Only the Podesta at his left heard the Bishop. The rest of the Council had at first been confused – firstly at why they were there and then by the monk's strangely sweet and calm manner – but now they were getting angry.

'A Borgia bishop! *Sanguis Christi*!' the fat Benedictine abbot flushed in outrage which the actual Bishop found mildly amusing, given the very many years of scarcely veiled animosity between them. Good to know it was better the devil you knew . . .

And so it went on. The monk stood, still and radiating beneficence whilst occasionally uttering the most seditious and terrible of things. On the dais, the Podesta was picking at his rough-cut nails. The Bishop stared sadly into middle distance. The others, frustrated that they had missed the *canticum* of the day before – near-hangings postponed by the last minute intervention of a magical horse with sharpened teeth! – let their passions froth over the edges of their common sense.

'He is surely possessed by some kind of demon!'

'Look at his face! Only fallen angels have such sweetness of skin and lips. Only *reprobi angeli* can stand so calm and still.'

'We need to have him in front of the Doge! This plot threatens Venezia too. We must call in the Avogadori, this is too much for our little Council. Or the Emperor! He is nursing vipers at his breast. He needs to be warned. Podesta, you must return to the Emperor at once and tell him every detail of this cursed conspiracy.'

'I think not,' grunted the Podesta who was very tired and wanted to be in his own bed with his own wife but who was also concerned that it might still smell of the Duke of Gandia's lust. It was well past Vespers, the light was leaving them, and by rights they should not even be holding an interrogation after night's fall. Was he Caiaphas to hide the darkness of his deeds in the shades of a dying day? He gave the Bishop at his side a scowl. This was all his fault. The prelates of this world demanded a share in temporal power, they insisted on sharing it with the secular authorities but in almost every case they did not have the ... the *aptitude*. No, they simply were not suited, even those with an admittedly fair work ethic and intellect like this one, sighing quietly at his elbow.

The Abbot seemed intent on turning this into some ecclesiastical investigation of demonic influence. There was only one way such an investigation would end and they simply did not have the time nor energy to indulge a heresy trial. Such things might excite the masses and the ignorant but it did a town no good at all. And feeding the Inquisition was horribly expensive. And for what? A pile of ashes and the taste of melted fat and scorched wood upon the air. No, this needed to be kept within the secular.

'Good Abbo, this case is not one of satanic influence ...'

'I disagree; I cannot see how such evil can be considered without . . . '

'You may well disagree but yours is not the *publica vox* of the Church at this Council, that great honour lies with our Bishop.'

The dark grey head nodded, almost somnolent. 'Thank you, Podesta. Yes, I agree. Brother Lorenzo, you do not claim the influence of Lucifer in your actions, do you?'

There was a brief second when the Bishop thought he might have given the man an even more horrible way to atone for his guilt. A flash of interest. Then gone and the quiet, simple contentment returned.

'No, my Lord Bishop. I cannot hide my ambition behind the skirts of the devil. I cannot claim that I was duped or suborned or magicked into the immoral labyrinth into which I walked. No, I walked in unaided. I wrote letters, passed letters, read letters, all of my own volition, supernaturally coerced by no one.'

'Thanks be at least,' said the Bishop, somewhat relieved. The Abbo seemed a little disappointed. Lord Cyprian however was leaning forwards and staring down at the man in the dark grey, the man who had married his daughter to the son of his enemy, the man who had given his daughter the sleeping draught which had stolen her wits.

'You say, *soi-disant* Brother, that you were encouraged by another, by some monk now dead and whose name you will not divulge. That you do not know the names of those at the Emperor's court who support the Scaglieri claim alongside the perfidious lord himself. But it seems to me that a plot like this needs a nobleman's hand, a mind full of intrigue and arrogance, a man already here in this poor city-state who like Odysseus' horse could open the gates of Troy to let the invaders in.'

The monk was thinking this line through carefully but the Bishop was quicker.

'No, Lord Cyprian, we shall not go there. There is no evidence of internal conspiracy beyond this foolish brother and the monk now dead. You will not bring your infernal feud back to life by harnessing its horse to a cart already equipped. No, you shall not.'

Cyprian was now on his feet. 'I shall be heard! My daughter, my nephew, my friend, all dead and none yet avenged. If you really see a Scaglieri plot devised in the minds of ignorant Dominican monks and not in ambitious noblemen then you are an innocent dupe and . . .'

'Enough my lord!' Now the Podesta too was on his feet, the monk momentarily forgotten. 'You shall not, my lord! You shall not drag us back to the dark days, *you shall not!* This ends here and it ends today. It ends with this sorry Dominican. You can have your vengeance, you can have your blood. But you shall not drag us back to those days when boys died in the streets and children killed themselves because of the world we had created for them. We shall not return to that place. *Manifestum est?*

Podesta and Bishop stood their ground, secular and spiritual, prelate and lord. Cyprian Capulet sat down. But as he did . . .

'If this sorry creature is to take the weight of treason upon his shoulders, then take it he must. No merciful beheading. No Chinese powder around the neck. If he is a traitor to this Republic, then he needs must pay for that in full.'

There was nothing to be said. Eight men nodded, eight men raised their hands and said their names, eight men signed upon the scribe's paper, eight men bade each other good night and went home to wives, brothers and children.

The Bishop took the condemned man out of the cathedral and led him home to the Basilica of San Zeno for one more night. It was getting cold now, the end of September was near and the clouds now scurried faster and heavier. There was a taste of winter on the tongue. A hint of fires in hearths, roasting meats, damp boots by doors. The few citizens still on the streets bowed as the great man passed, wondering who the elderly man at his side might be and what might be the cause of such a beatific smile. Zeno walked on Lorenzo's other side, ghostly fingers locking himself firmly into the monk's own. The citizens couldn't see him of course but still, something in the twilight air moved them to give the monk his space.

----------∞∞∞----------

When a young man dies of an enflamed appendix it is a most terrible death. When Uffizi of Santa Anastasia Abbey lay writhing and screaming on his last night on earth, the brother Physic and his two assistants knew that he was dying but had very little idea of what. And their ignorance was really the fault of Galen.

There was nothing in medicine that could not be found in Galen; his was a blessed received wisdom a millennium old. Galen's treatises via Avicenna had returned to Italy after a long dark absence and these were viewed as beams of light shining hope into the darkness. All Benedictine and Dominican physics read him avidly, took his advice to watch for imbalance in the four humours, to bloodlet regularly, to perform enemas if there was blockage. But Galen had been in many ways the sensitive soul; he had not dared nor wished to dissect humans, great anatomist though he was. And so he cut open and drew the mysterious inner workings of... Barbary apes. And Barbary apes do not have appendices.

Now if the anatomical works of Aristotle had survived... Aristotle had held no such squeamish niceties. A battlefield corpse was already dead, what harm to take it home and open it gently up? And look, there is that strange little worm again, that tiny tube of flesh hanging away from the caecum. But by the time poor Uffizi lies crying for his long-lost mother, the Great Philosopher's *On The Natural History of Men*—the only copy no less—had succumbed to a fire in the great library of Baghdad. All the learned men of Uffizi's time had was his *Natural History* and *On The Parts of Animals*, no use at all if one wants to learn about the appendix.

And so the three men of medicine staring white-faced over the young man's cot read desperately from Galen, from

Hippocrates and from Avicenna. The youngest of them–ambitious and daring–also had brought with him from Scotland a precious copy of Magister John Aderne's *De Arte Phisicali et Cirurgia*, shamefully recent at just half a century old but even John Aderne had not had the nerve to admit observing an actual dissected human body. He did however write a treatise on the *passio iliaca*, very likely one of the first ever documents detailing appendicitis. Alas, his descriptions were identical to, and thus confused with, any intestinal blockage–so those daring to open up a writhing, screaming body did not even know what they were looking for.

No, tragically for Uffizi and so many countless others like him, the appendix would not be identified for another sixty years when Berengario da Carpi of Bologna published his *Commentaria* in which he described an *addentramentum*–a small empty cavity–at the end of the cecum. The purpose of this strange little worm? Only the blessed God could know. But certainly it was the devil's own pocket for catching things.

Uffizi only knew what had been a high fever, a rumbling ache, a sharp incessant pain which then became a screaming knife, zig and zagging inside his belly. A hot blade under his very skin, burning and glowing and growing. A moment of sweet release when something deep inside seemed to have burst open, momentarily ending the terrible pain. He had slept awhile then, Lorenzo sleepless on the stool by his side, the chief physic looking on sadly for he had witnessed this little reprieve before and guessed rightly it would not last.

When the pain returned–worse and across the whole of his lower belly now–he awoke. The physics urged him to let them help him to the small sunken bath in the lavatorium which they would attempt to fill with hot oil. But by this time, moving him caused so much agonized pleading that he was soon back on the cot, knees brought up to his belly, one arm wrapped around himself, the other outstretched to hold young Lorenzo's hand.

The monks knew that there was an obstruction and so they gently and then not so gently turned him over, sobbing onto his front and tried to force warm water with oil into his anus to unblock the passage. This failing, they sat him up and forced lead pellets down his throat for what would push an obstruction out of the cloaca better than lead? Uffizi choked and hawked the lead up until they forced shut his flaring nostrils; down he swallowed three, perhaps four. They sat and waited. It was past Matins and he had been getting worse since the Matins of two days previous. Lorenzo had not left his side, save on one occasion when the Chief Physic thought of a treatise by Oribasius which was held in the chapter library of Santa Maria and Lorenzo ran through the street to get it. Bishop Barbaro, a timid, bad-tempered little man, had shoo'ed him away empty-handed with peevish assurances that if such a book existed, it would take him three days to find it by which time the boy would either have recovered or be taken by God's good grace.

The emetics, the enemas, the lead pellets, the herbal infusions, all to no avail so out came the fleam, the sharpened metal pen for bloodletting.

The Chief Physic was nervous now. 'The Holy Church has issued an edict against bloodletting,' he reminded them nervously.

'But Galen recommends it!' said the enthusiastic young Scotsman. 'This poor boy's humours are completely out of balance, he has far too much blood in his belly–look you can feel it rising above the skin now, feel how hot it is!–we need to reduce the blood so the yellow bile can be given a chance to increase. Quick, his arm. Hold the bowl.'

And so the blood was drained until Uffizi was almost too weak to moan. Blood spilled from the little bowl and soaked the rough sheets already sodden with oils and vomit and urine and shitty water. The tiny cell–for they had not time to move him to the infirmary–was fetid and the air hot and thick.

Lorenzo was beyond tears. He had prayed to every saint and again and again to Zeno. Uffizi's beautiful face was now beyond recognition; his eyes red and swollen, his lips drawn back like a wolf, his skin white and blotchy, sun-kissed hair now black with sweat and plastered to his skull.

'Pray for me,' he whispered as Lorenzo bent near, 'pray for my soul, light a candle every day.'

'Zeno will save you!' swore Lorenzo fervently even as the older physic sighed sadly for saints do not give us what we want but what we need and what we need is clearly a mystery.

As the night rolled towards Vespers, Uffizi became delirious, calling again for his mother, begging her not to send him away, calling for Lorenzo to hold him tight but when his friend tried, Uffizi pushed him away as if touch alone was fire. He then began to scream out for a knife, a blade to cut open his belly, begging the Physic to either do it or allow him to do it to himself.

'I can cut it out!' he shrieked like a wild animal in a trap, 'I can cut the demon out, just give me a knife, Lorenzo, please, please, let me open up a wound and the Beast will crawl out.'

'We dare not cut you, Brother,' the Physic was exhausted but adamant, 'The Mother Church does not allow it, your body is not your own, it is a holy temple, St Paul tells us this, your body is only on loan and now it is being returned to God, praise be.'

'Lorenzo, please . . .' There was no screaming now, no high animal squeals, just whispers. His fingers were still wrapped around Lorenzo's but they were weak and loose. 'Lorenzo, *amica mea perfecta,* please cut open my belly, let there be just a small hole for the demon to slip out.'

'You may not!' said the senior Physic suddenly looking very scared, 'We cannot risk an evil spirit in these corridors. It could run and hide anywhere, we would need to get the Bishop to exorcise the whole abbey and that could be too late, it could possess any number of brothers by then.'

Lorenzo looked at their stern faces and then down. He knew then of course that beyond Christ and Zeno, this was the only face he would ever love, certainly the only skin, hair, body, lips that he would ever hold and touch. Could he run to the refectory or kitchens and somehow get himself a sharp knife? Push himself past the physics, hold Uffizi down and push the blade into the taut, swollen skin of his belly? Perhaps. He half rose to do his heart's bidding. He tensed himself to force aside the other men, to do damage to his brothers, to risk excommunication from the monastery if it would only help his friend. But he didn't. Fear gripped him tight around the chest. He lay down upon the narrow cot, shifting Uffizi gently onto his side and pressed himself against his back, holding him as tightly as he was able.

Before Prime, came the harsh rattle of the last breath. Abbo was there by then to give extreme unction but Lorenzo lay there still and from compassion or perhaps fear of his reaction, they let him stay awhile.

And so, his heartbeats became the Hours of the monk's day. The hours became days and the months followed their godly rhythm of saints' days, festivals, seasons and the whole world gently turning. Brother Lorenzo read books, he kept his vows, he tended the herbarium, eventually becoming Chief Herbalist. Young novices joined and learned and grew, middle-aged monks grew old and feeble and died, the world and seasons turned.

Thirty years on now, Saint Zeno allows him another night of sweet images, smells and tastes. Brother Lorenzo wakes on the morning of his death, his belly steady, his heartbeat calm, his mind full of relief.

Thursday

CHAPTER TWENTY FOUR

In which an elderly monk finds peace in a strange place

We have already witnessed the death of this decent man through the eyes of the populace and the woman who had been set free from her dark airless room that very same morning. Certain facts remain the same. He is allowed to walk, rather than be carried on a litter, through the streets of the western city into the Old Town and across the Duomo piazza in front of Santa Maria Matricolore where simple wooden gallows have been erected. There are a few people lining the narrow street but not many. Most have already taken up places in the square. Those that wait and watch him pass by are, for the most part, very quiet. A simple indictment of his crime had been nailed upon Santa Maria's western wall the evening before but few can read it and those who can, do not really understand the charge. Visitors from the outlying villages make up most of the piazza crowd. They jeer a little as the small procession slips quietly, untriumphantly in through their midst.

It is all a little disappointing for those who have been on their feet since dawn. When two robbers-of-the-road had been executed in the spring, there had been singing, drinking, horse-shit thrown, a real carnival atmosphere. The roadrobbers had responded in kind–they knew the part Fate had gifted them and had chosen to take her final gift with alacrity – and there had been shouted jokes, insults towards the men, lascivious suggestions to the women and girls. The parade and theatrical tying of the nooses, the speeches, the confessions, the final song; it had all been most entertaining and had been well worth the journey. This little procession however is, as we have already said, very disappointing. A couple of deacons, not even the Bishop. Four Podesta guards, the Podesta himself scowling as he leads them in from the Porta Prima. A small grey man in their midst with a bowed head and tightly lined fingers. There had been rumours that Dido herself was to lead the guilty man to his death but there was no sign of her.

Next to the gallows is a long and sturdy trestle table, the city surgeon-cum-butcher standing behind, fingers playing upon the shining blades of his instruments as if preparing to play music. Which in a sense he is, for a man must do his job well on these occasions. It is the early afternoon and word has spread that a deacon has seen Zeno's face come alive and that the great saint spoke words of great encouragement for the city, that their future is bright and that God is smiling on them. After the massacre of Mordano and the battle of Fornovo – to say nothing of the deaths of the summer – the city can now return to prosperity, peace and agape. Already pilgrims are walking across the fields and forests to see Zeno in his crypt, to marvel at the silver mask and to pray that if they dropped a coin or two in the bucket at his wooden feet, then he might speak to them also. And so the crowd is a strange synthesis of the crudest need to see another man's humiliation and blood and the equally human desire for hope. There are also those who are subdued, for the man about to die had been Santa Anastasia's herbalist for decades and had helped cure the pains and ailments of so many. They could scarcely believe that he had procured poison in order to ferment discord and bring down their Podesta. But he had admitted his guilt before the City Council and he was walking quite calmly, no last minute protestations of innocence or desperate pleas for mercy.

We have already seen that the woman catches his eye and then as he bleeds upon the gallows platform, soaks up some of his blood to take home with her. We shall follow her another time and see where she goes but suffice to say for now that even she is surprised at how well her little subterfuge played out. Quite why the monk has admitted to a plot that never was, she does not know nor care, no doubt he was tortured. Her mind is cunning but there is little room in it for much more than survival and so she leaves the piazza with his blood in her shoes and soon casts the memory of him aside.

We however – painful though it might be – would surely like to be with Father Lorenzo the Friar as he breathes his last. For we know that as they help him up the crude wooden steps, as they read out the charges of fermenting disorder and plotting treason, as they secure the noose around his wrinkled neck and pull him up to strangle, we know that he is not alone but enveloped by a soft shimmering cloud of love. That on the one side, a dusty old saint brought out of a millennium's rest rubs ghostly hands up and down his arm, massaging his shoulder, supporting his neck as his throat throttles and his eyes bulge. And on the other side, there is a young man, firm of flesh, good of heart and quite beautiful, holding Lorenzo's hand tightly in his own as they do this thing to him.

Brought down still alive, they lay him upon the surgeon's table. The surgeon has orders from both Podesta and Bishop; *Cut this man as you must, let there be a great show of guts and blood but make the incision as small as you can, make it all show and little pain and as you hand him over to be strung up once more, cut the artery that leads from the heart, quick and sharp.*

And so, as the blade slices and the guts spill out, Lorenzo feels only a warm and welcoming pain, a sharp sting and then it is as if all the years and months and days and hours are flowing out of him, they are a mighty river which is his life and they flow like a torrent of water, joyful, hasty, the waves tumbling over themselves to get to the end. And as the waves spill over the cliff into a waterfall of shining crystal spray and deep dark depths below, he takes his last breath and cries out in pure relief as he passes over into absolution.

CHAPTER TWENTY FIVE

In which John Oldcastle says goodbye to Rosa, the old woman finds new employment and the Bishop wonders what it has all been for

John Oldcastle has enough trouble sleeping past dreams of his grandfather's burning without adding another godless execution to his collection of nightmares. He is good at compartmentalizing his thoughts – all lawyers must have this skill, building themselves mental libraries to store so many convoluted thoughts and facts – but the locked stronghold in the darkest reaches of his mental house is already full. One day he will open it up and set free the memory of what Juan Borgia did to Eleanor but not quite yet. And so he sits quietly by the river as they cut open an innocent man and hopes fervently that they were quick about it.

It is really too late in the year to be sitting outside, the earth smells a little damp, the grass still shines from a quick shower they only just avoided by ducking under an archway. But Rosa wanted to leave the Podesta house, no matter the weather. She wanted fresh air, she wanted – she said quietly and without fuss or explanation – to get the fetid stink of him out of that little room, for her and her sister to breath true again.

When she was a child, younger than Livia, she had fallen into this river. One of her cousins – *braggadocios* in the making, all of them – had given her a push, his foot had caught in a tussock, the push had been stronger, harder than he had intended. It had been spring and the snowrains were still coming down from the great *In Montibus Pallibus* range which sat grey and white and blue to the north of the city. The shock of the push, the cold, the pull of the current at and around her skirts; suddenly she was rushed away downstream, round the bend and under the Ponta Pietra. The shouts and screams of her cousins soon faded under the roar of water in her ears and up her nose. She could not swim – none of the girls could – and so she let the freezing waters carry her along, too full of shock to fight, her one tiny focus of self-awareness directed towards the next breath. And the next. And the next. It was a fortunate thing, they said afterwards as her cousins cried out from the hallway to the thrash of her father's belt, a fortunate thing that the river was so full and fierce that day. If it had been a slow and steady flow, she would have sunk to the bottom, no doubt about it. Sunk to the bottom and those damnable boys would be paying a heavier price than sore backsides. But the speed and strength of the current and the lightness of her body and inability to do anything but be carried, passively, along meant that as the swell rounded the river and passed under the Stone Bridge, she found herself rolled up onto gravel shore before the waters swept back down and carried on their way. The only cousin with any aptitude for learning had later tried to tell her than it was something called momentum. That the exceptional speed and weight of the river rounding the corner had resulted in an extra boost of height, landing her neatly and unharmed on the hard gravel of the opposite side just before the Porta Leoni. Aristotle was wrong, her earnest cousin had told her with wide myopic eyes, momentum was not the force of the air carrying a thing along but a force given, imparted, forced upon it. His tutor had a book by Pere Olivi the Franciscan, which showed this as a truth. A ball flies through the air because of the momentum given to it by the thrower, not by the air. And little Rosa flew through the water because of the force upstream of the narrow gorge and the great mass of rain squeezed through, it was not the water itself.

It felt like the water, she had whispered stubbornly. *Why am I so wet then?* Obviously perplexed by the stupidity of little girls, even cousins, the boy had shrugged. His tutor had that very day though been dismissed, Pere Olivi's treatises being on the Holy Mother Church's list of proscribed publications. The boy himself–she could not now remember if he had been a Mateo or a Mattia–had died the summer after as the Sweating Sickness descended upon the northern towns. She could scarcely remember his face nor his name and yet she remembered the word 'momentum' and she remembered lying, sore and grazed, in a hand's height of water, looking at a huge, white cloud. It had seemed to her that the cloud grew wider and thicker and seem to descend, enveloping her so that she could only see a white glare. No sky, no bridge, no Santa Anastasia on the other side of the river. Just soft white wool, gently wrapping itself around her. It became hard and harder to breath, her little nostrils were full of wool and the smell of lambs, her lungs began to hurt as she tried to suck in more air. She thinks, looking back fifteen years, that she might have died then. And that dying like that would not have been so awful at all. She remembered her heartbeat slowing down, a loud buzzing in her ears, a terrible panic and then the slow warm creep of acceptance, of peace. Someone had found her of course, shaking her drenched little body, turning her on her front, pushing hard upon her back so it seemed that she vomited up a whole river onto the mud. She went back to the river countless times after that, in a small city there were only rivers, streets and fields in which to play and the streets were denied her as too low. The water never scared her although she did not learn to swim. But sometimes she would lie on her back and look up at the clouds and feel a slight choke.

The three of them had a simple meal. A flagon of wine, Celestina's finest bread, some cheese, figs, the food was not important. There was a sharp, nipping breeze coming down the

River Adige, sweeping up little ripples, pushing aside the reeds, catching their throats so that they pulled their cloaks and shawls tight. But still they sat.

'Are you really leaving?' Rosa stared straight ahead. They were a decent hand's span apart but two of her fingers sat light and soft upon two of his.

'Yes. Tomorrow.'

'Back to England?'

Livia was lying on the rough woolen rug, eyes closed but she heard.

'I should like to come with you, John Oldcastle. We could all three live in London Town in the Great Tower. And then I could far more easily meet Prince Arthur.' Her voice was a little slurred and Oldcastle suspected that Rosa had given her sister her own dose of poppy that morning.

Rose stroked the little girl's hair. 'You are to live with the Podesta and I am to live with Saint Clare. This is the plan. Is it not the plan?'

He was well aware that the question was not directed towards the half-sleeping child.

'It seems like a good plan.'

'If you say.'

'I say that there are many plans in the mind of God, an infinite number I should imagine. And in one of these plans, yes, you spend your life content to be a Sister under vows to Saint Clare. And Livia grows to be a lady in the highest house in the city. But in another of God's plans, perhaps you marry the Emperor of China and live in a palace with a thousand slaves. In another, you grow wings like Icarus and fly to Atlantis . . . '

'Atlantis is under the sea, silly,' Livia yawned indignantly.

'But in this divine plan, Atlantis is renewed and Rosa lands safely, to the acclaim and worship of all.'

'Is there another?'

'I think perhaps in one plan you travel on a fine ship with billowing sails to London Town and marry a humble lawyer and live in Spitalfields which is not such a terrible place to be although you are colder there and need thicker clothes.'

'You think this might be one of the infinite plans in the mind of God?'

'I think it may well be.'

They sat in silence for a while for there was little else to say. Livia was now in a heavy sleep so when they had packed away the foodstuff, he carried her carefully over one shoulder through the street back to the Podesta's house where Celestina was waiting at the side door of the tower.

'You off then, Englishman?'

'I am, Mistress Celestina, I am.'

'Back to cold, wet Albion?'

'Yes. But first south to Firenze to see a friend. He is not behaving himself prudently and needs a stern but loving voice in his ear.'

'We all need that, Englishman.'

'Look after them for me, Celestina.'

'I shall,' She took the heavy weight of Livia, gently, almost reverently and went back inside the dark shadows of the tower. Rosa stared at her feet. He reached out to take her hand but then dropped his own back down.

'It will be a long time. Faith and patience, Rosa of the brown-as-black eyes. But remember how many plans are in the mind of God. A few must come true if we wait long enough.'

'I can wait.' And she raised her eyes, gave him a small smile and was gone.

John Oldcastle left the smallest of the Lombard city-states the next morning at dawn. He had booked himself on the same carriage that had carried him thither just one week before. He was leaving far richer than he arrived for he had won the case, done as commanded and Lord Cyprian's serving woman was free. But there had been a terrible price to pay and so he closed his eyes as his fellow passengers chatted and soon they left him alone.

---------- ∞∞∞ ----------

As John Oldcastle was carried along the rough cobbles towards the western Porta Palio and bridge, old Susanna, the woman at the centre of the *fabula tristus* stopped for breath. She was walking in the opposite direction to the Englishman's carriage and strangely enough heading for the Podesta's tower. There in that tall ugly building was a little girl, a little girl without mother or father, whose sister was soon to be dead to the world. The woman had been nurse to the little girl's cousin and had known both Rosa and Livia their whole lives. The Podesta's wife was a fine soul but she would need help, help experienced with the whims and wiles of children and young ladies.

As her wheezing lessened, the nurse looked around her. Her throat, indeed her larynx and whole neck, was a mass of red swelling; it hurt to swallow, to turn her chin, to breath even, God curse the young bastard. But God had been looking for her, aye, God and all the saints, even for one such as her. A few seconds to catch her breath, slow and gentle, a nasty rasp; Hell take the young bastard! The Pool of Hetaira was down the alley to her left, the Basilica of Zeno now at her back; she had another ten minutes walking before reaching the Roman Arena and the Castelvecchio. Almost forgotten, the gallows in Duomo Piazza would have been dismantled by now, the body quickly buried, the mess scooped up with sawdust. She wondered again if he had seen her. She had stared right at him but his eyes had seemed unfocussed, she could have sworn the old fool had been smiling. Well, she had been smiling when the guts fell out of his skinny white belly. There had been a sight! Well, he had deserved nothing less.

She started walking again, limping slightly from the pain in her hip. There had been no need for the Dominican to drag her into it, no need at all. Six dead and nothing to bring them back, nobody suspecting there had been a foolish secret marriage between children, who cared about lustful vows when there were dead bodies to bury? But the damned Dominican had opened his mealy little mouth, had spouted some long confession in the interests of truth and conscience. Truth and Conscience! Now there was two goddesses no one need bother with. He had done ***this***–so sorry, so sorry–then he had done ***that***–so sorry again–then ***this*** had happened and ***that*** had happened and all the while–half hidden at the back–she had held her breath, deep in the crowd, her name unsaid, her part untold. But then right at the end, he had damned well thrown her to the lions! *Oh Podesta, I am so sorry! Oh Podesta, yes I married them and gave her sleeping draught and encouraged the whole damned stupidity. But she knew too, Podesta, the Nurse knew too!*

Anger flooded her cheeks. Raf Salamanca's bruises were fading and almost disappeared beneath the rosy flare of rage but the new welts around her throat flushed bright. There had been no need! All had been settled, all forgiven, all judged. But for no reason than malice, he had thrown her to the lions. And so she had lost her home, her family, the roof over her head, her good name. All because a stupid old man could not keep his mouth shut on one tiny unimportant detail. She reached into the pocket of her long skirt to feel the still-damp pair of stockings. Every time she touched his blood, she felt strength flood back into her. It was like Jesus' blood they drank at Mass. It was lucky blood, lucky. She was a stupid fat old sow but she was lucky and so she was still here. Where was the fine Duke with his *barbari* friends? Where was the English lawyer so keen to believe her silly story? Where was her own mighty lord now he had no pretty daughter to bully? And where was the grey-haired old monk with the soft eyes and treacherous tongue? All reduced, all gone, all beneath her feet. She had won.

It seemed longer than she remembered, this walk through the city past the old Roman ring. But nearly there, her new little girl waiting just ahead on her left, the enormous castle with its seven great towers, its deep moat, its crenellated battlements with the glorious merlons atop every crenel. She felt like a queen. She *was* a queen! A queen of all that mattered. Her feet picked up their speed. She might be a fat old sow with only four teeth in her head but she had lost her darling daughter–two darling daughters really–her husband, her home and her job. She was damned well not going to lose this last chance too. And so the old nurse picked up her baggage for one last push, took a deep breath and walked on.

---------- ∞∞∞----------

And finally back to where we began, almost. The Bishop watches the Podesta shout at some poor boy–Horto is it?–as Paulo the Steward tries to create order from the chaos of a late-arriving set of trunks.

Well, my Lord Bishop, a result of sorts–*Horto, if that trunk is full of hose then do not unpack it here in front of the Lord Bishop, does the Lord Bishop want to see his Podesta's undergarments?*–if of course we might be happy with a result that is the complete opposite to the one at which we had aimed.

Yes, my lord. Aquinas would not be impressed by how well we have shot our arrows perhaps.

No, indeed, a midden of misadventurous mistakes, eh?

Yes.

But the populace got their execution, Lord Capulet his bucket of blood, that should keep him quiet or I swear I'll send him as ambassador to Cappadocia or somesuch place–*Paulo, we have had a devil of a week, get that Rioja in the small Calaburra casket up from the cellar*–and now that winter is coming, we should have fewer work-shy *otiosi* on the streets gossiping. This time next year the entire tragedy will be completely forgotten and wiped from the face of the earth.

Vellet Deus est.

What? Why the miserable face, Prelate? Your nose is even longer than usual. Which feast day we have coming up? St Bernard? We shall make a carnival of it! A celebration of this town and its populace. And I have a new ward, did you know, a new daughter to keep my wife happy and the lovely young thing that is her sister can devote herself to God with the Poor Clares. Too much trouble allowing a girl with a face like that to cause disorder amongst the young men, best put all the pretty faces in nunneries and only allow the plain ones to be seen.

It is an idea, my lord.

Paulo, where is that damned Rioja? God help me but I swear my household steal me blind. Still miserable, Bishop? Sit yourself down, you are towering over me as usual, wait until you taste this fine Spanish Red, you'll soon be smiling. *Paulo!*

You are right of course. And a carnival... let us call it a festival, carnival is too pagan but yes, a celebration of this city at the same time moving into the darkness of winter but also the light of a new beginning.

Good lord, what a poet you are. We must exchange verses. All I hear in the streets are sonnets and I am keen to explore new forms. Don't look askance, Bishop! Not all novelty is against God surely? *Damn, I cannot get this boot off–Horto, come back in and pull at my boot*–no, I am keen to settle this town into a stage of peace and order, now that we are part of the League and have expelled the French, a new Golden Age must be upon us, an age of new poetry and art and even philosophy for you, Bishop. *Ah, yes that's better, my boots are shrunken from the rain, I swear. Look at that toe, is it gangrene? I swear by Zeno that could be gangrene.'*

I am happy with the philosophy we already have. But you see yourself a Cosimo de Medici, my lord? *And he spoke 'my lord' as other men say 'my friend'.*

Hah! With far fewer funds but we shall see. Yes, yes, new bell towers certainly, we need a more impressive sky line. And frescoes, lots of frescoes. Firenze is full of new statues, ours are looking old and dirty, we shall commission new statues, perhaps we could visit the studios in Rome even?'

I have no wish to go to Rome.

Ah yes, our Borgia friend. And his even more Borgia father. But perhaps in a few months, the marks of Dido's teeth might fade… hah, I can see a slight smile, you cannot deny it! And I have to say that now we have persuaded the papal father to join the League and to recognise the sovereignty of the Lombard states, perhaps someone with Rodrigo Borgia's power and wealth might be a good thing for this poor land.

Hmm. You may be right. But your words remind me… I chanced to hear someone quote something of Juvenal the other day…

Juvenal! I am astonished, Bishop. The good Prelate of this town possessing a copy of Juvenal…

No, I did not say I possessed it, I simply heard someone ask me '*but who will watch the watchers?*' and it seems to me a very good question. We have our popes and bishops and podestas and doges but who will judge their actions and bring them to account whilst God is preparing for the Final Judgement? We over-ruled the wishes of the City Council yesterday, my lord, you know that we did. They wished the monk interrogated further, perhaps even by the Inquisition. But we felt we knew better and we over-ruled them. But we also knew that he was innocent and yet chose not to direct them to acquit. We allowed an innocent man to be butchered in the piazza so that the commonwealth might be served above his own interests. But who was there to look over *our* shoulders and into *our* consciences? Who was there to watch us? If we allow one man to die for the good of the nation, how are we better than Caiaphas? How are we any better than the hypocrites in Matthew who are whitened sepulchres full of dead men's bones? Who will watch the watchers?

Ah, here is the wine, no, this is not the best casket, this is not the Calaburro, oh for the love of the Lord it doesn't matter, just pour it out and go away. Here Bishop, take a good draught and then another. You are getting too philosophical about this whole sorry business. You know I have a funny story about Juvenal. Were you allowed to actually read the *Satires* in full at the seminary?

Of course not! There was a copy in the prohibited section of the chapterhouse library...

And you and your seminary friends sneaked a peak.

Absolutely not.

Well, I had a tutor who was as drunk as Bacchus and twice as fat – a Benedictine of course – and he would read me Juvenal to corrupt me and persuade me that nothing in this life was worth anything, aside of course from good health, an aspect of Juvenal he himself was assiduously ignoring. And I already knew a few short lines from my father – '*who will watch the watchers?*' he would boom at me and tell me that it was great advice from some revered Greek political philosopher debating the nature of power and responsibility. It was a line from a most serious study of civic government, of democracy, of sovereignty and of the people. So I told my tutor this, I said it had come from Plato or Demosthenes or somesuch Greek I could scarcely pronounce, all in the cause of Athenian morality and high ideals argued by the greatest of minds. So he laughed at me. Laughed and laughed, drank more wine, laughed again. And read from the Satires themselves. Did you know, Bishop, that Juvenal thought all women whores? That your wife will have sex with your friends and that if you keep her away from your friends she will have sex with strangers. And that if you keep her away from strangers, she will have sex with your servants. So you need a watcher to make sure she does not have sex with the servants. But then...

Who will watch the watchers?

Indeed!

You are sure that this great rhetorical question was not concerning the political ideology of the perfect civic government?

No, it was about stopping your wife having sex with the servants.

You are quite sure? Not concerning the responsibilities of kings so that they do not become tyrants?

Positive. I have a copy if you would like to check.

Hmm. Perhaps and yes, another glass of your fine Red.

It's not so fine, it's mediocre but have I cheered you a little? I think you have. And after another glass of this red I shall tell you a funny story about Saint Philomena. But before I do, tell me your ideas, dear Podesta, for this ... carnival you are planning. And for the grand rebirth of our little city state. More statues you say. And frescos? One of a giant black horse with sharpened teeth, I am thinking ...

The rain outside drizzles to a close, the night birds venture out and search for worms and slugs and other things dropped by the citizens of the day. A fine sliced moon, slivered but hopeful, balances herself gingerly upon a slate grey cloud as if she is not quite sure of her place. She quivers a little like an excited child, then settles and assumes a knowing air. The wind drops, the air grows still and the fires in the city hearths burn strong and kind and warm.

EPILOGUE

17th June 1497, the Ponte Fabricio, Rome in which we meet three, no four, old friends

On the Ponte Fabricio, right in the middle where the classical middle arch gently peaked, Signor Bauta the Highwayman met with Signora Gnaga, the Cat. Bauta had been waiting there a while. His long cloak was black and swept down to his ankles, it rose up also in a deep hood to cover his head. In the space within was the white glow of a full mask. Eye slits and a simple downward sloping mouth, a casual observer might mistake the mask for the full moon, floating a little low in the sky this night, silhouetted by darkness. Gnaga was resplendent in reds and golds, her tight bodice laced at the back in bold crosses, daring the admirer to unhook. Her mask was three-quartered; feline cheekbones, slitted eyes, pussy-cat ears but a very full and human mouth beneath. Chestnut hair slicked back in a chignon, she looked and moved like a dancer.

He gave a very deep and theatrical bow, cloak swirling like liquid. Gnaga curtsied, gave him her glove to kiss, long cat's claws painted on the leather. Then she gave a graceful *saltarello* step, step, small leap and step and he bowed again.

'Intriguing what one learns with the nuns of Poor Clare. I had not thought the humble cloister to be such an academy of skills.'

Gnaga did a slow, teasing pirouette. 'If one wishes to learn embroidery, peeling carrots and silent prayer whilst bruising one's knees, then the Academy of Saint Clare is the only choice. If however one wishes to learn how to live . . . then it would not be my suggestion for you.'

'No. I imagine not.' He came closer, reached out to run his finger along her unmasked jaw. 'You were always the cat. Just as Livia was the bird. How is she singing?'

'Loudly now and with no little joy. As you know, there was a time when we were fearful that she would not sing again. But now . . . well, the house is like a Greek chorus of voices except there is no tragedy but a celebration. And if Livia sings then so does Celestina and if Celestina sings then so does the Nurse but not so well. And then the old dog barks and it is all a calamity but a sweet one. Have you thought of me, John Oldcastle?'

The highwayman came close. 'I have had to turn to your countryman for the words. My accent will be poor, I fear . . . '

'Do not tease me, say the words.'

'Well then . . . *I look, think, burn, weep: and then she who destroys me is before my eyes, to my sweet distress: war is my state, filled with grief and anger, and only in thinking of her do I find peace.*'

'It is a much longer piece than that I think.'

'And I have learned it all. But I do not think we have the time until this night is done.'

'I shall hold you to this.'

'You must hold me to many things. Things I can only do if you have truly left the Poor Clares. Can you still return if you change your mind?'

'Of course. I am still Lady Rosa of House Marin. They need my money if not my devotions. But, oh John Oldcastle, I do not think I was made by Almighty God to be a nun.'

He leaned a little closer.

'*Sono tintinnabulum*
Repeto psalterium,

Gratum linquo somnium
Cum dormire cuperem,
Heu misella!
Nichil est deterius tali vita
Cum enim sim petulans et lasciva.'

'You know I speak hardly any Latin.'

'And you a good Sister.'

'Tell me.'

'The bell I am ringing,
The psalter am singing,
And from my bed creeping
Who fain would be sleeping,
O Misery me! O what can be worse than this life that I dree,
When naughty and lovelorn and wanton I be?'

There was definite smile beneath Gnaga's blank stare. 'So, I am naughty and lovelorn and wanton, am I?'

'I should very much like to think so. The very least of it is that you belong in the air and the sun not in the cell. Now, how do you like Roma?'

'Not at all. It is dirty, it smells of foul things, the people do not care if they walk over a dying child in the street. I had no idea that there were so many people in the world and yet no one here cares about another. They live pressed up against each one, nose to nose, but they turn their eyes away and say '*I do not know my neighbour. Did my neighbour fall ill yesterday? I had no idea. What is it to me?*'

'Most cities are like that.'

'No, this city is different. You can smell the cruelty in the air and taste it in the water. I think if you live on earth where thousands of people cheered and lusted for the blood of their fellows, then these cheers make a mark in the earth which we can still feel.'

'Like an echo.'

'Yes, an echo in the very soil. It gets into the water and the air and into your skin. No surprise that the people who live here are cruel and thoughtless too. How many good Christians died with their slaughtered children in their arms because the Romans could not accept their worship of one god? My Lord Podesta was telling me on the journey here that Christians were so persecuted that they were forced to live amongst the dead, in the labyrinths and catacombs below the very streets.'

'It is true. I have read the accounts. They were very brave.'

'And the Ancients very cruel.'

'And is it better now? Now that the Christians are in control of the Eternal City?'

She flushed. 'You know that it is not.'

'I'm sorry. I did not mean . . . '

'I know but it is true. A city like this allows a man like him. In fact, a city like this breeds a man like Juan Borgia. The city births him like a great monstrous beast spawns smaller monsters of her own.'

'Peter was also here. And Paul.'

'And look what happened to them!'

He sighed. 'But we must have hope that we are not on a plateau but an upward-facing slope. That the matter and morals of man will improve so that finally we shall be worthy to call ourselves Christians. But that upward slope is not the way of chantry prayers and pigs' bones dressed up as saints' relics and greedy, arrogant' – he was going to say *lustful* but stopped himself – 'prelates and priests acting like Nero and Domitian. The only way forward is to find the truth in the Scriptures. To allow people to hear the word of God in their own tongue and not have it filtered through the lying mouths of priests and popes who corrupt the message under the veil of Latin and Greek.'

'That will not happen in this city. Not in one thousand years.'

'I think you are right. No, all of our hopes lie with Germany, the Low Countries and perhaps even England. Rome is lost to us now.'

'I told you. The blood and wickedness is seeped into the very sod, the emperors began the terror and the popes continued with the same.'

He put his arm around her waist and they leaned back against the low bridge wall. Behind and ahead, the Tiber snaked slowly under and away, shining sharp triangles of light as the water ebbed and flowed against the walls of the city that had tamed it. The Pons Fabricius linked the ancient Campus Martius – now a sprawling ghetto where the city's two thousand or so Jews lived in no little squalor – to the Tiber Island in the middle of the river. Its two wide arches met in the centre of the river where a small concrete and brick mound, covered in wild vegetation, gave support. If it had been daylight they could have admired the still visible inscription declaring proudly that *Lucius Fabricius, son of Gaius, superintendent of the roads, took care and likewise caused this to be built.* But it was already very dark, heading close to the ninth hour and even if they had peered over the edge of the wall, they could not have read it.

'Whilst we are waiting,' he let his fingers press more firmly against her waist, 'let me tell you a story of the first Emperor Augustus, he who was Octavian.' He took her silence as acquiescence if not enthusiasm for she was already slightly wary of his long stories. 'There was a great but cruel and mean-spirited nobleman in Rome at that time, a man called Pollio. He made his fortune from land and from war in Spain, he was a poet of sorts and a historian, friend first to Caesar, then to Antony, then to Octavian, always on the winning side. When the wars ended, he retired to his villa in Tusculum in the Alban Hills not far from the city and built huge ponds and pools for his beloved fish. He had giant carp and strange fish from Persia with jewelry piercings in their gills. He called them his mermaids. And he had huge eels, eels so vicious they would eat a man alive and leave only the bones.'

'This is not a good story, John Oldcastle.'

'Pollio loved his carp and his exotic Persian mermaids but most of all he loved his eels. And if a slave displeased him, he would gather the *familia* around and have the offending one pushed in. And they would all have to watch as the flesh was torn bit by bit and then the muscles, eyes, organs.'

'And you are telling me these were not the cruelest of people?'

'One day he invited the Emperor Augustus to dine. Pollio was very proud and had to have the best of everything and he had just received a crate of the finest Syrian goblets, blown glass with silver vines climbing up the stems. They were said to be the most beautiful things in Rome, not even Augustus – who had simple tastes anyway – had anything like. So they reclined at table and drank and ate and Pollio recited some of his histories, no doubt flattering Augustus who was by this time well past leading an army or even fitting into his armour. During the meal a disaster occurs. A young slave serving the wine swings his arm too close to the table . . . a glass goblet falls to the stone and smashes. The slave knows of course that he is dead. Pollio his master is incandescent with rage. The slave falls to his knees before the Emperor. He does not beg for his life – he knows he is worth so much less than the precious glass goblet and that it is only right that he pays the price – but he begs Augustus *Not the eels, please! My mother is a slave here too, please do not let her watch me being eaten by eels.*'

'I hate this man. Why are you telling me this dreadful story?'

'Augustus was horrified. What kind of man is this fine noble Pollio that terrifies his slaves so, that forces them to watch each other being torn apart by vicious monsters? How can such a man be living in Augustus' golden new world? And so the Emperor ordered Pollio to do three things; he was to free the slave and his mother there and then. He was to fill in every single pool and pond and fishery with concrete, fish and eels and mermaids all. And then finally, he was ordered to take each and every one of the Syrian glass goblets and smash each one upon the floor.'

'Ah.'

'Better?'

'Yes, a little better. But I still think that . . . '

'Hush, I think he arrives . . . '

The only lights – for it was already gone Matins – was a pair of low burning braziers at either end of the ancient bridge. The sound of a horse's hooves upon stone, then a fine bay mare and a man leading her by the reins came out of the dark and into view, briskly crossing the slight incline to the centre point and stopping.

'Welcome, old friend,' Oldcastle stepped forward and held out his hand. Vincenzo di Casale took it firmly and smiled, light and quick. Nodding quickly to Rosa, he quietened the horse which seemed skittish. 'He is on his way. His horse broke a shoe as we crossed the Jewish quarter, Carlo went to wake someone up from the slum houses to fix it. He did not return. Borgia will make his way to this bridge, I have told him the person he wishes to meet is from the Jewish quarter.'

'And how is he?'

'Very drunk. He has been at his mother's all evening at her villa at Monte Martino, a few miles out of the city. They were all there; Cesare, Lucrezia, Gioffre and the wives and Lucrezia's husband.'

'How pleasant.'

'Not really. His mother, Vannozza, did her best but the four of them are not at all friendly with each other and each day it gets worse. They fight for their father's favour, she tries to bring them together again, the next day they are fighting. It has been going on forever. She feeds them the best food in Rome and pours wine down their throats but still they fight and argue and insult each other. It is very tiring to have to hear. I was positioned by the Duke at the door, I don't think he trusted his older brother not to send in some assassin to stab him as he ate. Every other guest was a food-taster, I think. And the younger brother, Gioffre, he spent the whole evening glaring at Gandia like a chained dog with a cat he just cannot reach. Gandia is having sex with Gioffre's wife Sansia. They all know it. Gandia flaunts it in Gioffre's face. Sansia sits all innocent like the Virgin Mary but I could hear them having sex in the gardens. Apologies, Lady Rosa.'

'How did you get him here?'

'He left with Cesare and a cousin, we got to the Castel San Angelo bridge when I told him the Jewish procurer had sent me a message at dinner. A new consignment from Syria. Very young girls. He told his brother he would see him in the morning, that he was out on Gonfalonier business! So it was just Gandia, Carlo and me.'

'And Carlo?'

'In the Jewish quarter still, in an alley just over there by the river walk. Not ever getting up.'

'Your devotion to our cause is beyond words, my friend. Now quickly, before he arrives … I know the worst of it, I have read the reports but you were there, you were with him at the end. Tell me how Giramo died.'

The Italian *sicario* nodded slowly. 'You know how many times the Borgia pope wrote him, warned him, threatened him? But he ignored every command. Even when the Commune's council withdrew their support, still he continued with the burnings. Statues, paintings, arras, women's gowns, embroidered waistcoats, people were walking naked from the Piazza della Signoria, naked and thinking themselves better loved by God because they had burnt their vanities. Then they woke up the next morning and found they had nothing to wear. And he could not stop. Books, so many books, you would have wept, Oldcastle, wept.'

'Go on.'

'You know the Papal Father had already excommunicated him. I think this was what Savonarola wanted but of course it meant he was unable to preach in any of the Firenzi basilicas. But as you remember he always preferred to speak out in the open anyway so he carried on. The order came to arrest him. The Pope threatened the entire city with excommunication if they did not hand him over. The people had grown tired, tired or afraid. He was not always speaking sense, John. The New Jerusalem, built in Firenze, sometimes it was already here, sometimes a thousand years from now. It was to be ethereal, it was to be stone and mortar, it was to be of air and water and fire. Women were devils, women were the New Jerusalem's angels. Books were God's word; books were the work of Satan. We should read the holy scriptures in Italian, we would be damned if we did.'

'We heard something about a trial by fire. I could not believe that Giramo would be so . . . superstitious.'

'I was not there for that, *gratias Deo*. I was here in Rome with Gandia. But yes, it was a farcical day. Two preachers trying to outdo each other and when words were not enough, turning to *Igne Judicii*. A most shameful and farcical spectacle. Two paths of coals were laid in the piazza and set alight for both men to walk barefoot upon. And then the good God saw fit to open his heavens and pour rain upon the coals, extinguishing the fires. They re-laid them and set the fires ablaze again but once more, from a clear blue sky, the heavens opened. The crowds watching saw this – quite rightly, forgive me, I know you loved him – as a sign from God that both Savonarola and his rival were wrong to display their pride in such a way. Days later the Holy Inquisition arrived in Firenze and he was lost to us. At his trial he seemed desperate for death, shouting out that Elijah would come and carry him to safety before the flames touched his skin.'

'But he did not.'

'No. It was a bad death. Not quick. I rode north when I heard and was in the crowd but they would not let me or any of his Piagnoni followers visit him before. I'm sorry. He was my master but I know he was your friend.'

'Yes. Thank you, Vincenzo, for being there for him. And for me.'

The Italian nodded. 'He is with God now. Such a great man. There can be no doubt surely? Despite . . . well, despite it all.'

There was a pause broken only by water and night birds. 'I'll wait by the foot of the bridge so that he can see me, as I say he is very drunk.'

The horse, who had settled, protested a little as she was maneuvered around in the tight space and then led back down the slope. Just beyond the brazier and its glow, they could dimly perceive Vincenzo and the bulk of the animal, just hear the occasional clatter of hooves on cobbles.

Oldcastle turned slightly towards the woman behind the cat's face. His forefinger tilted up her chin just slightly and tried to gauge her thoughts.

'You can re-consider.'

'Oh, I can? I can hide in the shadows whilst John Oldcastle takes my vengeance for me?'

'It is my vengeance too.'

'I know. So we shall do this thing together then.'

From the Jewish quarter came the occasional shout, a woman screaming, dogs barking, some unidentifiable musical instrument drifting in and out of the light summer breezes. More music, no it was singing, a man's voice, loud, holding the tune, a disgusting street song but held in a baritone that knew its cadence, rhythm and pitch. Oldcastle could feel Gnaga the Cat tense beside him. He stepped away from her, stretched his shoulders back and then relaxed, back again. Gnaga stepped carefully to the centre of the bridge.

The song stopped mid-verse and there was a shout of welcome. A low voice, a louder one, two horses recognising each other, high whinneys of something inhuman. Hooves again upon cobbles. The bridge was eighteen feet or so across but for some reason the man with the bay horse slowed her down so that the white horse led the way alone.

'Aha!' Gandia had now seen Gnaga who was holding the bridge, long skirts, narrow waist, provocative décolletage catching his inebriated attention, despite the gloom. He dropped the reins and held both palms outwards in a strangely aggressive display of submission to, presumably, her beauty.

'My Lena Giudia! What a pleasant surprise. I was expecting a gnarled old crone, bent down with the weight of her years and her gold. But here Phoebe has gifted me Gnaga herself.' His voice was slightly slurred but not disastrously so. He was not as drunk as they had hoped. Still and dark, the shadow of his hood over his mask, Bauta stood back by the wall.

Gandia dropped the reins, calling back but not dropping his eyes from the woman in the middle of the road.

'Vincenzo, *es stercus*! You have kept this filthy daughter of Moses to yourself and not shared her around! As your Papal Captain, I am most displeased, you disloyal *filius canis*. If the pimp is this beautiful, then my hopes are rising as to the quality of her little girls. And other things are also rising.' And he stroked his crotch, still holding her eyes.

Vincenzo was very quiet as the best *sicario* had to be. Slipping beside the Duke's white Sabino gelding, in one smooth move he had Gandia's arms pinned behind his back whilst the Gonfalonier's legs were kicked out from under him. A strap secured the wrists even as the Duke very nearly sprang back to his knees, blood on his cheek where his face as hit the floor.

'With this.' Gnaga took a silk kerchief from her bodice and Vincenzo swung the other man around even as kicked out and knocked him back to his knees. As the fallen man concentrated briefly on the agonizing pain in his kneecaps, the cloth was tied tightly around his mouth and secured with a viciously tight knot.

'He is a kicker,' said Gnaga quietly, 'Best tie his ankles too.'

Gandia was clearly threatening them with the very wrath of God and despite the gag, still making a great deal of noise. Fortunately, the Jewish Quarter was a notoriously loud and lawless place and few people crossed the Ponte Fabricio after dark.

Gnaga took a thin stiletto blade from the inside of her boot. Gandia at first looked wary but there was something in her inexpert, even nervous handling of the weapon that brought a cunning to his eyes and his body relaxed a little. He motioned for Vincenzo to lose the gag, keeping his body very still.

'My lord, if you shout out we shall cut your throat,' said his erstwhile servant, 'This is but a robbery. You have at least thirty ducats in your purse there and I have to leave your service unexpectedly. Those thirty will see me to Greece. But if you shout out, my *pulcra amica* here will slit you from ear to ear.'

Gandia could see, even in his drunken state, that this was not a woman able to do what Vincenzo had threatened. But Vincenzo was perfectly capable of it and more. So he nodded.

'I am going to tie your feet, not because I think you are going to run but because – as my lady says – you are a kicker and I like my nose the way it is.'

Another nod. Vincenzo slipped the short length of rope, which had been serving as a belt, from his waist and tied the soft leather boots. Then the spit-soaked gag was eased gently – for this Duke was also a biter – from the man's mouth.

'Well, Vincenzo, you have more cajones than I ever gave you credit for.' Gandia spat out some threads of cloth. 'Raf Salamanca – you remember Raf? – always told me he had doubts about you. Never trust an Italian, he said, stick to Castilians, blood runs thicker than gold. Who are you running from, my friend? You know I can make them disappear.'

He had not noticed up until now the dark shape on the other side of the bridge. As Bauto the Highwayman slowly walked across to the opposing wall, Gandia's eye narrowed.

'A friend. I see. This is a more disturbing situation than I had at first assumed . . . a beautiful Gnaga cat and a mysterious Bauta of the night. But fitting. If you are to rob me, Vincenzo, a thief of the roadway is a good co-conspirator.'

'We are not going to rob you, Juan Borgia. We are going to kill you.' Oldcastle was slightly muffled by the mask but clear enough. Gandia's eye darted from one side of the bridge to the other. He had grown a light, curly beard since their last meeting.

Oldcastle could see froth and some blood on his chin but the Duke seem very calm and self-possessed.

He nodded. 'Ah, kill me. Quite right too. I am most certainly deserving of death. I have done some truly horrendous things although I assure you that many are slanders by my enemies and many are things done whilst Bacchus was in control of my faculties. I can also assure you that I have done full and honest confession for them all, with absolution each time.'

'Priestly absolution means nothing. It is a fraud, invented and perpetrated by tyrants like your father. There is no mention of the *soi-disant* sacrament of confession in Scripture.'

'Ah! A heretic! A Poor Spiritual perhaps, given your costume. Your mission to spread Waldensian lies and redistribute gold to the poor. I am sorry. I thought you the cuckolded husband of some slut I had tumbled. I did not realise that this was to be a theological assassination. How very . . . *theatrical* of you, Bauta.'

'Do not flatter yourself. This will not go into the papal annals as some kind of philosophical martyrdom. You are no hero of ideas, you are not Socrates. You are a rapist. An abuser of children. You are an abomination, cursed and damned. You are God's mistake.'

'*Errorem Dei*? Strong words for a *vix hominem* who hides behind a braver man's face. And rapist? I am Papal Gonfalonier, Duke of Gandia, Duke of Sessia, Grand Constable of Napoli–why would any woman not want to spread her legs for me?'

'My sister did not want to.'

'And neither did mine.' Gnaga the cat stepped closer. Gandia could see that the slim fingers holding the stiletto blade were now very steady. In a strangely calm way, he realized at that moment that he was certainly and without doubt going to die. He had no idea who this woman was, no idea of Bauta's identity either although there was something nagging at the back of his mind about the man's accent. But a cool chill was spreading outwards from his stomach up to his throat and down to his guts and legs.

But he was resourceful, the young Duke of Gandia. He had two children just off the breast and another on the way. There was no luxury, no opulence, no depravity, no excess not available to him and he had planned a long lifetime enjoying them all.

'As I say, I am a sinner. And you are right, Heretic, no doubt there is a circle of Hell close to the very centre in which I shall be thrown. But I am also the Papal Father's son. And if my dead body is found face down in the Tiber, Rodrigo Borgia will not rest until you three are hunted down. There will be no sanctuary on the face of this earth that will be safe from his rage and grief.'

'When your dead body is found face down in the Tiber, your papal father will assume that your brother Gioffre has finally got tired of watching you fuck his wife,' said the Highwayman quietly, 'And if Gioffre convinces him of his innocence, the papal finger will then point towards Cesare who has hated you since you were born, I hear. And if Cesare is innocent, then the light will fall upon the Orsini clan who you have upset so much in recent months. There will then be other candidates, Borgia. Because you have spent your twenty years making so many enemies, the wide expanse of all infinity could not contain them.'

Gnaga could contain herself no longer, her hands and arm were still but her voice was strained.

'She was a *child.* A little girl. You . . . hurt her. There are no words to describe what you did. There is no place even in the seven circles for you.' Each word was clearly painful. But even now, even this close to his own oblivion, to the last beat of his heart, even now Gandia found himself appraising what he could see of her body.

'What has been done cannot been undone. But these . . . girls of whom you speak, their lives will surely be enriched by what I can give them. The thirty ducats in my purse is nothing compared to what they can have for the rest of their lives. This is empty vengeance; this is foolish . . .'

'It does not feel empty,' said Rosa as she pushed the stiletto as hard as she could into the side of his throat. The thin needle pierced skin, muscle and entered through to the oesophagus, filling it with blood. Gandia began to choke, feeling hot liquid spread down into his lungs and up through his mouth and nose.

'Eleanor,' said the Highwayman with some emotion Gandia could not identify. And then there was a sharp thrust to his chest, forcing between ribs, splitting some organ he knew not what. There were other stabbing blows, seven, eight, he had choked almost to oblivion by the end of it. And so when the knife came to roughly cut his throat from ear to ear, and when he was pushed back so that the night sky and the air and the stars tumbled over his head and down, down until the hard crash of his body hit the slow solid mass of the Tiber, by that time he was in darkness and then he was nothing.

---------- ∞∞∞ ----------

Vincenzo was gone with both horses, Rome would not see him again and neither would they. Rosa was shaking a little and he held her close to him so that the black of his cloak covered them both. So dark was the middle of the bridge that anyone crossing would have almost walked into them before realizing that they were even there.

'We need to leave,' he said at last. He could feel her head slightly nod.

He was not an aggressive man, not one to force his will upon others but at this moment he sensed that she wanted some clear direction, if not from him, then from Fate itself. And at this point he knew for certain that no one was going to be her Fate but he.

'There is a good little house in Spitalfields, close to the great cathedral of St Paul's which needs you. It is not a fine Italian palace with balconies and topiary beasts, I have only two serving women to clean and cook and an apprentice under my feet all day long. I also have a common law wife of twenty years although she is happy to find herself another household. I am not offering you luxury and I am bastard-born which limits my future somewhat. I cannot offer you the life the Podesta of Verona can offer you. But I can at least give you more than life as a Poor Clare. I have built up a decent income from my practice and have every expectation of increasing my yield…' She stopped his mouth with her forefinger and left it there.

'Rosaline…'

'Enough John Oldcastle of London Town. Let us find ourselves a ship with billowing sails and escape this terrible place. I shall set up home with you and marry you and have your children and they shall not be bastards. And one day we shall send for Livia and she can find herself a Prince Arthur if the real one will not have her. This is my choice.'

The choice made, the pair uncoupled from beneath the cloak and crossed onto Tiber Island and from there they passed by St Bartholomew's basilica, walked over the Bridge of Cestius and disappeared into the labyrinthine streets of the Trastavere.

---------- ∞∞∞ ----------

Saint Zeno follows them into the deep dark shadow of St Bartholomew's and then stops; he has no need to watch them further, they are beyond his touch now and so he lets them go. He can sense all around him the frayed dusty spirits of the dead; beneath his feet, in the tombs of the churches, cramped and forgotten in the very stones and bricks of the walls and bridges. There are saints here too, his brothers and sisters. But when he calls out tentatively for their companionship, for them to welcome him into their city, he receives just a soft, grey breeze of quiet disinterest. They are tired, they are old, they can scarcely remember how to drift up out of their bones and blackened skin and float through the streets they once strode along. Zeno waits. There is a man playing a Vielle somewhere back over the Castius and Fabricius bridges. Over towards the ghetto. He is playing a sweet low tune on all five strings, nimble fingers and a strong, safe bow. Zeno listens for he thinks he has heard the tune before. To the north-west, he lets his gaze float above the sleeping face of Rodrigo Borgia whose grief tomorrow on seeing the body of his favourite child is going to know no bounds. Even further north-north-west, the ashes that once were Girolamo Savonarola are now scattered in the corners and the cracks of Firenze's Piazza della Signoria and beyond. They are carried by Firenzi boots and slippers and paws, they seep into the mud and are carried by birds and crawling things to nests on high and to the waterways. Soon he will be nowhere but also everywhere. Which, thinks Zeno, is probably what he would have wanted.

He takes a deep breath and casts himself up on the night air, slightly to the east, following the spine of the great boot but before he reaches the city of canals and the sea, he hears a bird singing. It is past midnight now and the time for singing is long gone but she keeps her voice quiet so only she and Saint Zeno can hear. The child with the tousled hair casts up her song to a ceiling that has one too many plaster leaves but she does not care that even numbers bring bad luck because birds who sing like her can make their own.

AUTHOR'S NOTES

Juan Borgia, (1476-1497) son of Rodrigo Borgia (Pope Alexander VI) went missing on the night of 14th June 1497. His body was fished out of the Tiber a day later with multiple stab wounds and a slit throat. At first his grief-stricken father blamed the Orsini family but a few days later the accusations fell silent. Most historians view this as indicating the Holy Father's realization that responsibility for the murder might lie closer to home, most likely Juan's brother, Gioffre. Juan Borgia left behind twins – Juan and Francesca – and a daughter, Isobel, born posthumously. Pope Alexander reigned for another six years whilst his surviving children left their names indelibly in the ink of history.

Our Bishop is loosely based on **Bishop Giovanni Michiel** (1446-1503). He came from an illustrious Venetian family and was nephew of Pope Paul II, living as a young man with his uncle in the Vatican Palace. After holding many high offices, he fell foul of Venetian politics and was forced to resign many although he remained influential in Rome. Although a one-time supporter of Alexander VI (Rodrigo Borgia), he was poisoned by Cesare Borgia in 1503. The motive for this murder is not known.

Sir John Oldcastle (died 1417) was a close friend of the young English king, Henry V, fighting alongside the Plantagenet monarch in France. He became leader of the Lollard group of heretics who followed the teachings of John Wcyclif and who are now viewed as early Protestant reformers. Oldcastle became

Baron Cobham through his marriage to the heiress Joan and the pair left at least four legitimate children who inherited the title and surname Brooke. Oldcastle was arrested for his beliefs but with the assistance of the king, escaped twice only then to mount a rebellion against the crown. Captured again, he refused to recant and was burnt at the stake. Shakespeare included the character of Oldcastle–best friend to the king–in his play Henry V but the Cobham family complained at this reminder of their less than illustrious past and the character's name was changed to Falstaff. John Oldcastle and Joan Cobham's descendants used the surname Brooke and were Lords of Cobham until they were indicted under Bills of Attainder for their part in the Main Plot against King James I in 1605. John Oldcastle (bastard) is fictional.

Girolamo Savonarola (1452-1498) was an Italian monk and preacher, burnt at the stake for defying the Papacy of Alexander VI. He preached that Florence was the New Jerusalem and that the people must burn their vanities upon bonfires to be saved. Under his direction, the Medici family was expelled from Florence which then declared itself a free republic. Excommunicated, Savonarola performed many trials by fire to try to prove God's support but was eventually burnt in the Piazza della Signoria. His anti-clerical revolutionary ideas were continued by his devoted disciples, the Piagnoni, and were adopted by the next century's Protestant reformers.

Rosaline, Livia, Brother Lorenzo, Podesta Escalus and the **Nurse** are of course shamelessly purloined from another source. Setting their fictional lives in 1495 serves to distance their new story from the original but also is in keeping with many scholars' beliefs that the romantic tragedy was actually set a century earlier than its creation.

---------- ∞∞∞ ---------

Printed in Great Britain
by Amazon

46622529R00222